WANNA GET LUCKY?

WANNA GET LUCKY?

LUCKY O'TOOLE VEGAS ADVENTURE: BOOK 1

DEBORAH COONTS

Chestnut Street Press

Published by Chestnut Street Press

eBook ISBN: 978-0-9857925-1-0
Paperback ISBN: 978-0-9857925-8-9
Hardcover ISBN: 978-1-944831-71-4
Audiobook ISBN: 978-1-944831-41-7
Large Print ISBN: 978-1-944831-57-8

Cover design by Streetlight Graphics
(www.streetlightgraphics.com)

Formatting by Kate Tilton's Author Services, LLC
(www.katetilton.com)

To Tyler

CHAPTER ONE

*a*S HER final act on this earth, Lyda Sue Stalnaker plummeted out of a Las Vegas helicopter and landed smack in the middle of the pirates' lagoon in front of the Treasure Island Hotel, disrupting the 8:30 p.m. pirate show.

The video ran as the lead-in for the 11:00 p.m. news. I caught it on a television in the sports bar. Actually, it was amazing I caught it at all. My name is Lucky O'Toole, and I am the chief problem solver at the Babylon, the newest, most over-the-top mega-casino/resort on the Las Vegas Strip. I'd been fighting my way through the crowds packing the casino on my way to Stairwell Fifteen to deal with a naked man asleep under the stairs, when I caught the television feed out of the corner of my eye.

A grainy video of a helicopter with the Babylon's script logo painted on the side appeared on the screen with a small headshot of Lyda Sue in the corner—it was Lyda Sue's sweet smile that actually captured my attention. I leaned over the backs of two guys playing video poker at the bar, a sinking feeling in my stomach. In Vegas, nobody gets their picture on the news unless they've committed some grisly crime or have been a victim of one themselves.

Of course, I couldn't hear what the talking heads on the television were saying. The clamor of excited voices from the casino combined with the pinging from the video machines and the piped-in music to create a cacophony of excitement that made it not only impossible to talk, but to think as well.

Eyes wide, I watched as the station ran the video again—this time the full version as part of their newscast.

Hovering above the lagoon as the show began, the copter began to buck and roll. A body tumbled out, backward or forward —it was hard to tell. Thankfully, the final impact with the water was hidden behind the pirate ship advancing toward the British with cannons belching fire and smoke. The picture tilted, then went dark—a head shot of Lyda Sue taking its place.

"Ms. O'Toole?" My Nextel push-to-talk vibrated at my hip. "Are you coming?"

I grabbed the device and pushed the direct-connect button to shout. "What?"

I pressed the thing to my ear as I tried to hear.

"Ma'am, this is Sergio at the front desk. The doctor's with our naked guy. He's fine—apparently sleeping off a bender. But we got another problem—some guy in Security by the name of Dane is insisting we call the paramedics just to be on the safe side."

I stared at Lyda Sue's picture on the television, my mind unable to process what I saw. The video switched to the police and a body covered with a white cloth, one delicate hand dangling from the stretcher as they loaded it into the back of an ambulance. Nobody was in a hurry.

"Ma'am, are you there?"

The question snapped me back. "Sorry. Naked guy in the stairwell, right. Do *not* call the paramedics unless the doctor wants them. We don't need to cause a scene and have this guy splashed across the pages of the *Review-Journal* in the morning—I'm sure he'd love that." Trying to steady my nerves, I took a deep breath. Instantly, I regretted it. Smoke-filled air assaulted my lungs, bringing tears to my eyes. "I'll be right there, and I'll deal with Dane." I choked the words out as I struggled to catch my breath.

"Yes, Ma'am."

I reclipped the Nextel at my waist.

I fought to not only clear my lungs, but to clear my thoughts as well—a Herculean task as hundreds of questions pinged around inside my head.

Lyda Sue, dead? I'd seen her just last night, holding forth on the end stool at Delilah's Bar. We'd talked for a minute or two; her world had seemed stable enough. Twenty-four hours later, she took a header out of our helicopter, landing smack in the middle of the 8:30 p.m. pirate show. What had I missed?

Damn. Lyda Sue was dead. *Double damn.* She fell out of *our* helicopter. The Babylon would be big news. My job was to keep the Babylon *out* of the news. Or to take the fallout when I failed. The Big Boss was not going to be pleased.

Tonight was shaping up to be a doozie.

I muscled between the two guys intent on their video poker monitors and leaned across the bar so the bartender could hear me. "Get the news off that television. Find a sports feed or something."

The real world had no place in this fantasyland.

My mind clicked into gear. I couldn't wait to get my hands on that pilot. He should have called me right away. Lyda Sue hit the lagoon at 8:30. Damage control was tough enough without giving the newshounds and gossip mongers two and a half hours head start. I had a feeling that nothing short of an overnight nuclear test at Yucca Flats would keep us out of the morning headlines now.

Nevertheless, I grabbed the Nextel, and started in. "Jerry?"

"Yo," our Head of Security answered in his laid-back manner.

"I want our pilot in my office right now—handcuff him and drag him there if you have to. Next, get over to Channel Eight. I want all copies of a tape Marty ran on the eleven o'clock news of a

3

woman falling out of our helicopter. If he refuses, remind him of that awkward little situation at the opening gala—he'll know what you're talking about. Bring the tapes to me when you get them."

"I'm on it."

"Oh, and Jer? I almost forgot. What's the status on the mega-millions winner? Did she actually hit it?"

"We're working on it. I'll have an answer for you in the next half hour—our plate's sorta full."

"Welcome to the club. Thanks."

I disconnected, then scrolled through the stored numbers looking for Dane's as I turned to head toward Stairwell Fifteen. Paramedics! Was the guy nuts?

As fate would have it, his number didn't matter. Two steps with my head down focusing on my phone and I ran smack into the rather solid chest of the man I was looking for—Paxton Dane, the new hire in Security.

At a couple of inches taller than my six feet, Dane was the poster boy for the testosterone-laden, ex-military, jet-jockey set. Square jaw, soft brown hair, green eyes, great ass, and an attitude —which I didn't need right now.

"Did I just hear you tell Jerry to threaten to blackmail the manager of the television station?" His voice held the soft traces of old Texas, yet the sexy timbre of a man confident of his appeal.

"I never threaten. I offered him a deal." I had neither the time nor the patience to educate Dane tonight, but it seemed that was in the cards.

"A rather fine distinction."

"Dane, you'll find those black-and-white lines painted so brightly in the rest of the world blur to a nice shade of gray in Vegas." I put a hand on his chest and pushed him away, since his nearness seemed to affect what rational thought I had left at this time of night. "I was already up to my ass in alligators, and the suicide dive just upped the ante. I really do have to go."

I pushed away the images of Lyda Sue's final moments. If I

kept them at a distance, maybe, just maybe, I could make it through the night. If I spoke of her cavalierly, maybe I could hold back my emotions.

"What makes you think she was a suicide?" The soft traces of old Texas disappeared. Dane's voice was hard, flat, and held an edge like tempered steel.

The question and his tone stopped me cold. What did he know that I didn't? "You got any reason to think otherwise?"

Murder, now that *would be a real problem.*

He waved my question away, arranging his features in an expressionless mask. "I need to talk to you about one of our whales. Apparently, the guy had a mishap in one of the Ferraris. If you want me to handle it, I can, but you'll have to make the call as to what the hotel is willing to do. The whale in question is..." He consulted a folded sheet of paper he had extracted out of his back pocket and gave a low whistle. "A Mr. Fujikara and he seems to be quite a whale—he keeps several million in play during his monthly visits."

"I know Mr. Fujikara well."

Dane glanced up, one eyebrow raised, but he didn't ask the question I saw lurking there, and I felt no need to explain.

"We also have a Pascarelli. Apparently, he wants a hug from you," Dane continued, not missing a beat as he absently rubbed his chest where my hand had been. "And the naked guy..."

"He's all mine as well," I interjected to speed up the conversation. With major problems to solve, I had little time and even less patience. "And, Dane, for the record, never call the paramedics unless it's an all-out emergency or the doctor wants them. Casinos are closed worlds here—we protect our own—and we zealously guard the privacy of our guests. Remember that. Outsiders are allowed in to help with problems only, and I repeat, only when the problem gets out of hand."

Dane's eyes narrowed—his only response. A tic worked in his cheek.

I rolled my head and rubbed the back of my neck. "I need to take Mr. Fujikara as well; this is a game we play. For his millions, he likes some personal attention—apparently I'm the anointed one. You can help me with one thing, though. We had a lady hit the mega-million, but we need to make sure she played the six quarters. Jerry's shut down the machine and is reviewing the tapes. While we're in the process, why don't you offer the Sodom and Gomorrah Suite to the winner and her friends for the night? Make double sure that she understands her winnings have not been confirmed. I'll follow up with her when I get the results of the diagnostics from Jerry."

"And who will authorize the comped suite?"

"I thought I just did." My words sounded harsher than I intended. "Sorry. If Sergio wants confirmation, have him call me."

"Right. Oh, and The Big Boss wants fifteen minutes of your time. He's in his apartment."

"He'll have to get in line."

"He told me now," Dane said, as he rubbed his eyes.

"I said, he'll have to wait." Now that I took a closer look, Danes eyes were bloodshot. The guy looked totally wrung out. I put a hand on his arm. "Are you okay?"

"Fine." Dane shrugged my question off, then shrugged out of my grasp. "You leave The Big Boss hanging, it's your funeral."

"It'll take more than that to put me six feet under."

My relationship with The Big Boss was none of Dane's business. I turned and took off through the casino with more questions than answers bouncing around in my skull: Why the swan dive, why did The Big Boss send Dane to bring me to heel, and why did Dane sidestep my question?

Murder! What made him think Lyda Sue was murdered?

~

THE CASINO AT THE BABYLON IS MUCH LIKE ANY OTHER. AN intimate labyrinth, subtly decorated, windowless and, tonight, jam-packed with people all paying and praying for whatever it was they hoped to get in Vegas. A thin layer of smoke hovered over the crowd, as the slot machines sang their come-on songs and occasional shouts arose from the tables. Cocktail waitresses wearing painted-on smiles and little else darted in and out delivering fresh libations and collecting the empties. Young women paraded around in tight-fitting clothes they wouldn't be caught dead in back home. Pierced and tattooed young men, their jeans hanging precariously across their butts, followed the young women. How the boys kept their jeans from falling straight to the floor was an enduring mystery.

The nightly line of the young and the beautiful snaked from the entrance to Pandora's Box, our popular nightclub and body exchange. Pulses of dance music escaped each time Ralph, our bouncer, opened the door to let one of the hip and trendy in or out. The entrance to the adjacent theatre was empty; the 10:30 show was well underway.

I knew where to find Mr. Pascarelli—thankfully he was on my way to Stairwell Fifteen. Like all serious gamblers, Mr. Pascarelli was a creature of habit and superstition. Dressed in the same shirt, a now-threadbare Hawaiian number his wife, Mildred, "God rest her soul," had given him decades ago when I guessed he weighed forty pounds more than he did now, he always started his night of play at the third slot machine from the end of the third row.

A gnome-like eighty, Mr. Pascarelli was cute as a bug, bald as Michael Jordan, a night owl and, I suspected, a bit lonely. Three was his lucky number, and I was his good-luck charm.

Lucky me.

Truth be told, giving Mr. Pascarelli his hug was usually the high-point of my night, a fact that—had I time to think about it— would probably have concerned me.

"There you are, my dear!" He waved his glass at me. "I was beginning to worry."

"Worry? Don't be silly, but this one will have to be a quickie." I gave him a squeeze, careful to not crush him too tightly.

He laughed at the innuendo. "Hard night?"

"You don't know the half of it."

"Little Lyda taking a header out of the helicopter?"

"Bad news travels fast. You knew Lyda Sue?"

"Sure. When she wasn't busy, she used to pull up a stool and talk to me for a while. Sweet kid, from somewhere in Texas, I think." He shook his head and crinkled his brow. "She'd been sorta jumpy lately."

"Did she say why?"

"If she did, I don't remember."

"Do me a favor—try. When she sailed out of that helicopter, she landed right in my lap. I could use some help on this."

He nodded, his eyes serious.

I patted Mr. Pascarelli's shoulder. "Go easy on us tonight, okay?"

"Sure, honey," he said with a wink.

Mr. Pascarelli was the only man on the planet who could call me "honey," wink at me, and live to tell about it.

I dove into the crowd and wove my way on toward Stairwell Fifteen. I threw my weight against the stairwell door and came face to face with the normally unflappable Sergio Fabiano, our night-shift front-desk manager. Dark hair, olive skin, a face a photographer would love and a body to match, Sergio was the Babylon's resident Greek god. Women were drawn to him like sharks to an injured seal. Thankfully, the women were nowhere in sight. Neither was Security. Apparently, Dane had done as I asked and called off his posse.

"Thank heavens!" A scowl creased Sergio's otherwise flawless face, but his dark eyes danced with merriment. He gestured disdainfully toward the space under the first flight of stairs.

"Good God!" The words escaped before I could stop them.

"But not a merciful God," announced Sergio.

Our naked guest must have weighed four hundred pounds, with pasty white skin and more hair sprouting on his body than his head. Thankfully, he was curled in the fetal position. And he was still out cold. But, judging from the way his ass was twitching, his dreams were good ones.

"We don't know who he is?" I managed to choke out. I kept repeating, *I will not laugh at this* over and over in my head until I felt confident I would do as I told myself.

Sergio shook his head, his jaw clamped tight, his lips compressed together. He didn't laugh, not even a smile, or a smirk. Amazing.

I keyed my Nextel. "Security, any missing-person reports for tonight?"

"Excuse me?" The unmistakable voice of Paxton Dane. Did the guy ever stop? Like the Energizer bunny, he just kept going and going, handling everything, everywhere.

"Dane, have you guys had any calls from anyone looking for someone who matches the description of our guy in Stairwell Fifteen?"

"Already checked that. And, to answer your question, no."

"Okay, then send four..." I looked at the inert shape again. "Make that five of your strongest guys to Stairwell Fifteen, ground floor."

"On their way—again."

Taking the high road, I ignored the jab. "And, Dane, remember, a bit of discretion here. This man is most likely one of our guests. We wouldn't want to see him on the news, okay?"

"You mean one appearance on the nightly news is enough?"

Did the guy take a class on how to be a jerk or was it something that just came naturally?

"Dane..." I started in on him, then realized I was talking to dead air.

9

Sergio looked at me, his eyes round black saucers.

I snapped my phone shut. "Sergio, take care of this guy," I said as I reclipped my phone, glad that Dane had retreated. I was too wrung out to do the whole verbal thrust-and-parry thing. "You know, the usual routine."

"Right," Sergio began. "First, get a robe that'll fit him—preferably one with another hotel's logo on it." He paused to flash me a grin, then continued as if he'd memorized it all from the employee handbook and hadn't actually learned it from me. "When Security gets here, have them carry him through the back corridors to the worst room open tonight. Take all the bedsheets, the towels and the robes—anything he can put around himself when he wakes up, so he can't sneak out on us."

"You've got it. But you might see if Security can spare someone to stand outside the door, just in case our friend—" I pointed to the guy on the floor, now snoring loudly. "—has an accomplice to bring him some clothes."

Sergio nodded.

"And the doc is going to check on him?" I asked.

"Every half hour."

"Good work." Another problem down, how many more to go? I'd lost count. "Sergio, another thing..."

Again those black eyes focused on me.

"I need you to alert your staff at the front desk, the bell staff, and the valets. If anyone comes around asking questions about a girl falling out of our helicopter, they are to be directed to my office. That includes the police. Our staff is not to answer any questions or to give any information. Is that clear?"

"Yes, Ma'am." Sergio's eyes grew a fraction wider, but he kept his composure.

"And if anyone is poking around, let me know, okay? Just because you send them to my office doesn't mean they will actually do as you suggest."

I gave one last look around. I couldn't think of anything else.

Satisfied Sergio could handle the problem from here, I turned to go—

After all, it's not as if this was our first naked drunk sleeping in a stairwell.

∽

THE ELEVATORS LURKED JUST INSIDE THE FOYER OF THE BABYLON, separating the casino from the hotel. The foyer was the Babylon's showpiece. Designed to draw all passersby inside, the grand ceiling was covered with millions of dollars' worth of Chihuly blown glass. The Bellagio had glass flowers, we had butterflies and hummingbirds—thousands of them. Personally, they made me feel like we all were in a remake of the film *The Birds*, but obviously no one shared my opinion. As usual, a crowd clustered under them, oohing and ahhing.

Numerous walking bridges arched over a lazy river, our interpretation of the Euphrates, which snaked throughout the ground level. Tropical plants and trees grew along its banks, lending shade for the colorful fish, swans and ducks that swam in the clear blue water. Somehow, I doubted whether the birthplace of civilization ever had a river quite like our Euphrates, but The Big Boss wanted it, so there it was.

Off to one side of the lobby, behind a wall of twenty-five-foot windows, an indoor ski slope with real, man-made snow descended from high above. Again, I wasn't sure whether the original Babylonians had ever strapped on a pair of K2s and flown down a snow-covered hillside, but in keeping with the relatively recent adage "If you build it, they will come," The Big Boss had built it and, indeed, they came. Another crowd gathered there, watching the folks who had paid an exorbitant sum to ski indoors on the desert slide down the hill.

The other side of the lobby boasted the entrance to the Bazaar. There one could slide behind the wheel of a Ferrari, buy a six-hundred-thousand-dollar pink diamond ring, a two-thousand-dollar pair of Versace jeans, or load up on five-hundred-dollar Jimmy Choos. A constant line of customers with fat wallets trailed through there like ants bearing gifts for the queen.

The Big Boss was an expert at separating tourists from their money.

Ah yes, The Big Boss—he was next on the list.

I shouldered my way through the crowd, ignoring the man yelling at one of the bellmen—a front-desk clerk was already interceding. Paxton Dane was giving a woman a hug—probably the mega-millions lady. He caught my eye over the lady's shoulder and gave me a discreet thumbs-up. For this brief moment in time, we appeared to have things under control, which, of course, was an illusion. Life in Vegas was never under control; it walked, trotted or galloped, as it chose, and we merely hung on for the ride.

Tomorrow, the Trendmakers would arrive for their annual week of spouse swapping, the stars of the adult movie industry would descend on us for their annual awards ceremony, Electron-iCon started Tuesday, and I would have to deal with the fallout from Lyda Sue's dramatic exit, which would surely hit not only the morning papers but the Internet as well.

Whoever thought up the tagline "What happens in Vegas, stays in Vegas" got it backward—Vegas was always news. Heck, the video of Lyda Sue's final dive was probably playing on YouTube by now.

I was a fool to think I could corral this one.

I rounded the corner, pushed the up button, and pondered the reflection that stared back at me from the mirrored surface of the elevator doors. I looked like a hundred miles of bad road. Barely over thirty, and I could pass for my mother's sister. *Haggard* was the word that leapt to mind. Thankfully, the doors slid open and I was no longer nose to nose with myself. Why people want mirrors everywhere is beyond me.

I stepped inside the empty car, inserted my security card in the slot, and pressed the button marked "private." Self-consciously I patted my bottle-blonde hair, my one concession to the land of the beautiful people. Attractive enough, I guess, I'd never be considered beautiful or buxom—at least not without serious surgical intervention—but I damn well could be tall and blonde. Self-consciously I smoothed my dress, pinched my cheeks to get some color into them, then wiped at the black smudges I had seen under my eyes. I threw back my shoulders and adopted what I thought was an air of confidence.

"Who you trying to fool?" The voice emanating from the ceiling startled me.

I looked up at the "eye in the sky," the small video camera hidden discretely in a plastic bubble partially recessed into the ceiling of the elevator car. Security monitored the video feeds from thousands of similar devices located all over the property. The voice belonged to Vivienne Rainwater, one of our Security team.

"You know what they say, image is everything." I forced a smile for the camera. "I'll be unavailable for a few."

"You go, girl."

"Over the line, Viv."

"I thought there weren't any lines in Vegas, just shades of gray."

"And you shouldn't listen to conversations you're not invited into."

"You'd be amazed at what you see and hear up here."

Not long ago, I had sat where Vivienne now sits, and received a quick lesson into my fellow man, one I assumed Vivienne was now learning. "Titillated? Maybe. Amused? Possibly. But amazed? No. Now, go away and spy on someone else."

The elevator whirred seamlessly to a stop at the fifty-second floor and the doors slid open. Every time I made this ride, I thought of Dorothy leaving Kansas in a tornado and waking up in Oz. Thirty seconds and I was transported from the semicontrolled chaos of the lobby to the quiet, serene living room of The Big Boss's penthouse.

The muted lights cast a warm glow on leather-finished walls. The rich sheen of the hardwood floors framed hand-knotted silk rugs from the Middle East. Each was tastefully arranged and supported a cluster of understated furniture made from the hides of exotic beasts and woods from faraway lands. Lesser works from some of the great Masters graced the walls—sketches by Picasso and smaller works by Van Gogh and Monet. I couldn't identify the others—apparently my high school art history teacher had overlooked them—but I was sure they were all very expensive and "important." The whole effect made a three-thousand-square-foot box of a room cozy.

The Big Boss stood silhouetted against the wall of twenty-foot windows backlit by the lights of the Strip below. He warmed his hands in front of a gas fire dancing merrily in a freestanding fireplace. He explained to me once that he kept the air-conditioning on full blast so he could have his fire. Something about the ambiance.

The Big Boss, Albert Rothstein, was a Vegas legend. He had started as a valet at the Flamingo, caught the Mob's attention—he never would tell me exactly how—and then worked his way to the top of the heap. A short man with a full head of once black, now salt-and-pepper hair, he kept himself trim with thrice-weekly personal training sessions. His smile could light up a room and his manner made you feel like you were the most important person in his world. He had a penchant for stiff whiskey, tall blondes, and big stakes. When I was fifteen, I'd filled out an employment application, stating my age as eighteen. The Big Boss hired me on the spot, even though he had known I was lying.

More than a little peeved at being summoned through the new flunky, I started in as I strode toward him. "Lyda Sue made a helluva splash, but I've got everything under control: Jerry's on his way to get the tape from the station, the front entrance staff has been alerted to direct all inquiries to me, and once I actually make it to my office, I'll work on keeping us off the front page."

I stopped in front of him, but The Big Boss didn't look at me. Instead, he continued staring into the fire, then he reached into his back pocket, extracted his wallet and pulled out what I knew to be a one-hundred-dollar bill. He put his wallet back, then started working with the paper money, smoothing it, lining up the sides, meticulously folding it again and again. The silence stretched between us, then he finally said, "Bring all the copies of the video to me."

"You don't want Security to go over it? May I ask why?"

Now he eyed me over the top of his reading glasses perched on the end of his nose. His eyes were red. He looked like hell. "For once, just do as I say."

"Okay." First Lyda Sue, then Dane, now The Big Boss. Had I suddenly stepped into the Twilight Zone? Nothing about this night added up. "Aren't you interested in what the pilot has to say?"

"The pilot?" he repeated, as if stalling for time.

"The pilot's story should be a doozie."

His hands shook as he folded the bill over and over. "Of course, what did Willie have to say?"

Okay, now I was sure I smelled a rat. "How did you know it was Willie? We haven't found him yet."

The air seemed to go right out of The Big Boss. He closed his eyes, took a deep breath, and let it out slowly. "Lucky, you can truly try a man's soul."

"And you're stonewalling me." I laid a hand on his arm. "Boss, it's my job to solve problems, but I can't do it unless I know what the problems are."

"I was solving problems long before you showed up. This one's mine. I'll solve it myself, my own way." He shrugged out of my grasp.

The second man tonight to do that. Clearly, I was losing my touch.

"Just bring me that tape and keep me in the loop," he growled, looking like a pit bull ready to take a bite out of somebody's ass.

I had no idea how to reason with a pit bull—assuming it could even be done—so I bailed. "You're the boss. Anything else?" If I couldn't go through him, I'd just go around him.

Again the silence stretched between us as he worked, folding and folding. Finished, he took my hand, and closed my fingers around the small shape. He didn't let go. His eyes looked at our hands, then reluctantly met mine. "Trust me on this one."

"Sure." I looked at the shape in my palm. The Big Boss had folded the bill into a small elephant. I extracted my hands from his and dropped the figure into my pocket. "Look. Right now I got more fires than California in the fall and they are spreading by the minute. May I go now?"

"Give that to the first kid you see in the lobby." His voice was tired. His eyes, distracted.

"Boss, it's midnight. If there're any kids around, somebody ought to call Child Services."

"Right." He stepped around me and headed toward the bar. "Tomorrow then." He pulled a bottle of single malt off the shelf and raised it in my direction. I shook my head. He poured himself a drink. He raised the glass to his lips, took a long pull, and then said, "We've got another problem."

That much I knew. In fact, I thought we had several.

"And what might that be?"

"Paxton Dane."

Now *that* I didn't expect.

The Big Boss turned and stared at me, apparently awaiting my response.

If I didn't know better, I'd say he seemed nervous, a little antsy even, as he shifted from foot to foot.

A cold chill went through me. Whatever was bothering him, it must be bad—real bad. I'd only seen The Big Boss this way once before, and we both darn near went down in flames.

"He was your hire. What's the problem?" How I kept my voice even, I don't know.

"I hired Dane so we could keep an eye on him," The Big Boss said, his eyes drifting from mine.

For a moment I was speechless, unable to comprehend what he had just told me, then I found my voice. "Wait, let me get this straight. You put somebody you don't trust in one of the most sensitive positions in the house? Do you think that's wise?" I tried to keep my voice low, my tone smooth, but even I could detect a hint of panic around the edges.

"Probably not, but it was the best I could think of on the fly." The Boss took a slug of scotch. "Jerry knows. He's keeping tabs on Dane, and I want you to help him."

"Why?"

"He asked too many questions and was snooping around like he was trailing after something or someone. It doesn't seem hiring him has put him off the scent. I want to know what he's looking for and who's holding his reins. So, keep him close, okay?"

"Why me? I'm not in Security. I'm the customer relations person, remember?"

"I know it's asking a lot." He turned. His eyes locked onto mine. "But, Lucky, you're the only one I can trust."

CHAPTER TWO

ONIGHT'S PILOT would have to be Willie the Weasel. I fumed as I rode the elevator down from The Big Boss's suite. As far as I knew, I was the only person who referred to Willie as the Weasel, but knowing Willie, there were probably hundreds, if not thousands, out there who felt the same way I did. We had history, the Weasel and me. As my mother was so fond of pointing out, the Weasel had been one of those "learning experiences." I learned all right. If I had it to do over again, I would have shot him and put him out of my misery.

Unfortunately I hadn't been smart enough to shoot the Weasel, and now I had to find him.

The Big Boss was stonewalling me, I'd been reduced to Paxton Dane's babysitter, and now the Weasel was back in my life. What a great night this was turning out to be.

I had worked myself into a lather when my phone rang, interrupting my pity party. I grabbed the offending device from its perch on my hip, flipped it open and snarled, "O'Toole." I didn't look at the caller's number first.

Big mistake.

"Lucky, you're never going to catch a man with a bark like

that." My mother's voice was flat, emotionless, authoritative, and just enough to push me over the edge.

"Mother, you make dating sound like the greased pig contest at the state fair. That's not fair to the pigs. Besides, my bite is worse than my bark."

"I know some nice men I could introduce you to." Even after all these years, she refused to quit.

"Mother, the men you know are not nice. They pay for sex."

"You're way too picky, honey."

"It's my cross to bear." The elevator doors opened on the mezzanine. I stepped out and took a few steps to the railing of the balcony overlooking the lobby. "It's pretty late for a social call, Mother. Everything okay?"

I thought I heard a sniffle. "Mother, are you crying?" My mother never cried. She made other people cry.

"Oh, Lucky! I saw the news. Poor Lyda Sue! And it's all my fault." Mother really was crying. She had my full attention now.

"How could it be your fault?" I leaned against the railing and watched the sea of people below. "Lyda Sue quit working for you some time ago."

Mother took a deep, ragged breath.

"Oh, Lucky, you're going to be so mad at me."

I shut my eyes and counted to ten. It didn't work; I was still mad. "Mother, I'm not sure you could make this night any worse, so why don't you just give it to me straight?"

"Well, a couple of months ago, Lyda Sue came out here and asked me if I would bend the rules for her a little bit."

"How little?" I had a real bad feeling I knew what was coming.

"She said she had a big fish, a real high-profile guy, and he didn't want to be seen meeting her. So I let her meet him here."

"And you didn't check him out, right?"

"It was Lyda Sue, honey. She'd never gotten into any trouble before, and she was one of my favorites. She always came to visit and cheer up this old lady, unlike somebody else I know."

19

"Guilt doesn't work with me, Mother." Taking a call from Mother was like stabbing myself in the leg with a sharp knife—extraordinarily painful but not life threatening. "So you have no idea who he was, and nobody there saw him?"

"No, but I do know each time he met her here he arrived in the Babylon's helicopter."

Okay, I was wrong, she *could* make my night worse.

"Tell you what, Mother. Why don't I come for lunch tomorrow, and you can tell me all about this then?"

"That would be wonderful! Will you bring a beau with you?"

"Mother, give it a rest."

"You know, Lucky, your Aunt Matilda was right. We should have had sons. They're much nicer than daughters."

~

For years I'd been telling The Big Boss that to have an office for me was a waste of time. All I needed was my Nextel and a pair of track shoes. He'd responded that maybe that was so, but my assistant needed a little corner of the world to call her own, and we couldn't very well put her in the lobby. Unable to think up a pithy reply, I caved. I had to admit, though, the office he shamed me into using was a better place to store my stuff than an employee locker.

Consisting of an outer reception area policed by my assistant, Miss Patterson, a small kitchenette, and a room where I stored my stuff and pretended to be important, my office occupied a section of the mezzanine level. With its wall of windows overlooking the lobby, I felt as if I were living life trapped behind glass, like a snake at the zoo, just another of the many attractions at the Babylon.

Miss Patterson, on the other hand, loved it and ran her own little fiefdom from her desk in the outer office, her very own pulpit of power. From there she corralled all of the worker bees, wayward guests, occasional disgruntled losers, reporters looking for a juicy tidbit, gaming inspectors, policemen and women, and anyone else who wanted a moment of my time.

I'd inherited Miss Patterson from my counterpart at one of The Big Boss's lesser properties. I was less than impressed when I met her. Fiftyish and frumpy, she dressed as if she had given in to getting older. In Vegas, that was tantamount to a cardinal sin. Every day, she hid her body under a long skirt, oversized blouse, and tattered sweater. She wore her salt-and-pepper hair in short, soft curls framing her round, impish face. All in all, she didn't exactly inspire confidence. I never suspected she possessed the most finely tuned bullshit meter of anyone I'd ever met. Looking back on it, I would have been money ahead had I paid her twice what she asked.

She was waiting for me just inside the outer door with a cup of hot coffee and a frown. "Two Metro detectives are in your office," she said. "They wouldn't tell me what they wanted." She sniffed, as if the snub was a personal affront.

I took the proffered coffee and inhaled deeply, savoring the vanilla nut aroma, then sipped. Hot, but not enough to take my skin off, so I drank deeply. I couldn't remember the last time I'd eaten. A headache was forming just behind my right eye. I hoped the caffeine would help. "If Pierce Brosnan walked in here and wouldn't give you the time of day, I'd understand you being miffed and fairly disappointed. But two of Vegas' finest?" I made a rude noise with my lips. I didn't even get a smile. She was one tough audience. "And the reporters?"

"Several have called. As usual, I've given them the standard—this is an ongoing investigation, we don't know anything yet—and referred them to Metro."

"What does this place need me for?"

"To handle the police," she deadpanned.

"Thanks." I noticed Miss Patterson looked as tired as I felt. "It's late. You should go home."

"I'll go when you go."

I think she harbored the secret opinion that I couldn't do my job without her. And, secretly, I agreed with her.

"Oh, and Jerry dropped off a package, which I put in your purse," she added.

I nodded. So Marty had seen the light. Now I owed him a big favor.

Girded by the jolt of caffeine and a sense of impending doom, I opened the door to my inner office and stepped inside.

Both detectives turned at my greeting. One stood at my wall of windows, legs spread, hands on hips, surveying the activity in the lobby below. The other, much younger detective, held one of the photographs from my credenza. He hastily replaced it. A sheepish grin briefly split his face, then disappeared.

He had been holding my favorite photograph, a black-and-white picture that showed a four-year-old me and my mom with Dean Martin and Sammy Davis Jr. Dean Martin held me as I smiled and reached for the camera. In short-shorts with one of her heels kicked up, my mother had thrown her arms playfully around Sammy Davis's neck. She was beautiful—so young and full of life.

Another time and place.

Both of the cops were dressed as if they'd come straight from the set of one of those police dramas on television—cheap suits, rumpled jackets, and serious expressions.

"We're looking for your helicopter pilot who was on duty tonight," said the older one. "I assume you know why?"

"And you are?"

"Detective Richards." He reached inside his jacket and pulled out a badge, which he flashed. Then he pulled out a business card and shoved it at me. He jerked his head at the young guy. "That's Detective Romeo."

I looked at the younger one. He must have seen my amusement, as his face flushed crimson, and I instantly felt like a pig. I was ashamed of myself, sort of. It was late. I was tired. My head hurt. And I'm shallow—I find amusement where I can.

I turned back to Detective Richards in time to watch his gaze wander from my face down my body then back again, apparently missing the fact that my eyes had turned into little slits at his obvious undressing. "We were told you might be able to help us." He sounded dubious.

"I work mainly the on-property problems. Young women jumping to their deaths at another hotel are a bit out of my purview." The truth, but not the whole truth.

"So, you won't help us?"

"Can't help you. I haven't a clue where the pilot is. Believe me, I'm looking for him myself." I could feel the detective's eyes follow me as I moved behind my desk and sat down.

The guy was starting to creep me out. Still, as far as creeps go, he was a benchwarmer in the minor leagues. I played in the majors. I'd come up through the ranks of violently drunk customers with projectile vomiting, groping hands and foul mouths, plus card sharps, thieves, petty thugs, mashers and various other minor criminals. Just imagining this pompous detective dealing with the vomiters made me smile.

That clearly wasn't the reaction Richards expected. He glowered at me.

Romeo shifted nervously from one foot to the other, his eyes fixed on his partner as if watching for his cue.

I was wondering if I was going to get the whole good cop/bad cop thing, which semi-amused me, but then I decided I was too beat to stick around and play. "Gentlemen, I'm tired. I have a headache. And—" I motioned with my arm toward the wall of glass. "—out there is a hotel and casino full of problems, all of which I have to address before I get to call it a night."

"So, you won't tell us where the helicopter pilot is?" Detective Richards asked again.

"I told you, I have no idea. Why don't you try the dispatch

operator, he or she may know more. You'll find the dispatch desk in Guest Services."

Detective Romeo pulled out a pad and started taking notes.

"And the video of the suicide, did you know the television station apparently taped over it after it ran on the eleven o'clock news?" Detective Richards continued.

"Erased? Too bad." *Bless you, Marty.* Good thing for me, lying by omission wasn't a capital offense in Nevada—at least I didn't think it was. "Now, please, if that's all you want, you're talking to the wrong gal."

"You're not being very helpful," said Detective Romeo.

I turned to look at him. He shrank back, then reddened again — apparently he was smarter than his partner and noticed my slitty eyes. "My contract says I don't have to be helpful after midnight." I spoke slowly, then smiled and batted my eyes at him. I know, I know—I should pick on someone my own size. After midnight I have no self-control.

"You tell us if you find him," Detective Richards said in his best "do as I say" manner. "You have my card."

"*If* I find him, I'll tell him you're looking for him." For a moment, I held the detective's steady gaze, then I stood and moved toward the door. "Gentlemen, if you please, I'm needed in Delilah's Bar."

I opened the door and ushered them out.

~

ONCE THE DOOR HAD CLOSED BEHIND THE DETECTIVES, I PAUSED AT Miss Patterson's desk long enough to kick off the flats I had been wearing and grab a pair of killer Jimmy Choo's she kept stashed for me in her bottom drawer. With their delicate silver straps and six-inch heels, they were the best "knock me down and fuck me shoes" I owned.

The phone rang incessantly—all three lines were lit. We both ignored it. "Have the dispatcher call me on my cell." I sank into one of the chairs across from Miss Patterson's desk. She grabbed a notebook and pen as I tried to stuff my already tired and swollen feet into the strappy shoes. "I told Jerry to keep Willie in Security, but now that the police have gone, tell Jerry the minute Willie shows his face around here, I want him strung up by the balls and brought to me. I'm going to hang him on a spit and roast him over an open fire." The mental image of a well-done Willie brought a smile to my face.

I tightened the straps on the shoes, then I arranged my décolletage to show a bit more cleavage. Fuck-me shoes and cleavage—the perfect costume for my part in Mr. Fujikara's production. "Tell Operations two detectives are on their way to dispatch. Get rid of them quickly and for God's sake don't let them run into Willie, assuming, of course, we actually find the bastard."

I took a deep breath, steadying myself. My mind was whirling. "See if Felicia Reilly is working tonight. She's a cocktail waitress and usually works in the high-stakes room—the same place Lyda Sue worked. Miss Reilly is Willie's latest conquest. If she's on the property, I want to see her in my office in thirty minutes." I paused to let Miss Patterson, who scribbled fast, catch up. "Then see if you can find the Beautiful Jeremy Whitlock."

"The Beautiful Jeremy Whitlock?" Miss Patterson's normal dour expression brightened.

Hmmm, did Miss Patterson harbor a secret crush? I nodded. I'd probably have a crush on him too, but I'd sworn off men. They were all pigs and to be pitied.

Nobody ever referred to the private investigator as just Jeremy —he was always the Beautiful Jeremy Whitlock. And, I had to admit, the name fit. "See if he can come by tomorrow afternoon."

With both shoes firmly strapped on, I grabbed the edge of the desk as I carefully rose to my feet. Wearing high heels had never been my forte. Walking in them even less so. I took a tentative step, then another, gaining confidence by the time I reached the door and pulled it open.

I had made it to the elevator when my Nextel spoke my name. I pulled it from its holster and pushed the direct-connect button. "O'Toole."

"Ms. O'Toole, this is Ben Hawkins in Guest Services. I worked dispatch tonight. Miss Patterson told me you wanted to talk to me."

I didn't know Ben. He sounded young. His voice shook. I couldn't be that scary, could I? "Yes, Ben. Thanks for calling so quickly." I stepped into the waiting elevator, thankful to have a wall to lean against. Normally, I took the stairs—the casino level was only one flight down—but not tonight, not in these shoes. "Have you guys had any luck locating William, the helicopter pilot?"

"I wish. The whole world wants to talk to him. I keep calling him on the radio. I've even tried his cell, but he doesn't respond."

I knew the answer, but I had to ask. "Why are you calling him? Isn't he back yet?"

"He never came back."

Ever hopeful, I asked, "Does the FAA have any reports of a crash nearby?"

"No, Ma'am."

Bummer. Of course Willie couldn't have just crashed and burned, saving me the trouble of tracking him down. He never was helpful that way.

I glanced at my watch—12:35 a.m. A bit under four hours since Lyda Sue hit the lagoon. I didn't know how much fuel Willie'd had onboard the helicopter, but it couldn't have been more than three hours' worth. I thought I remembered Willie explaining they usually went light on the fuel so they could carry more paying customers.

Willie the Weasel had vanished.

And he took our friggin' helicopter.

❀

As the elevator doors opened and I headed for Delilah's Bar, a wall of sound hit me. The night in full swing, gaggles of folks wandered about, drinks clutched tightly. Of course, it could have been any time of day or night in the windowless, hermetically sealed casino. Casinos are designed to trap gamblers and keep them wagering until they dropped, and, in our case, that strategy seemed to be working. With flashing lights, snippets of music, and an occasional siren, the slot machines vied with each other for players. The tables were all in play, with people packed at least two deep around each. Other folks wandered between the tables and the machines.

Glasses in hand, they ogled the other wanderers, apparently looking for a different kind of entertainment. Energy shimmered off the crowd.

The air was so full of smoke it amazed me anyone could breathe the stuff and actually survive. My eyes watered and my lungs screamed. Ah, Vegas!

So, how was I going to find a missing helicopter? I hadn't a clue, but I knew it wouldn't be easy. Vegas was a tiny oasis in a vast desert. The Weasel could have refueled and be halfway to L.A. by now.

Think, O'Toole. How would the FAA look for a missing aircraft? I had no idea, but I knew who might. As I navigated toward the bar, I keyed my Nextel. To be heard over the din, I held it close to my mouth. "Dane, are you there?"

His response was quick. "This is Dane, over."

"Lucky, here."

"Lucky me."

"Truer words were never spoken. You're a pilot, right?" I thought I remembered Jerry telling me something about Dane's military service that included flying. I hoped I remembered right.

"Yeah."

27

"Would you have any idea how to find a missing helicopter?"

"I'm already on it. I figured the guy might get scared and bolt. I've put in a few calls and am waiting to hear back. Shouldn't be long. Can you give me fifteen minutes or so and I'll get back to you?"

"Sure. I'll be in Delilah's with Mr. Fujikara."

"Roger."

~

DELILAH'S BAR WAS A COMFY OASIS SET ON A RAISED PLATFORM smack in the middle of the casino. Here, surrounded by palm trees and trellises of trailing bougainvillea, one could rest from the rigors of wagering, slake thirst, fortify resolve, and hit the ATM. The stench of the tropical flowers diluted the natural, organic purity of the cigarette aroma, and hit me in the face as I teetered up the steps. Someone had definitely gone a bit overboard on the flowers.

Mr. Fujikara and his three friends rose as I approached. They were all short men. In these heels, their eyes were level with my chest. I think that was part of the game we played. Standing there surrounded by short men reminded me of junior high school; I was an Amazon and everyone else, especially the boys, were pygmies. I stifled that familiar feeling of awkwardness as I dropped into a small bow. "Mr. Fujikara, how nice to see you again."

"Ms. O'Toole," he said, as he bowed in return then motioned to the chair next to his. "Please, sit."

Mr. Fujikara introduced his friends as I took my seat. I nodded to each in turn. I noticed they were well into a second bottle of wine. "Are you enjoying yourselves?"

A smile spread across Mr. Fujikara's face. "The suite is magnificent! From the balcony we can see all the way up the Strip. And the service has been impeccable."

I reached over and touched his knee, then leaned into him. "I'm so glad you're satisfied." I turned toward Mr. Fujikara's friends. "Mr. Fujikara is a very important guest of ours...of mine." I gave him a smile and squeezed his arm. "And you like the wine?"

"It is sublime." He beamed. "But I think now your presence calls for a bottle of champagne." His eyes twinkled. "What do you think? Perhaps a nice bottle of Dom Perignon?"

I smothered a smile. Mr. Fujikara was going to play this for all it was worth. I thought for a moment. The insurance deductible and the value of lost rental time on the Ferrari would run six or seven grand, so I could afford to give him a couple of bottles of four-hundred-dollar wine, a five-hundred-dollar bottle of bubbly, and a bit of attention. "Of course! Perhaps the '95?"

"Splendid!"

I motioned to the waitress hovering nearby. "Kimmy, a bottle of the 1995 Dom Perignon, please, and four glasses."

"You're not going to celebrate with us?" asked one of Mr. Fujikara's friends.

"Unfortunately, my workday isn't over." I sighed dramatically. "It's been a very long day, and I still must see to the Ferrari."

Mr. Fujikara's smile disappeared. A look of concern replaced it.

"Yes, the car. So silly of the valet to injure such a fine piece of machinery."

I nodded.

"I had driven it to Carne, the steakhouse on Charleston Boulevard. I'm sure it was fine when I brought it back."

"I *am* sorry," I said with as much sympathy as I could muster.

"Will your Boss be angry?"

"Most likely."

"Will he be angry at you?"

"He does hold me accountable for these sorts of transgressions." We both knew it was a lie, but that was part of the game.

Mr. Fujikara puffed out his chest in indignation. "Well, we

can't have that. I will pay for the car!" We both knew he was only agreeing to pay the few grand of the deductible, a paltry sum in his world, but his friends probably didn't know that.

"Oh, Mr. Fujikara! Do you mean it?" I reached over and grabbed his hand in both of mine. "What a kind and generous man you are!"

Mr. Fujikara beamed. His friends looked suitably impressed.

"Mr. Fujikara, you are indeed one of my favorites!" I leaned over and planted a kiss on his cheek.

"Now, now. It is but a small thing," he stammered.

I rose as Kimmy arrived with the champagne. "Gentlemen, enjoy." I smiled and bowed at Mr. Fujikara. "I'll look forward to seeing you soon. Perhaps dinner this week sometime?" I thought I caught a wink as he nodded in return.

Waving Kimmy away, he turned to his friends and proffered the bottle of champagne. "Let's drink!" He popped the cork and began to pour.

They all stood and bowed as I took my leave. It was very awkward, all this bowing—I'd never gotten used to it. Finally, I turned and tottered toward the steps. I almost made it to the casino floor. On the next to the last step, my ankle twisted. I yelped and grabbed for the rail, which slipped by, just out of reach. I started to fall. Out of nowhere, a pair of strong hands grabbed me.

"Whoa. Steady there."

I looked up into the twinkling eyes of Paxton Dane. Eyes that took in my cleavage, and my fuck-me shoes.

"Very nice," he said as he easily set me right. "And well played." He cocked his head in the direction of Mr. Fujikara, who, thankfully, was out of earshot. "Would you like to practice on me sometime?"

Intensely aware of the warmth of his hands on my bare arms, my heart tripped. *What is it with my taste in men?* Regaining my balance, if not my pride, I stepped away from him and smoothed my dress. "That's just a game Mr. Fujikara and I play."

"And you played him pretty well." Dane smirked.

"I've had a lot of practice." I grabbed his elbow and drew him into the crowd and away from the bar. I looked back at Mr. Fujikara and his friends. They were laughing. Mr. Fujikara caught my eye and raised his glass in a silent toast. I smiled and nodded in return. "I helped him be a big man in front of his friends. What's so bad about that?" Realizing I still had hold of Dane's arm, I let go and stepped back.

"If word of your personal touch gets out, we may have a rash of whales with fender benders."

"Not likely. Now, how do we go about finding a missing helicopter?"

"Want to go for a ride?" Dane asked.

"Don't tell me you found it already?" Just thinking about getting my hands around Willie's neck made me salivate.

"Unfortunately, no. But my contact arranged for us to view the videotapes of tonight's air traffic at the control tower at McCarran. Maybe we can figure out where the pilot went."

"I'm in, but I've got to do a couple of things first. Can we meet out front in a half an hour?"

"You got it."

I watched Dane walk away. When he was out of earshot, I keyed my Nextel. "Jer, what do you have on the mega-millions lady?"

"Mrs. Paisley? The tapes and machine are in agreement—she only played two quarters."

"What did she win?"

"Three hundred and sixty-five thousand."

Not a bad payday, but nowhere near the eighty-five million she would have won had she played six quarters. And I was going to be the bearer of the bad news. On nights like this, being the messenger not only put me in the line of fire, but also put me in a bad mood.

"You want me to tell her?" Jerry asked.

"You're a sweetheart, but this is what I get paid for." Reluctantly, I headed for the elevators.

Soon I was standing in front of the gilded double doors of the Sodom and Gomorrah suite. One of our best suites, it encompassed half of the top floor of the northwest wing. With its three bedrooms, great room with a bar, dining room for private dinners, and a large, Roman-inspired bath with a hot tub for you and ten of your closest friends, the suite was a favorite with the Hollywood and professional athlete crowds. Decorated in an over-the-top Egyptian motif, with gold columns, huge potted palms and clouds painted on the ceiling, the suite reminded me of the set of an old Egyptian horror movie. I had no idea how anyone could sleep in there—not that anyone spent much time sleeping in Vegas. In my opinion, the view was the best part, looking straight up the Strip.

I *so* didn't want to do this. The Big Boss would probably fire me if he knew how badly I wanted to give away eighty-five million dollars. I forced myself to pull the rope beside the door. Deep inside, a bell chimed. I stepped back, half expecting a tall, scantily dressed Nubian to appear at my summons.

Instead, the lady who opened the door couldn't have been even a fraction over five feet tall. And she was most definitely not Nubian; she was more like middle North American. Almost as wide as she was tall, she sported a cap of graying curls and the best set of dimples I'd seen in quite a while. Wrapped in one of the Babylon's terrycloth robes, which looked to be about three sizes too large, sleeves rolled up, and hem dragging the ground, her feet bare and her eyes bright, the little lady flashed a big smile.

"Mrs. Paisley?" I asked.

"For heaven's sake, call me Velma. Mrs. Paisley is, or was, my mother-in-law." She stepped back, opening the door wider and motioning me inside. "You must have drawn the short straw."

"I'm Lucky O'Toole, and I'm in charge of customer relations here at the Babylon. My job entails a lot of short straws."

"It can't be much fun coming to tell me I didn't win the eighty-five million."

So she knew. "No, this is not one of the better parts of my job."

Her three friends, also dressed in oversized robes, gathered around us. They all looked flushed, as if they'd been enjoying the hot tub.

"Goodness." She laid a hand on my arm. "Don't worry yourself. I knew I had only played two quarters. I'd been playing six most of the evening, but then, about a half hour before I hit, I switched to two quarters per pull."

"How much did you win, Velma?" asked one of her friends.

All eyes swiveled to me.

"Three hundred and sixty-five thousand," I said.

"That's wonderful!" Mrs. Paisley positively beamed. "After taxes that should be almost enough to get my grandson through Harvard."

"You have a grandson at Harvard?" I asked.

"Not yet. He's applied, but hasn't heard. He's wanted to go there practically forever."

"You don't seem upset about hitting the big one, but not winning the eighty-five million."

Mrs. Paisley held onto my arm as she directed me to a couch in the great room.

I took a peek at the fabulous view. The lights of the Strip stretched off into the distance. For some reason, I felt like shouting, "I'm king of the world," but that had already been done.

"Sit, Ms. O'Toole. May I offer you a drink?"

"Please, call me Lucky. Perhaps a small one." I was entitled to a drink; I'd spent the better part of the last sixteen hours at work—above and beyond by anyone's definition. But I hadn't eaten in a while, so the drink had better be small or I'd find myself sleeping it off in a stairwell just like our naked guy.

At the clap of Mrs. Paisley's small hands, a buff blond guy dressed in a loincloth appeared.

"Chad, bring Ms. O'Toole whatever she wants." Mrs. Paisley sounded imperious and impish at the same time. Who wouldn't enjoy having buff-body Chad waiting to grant their every wish?

"Scotch, neat."

Chad nodded and disappeared.

Mrs. Paisley settled in next to me. Her friends took the chairs across from us.

"Eighty-five million is a life-changing amount," Mrs. Paisley announced. "Some lives don't need that much changing. Mine's one of them. Mr. Paisley left me well taken care of. After he passed, I was bored, so I started baking pies for the local restaurants back in my hometown of Griffin, Indiana. Do you know of it?"

I shook my head. "Sorry, no." Chad reappeared with my drink. I took a long sip, gasping as the liquid burned down my throat.

"It's a small town, mostly farming folk, but we're on Interstate 70, so we get a fair amount of traffic." Mrs. Paisley wiggled like a puppy, clearly enjoying her moment in the spotlight. "My pies were pretty popular, and then Margaret over there..." She pointed to one of the ladies sitting opposite us. "Well, she was taking names of the out-of-towners who would call asking for us to send them a pie. After the names started adding up, she convinced me, and Paisley Pies was born."

"Paisley Pies?"

"We're small, but growing. All my kids and most of my grand-kids, at one time or another, have worked with me. My friends process the orders and handle all of the shipping. According to my grandson, I even have a 'Web presence.' I'm not sure what that means, but he seems thrilled. And the orders are increasing almost faster than we can keep up. So, Lucky, what more could I possibly want?"

"You're a real glass-half-full kind of woman, aren't you?" I took another sip of my scotch, enjoying the warmth—as much from Mrs. Paisley as the alcohol—spreading through me.

"Most folks only think about what they don't have. I know what I've got. Eighty-five million wouldn't make it any better."

I patted Mrs. Paisley's knee. "You are a breath of fresh air. And you have made my night." I pulled one of my cards out of my pocket and turned it over. "Does anyone have a pen?" I put my drink down on the side table. I'd just about polished it off.

One of the ladies found a pencil and handed it to me.

"Velma, what's your grandson's name?" I asked, pencil poised. "The one who wants to go to Harvard?"

"Pete. Peter Paisley the Fourth. He's named after my late husband and the other Paisley men before him."

I noted his name and put the card in my pocket. "Ladies, I must go. Meeting you has restored my faith in humanity. Please, order anything you want from the restaurant or partake of any of the spa treatments, on the house, with my compliments."

CHAPTER THREE

I DUCKED into my office. A change of shoes was definitely in order.

As I suspected, Miss Patterson still manned her desk. Her eyes twinkled as she handed me my flats. "I trust everything went smoothly with Mr. Fujikara?"

I nodded, and with a grateful sigh, I sank into the chair opposite her desk. "A bit more expensive than I thought it would be. Can you believe the little shyster tagged me for two bottles of very nice wine *and* a bottle of Dom Perignon?"

"I could take lessons from him," she said.

I snorted. "Be careful. You just might clever yourself right out of a job." We both knew it was a hollow threat.

"I've spent the last hour cleaning up your e-mail. You had another job offer from the Athena. The salary and benefits they're offering border on the obscene."

"My salary is already off the charts. The Big Boss will have to fire me if he wants to get rid of me. This is my home; I'm here to stay."

She visibly sighed with relief. "I prepared your response, but I haven't sent it."

"A simple 'thank you, but, hell no' will do."

She smiled. "I figured that's what you'd say."

My feet practically shouted with glee as I tucked them back into my comfy flats. "You know me well. Now, go home. I don't want to see your frowning face for at least twelve hours."

"Are you going home as well?"

"Soon, God willing, but I have to swing by the airport first. Oh, before you leave, could you have Paolo meet us down front?" Paolo drove one of the company limos, and he usually worked the graveyard shift.

"Us?"

"Paxton Dane is going with me. Paolo can be my chaperone." I had no intention of riding around Vegas at this hour of the morning alone with Paxton Dane—like I said, after midnight I have no self-control.

"I see." Miss Patterson's expression didn't change. "That could salvage the evening. Mr. Dane *is* a tasty bit of eye candy."

"I think I'll leave that comment alone." Weak, I know, but my skills suffer when I'm low on fuel and it's late in the game.

With a bland expression, but victory in her eyes, Miss Patterson handed me the satchel I called my purse. It actually was a prized possession—an Hermes Birkin bag. Obscenely expensive, sickeningly fashionable, it had been a gift from The Big Boss. "Jerry's package is in your bag, and the Beautiful Jeremy Whitlock will be by tomorrow afternoon around two."

"Right. Thanks. And what about Felicia Reilly? I assume she isn't on the property or she would be here."

"She called in sick."

"When was her shift to start?"

"Midnight."

"I see," I replied, but I didn't see at all. Another piece to the puzzle, but I had no idea how it fit. "Thanks again. And remember, twelve hours. Go home. Get some rest."

I charged through the office door and raced for the elevator.

∽

PAXTON DANE WAS WAITING JUST OUTSIDE THE FRONT ENTRANCE. He gave me the once-over as I walked up. "Your car or mine? And, for the record, I liked the other shoes better."

"You don't have to walk in them." I breezed past him and motioned to Paolo. "You probably drive an old pickup with a gun rack and a coonhound slobbering out the window. Let's take the company car." I didn't look at Dane as he stepped to the curb beside me. Something about the man kept me just a bit off balance. He practically oozed sex. I remembered the feel of his chest, his hands on my arms, his breath on my cheek.

I may have sworn off men, but my body apparently hadn't gotten the memo. My mind wasn't exactly cooperating either.

A sleek, black limo eased to a stop in front of us. Paolo jumped out and ran around the car to greet us. "Ms. O'Toole, what a pleasure!"

I liked Paolo, but, like a bright light, I could take him only in small doses. Dark and Latin, he had so much energy he seemed to bounce when he walked. Sporting an ever-ready smile, he opened the back door with the flourish of a matador taunting a bull.

"Paolo, how are Maria and little Javier?"

"Ms. O'Toole, you are so kind to remember my family," Paolo gushed. "They are wonderful. Thank you."

I ducked inside the cavernous automobile. I've never felt comfortable in the back of a limo—they were for celebrities and people trying to attract attention—and I struck out on both counts.

Dane took the seat directly across from me. So now I had to look at him or out the window. Great.

Before Paolo could shut the door, I remembered the little elephant The Big Boss had given me. I pulled it out of my pocket. "Here's something for Javier."

Paolo took it gently. "Thank you, Ms. O'Toole!"

"You're welcome. We need to go to the control tower at the airport. Do you have any idea how to get there?"

"I will find it. You can trust Paolo!"

As the car eased away from the curb, I leaned back and shut my eyes—that way I avoided looking at anything. The little headache that was forming earlier behind my right eye had bloomed into a thumper, the whiskey had left a bilious brew in the pit of my stomach, and I was hungry. I bet the three were related.

Without opening my eyes, I found the intercom button. "Paolo, are we too late to make a swing through In-N-Out before they close?"

"They turn out the lights at one thirty. We should be able to get to the one on Maryland Parkway by then."

"See if you can make it; I'm starved." I opened one eye and looked at Dane. He was watching me with a bemused expression on his face. "What? You don't mind, do you?"

"Now that you ask, no."

The lights were still on when we pulled into the drive-thru. Maybe my luck was turning—I was about due for something to go my way. I pressed the intercom switch. "Paolo, I want a combo with a large Diet Coke. Oh, and make it animal-style." I let off the switch. "Dane, what do you want?"

"I've never done 'animal-style'," he answered, his face an inscrutable mask.

I'll bet. He was just the sort who'd want to do the doggy. God, was my brain determined to stay in the gutter when I was around him? "'Animal-style' generally means they add grilled onions. What do you want?" I was way too smart to ask him what he wanted to eat.

"What are my choices? I've never dined at this fine establishment."

I leaned back and watched him as he perused the limited menu. "Don't let appearances deceive you. In-N-Out is a mecca.

Three times a day junk food addicts prostrate themselves in front of the counter willing to sell their grandmothers for a burger animal-style."

"You mean hamburgers aren't just for breakfast anymore?" he fired back with a grin.

"This is Vegas. We don't eat meals here; we grab food when we can find it."

"When in Rome..." he said with a smile. "Animal-style it is."

I depressed the intercom switch again. "Okay, Paolo, make that two number one combos, animal-style, both with large drinks. Mine's a Diet Coke, and Dane wants..." I cocked an eyebrow at him.

"Do they have Dr. Pepper?"

"And Dane's will be a Dr. Pepper. Then order whatever you want." I dove into my Birkin, rooting around for my wallet.

Dane stopped me. "Here." He pulled a couple of crumpled twenties out of his pants pocket. "Allow me."

I didn't come up for air until I had inhaled half my burger and almost all of my fries.

"Impressive." Dane, a half-eaten burger in his hands, watched me with a look of wry amusement and awe.

"Lunch was a long time ago." I could feel the heat rise in my face. Eating in front of people was hard for me. I'd never been petite, or small, or even medium-sized. In Las Vegas, a city where all the Barbie-sized clothes sell out first, I was a giant living in the land of the munchkins. Of course, when I deigned to shop, I had no trouble finding clothes in my size, which was a plus—literally. A saleslady once told me they stocked my size for the transvestites.

I took another bite of hamburger. "Besides, In-N-Out burgers and fries are two of the four major food groups."

"And the other two food groups would be...?"

"Krispy Kreme doughnuts and any kind of M&M's."

Dane threw back his head and laughed. "I like a woman who

relishes her food. Those dainty little eaters who order a whole meal then push it around their plate aren't for me. If you can add barbeque and beer to your list, we could be good friends."

Damn, now along with lusting after him, I was starting to *like* the guy—for sure he'd turn out to be a bum; it never failed. "A list to horrify a cardiologist—I guess we'll die young. But happy." He tucked into his fries with gusto.

~

MCCARRAN AIRPORT FRONTED THE SOUTHERN END OF THE STRIP on the east side. The airport worked in opposite rhythm to the city—when night fell, the Strip fired up and the airport wound down. Few flights operated at this time of the morning, although there were the obligatory red-eyes to the East Coast and Hawaii.

Paolo found the control tower in the web of access roads and runways, and pulled into the parking lot. I rolled down my window, stuck my head out, and looked at the dark tower looming above us. "So, what do we do? Knock three times and ask to see the wizard?"

"Do you ever turn it off?" Dane asked.

I donned my most innocent expression. "What?"

"Never mind." Dane wadded up the refuse from his meal and stuffed it back in the sack. "Coming?" he asked, as Paolo opened the door. Dane unfolded himself from the back of the limo and extended his hand to help me out.

I let him help me out of the car on the off chance he might turn out to be one of us good guys.

"We aren't exactly going up to the tower," he said. "We are going down to Las Vegas TRACON."

"I love it when you talk dirty." Jesus, was I flirting with him?

He shot me a grin.

"And what is TRACON going to tell us?" I asked, forcing my mind back to the business at hand.

He shrugged. "Don't know. The radar tracking files may show us where our helicopter went after depositing Lyda Sue in the pirates' lagoon." He identified himself into a speaker beside the door, then it opened.

I followed him down the stairs to the basement. TRACON was housed in a large, windowless room that reminded me of a huge, darkened theatre. Two banks of computers were arranged in concentric semicircles. In the dark, I could just make out several hunched-over figures, their faces illuminated by the displays in front of them. The figures spoke into headsets, their voices modulated so they blended into an indistinguishable background murmur. Additional displays hung at intervals on the wall, each showing various symbols that looked to me like Sanskrit...or Klingon.

"Beam me up, Scotty," I muttered, unable to help myself.

"Behave," Dane whispered through clenched teeth. "These folks take their job seriously."

"Oh, sorry." Pricked by his chiding, I feigned sincerity. "I must have missed the No Humor sign."

"You clearly missed the No Sarcasm sign as well." Dane shot me a dirty look. "Stay here, I'll be right back," he ordered, as he took off like a scalded dog, making straight for a guy sitting behind a desk in the far corner. Clearly, Dane thought there was no need to inflict me on an unsuspecting civil servant. Once in a while, I had to agree with his judgment.

I held up the wall near the stairs. From here, I could watch Dane unobserved. He was bent over a display, his ass pointed in my direction. My mind was just beginning to wander into forbidden territory when my Nextel vibrated at my hip. I was smart enough to have put it on silent. Its normal wail would shatter the silence in this techie mausoleum. Everyone in the joint would probably have a coronary and planes would fall out of the skies.

I pushed-to-talk as I bounded up the stairs, two at a time.

"Hang on," I whispered. I raced up the stairs and back outside, and stuck a foot between the door and the door jamb so I didn't get locked out. "O'Toole here."

"Hey, Lucky. Where you at?" Jerry was apparently pulling the night shift in Security.

"I'm hot on the trail of a missing helicopter."

"Then you're gonna like this. I just got a call from some irate Mexican dude—he kept cussing at me in Spanish like I was too stupid to understand." Jerry chuckled. "The dude was really hot. Even *I* learned a few words."

I gritted my teeth and kept quiet. Jerry loved to string me along when he had something really good to tell me.

"Anyway, it seems this guy works as security at Spanish Trail," he continued.

I couldn't stand it any longer. "Jer, I'm getting older by the minute."

"Right. Our missing helicopter is sitting on the ninth green of the Lakes golf course at Spanish Trail Golf and Country Club. Doors are unlocked, but no pilot. I promised the security guy a hundred bucks for not calling the police."

"I could kiss you!" I reclipped the Nextel just as Dane materialized at my elbow.

"Who could you kiss?" he asked.

"Jerry. He found something for me. Did you find out anything from Captain Kirk in there?"

"I'll show you mine if you show me yours," Dane said with an evil grin.

"Okay, smart-ass. You first."

We both walked toward the waiting limo. "It seems our boy circled around for a while after the gal took a header. Then he asked for clearance to Northtown."

"Northtown?" I asked, as Dane waved Paolo away and opened my door. We both settled in, this time side by side.

"North Las Vegas Airport, a general aviation field off Rancho."

"I know the place."

"My buddy checked with their tower. It seems the chopper landed there, but only stayed for a few minutes. The guys in the tower either couldn't see or didn't notice whether anyone got on or off. Once he was airborne again, they cleared him to the west. From there, the trail goes cold. After the chopper exited the airport's airspace, the pilot turned off his transponder and disappeared off the radar."

"Transponder?" I asked, then thought better of it. I could get a lesson in air traffic control some other time. "Never mind."

"Now I get to see yours," Dane reminded me.

"Well," I said, as I settled into the deep seat. "Before I turn my cards over, I call and raise you one dinner at the restaurant of my choice."

He whistled. "It must be good." He narrowed his eyes as he looked at my face. "Or you're bluffing." He waited a moment, then said, "Okay, I'll play. What do you have?"

I smiled and pressed the intercom switch. "Paolo, take us to Spanish Trail, the east entrance, please."

~

"REMIND ME NEVER TO PLAY POKER WITH YOU," DANE SAID, AS HE and I stared at the Babylon's missing helicopter, silhouetted by the eerie yellow glow of the streetlamps.

We were standing on what I had been told was the ninth green of the Lakes course at Spanish Trail. And sitting right in front of us, big as life, was our missing helicopter. In the dark, the faint glow of the streetlights reflected off its bubble cockpit. With its rotors sagging limply, the helicopter looked like a giant dragonfly.

A man emerged from the shadows. He wore the uniform of the security guards at Spanish Trail. "You guys from the Babylon?"

"I understand I owe you a great deal of thanks," I said, as I rooted around my Birkin. I was able to find three twenties, a five, and four crumpled ones. I felt like a kid amassing his allowance. I led Dane a few steps away. "Do you have two twenties?"

"What?"

Clearly, he hadn't been paying attention. I nodded my head toward the security guard, who waited patiently, not facing us, as if money were beneath him. "Two twenties."

"Oh. Let me see." He opened his wallet. "Two tens in here." Then he started pulling things out of his pockets. "Here, hold this stuff."

I extended my cupped hands. In them, he deposited several overladen key rings, two handfuls of coins, two rifle bullets, a roll of antacids, multiple wadded-up receipts, and several crumpled bills, which he extracted. All of it weighed more than my Birkin.

"With all this stuff in your pockets, what keeps your pants up?"

"The dictates of fashion."

I made a rude noise. "There are no dictates of fashion in Vegas."

"Good point. How about several local laws and the presence of an unwilling female, not to mention the security guard lurking in the trees? Will that do?" He smoothed the bills, then held them out for me. "Two twenties, as requested."

"Unwilling female?"

"You haven't exactly extended the welcome sign."

"This is Vegas, Tex. If I threw myself on my back in front of every pretty boy I see, I'd never get any work done."

"Yes, but all work and no play—"

"Makes Lucky a dull girl, I know. Now, about work. Take those twenties and the other money buried under your stuff here and give it to the guard."

"What are we paying him for?"

"Just do it."

He did, and the guard melted into the shadows.

When Dane returned, I handed him all his stuff back, dropping only a few coins in the process. "Sure makes it easier to find lost helicopters when someone calls and tells us where it is." Yes, I have a knack for stating the obvious. "So, what do we do now? Should we call the police?"

He walked slowly around the helicopter. "Eventually. But what do you say we take a look inside first?"

"After you. But don't touch anything," I said. Working in a casino, I'd seen my share of crime scenes. I knew the drill.

Dane pulled a handkerchief out of his shirt pocket, covered his right hand and reached for the door.

I grabbed his elbow, stopping him. "What if somebody's in there? Do you have a gun?"

"It's hanging on the rack in the back of my pickup."

"Guarded by the coonhound, no doubt. But, I'm serious, what if there's a body in there?" A vision of Willie having met his demise in a prolonged and excruciating way popped into my head. I crossed my fingers.

"If it's a body, we certainly won't need a gun." Dane threw the words over his shoulder as he turned to examine the helicopter.

I was right behind him. A shiver chased down my spine—I looked over my shoulder, but saw no one. This whole thing was creeping me out.

Using the handkerchief, and touching only the edge of the handle to avoid smearing any prints, he lifted the latch of the rear door on the right side. "If I remember correctly, Lyda Sue went out this way." He eased the door open, then flashed the beam of a flashlight Paolo had lent him around the interior.

Half expecting another dead body to fall out of the thing, and half hoping it would be Willie, I held back, keeping Dane's body between me and the helicopter.

"Nothing unusual here," Dane muttered.

Drat, no dead Willie. In fact, no Willie, dead or alive.

Dane then trained the beam of light on the door latch. "Hmmmm…"

"What?" I leaned around him to get a peek at what he was looking at.

He pointed to the inner workings of the latch. "See how this bit of metal is shinier than the rest? It almost looks like someone filed it so that..."

I could just make out what he was talking about. "Yeah?"

"And these striations in the metal?"

"Barely." I drew back. "What does it mean?"

Dane stood and looked at me. The look on his face frightened me.

"Murder."

⁓

THE NEXT HOUR WAS A BLUR. WE CALLED THE POLICE AND THEY arrived with sirens blaring, which, I'm sure, endeared us to the sleeping residents of Spanish Trail. We gave our statements—several times—then finally, were allowed to leave.

The clock struck three bells as I dragged my sorry ass through the front door of The Babylon. My brain had ceased working an hour ago, and my body was threatening mutiny. I had one last thing to check on before I headed home.

My luck appeared to be holding. Sergio still manned the front desk.

"Can you give me a quick rundown before I quit for the night?" I asked, as I propped myself up against the check-in desk.

"The mega-millions lady and three of her friends are ensconced in the Sodom and Gomorrah suite with their three masseurs—they requested tall, blond and decidedly male—and a feast fit for a king. I have the Ferrari waiting for the body shop to open." He ticked them off his fingers as he recited. "Let me see, there was something else..."

I wish he hadn't told me about the masseurs and Mrs. Paisley and friends. I'm very visual. I closed my eyes and tried to shut my mind to the images flashing across it. Were the young men part of the feast fit for a king? "What's the latest on the naked stair dweller?" Another wonderful image. If I ever got to sleep, my dreams were going to be doozies.

"Ah, yes, Reverend Peabody."

"*Reverend* Peabody? You're kidding, right? Of what church? The Church of the Seven Virgins?"

Sergio offered a tired smile. "As of last hour, the doctor had checked on him several times, and each time he was resting peacefully. However, I don't envy him the headache he'll have in the morning."

"So, he's all right?"

"Yes. The doctor will keep checking on him." Sergio paused. A slight frown creased his flawless face.

"How did you figure out who he was?"

"Security gave me the name he registered under. Needless to say, it wasn't his real name. I put two and two together when I kept fielding calls from a lady from Iowa looking for her husband. She said he was supposed to be in his room, but he hadn't called, and she hadn't been able to reach him."

"You've checked his room?"

Sergio nodded. "Empty. And I confirmed his identity with her —she described him to a T. At first, the wife was unwilling to tell us who he was, but I convinced her I needed to know his real name so that I might find him."

"Did you tell the wife we had him?"

"Of course not. I wanted to talk to you first."

"Perfect. Next time she calls, tell her that half our phone system is on the fritz, including the phone in her husband's room, and that you personally checked on him. He is, in fact, asleep and you didn't see any need to awaken him. In the morning, when our Reverend Peabody from Iowa awakens, give him coffee, intravenously if necessary, a hand towel for modesty's sake, and some aspirin, then have someone bring him to my office. I should be in by nine at the latest." I looked at my watch. "I may not be functional, but I'll be here."

I stepped through the front door and out into the night air. The artificial daylight created by the lights of the Strip held the darkness at bay. I paused and took a deep breath. The heat of the midsummer's day had given way to the coolness of a high desert night. Dry and still, the air was like wine, and I drank my fill.

My nerves were as frayed as the end of a broken rope.

Try as I might, I couldn't shake the image of Lyda Sue's body flailing like a broken rag doll as it hurtled earthward. Could it really be murder? And on top of that, add The Big Boss's strong hint that Paxton Dane was something less than the good guy he appeared to be.

I was toast.

My thoughts shifted to Paxton Dane. I had a hard time believing he was a bum. He seemed fine to me—more than fine, in fact. However, I learned my lesson long ago—my taste in men sucked. Since I was unable to stop fantasizing about Paxton Dane, history dictated he would turn out to be a bum. So, no welcome mat for Mr. Dane.

A nice walk and I'd be home.

A voice interrupted my reverie. "Ms. O'Toole?"

I recognized Paolo's voice. I opened my eyes, which took longer than normal to focus. When they did, I saw Paolo, his smile a beckoning beacon, standing at attention next to the open door of the limo.

"Need a ride home?"

I sighed with relief. "You, my friend, are a prince among men."

～

HOME FOR ME WAS THE WHOLE THIRTIETH FLOOR OF THE PRESIDIO, Las Vegas' premier multistory residence—or so said the sales brochure. A tower of glass, The Presidio was home to professional athletes, entertainers, extraordinarily rich foreigners...and me. My best friend, Teddie, occupied the penthouse one floor up.

In contrast to its exterior, the lobby was warm, with wooden floors covered with thick luxurious area rugs in rich shades of orange and red. Lush landscapes graced the faux-painted walls. The spa and fitness facilities were reputed to be the best in the city. The Presidio also housed the Silver Club, again supposedly Las Vegas' best private club. Who made these pronouncements, I didn't know, but you couldn't verify them by me—I'd never been to either one. I worked for a living. No, to be more precise, I didn't actually have a life. I worked and slept—not "a life" in anybody's book.

Forrest, the security guard, nodded as I staggered though the doors. A mountain of a man, all sinew and bulging muscle—he was the security guard from central casting. Rumor had it he'd played in the NFL for a couple of years, then blew out a knee. A nice guy, but I had no intention of ever making him mad.

"Ms. O'Toole. Tough day?"

"A little tougher than most."

"Yeah, I caught the news."

All I could do was nod. "Is Teddie home yet?"

"Not yet."

Teddie's show would have been over hours ago. I guess he'd gone out after. Everybody had a life except me.

I nodded as I stepped into the elevator, waved my magic key card over the pad, and punched the button for home.

The elevator deposited me in the middle of my living room.

"Where you been, bitch?"

God, I'd forgotten about the bird. My one foray into pet ownership and it had to be a belligerent macaw with a foul mouth. I walked over to Newton's cage. "Glad to see you, too, my pet."

The bird eyed me warily. "What's for dinner?"

"The usual." I stuck a stick of celery through the bars of his cage.

He attacked it with relish.

I wish I felt that way about celery. Weight control would be so much easier.

Despite Newton, my apartment was my sanctuary...walls of windows, high ceilings, and large open rooms decorated minimally with brightly colored contemporary furniture and modern art in brilliant hues on the walls—what few there were. The kitchen, so I was told, was a work of art. I wouldn't know. Give me a phone to order takeout, a microwave to heat it, and a fridge to store what's left, and I'm happy. On the other hand, the master bath was critical, and it was a masterpiece.

I may not have a life, but I have a great place to take a bath.

However, first I needed a drink. The bar was hidden behind a panel in the far wall next to the fireplace. I pressed the secret button and, voilà, a fully stocked bar appeared.

My hands shook as I poured a stiff shot of Wild Turkey 101 into a Steuben tumbler, added a single cube of ice, then drained it in one gulp. This was becoming a habit, a bad habit. I'd had more hard liquor today than I could remember drinking in quite a while. Of course, the drinking affects the remembering...Again, the amber liquid traced a fiery path down my throat, landing with a warm explosion in my stomach. The warmth radiated to the tips of my fingers and toes. I closed my eyes and embraced the relaxing heat, but I couldn't escape reality.

Lyda Sue was dead.

What the hell had she gotten mixed up in?

I hadn't a clue.

"So, what do you think, Big Guy?" I picked up a piece of browned apple and pushed it through the bars of Newton's cage.

"Screw you," said Newton, as he jerked the apple out of my hand.

"Bad parrot."

"Asshole!"

I laughed out loud. The bird actually sounded like he meant it. I'm sure a shrink would have a field day with me. Not only did I talk to my parrot, but I took shit from him as well.

"Enough out of you, Big Guy. It's time for you to rest." I slid the cover over his cage. "And way past time for me to sleep."

CHAPTER FOUR

"*R*ISE AND shine!"

Bright light flooded my bedroom. I rolled over and groaned as I squinted at the clock, then slammed my eyes shut again.

Seven a.m. Pretty early for Teddie to be sounding so chipper. He usually arose in time for cocktail hour.

"Okay, I can see we need to work on rising first. You look like you were run over and left for dead. Here, this ought to help." I caught the aroma of coffee and breathed deeply. "It works better if you drink it."

I pried one eye open, then the other as I pushed myself to a sitting position. Grateful, I grabbed the proffered mug and took a big gulp. I narrowed my eyes. "Are those my Manolos?"

Teddie stepped back, hiked up the hem of his gown and showed me the shoes. "Don't they just make the whole ensemble? I came down and borrowed them last night before the last show. I would've asked, but you weren't home."

Teddie was in full makeup, a long black wig, and chandelier earrings that brushed his shoulders. He wore a skintight, silver-sequined strapless sheath with a split on the side that bordered on the obscene, a hot pink boa around his neck—and my Manolos.

"You know how I hate it when you wear my shoes; you stretch them out."

"Oh, don't grouse." He pretended to pout. "I let you borrow my Chanel."

"You have a point." I inspected him over my coffee cup. "What keeps that dress up?"

"Modesty."

"Good line." That was the second time in the last few hours I'd asked a man what kept his clothing where it was supposed to be. What was up with me lately?

"I stole it from *American in Paris.*" Teddie, or as the world knew him, the Great Teddie Divine, was the premier female impersonator in Las Vegas. We'd hired him away from the Flamingo, and he packed his new theatre at the Babylon five nights a week, Wednesday through Sunday.

"I thought I'd heard it before." We both loved old movies. Tuesday nights were movie fest nights at my place. Teddie brought the movies. I made the popcorn—it was the only thing he trusted me to make and not poison him. "Are you trying to channel Cher in that getup?"

"I've added her to my act. What do you think?" He pirouetted in front of me.

"Sing something for me."

Teddie broke into a stirring rendition of "I Got You, Babe."

After a couple of verses, I held up my hand. "You got her down. But that's a duet. Who plays Sonny?"

"I was hoping I could talk you into it."

I snorted. "I'm a foot too tall, and you know I can't sing. Did you go out looking like that, or is all of this for my entertainment?"

"I did a private party after the late show. We sorta got carried away. I'm just getting home." He sat on the edge of my bed. "It seems you had a busy night as well. Everyone was talking about the girl and the pirate show. Was it suicide like the morning paper said, quoting you as the source, by the way?"

"Tell you what. Why don't you go change into the Ted Kowalski I know and love, and let me take a shower? I'll meet you in the kitchen in twenty minutes."

"You got it. I'll bring down some eggs and bacon for breakfast. The stuff in your fridge is green." With a toss of the boa over his shoulder, he sashayed out of the room in my Manolos.

I had to get him to teach me how to walk in those things.

∽

TWENTY MINUTES LATER, WRAPPED IN MY ROBE, I CRADLED A FRESH mug of coffee as I stood looking out the picture window in my kitchen. In the daylight, the sun seemed to suck the energy from Las Vegas until the city blended with the desert that surrounded it, where it waited to be reborn again in glitter and high-energy glory when the sun went down.

Fresh-faced, Teddie had traded his gown for a baggy pair of jeans and a Harvard sweatshirt that had seen better days. He wore his platinum hair short and spiked. His blue eyes—bracketed by lashes a girl would kill for—always seemed to dance at some private joke. And when he chose to flash it, his megawatt smile could stop male or female at a hundred yards. With a strong jaw and high cheekbones, I guess he could be considered pretty or handsome, depending on which way he played it.

I noticed his feet were bare, my Manolos conspicuous in their absence, as he busied himself over the stove.

I let him cook for me—he enjoyed it. Besides, I didn't know any restaurants open at this hour with a delivery service.

He put a plate of steaming eggs and bacon on the counter. "Come and get it."

I hoisted myself up and onto the high stool. "God, it smells delicious."

Teddie put a plate for himself down next to mine. "I'd make someone a good wife."

I tucked into my food as if I hadn't eaten in months. "No doubt," I said through a mouthful of eggs.

"How about me being yours?"

"I could never marry a man with better legs than me."

When Teddie played around like this, I never knew whether he was kidding or not. We were such good friends. Why screw it up?

"Okay, time to dish." Teddie sidled onto the stool beside me. "I want to know everything. What do you know about the girl who took the dive?"

Relieved that he'd changed the subject, I launched in. "Her name was Lyda Sue Stalnaker. I didn't know her that well, but she used to stop and gab when she caught me in the casino or Delilah's. She was from some small town in west Texas, and I think she was a little lonely."

"How'd a kid from small town Texas end up in Vegas?" Teddie asked with his mouth full.

"Same story you've heard a million times. She screwed up in high school, got knocked up. That screwed up her relationship with her folks. The abortion screwed her up." I passed my cup to Teddie. "Pour me another, would you? You're closest to the pot."

Teddie freshened my coffee.

"She came to Vegas to be a dancer and ended up a hooker. All in all, she was sick of screwing...up or otherwise. At least that's what she told me last night. She wanted to go home."

"So, why do you think she jumped?" Clearly engrossed in the story, Teddie cupped his chin in his hand, his elbow resting on the counter. He did love his gossip, but if I didn't want him spreading it all over, he wouldn't.

"I'm not sure she jumped."

Teddy straightened, his eyes grew big. "What are you saying?"

"I think she was pushed."

~

AT 8:50 IN THE MORNING, THE CASINO RESEMBLED A BEAUTY QUEEN after an all-nighter—tired, bedraggled, sullied. The cleaning crew ran vacuums and spot-cleaned the carpet. The smell of cigarette smoke, now stale, lingered, mixing with the odor of spilled liquor and other, nastier things I didn't want to think about. A few bleary-eyed stragglers, cigarettes dangling from their lips, fed coins into the slots, but for the most part the casino was empty.

I stood in front of my office door, rooting in my Birkin for my keys; the damn things always managed to hide in the bowels of the bag. I had found one half-eaten, slightly stale Oreo, three pieces of used gum wrapped in tiny bits of paper, and one squashed protein bar left over from my very brief personal-trainer phase, when my fingers brushed metal. "Ah ha! There you are, you little buggers." I was leaning over to insert the appropriate key in the lock when the door flew open.

I leapt back.

Miss Patterson stood there looking at me with that damn inscrutable expression of hers. "The door was open."

"I thought I told you I didn't want to see your face for twelve hours." I brushed past her.

She followed me into my office. "And good morning to you, too." She took my Birkin and deposited it in the closet. "You have an appointment..." she glanced at the clock "...in three minutes, with the Most Reverend Peterson J. Peabody. Security has been calling. They want to know if they should give Reverend Peabody his clothes or if they should bring him 'as is.'"

"The *Most* Reverend?"

Miss Patterson nodded, this time a fleeting wisp of a smile on her face.

"Oh, give him his clothes. I'm evil, but I'm not mean. Besides, it's way too early to see Reverend Peabody in his altogether again."

"I'll get you some coffee."

"After Reverend Peabody, I don't have anything else until two, right?"

"Right, the Beautiful Jeremy Whitlock at two, then your friends from Hollywood are due to arrive around three, with the Trendmakers shortly thereafter."

"Ah, yes, how could I forget?" I walked over to my closet and opened the door. "Let me know when Reverend Peabody arrives."

I stared at my reflection in the full-length mirror that hung on the back of the closet door. Teddie had kept me until the last possible minute. I'd had to race to get ready and out the door. I definitely looked like I'd had three hours of sleep, but I was semi-presentable in my new Diane Von Furstenberg wrap dress and sassy little sandals—another day saved by good clothes. The hair was a bit wild, and the makeup—well, I'd have to get Teddie's help there, too.

Satisfied I wasn't going to scare anyone, I shut the closet and retreated behind my desk. Miss Patterson, bless her, had set a cup of steaming java next to a stack of papers sitting there—I didn't remember the pile being so high last night. I grabbed the papers and a pen, hunched over my desk, and started in on the day.

I had almost made it through the lot when my intercom buzzed and Miss Patterson announced the Most Reverend Peabody's arrival. I depressed the intercom switch. "Show him in." I rose and smoothed my dress as I stepped around my desk to greet my guest. I had never met a Most Reverend before.

As the door opened, I extended my hand. "Reverend Peabody." I tried to keep my eyes focused on his face. For some reason, I was a bit embarrassed. Sorta like when you face a one-night stand the morning after.

I already knew he was a big man, but he carried all that weight on a frame about the size of mine. Like a fallen halo, a neat fringe of gray hair circled his head. Apparently, Security had given him a comb but not a razor—day-old stubble dotted his jowls. Dressed in khakis, a button-down, and Nikes, he looked every inch a respectable patron from out of town. No self-respecting Las Vegan would wear that getup unless he hadn't yet adopted the local customs or he was on his way to play golf. We're a bit edgier here in Sin City. Or tackier, depending on your point of view.

He shook my hand, but wouldn't meet my eyes. "Call me Jeep." His voice was soft, almost childlike—a far cry from the fire and brimstone I was expecting.

"Jeep?"

He shrugged. "I was always...big. In high school, they used to say I was as big as a Jeep. The name stuck."

"I see." Stifling a smile, I motioned to the sofa on the far side of my office, away from the windows. "Take a seat."

If it was possible for a four-hundred-pound man to slink, then the Most Reverend "Jeep" Peabody slunk over to the sofa and lowered himself to perch on the edge. He fidgeted with a button on his shirt.

I took the chair across from him, taking a deep breath and letting it out while I looked at my guest. "You gave us quite a scare last night."

This time, his eyes met mine. His eyes were bloodshot and blue, yet kind. "You're not going to throw me out of the hotel, are you?"

"Of course not. It's my job to take care of our guests. You seemed to have gotten in over your head. Did you just tie one on and go out the wrong door looking for the bathroom? You wouldn't believe how many times that's happened."

He turned his wedding band around and around. "I've gotten myself in a bit of a bind. Thought I could work it out. Guess I was wrong."

"What sort of a bind?"

"It's pretty simple really. My wife and I are swingers—Trend-makers. You know the group?"

I nodded, my expression unchanged. I'd learned long ago books couldn't be judged by their covers—especially in Vegas.

"We've been members for years, but we've been discreet." He paused. "Come to think of it, I never register as Reverend Peabody. How did you know my name?"

"It was given to me. I believe our front-desk manager got it from your wife, who called frantically looking for you." I held up my hand, stopping him before he asked. "We didn't give her any information other than that you were sleeping."

He nodded; I saw relief in his eyes.

"Why don't you continue with your story?"

"Well, someone got wind of our involvement in the group and started blackmailing me. I can tell you the church would take a dim view of a swinging lifestyle, and my parishioners...well it's pretty hypocritical on my part to preach monogamy, then not live it."

"I see what you mean."

"I know I'm taking quite a risk, but I'd never quit the group; they've done wonders for my self-esteem. I never knew how many women would jump at the chance for a roll in the hay with a big guy."

I really wished he hadn't said that—that whole visual thing again.

"They really were a godsend."

"God works in mysterious ways," I countered, pretty much at sea. "Now, can you tell me anything about your blackmailer? For instance, male or female?"

"Female. I'd never met her before."

"So, what happened last night?"

"I'd been attending a bishops' conference in San Fran. My wife wasn't with me; she's meeting me here this afternoon. I thought I would come a day early and arrange a meeting with the black-mailer, try to pay her off or talk her out of it. I don't know what I was thinking. We met in my room, 10123."

"What time?"

"Ten last night."

"The blackmailer actually showed?"

"Yes. Why?"

"Blackmailers usually try to keep their identity a secret. Was she on time?"

"Ten o'clock, sharp."

I depressed the intercom. "Miss Patterson, could you please call Security. Tell them I want to see the tapes of the main elevator bank and the service elevators in the main tower. Also any tape of the tenth floor in the southwest wing. The time frame I'm interested in is around ten p.m. last night."

"Right away."

I released the intercom switch and turned my attention back to Reverend Peabody. "Everything in this hotel is videotaped."

"Everything?" He blanched.

"Pretty much." I watched him wilt. "Now, go on."

"There's not much more. I had ordered a bottle of wine. She insisted on pouring. We talked." He paused and shut his eyes. "She laughed at me—I do remember that, but I don't remember much else until I awoke in a strange room with no clothes on. And then they brought me here."

I didn't have the heart to tell him his blackmail problem was probably much worse now. I'd bet my reputation that whoever met him last night had taken some interesting pictures after she slipped him the mickey. "Was the blackmailer working alone?"

"Couldn't say for sure, but I got the distinct impression she had an accomplice. She was nervous, and almost apologetic. Not at all what I thought she'd be."

"What did she look like?"

"Medium height, say five-foot-six or so. Trim with blue eyes. Her hair was blonde, but it looked like a wig."

I rose. Reverend Peabody followed my lead. "Reverend..."

"Jeep, please."

"Jeep. Let me work on this a bit from my end, see what I can find out. I assume you would recognize your blackmailer if you saw her again?"

"You bet."

I led him toward the door. "I'll be in touch. If you think of anything else, call me, okay? I'll give you one of my cards."

"Sure. Don't guess you could help me with my wife? She's going to be pretty perturbed at me for not calling her last night. I'm sure she stayed up till all hours trying to track me down."

The way the guy said "perturbed" made me think the woman was going to start lopping off vital parts the next time she saw him.

"Already taken care of. When she called last night, and we finally put you and her together, I had the front desk tell her half our phone system was on the fritz, that you were indeed in your room, but you were sleeping and they didn't want to disturb you. I think she bought it; I haven't heard otherwise. If I were you, I'd give her a call. Maybe apologize for not being able to call out. Do you have a cell?"

He shook his head.

"You're probably the only man on the face of the planet who doesn't, but the story should hold water then."

"I owe you one. How can I repay you?"

I ushered him out the door, stuffing my card in his hand as he was leaving.

"We'll think of something."

I turned to Miss Patterson. "Got anything for me?"

She adjusted her glasses on the end of her nose and consulted a notepad, which she still had to hold at arm's length to read. "Three suites with appropriate welcome gifts are prepared for your friends from Hollywood. The menu is set for their awards dinner—you are Mr. Jones's date, by the way. CNBC has been given the Golden Fleece Room. They are setting up their equipment as we speak. You have a meeting with the Beautiful Jeremy

Whitlock at two. The Trendmakers are coming by bus this afternoon around four. We will have refreshments for them in Delilah's."

"Another day at the zoo." I blew at a strand of hair tickling my left eye. "Call Bert at the dealership; ask him if he could lend me something fast. I'll have it back by two."

I stepped around the wall that separated the reception area from a small coffee bar and opened the fridge. Raising my voice to be heard, I continued. "Call Human Resources. Tell them I need a couple of copies of our file photos of Felicia Reilly and the Weasel. On second thought, get me a couple of Paxton Dane also." I grabbed two bottles of water, shutting the fridge with my foot. I rounded the corner just as the front door opened and Paxton Dane himself stepped through. I was glad he hadn't arrived a few seconds earlier.

"I caught you. Good," he said. "I have some news, and you're not going to like it."

"I knew this day was going too well." I stuffed the water bottles in my Birkin and slung it over my shoulder. My baseball cap hung on the hat rack in the corner. I grabbed it and slapped it on my head as I handed my Nextel to Miss Patterson. "You know the drill," I said to her.

"Don't call you unless someone has a gun pointed to my head."

"Right." I turned my attention back to Dane, who was waiting not so patiently. "Now, what's got your knickers in a twist?"

He cocked an eyebrow at me. I wish he'd quit doing that.

"You know those security tapes from last night you requested? The ones of the elevators and tenth floor?"

"Of course."

"Well, they're missing."

"Missing?"

"We looked everywhere. They're gone."

"I see." It seemed I'd been saying that a lot lately, when in fact, I didn't see at all.

Finally, Dane noticed the hat on my head and the bag on my shoulder. "Going somewhere?"

"For a drive. Want to come?" The Big Boss had said to keep him close. Besides, we needed to talk.

"You're leaving so early in the duty day?" he said with a smile. This time the smile reached his eyes.

"Call me irresponsible."

"I have a security briefing in a few minutes," Dane said, looking a bit torn.

"You can miss it. I'll fill you in."

The phone rang and Miss Patterson picked up. She listened for a bit, then said, "That was Bert. He said, and I quote, "'your chariot awaits.'"

I grabbed another hat off the hat rack and handed it to Dane. "Here. If you're going to play hooky with me, you'll need this."

〰

MY CHARIOT TURNED OUT TO BE A BRIGHT RED FERRARI F-430 Spider with the roof retracted. I slipped behind the wheel. "You're riding shotgun."

Dane whistled low. "Some ride. Apparently your salary has a few more zeros than mine."

"There are some perks to working for The Big Boss."

"You must do more for him than I do."

"No, I've just been at it longer." I looked at Dane, trying to determine whether he meant the implied insult or not.

Apparently oblivious to his faux pas, he was consumed by the car. His eyes shone with lust as he ran his fingers over the wood accents and the fine leather. Whoever said the way to a man's heart is through his stomach had never watched a grown man with a Ferrari.

We climbed in and pulled the seat belts tight. I hit the start button and the engine caught with a low growl. "I've got a stop to make on our way out of town. Hope you don't mind."

I threw it into gear and gunned the engine, drowning out his reply.

~

SMOKIN' JOES XXX ADULT VIDEO PARLOR AND SEX EMPORIUM occupied a warehouse that encompassed an entire city block on Tropicana just west of Interstate 15. Las Vegans referred to the interstate, which bisected the town north to south, as "the 15," and those who lived on one side rarely ventured to the other, for reasons I never understood.

Several women leaned against the building as I pulled into the parking lot. They were dressed in boots, tiny tubes of spandex— one for the bottom half and one for the top—heavy makeup, and hollow stares. The car did seem to pique their interest a bit. Or maybe it was the combination of the car and the male sitting beside me. "This'll only take a minute."

"*This* was the stop you needed to make?" Dane asked, unable to keep a straight face.

"Just sit. I'll be back." I maneuvered the car into a space and killed the engine.

"Want me to come in with you?" he said, as he flashed me a wicked grin. "I don't mind sharing a booth."

"Perhaps another time." I couldn't believe I said that. I pushed myself up and out of the low-riding car.

"I'll look forward to it, but in the interest of time today, I could help you shop."

The hookers had left their wall and were sidling over to the car.

"Or maybe," he continued with a leer. "I can do my shopping out here."

"Suit yourself," I shot back. "But I'll only be a few minutes and, unless you're Superman, you won't get your money's worth."

As I passed the women, I said, "Ladies, the car is off limits. Anything else that interests you is fair game."

Smokin' Joe himself was behind the counter when I walked in. Native American, rail thin, Joe had soulful brown eyes, thin lips that never curled into a smile, and tattoos that covered almost every inch of his exposed forearms. He even had "MOM" tattooed on the three middle fingers of his left hand, one letter on each finger. A hand-rolled cigarette dangled from his mouth. I suspected he'd done more than a little hard time. For some reason, Smokin' Joe seemed to like me. I tried not to be bothered by that.

He cocked his head toward the rear of the store. "New stuff's in back." He rooted through some papers on his counter and extracted one, which he extended toward me. "Here's a list of the good ones. Didn't pull them cuz I didn't know you was comin'."

I took the proffered list. "No problem. I'll get them myself. Thanks."

The back of the store was a city block away. I took the outside aisle, the one that separated the row of private viewing booths that lined the exterior wall from racks and racks of dildos of all shapes and sizes, vibrators, and other foreign objects. For a small fee, on top of the normal movie rental charge, you could rent one of the viewing booths by the hour to watch the movie of your choice and do whatever, out of sight of the other patrons.

Out of sight, but not out of hearing—a fact I discovered as I walked past the third booth, where a woman dressed in scrubs waited outside. Moans and groans and an occasional scream emanated from the booth. My cheeks flushed as I walked past and stepped around the waiting woman.

I'd made it a few steps before I stopped and turned around. My mother always told me my curiosity would get the better of me someday. "I know I'm going to be sorry I asked this, but why is there a line for this booth?"

"Oh, I'm not waiting to go inside," the woman said. "I'm a midwife, and my client is two weeks past her due date. It's an old trick of my trade. Sexual arousal seems to stimulate the birthing process. She was miserable, so we thought we'd give it a try."

"I had no idea." I listened to the moans coming from the booth. They were coming quicker now. "Seems to be working." I turned to go, then stopped. "What movie is she watching?" The woman gave me the name. I checked my list for it as I hurried toward the back of the store. Bingo.

When I passed her again, my arms laden with DVDs, a male voice tinged with panic shouted, "The baby's coming!" Better the baby than his wife at this point, I guess. The midwife disappeared inside the booth. A man stepped out as she went in. Pale and shaken, he took her place as sentry.

All I could think of was the story that kid was going to have when he or she grew up. Being born in an adult video store had a certain panache, a *je ne sais quoi*, if you will. I wondered if the parents would actually share the story.

I deposited my choices on the counter in front of Smokin' Joe. "Put it on my account, okay?" I was the only person I knew who ran a tab at an adult video store.

Outside the building, the hookers were again leaning against the wall. "That boy's got a bite," one of them hissed at me as I passed.

"You scared the locals," I said to Dane as I nodded toward the hookers.

"I was in the Navy. Hookers, I can handle."

I dropped my bag with XXX in big red lettering on the side in Paxton Dane's lap as I got into the car.

He took a peek inside, then shut the bag and looked at me with a thinly disguised leer. "You *are* a surprise."

"Those aren't for me." I started the car, gunned the engine, and piloted us out of the parking lot. "Those are for my mother."

CHAPTER FIVE

"*Y*OUR *MOTHER?*" Paxton Dane shouted to be heard above the wind.

"Contrary to popular opinion, I was not hatched from an egg," I said.

"Did you spring fully formed from The Big Boss's head, like Athena from the head of Zeus?"

"No, although I like that analogy. Unfortunately, I do indeed have a mother." Driving a bit too fast, I darted in and out of traffic on the 15. I noticed Dane's white-knuckled grip on the armrest, but I didn't slow down.

"Miracles never cease," Dane remarked. "But I wasn't really commenting on whether you have a mother or not, but on the fact that you buy porno movies for her. Most people I know spend half their lives hiding smut from their mothers, not buying it for them."

"My mother is unique." And a good thing, too—the world would never survive more than one Mona.

I slowed, but not much, took the off-ramp for the Blue Diamond highway, then hung a right, heading west out of town.

The Blue Diamond highway is another Las Vegas exaggeration. A four-lane with traffic signals every few hundred yards, at the edge of town it shrinks into a two-lane blacktop that bears little resemblance to a highway and has nothing to do with blue diamonds. Stretching across the Mojave Desert, it snakes through the Spring Mountains (another bit of wishful thinking) before dropping into the desert again.

We said nothing as we inched through traffic and around seemingly endless road construction. The heat of the beating sun radiated off every surface, smothering, suffocating, and turning the convertible into an oven of stagnant, superheated air almost impossible to breathe. Thirst, a mere discomfort anywhere else, triggered a survival instinct impossible to ignore in the desert. I pulled the two bottles of water out of my bag, handing one of them to Dane. We both drank deeply.

Finally, we reached the edge of town. The transition from city to abject desert startled me each time I ventured out of civilization. Without water, the desert quickly reclaimed all that man abandoned, and the land reverted to uncovered sand, dotted with patches of low grasses and prickly cacti. Everything about the desert was inhospitable, if not downright dangerous, including some of the flora and most of the fauna—a lesson I learned at an early age when I decided to run away from home.

Most of the traffic had filtered away when the highway narrowed, and I found myself faced with an open stretch of blacktop. A slight pressure on the accelerator and, like a horse ready to run, the car surged forward. The speed climbed. The dry desert air raced past, bringing tears to my eyes.

The fast car was my sin, Mother, my penance.

"You going to tell me where we're going?"

I glanced at Dane. He still gripped the armrest, but his knuckles weren't as white as before.

At first blush, I'd pegged him as a fast-car, fast-woman kind of guy. The look in his eye told me I was right about the fast-car part. "Pahrump. It's a small town just across the county line. Mother is expecting us for lunch."

"I hope she's not going to make us watch videos."

"First lunch, then a movie? You never know with Mother. She does like to shake things up."

"The apple didn't fall far from the tree then," Dane said through clenched teeth as we reached the mountains and I threw the car into the curves.

Too soon, we dropped down to the desert floor again and, thinking of the looming meeting with my mother, I eased up on the throttle.

"Tell me about this mother of yours."

"She can't be described. She has to be experienced."

Dane released his grip on the handles, then, like a kid, stretched his arms up into the flow of air. "Okay, she likes porn, and she defies description. Does she work?"

"She's owns a business called Mona's Place."

His head whipped around, his eyes big as saucers. "You're shittin' me. *The* Mona's Place?"

"Guess you've heard of it." I refused to ask him if he'd been there—I didn't want to know.

"Heard of it, who hasn't? It's the best whorehouse in Nevada." Incredulousness crept into his voice as the light dawned. "Your mother is *Mona?* I'll be damned."

"You and me both." I eased off the accelerator as we approached the outskirts of Pahrump. "And, if you value your manhood, I wouldn't refer to her place as a whorehouse."

Dane made a rude noise. "What does she prefer? Bordello? Pleasure Palace? Fuck for a Fee? The Bang Barn?"

My fingers worked the paddle shifters, dropping the car through the gears until I hit second, holding the twenty-five-mile-an-hour speed limit. "You know, you've got a real bad case of foot-in-mouth disease."

"Sorry, it's a gift," Dane said, not looking the least bit sorry.

"That's not exactly what I would call it. She is my mother—remember that. And bordello will do."

"While I extract my foot from my mouth, why don't you tell me a bit about Mona?"

"She's a businesswoman running a legitimate, legal business and she expects to be treated as such."

"You make running a bordello sound like owning a Jiffy Lube."

"It's closer than you think. The bordellos pay licensing fees and purchase business permits. The girls all must be registered with the sheriff's office, and they too buy business licenses. In fact, the survival of many of the rural counties in Nevada depends on revenue from the bordellos."

Out of the corner of my eye, I caught Dane squirming in his seat. An often uncomfortable topic, prostitution polarized everyone.

"Mona's Place is the most successful house in Nevada, and she's proud of that," I said.

"If you believe the papers, the bordellos are all jails where the girls are trapped and forced to do things they don't want to do."

"I've never seen one like that, and Mother would rather walk stark naked down the Strip than have people thinking that's the kind of place she runs. In fact, she believes she's running a halfway house for hookers. She takes in girls off the streets, cleans them up, and gives them a safe place to live and work. In addition, she makes them go to school, so those who want out can get out and not end up back on the streets."

"They have a school for hookers?"

I shot him a warning look.

He held up his hands. "Sorry."

"The girls who are in school work at night to pay for their room and board. Believe it or not, most of them earn their GEDs, then enroll in either a trade school or job program. Some have even made it through college."

"A madam who helps her ladies get out of the trade—that's an interesting business model."

"She keeps the ones who want to stay, and she feels good about the ones who leave."

"And it works?"

"More or less." Lyda Sue had me feeling a little less confident about Mother's exit strategy.

"A halfway house for hookers?" Dane shook his head. "Is everyone in this town one bead out of true?"

"Just a bunch of square pegs. Mother's latest project is to become classified as a charity. Income taxes really cut into her bottom line."

"I can't tell if you're feeding me a line or not."

"Ask her yourself. She got this whole charity idea after reading a story about a guy who personally 'donated' his sperm to interested females. Apparently, the guy felt his services were of a charitable nature—I guess he screwed only women who couldn't get it anywhere else; I don't know. Anyway, I have no idea how all of that turned out, but it got Mother started, and once she gets the bit in her teeth, she can't be stopped."

Dane stared at me. "Do you ever feel like you've been transported to a parallel universe?"

"All the time."

Pahrump had been a small town when I lived here. Now, fueled by the recent double-digit annual price escalation in Vegas, houses were sprouting like weeds on the outskirts of town and extending across the desert. Like a new Detroit, Vegas real estate had out priced its workforce. Pahrump, and a few other outlying towns, gratefully absorbed the overflow. The town had certainly changed, with new schools, a championship golf course, brand-name fast-food joints—the streets had even been paved. The locals were all atwitter over the arrival of a Walmart Supercenter. A long time coming, civilization had found my hometown, and I'm not sure that was a good thing.

Despite all of the changes, Mona's Place was still hard to miss. A rambling, three-story, bright purple Victorian, it sported hot pink trim, a wraparound porch, and a neon sign announcing the daily special. Today apparently was "two for one" day. I didn't even want to know exactly what that referred to. I prayed Mother wouldn't tell me and that Dane was smart enough not to ask.

As I pulled into the half-full parking lot, angled the Ferrari across three spaces and cut the engine, Mona burst through the bright yellow front door. Dressed in a tailored gray business suit that had "designer" written all over it, no blouse, a lacy black bra, and purple high heels—this season's Ferragamos—she stopped at the edge of the porch and waved. Her long brown hair was taste-fully pulled back, her makeup understated and impeccable. Huge square-cut diamonds twinkled at her earlobes and a single strand of peach-colored South Sea pearls ringed her neck and dropped strategically between her breasts. Not a trace of yesterday's tears remained.

Next to her, I felt invisible.

Mona was only fifteen when I was conceived. It had taken her years to figure out how to be a mother, and by then I'd left. We had made our peace, but some of the old scars remained.

I waved back. I'd inherited her height, but not her figure; her brains, but not her discernment—especially when it came to men; her high cheekbones, but not her smoky gray eyes; her long legs, but not her tiny ass. I have never met my father, but if that ever happens, he has some explaining to do.

"*That's* Mona?" Dane hissed.

"My mother, the poster child for plastic surgery. I hear she's in a neck-and-neck race with a woman from Brazil to see who can have the most procedures before they die. The Brazilian had a head start, but Mother's pulling abreast."

Dane opened his door and levered himself out of the car, then leaned in so I was eye to eye with his emerald greens. God, he even smelled good. "You weren't by chance the inspiration for the slogan 'Sarcasm, just another service I provide'?"

"If not, I should have been." I felt the heat rise in my cheeks under his penetrating stare.

"They say sarcasm is a defense mechanism."

I stepped out of the car, grabbing the sack from Smokin' Joe's. "I prefer to think of it as the armor I wear. Makes me sound more well-adjusted."

We both tossed our ball caps into the car. I fluffed my hair—Mother would not tolerate hat hair, and I didn't want to hear about it.

He took my arm, leading me across the parking lot toward the porch steps. "Or it's the wall you hide behind."

So, he was smarter than he looked. Men are pigs; smart men are dangerous pigs. Perhaps The Big Boss knew more than I did. However, I let Dane hold my arm. It felt good.

"Lucky! Sweetheart! Miss Patterson told me you were bringing a guest, but she neglected to mention he was such a dish." Mother gave me a squeeze, one that lasted just a fraction longer than necessary.

I squeezed her back. "Mother, this is Paxton Dane. He works in Security at the hotel."

Her eyes narrowed slightly as she leveled her gaze on him, then she shook his hand.

Mother could size up a man in a millisecond. If she could bottle that, we'd all be rich. "Mr. Dane."

Dane nodded in return.

I handed Mother the sack. I knew better than to come to Mother's house empty-handed. Today I brought her two treats—new porn and a handsome man. Maybe I'd get extra daughter-of-the-year points, although I doubted it. "Here's the new batch. Smokin' Joe put three stars next to *Going Down on the L.A. Subway*. Guess he thought it was the best."

"Sweetheart, how thoughtful! The girls are so tired of the last batch you brought."

"These ought to liven things up."

"I thought you might forget or not have time. I called Miss Patterson earlier to remind you, but you had already left and you know there is no cell service between here and Vegas."

"I'm afraid we don't have too long. I have to be back for a two o'clock meeting."

My mother nodded.

For a moment, I thought I saw disappointment in her eyes.

"I understand, dear. You two must be parched from the trip. Why you insist on riding in that car with the top down, I'll never know. That dry desert air sucks the moisture right out of you. If you're not careful, dear, you'll be a wizened old prune by the time you're fifty."

"Something to look forward to," I said.

Mother gave me a disgusted look. "You know, sweetheart, sarcasm is so unbecoming."

"I play to my talents."

"I guess you have to make the most of what you have," she shot back.

"Did somebody declare it Pick on Lucky Day, and I missed it?"

She opened the front door and motioned us inside. "I have lunch set up in the solarium. I thought that would be nice."

The main floor of the house was empty as we trooped through the foyer with its grand sweeping staircase, white Italian marble floors, and gleaming white walls. It smelled of gardenias and Pine-Sol. Snatches of music drifted down from the upper floors.

Mother had spent hundreds of thousands updating the decor to resemble a contemporary, luxury home. Two VIP suites with fireplaces, plasma televisions, DVD players, and state-of-the-art sound systems occupied most of the main floor, in addition to the kitchen and a playroom with a whirlpool bath. Each girl had her own room, some in the main house and others in the additional building out back, with a shower and bath and maid service from one in the afternoon until six in the morning. A gourmet chef and a small army of drivers, with cars to pick up patrons and then return them when they wished, rounded out Mother's staff. In the interest of protecting clients' identities, Mother had even installed a private VIP entrance and helipad so high rollers could come and go undetected. I had a feeling this feature was turning out to be more of a liability than an asset.

A table replete with white cloth, silver, and crystal awaited us on the screened porch, or the "solarium" as Mother called it, that stretched the length of the back of the house. Once seated, and Mother was satisfied with the arrangement, she picked up a small bell from the table and shook it demurely.

A young lady I had never met before appeared like an apparition. Skin the color of coffee ice cream, silky dark hair, and piercing blue eyes that challenged rather than welcomed, she was tall and lithe and couldn't have been a day over sixteen.

I raised my eyebrows at my mother.

She shook her head. "Don't be silly, dear. This is Tamara. She helps out around the house when she's not in school. Right now, she's home for lunch. Tamara, honey, would you bring us some nice iced tea? Maybe with some of that mint you picked this morning?"

The girl nodded, then drifted away like smoke on the wind.

My mother, the rescuer. After I left home at fifteen, a parade of girls about the same age took my place. They usually lasted through high school. Mother sent to college the ones who wanted to go. None of them were ever allowed to return and work for her when they became of age.

"Mother, you look divine in your battle dress. Whom are you crossing swords with today?"

"I have to be up in Carson City tonight. The legislature is back in session. There's a possibility they will hear arguments on the tax bill this week or next." She smoothed her pencil skirt and checked her cleavage, then she turned in her chair to extend her legs out from under the table. Her legs always were her finest asset, and she used them to full advantage. She crossed them suggestively, her short skirt riding even higher on her thigh.

Dane's Adam's apple bobbed up and down as he swallowed. He shifted in his seat, crossing his legs. Apparently, he was no different than all the others.

I hadn't yet met a man immune to Mother. She feasted on men like a lioness on baby gazelles—hungry, but indifferent. Why couldn't somebody develop a Mona vaccine? Competing with her for men totally sucked.

"The tax bill?" Dane finally found his voice.

Unable to help herself, Mona preened at his attention. "The legislature is thinking of taxing our business much as they do all the other businesses."

"Mother is a lobbyist for the Nevada Brothel Association," I added.

Dane looked dumbfounded, but retained his composure. "I see. And you are working to defeat the bill?"

"Oh, no. We want to be taxed like everyone else. That would give us some respectability, some legitimacy, if you will. At least that's the general consensus."

"Do you think you have a chance this time?" I asked.

"There's always a chance, dear, but it's not looking very good. Prostitution is still such a hot potato. The counties love the income, but the politicians like to pretend we don't exist. Afraid to be seen as proponents of the industry and afraid to outlaw such a revenue maker, all of them have parked their fat behinds on the fence."

"That explains why they all walk around like they have sticks up their asses," I said.

Mother hid her smile behind her napkin. "Crude, dear, but accurate."

"I need some help here," Dane said. "You *want* to be taxed?"

Mother shrugged. "It's tiresome always being the bastard child." She reached over and patted his hand. "You'll get used to Sin City. The people who don't fit anywhere else find their spot in Vegas."

"Square pegs and round holes?"

"Precisely."

"Lucky, too?"

"Good heavens, no. She's my iconoclast—she strives to be normal."

Dane threw back his head and laughed. "Exceptional, maybe. But normal? Never."

He thought I was *exceptional*—okay, maybe exceptional? Who knew? For some reason the thought pleased me. I tried to remind myself that all men are pigs, but I was having a hard time believing myself.

My mother settled back in her chair, a smile lifting one corner of her mouth. "I think I'm going to like you, Mr. Dane."

High praise indeed.

Tamara materialized with three frosty glasses of tea decorated with sprigs of bright green mint. The tablecloth, silver, crystal, and now the mint, I had no doubt our lunch would be dainty and served on bone china. My mother was seriously entrenched in a Southern-belle phase. I had no idea what she was trying to prove —nor to whom.

I took the opportunity to alter the course of the conversation. "Mother, can you tell us about Lyda Sue?"

Dane snapped to attention. "Lyda Sue?"

"One of the reasons for our visit. She used to work for Mother, and apparently she'd been coming out here to meet a high-rolling John. I'll let Mother explain."

"You keep your cards close to your vest, don't you?" Dane said out of the side of his mouth.

"Vegas survival skill."

The look he threw my way gave me the impression he was

rethinking that "exceptional" remark. Ah me, it was nice while it lasted.

Mother waited for us to finish before she started. Basking in the klieg-light glow of our attention, she patted her hair, sat up straight, played with her pearls until they hung just right, then satisfied, she held us spellbound, she began, "Lyda Sue—"

"Wait. Her *John?* You mean she was a *hooker?*" Dane interrupted.

Mother hated being interrupted. She cast an imperious look down her nose. "Mr. Dane, I can assure you, this is not the place to trot out your prejudices."

"Sorry, Ma'am. That's not what I meant. I'm just surprised, that's all."

"I see. And why are you surprised? Did you know Lyda Sue?"

I knew I could count on Mother. Arms crossed, we both looked at Dane and waited.

Gazing over Mother's shoulder, he cleared his throat and shifted in his seat. "Of course not. I'm just not used to this whole prostitution thing and sex being so out in the open here, that's all."

It was a lie, and all three of us knew it.

Mother and I said nothing. We waited.

Most men don't last twenty seconds under the heat of Mother's stare, but Dane was made of sterner stuff—he lasted a full minute. "Okay, here's the deal. Lyda Sue was from my hometown. Her older brother married my kid sister. A couple of weeks ago, Lyda Sue called her parents, said she was in some kind of trouble, but wouldn't give any details. She told them she'd work it out, then come home."

"And you chose not to tell us because…?" I asked.

"I do better running under the radar."

"I see." This time I did see—pretty clearly in fact. He didn't want us to know what he was doing. "Are you going to share what kind of trouble Lyda Sue was in?" I asked.

"She didn't say, and I didn't have time to find out before she was pushed out of the helicopter."

"Pushed?" Mother asked, her voice hushed.

"It's just Dane's theory right now." I patted her knee. "And just for the record, Dane, taking a job under false pretenses and snooping around behind people's backs isn't the best strategy if you want to get them on your side."

"How did I know I could trust you?"

"Oh, like the higher-ups at a multibillion dollar casino conspired to kill a lowly hooker."

"*Ex*-hooker." Mother's words landed with a thud, then their meaning exploded through my consciousness.

"She wasn't hooking?" I'd given her a part-time job as a cocktail waitress for the high rollers, but I'd thought that was just supplemental income for her. I had no idea she was trying to put her past behind her.

Mother shook her head. "The last she'd told me, she was in the running for a very prestigious, high-profile job at one of the big hotels—her chance at a real life, she said."

"Then why meet someone here?"

Tears sprang to my mother's eyes. She dabbed at them with the corner of her napkin. "It was a cry for help, and I didn't hear. It's all my fault; I killed her."

"Trust me, it's not your fault," Dane said, a vicious undertone to his voice. "You weren't in the helicopter, were you?"

Mother shook her head.

"Then you didn't kill her." He leaned back in his chair surveying both of us. "And we need to figure out who did. Tell us everything you can remember."

Mother took a deep breath, collecting herself. "Once a week or so, Lyda Sue would show up, generally unannounced. She'd go to the back building and wait for the Babylon helicopter. I never saw who came to see her. They'd meet briefly—no sex was involved— the room was still clean when she left."

"Did you quiz the girls?" I asked.

"Tamara helped me, and between the two of us, we've talked to all but a half dozen. We'll get to them today. So far, nothing. However, I do know someone you need to talk to."

"Willie the Weasel," I said, stealing her thunder. This was rapidly becoming another one of those days.

"How did you know?"

"Somebody had to fly them here, and this has the Weasel's fingerprints all over it."

My mother nodded, her brows crinkled in thought—apparently she was due for her regular Botox injection.

"After what he did to you, you should know."

～

DURING THE REST OF OUR VISIT AS WELL AS THE RIDE BACK TO Vegas, I succeeded in steering the conversation to more pleasant topics.

Thankfully, Dane hadn't pressed me about Willie. The memory of past humiliation was tough enough without being dragged through it all over again.

Lunch, if you could call it that, had consisted of finger sandwiches—cream cheese and watercress, I think, but I wasn't sure—a cup of vichyssoise, and one tiny lemon bar for dessert. Mother was really taking the whole Southern-belle thing to heart. Next thing I'd know, she'd want to join the Junior League. The thought made me smile. I'd pay good money for a ticket to watch Mona and the Junior Leaguers.

Dane had prevailed upon me to swing through McDonald's for fortification. I was a willing accomplice. Nothing was quite as much fun as driving a fast car across the desert while stuffing my face with a quarter-pounder. I have to admit, though, having a handsome male sharing the fun made it that much better.

81

~

UNDAUNTED BY THE SUMMER HEAT, THE BABYLON HAD AWAKENED and was in full swing as we pulled up the long circular drive to the front entrance. A horde of photographers materialized and swarmed around the car. Flashbulbs popped as they took pictures on the off chance that we were somebody. Ignoring the paparazzi, I hopped out of the car and tossed the keys to the valet. The crush of people, all pointing cameras and shouting at me, closed in.

Dane appeared at my elbow. "People! Out of our way!"

He took my arm and, like a hot knife through butter, slid me through the crowd.

"Impressive."

"Rescuing damsels in distress is one of my many talents." He gave a low bow as he opened the front door and invited me through.

People packed the lobby—nomads seeking an oasis of cool air. The lines at registration, easily twenty deep, snaked across the vast expanse. People shifted from foot to foot, but waited patiently in the conditioned air. Cocktail waitresses worked the captive crowd, which I'm sure added to their good humor. Reporters, followed by men shouldering television cameras, who in turn were trailed by minions working the cables, trolled for somebody "important."

I took one look at the swarm in front of the elevators and headed toward the stairs.

"What is all of this?"

"Welcome to Hell Week." I threw my weight against the stairwell door.

"Hell Week?"

"Let me fill you in on what you missed by skipping out on the security briefing this morning. This is the week that the entire porn industry descends on Vegas for their annual awards banquet —sort of the Oscars of adult film. The banquet alone seats thirty-five hundred. Add a couple thousand more fans who couldn't score a ticket to the main event. On top of that, ElectroniCon starts tomorrow." I took the stairs two at a time.

"ElectroniCon?" Dane matched my pace.

"The high-tech industry's annual gathering. Picture a hundred thousand geeks gone wild."

"Whoa."

"That's just the beginning. In addition to the awards banquet, there is a trade show. Every manufacturer, distributor, and purveyor of dildos, sex toys, vibrators, and herbal sexual enhancements will be here. The film stars hawk the products. The geeks come to gawk." We hit the door to the mezzanine. "If that wasn't enough, this is the week the Trendmakers hold their annual confab of spouse swapping. All the regular shows in town go dark; X-rated shows replace them."

Dane and I paused at the railing. Below us teemed the controlled chaos in the lobby.

I bent over to catch my breath, then straightened. "This"—I swept my arm toward the crowd below—"is only the beginning."

"Damn."

I was glad to see Dane struggling to catch his breath as well. "Don't expect to get much sleep, but now I gotta go. I'm already a couple of minutes late for an appointment and I've left Miss Patterson holding the bag too long already. If she quits on me, I'm screwed."

"Thanks for lunch—both of them. It's been a most enlightening day."

"Sure. Keep looking for Willie, would you?"

"Your wish is my command." Dane started to go, then paused. "Say, you wouldn't want me to see if I can score a couple of tickets for us to the porno awards, would you? As I recall, I owe you a dinner."

"A dinner of *my* choice, I believe. And, you're too late. I'm sitting at the head table with Subway Jones, the porn industry's biggest star." I held up my hand, silencing him as he opened his mouth to speak. "I didn't make that up, and no, I can't attest to the truth of the statement—at least not from personal experience."

"I *know* you're shittin' me now."

"Trust me," I said. "The dinner is the highlight of the whole week. I wouldn't miss it."

"How'd you get so lucky?"

"I wish I could say it was my innate beauty and captivating charm, but the hotel buys a lot of adult films for the in-house movie channels. It's my job to vet them all—wouldn't want to offend anyone's sensibilities now, would we?"

"So you *do* watch those movies." Dane's eyes lit with mischief.

"Actually, I take Smokin' Joe's advice. There are just so many hours in the day." I started down the hall toward my office.

"Wait." Dane stopped me. "I know I'm going regret asking this, but *Subway?*"

"Subway." I held my hands up in front of me, palms facing, twelve inches apart. "Because it's a foot long."

I left Dane standing there with his mouth open.

CHAPTER SIX

"*A*M I interrupting?"

The Beautiful Jeremy Whitlock sprang to his feet from his perch on the corner of Miss Patterson's desk, guilt written across his reddening features.

Miss Patterson busied herself rearranging the papers on her desk. She didn't meet my eyes immediately, but when she did, I caught a reddening in her face as well. Without a word, she handed me my Nextel.

"Ah, my ball and chain. Thanks." Stifling a smile, I glanced at the offending device—twenty-seven messages. I tried to scowl at Miss Patterson as I handed the damn thing back to her.

Miss Patterson gave me a goofy grin, which ruined any chance I had at mustering that scowl. Had a guy ever put that look on my face? Maybe, but white knights and good guys were the stuff of grade-school crushes, and that had been a long time ago.

I pointed to Jeremy, then cocked my head toward my office. "You, in there."

He bolted in ahead of me and immediately retreated to a chair opposite my desk.

I shut the door behind me, then settled into my chair. The desk between us, I leveled my gaze on the Beautiful Jeremy Whitlock. This time, I mustered that scowl.

Shaggy brown hair, baleful golden brown eyes, chiseled features and a lopsided grin, his name fit—under any definition of the term, Jeremy was definitely beautiful. Not many women were cold to his outward charms, but, if they were, when he opened his mouth, they were toast. Handsome men with Australian accents had a magnetism that American women—present company excluded, of course—seemed unable to resist.

He flashed that grin at me, then said in his delicious accent, "You summoned me?"

"I'm not sure I'd put it quite that way." Although, I had to admit, the thought of having the Beautiful Jeremy Whitlock at my beck and call did have some appeal. "Before we get down to business, a word to the wise. Miss Patterson may work for me, but she is also my friend. Break her heart with all that Aussie surfer-boy charm, and I'm all over you. Got it?"

Jeremy opened his arms wide, his face falling into a mask of innocence. "Hey, I like her. She's got moxie, and some smarts, too. That's more than I can say about all the bubble-brains who parade around here hoping to catch big money with their plastic tits."

I crossed my arms, leaned back in my chair, and took in all of the Beautiful Jeremy Whitlock. Miss Patterson might have a great bullshit meter, but I'd learned, when it comes to personal stuff, those meters can give you false readings. She was my friend; I had her back.

He squirmed under my perusal. "She's fair dinkum, and certainly no dog."

Even though I had only the vaguest idea of what he just said, he wasn't registering on my meter. He could live another day.

"A real nice lady, you know?" he said, each word pregnant with sincerity.

"I know. I'm just making sure *you* know."

"Of course I know. I know everything. How do you think I got rated the best private investigator in all of Las Vegas by the *Review-Journal* last year?"

"It certainly wasn't your emphasis on keeping a low profile."

"You can't get business if nobody knows who you are." Apparently satisfied I wasn't going to skin him alive, Jeremy settled back into the chair. Crossing one foot over the other knee, he held his leg in place with both hands while his foot bounced with nervous energy.

"A valid point. And, speaking of business—" I sifted through the pile of papers in front of me and found the pictures I had requested. I extended one set to him. "Here are photos of three of our employees—Felicia Reilly, Willie the Weasel, and Paxton Dane. I want you to input them into your magic machine, then tell me if any of these folks show up, where they appear, and where they go."

"So, you actually believe my—let me see, what did you call it?" He flashed that damn grin again. "I remember. I believe you called it my 'hocus-pocus machine.' So now you think it works?"

"I'm willing to suspend disbelief. And it's not so much that it doesn't work, it's that it seems so...personally violating."

He laughed. Unfortunately, he had a deep, throaty, wonderfully male laugh. A laugh that seemed to imply we were both in on a secret.

I shifted in my chair. Okay, I lied. I'm not immune to the whole Aussie thing. I chanted, *All men are pigs,* over and over in my head. It didn't work this time either.

"You don't have to believe me," Jeremy continued. "The NSA is using the same software. They actually take pictures of all of us through cameras strategically located in most of the major cities, then compare us to an international database of known bad guys."

"Jesus, George Orwell was right. And, come to think of it, so was I."

"Huh?"

"Big Brother really is watching." I found that little bit of reality totally depressing. "Talk about personal violation!"

"You have no idea." Jeremy nodded, his eyes big—their gold flecks catching the light, momentarily distracting me. "This is just the tip of the iceberg. Don't get me started on cell phones used as listening and tracking devices. And then there are satellites. Did you know they can read your license plate using those things?"

I held up my hands. "You mean they can see our faces, our...everything?"

The Beautiful Jeremy Whitlock nodded, a serious look on his face, but a twinkle in those gold-flecked eyes. "Takes voyeurism to a whole new level, doesn't it?"

Why I ever leave the house in the morning, I don't know. "Are they allowed to do that?"

"Are *we*?"

I shrugged. "You have a point."

Jeremy nodded. "Anyway, we all have a unique set of facial measurements. The machine compares them, that's all."

"Like fingerprints."

"Exactly, but now Big Brother doesn't have to stop everyone on the street and ask them to roll ink on their fingers. In fact, we don't have to ask them for permission at all."

"People on the streets or everyone in a casino."

"Precisely." Jeremy nodded.

"Scary."

"But helpful."

"I'll go along, but only if they take pictures of everybody else." Call me morally corrupt, but I wasn't above letting the end justify the means—as long as I was the one pulling the strings.

"I do this for all of the casinos. The images come right from their security videos. It actually works quite well. We've caught a fair number of cheats and card counters. No terrorists, yet." He actually sounded disappointed about the terrorist part. "But, if it makes you feel better, I'll make a note—no pictures of Lucky O'Toole."

"Please do."

"You got it." Jeremy flashed that grin again as he took the pictures and stood.

Damn, he even had dimples. What was it with me lately? A handsome guy flashes me a grin, and I melt into a puddle. And a handsome guy who was off limits at that—I would never pull the rug out from under Miss Patterson. I must be hormonal.

"The normal fee?"

"There's a bonus in it if you start right away."

"That important?" He looked like he was going to perch on the corner of my desk, then thought better of it. "This wouldn't have anything to do with a certain helicopter, would it?"

"This has everything to do with that frigging helicopter."

"Right. I'll fossick through all the feeds myself. I'll let you know when I have something." Jeremy hurried out. He didn't linger in the outer office.

The man sure had a way with words.

For a fleeting moment I felt bad siccing Jeremy on Paxton Dane. Although Dane was charming, and I wanted him to be one of us good guys, he'd lied once—that I knew of. Lies were sorta like cockroaches: where you saw one, there were probably a thousand lurking out of sight. What was that old adage my mother pounded me with? *Fall for it once, shame on you. Fall for it twice, shame on me.* I took another set of the three pictures, folded them, and stuffed them in my pocket.

I was just rising to leave when Miss Patterson peeked around the doorway. "Could I have a minute? I won't take long. I know you have the Hollywood crowd in about a half hour."

I sank back into my chair and motioned for her to take a seat.

Like a bird at a feeder, Miss Patterson perched on the edge of the chair, which probably still held the warmth from the Beautiful Jeremy Whitlock's butt. I squeezed my eyes shut in an effort to block the images that thought conjured up.

"Do you have a headache? There's some aspirin in the cabinet. I could get you some."

I sneaked one eye open. No mental images of Jeremy's butt. I eased open the other eye. Miss Patterson, her feet and knees demurely touching, her hands resting in her lap, was the very picture of propriety. Concern clouded her eyes.

"Aspirin wouldn't put a dent in the kind of headaches I'm dealing with."

"Oh, am I going to have to lock up all the weapons again?"

I couldn't even muster a smile.

She started to rise. "I've caught you at a bad time."

"Sit. Sit." I rubbed my temples and took a deep breath. "You know how I get after a trip to Mother's."

"She does seem to dampen your normal effervescence."

Effervescence. I don't think I had ever before heard anyone use that word and my name in the same sentence. My smile fought with my foul humor. My smile won.

"Hah! I knew you were in there somewhere hiding behind that scowl." Miss Patterson looked triumphant.

"You've done your good deed for the day. They'll be proud of you at the next Girl Scout meeting. Are you working toward a good deed badge or something?"

"If they had such a thing, my chest would be covered with them by now."

"And you'd be well on your way to sainthood. So, you don't really think I'm effervescent?"

"Not today."

"A diplomat to the end. So what can this lowly grump do for you?"

"I need some advice."

"It'll be worth what you pay for it."

"I'll take my chances."

"It's your funeral."

"Would you stop?" Miss Patterson finally threw up her hands

in submission. "I don't want your bad mood, but that's what I'm going to get if you keep up this verbal parrying."

"It takes two to play," I mumbled.

She smoothed her skirt and harrumphed a bit more. "You can be so difficult."

"So I've been told."

"Anyway, I came to ask your opinion."

Opinion. I hated that word. My mother once gave me a tee shirt that said, "Everyone is entitled to my opinion." She said it was so *me*—opinions were my best thing. All these years later, I'm still trying to figure out what she meant by that. Was it a good thing or a bad thing? Why did I care? "It's Jeremy, isn't it?"

"Is it that obvious?" She looked embarrassed.

"Only to me," I lied.

"Good." She picked at an invisible piece of lint on her skirt. "Do you think I'm...overreaching?"

Miss Patterson, a cougar? Wow. An image of a wolf in sheep's clothing popped into my head, but the wolf was a she. The tables were turned. I liked it.

I tried to keep my face arranged in a benign expression. "Absolutely not!"

She went to work on that invisible piece of lint again. After a moment, she raised her eyes to meet mine.

I'd never noticed her pale blue eyes; the glasses didn't do much to bring them out. Her hair was a pretty color of brown. We could get rid of the few traces of early gray...Those changes, coupled with her peaches-and-cream skin, impish smile, and maybe a new wardrobe and she'd be in business. A makeover—that would be fun! Yes, we should start with the hair.

"I was going to ask you to make me an appointment with Linda," I said, as if I'd been thinking about it all along. "She's a magician when it comes to hair. Would you like her to look at yours as well?"

"She's the most expensive in town."

"Because she's the best. What do you say? My treat?"

Miss Patterson nodded, a smile tickling her lips.

"You book it. And make it soon, I think birds have come home to roost in my hair." I rose. Miss Patterson followed my lead. "Clear my schedule, and we will drink champagne while Linda makes us beautiful."

Lost in thought, Miss Patterson seemed to float out of my office.

I heard her on the phone making our appointments. Next, I hoped she would tackle the accumulated messages on my Nextel. I thought about leaving, but the pile of papers on my desk called to me. The damned things seemed to propagate every time I turned my back. If I didn't at least try tackling them now, there'd be twice as many to deal with tomorrow. I had twenty minutes before I was due out front. That should be enough time to at least make a dent.

I hadn't even gotten started, when Miss Patterson buzzed me. "Yeah."

"Detective Romeo to see you. I told him you are very busy."

First the morning with my mother, now the afternoon with the police. God was punishing me. "Five minutes, that's all I've got."

I didn't even look up as he walked in the door.

"You must've gone home. You've changed clothes." As greetings go, his was certainly unique.

I looked up and motioned for him to take a seat. "No need to go home. I just step into the nearest phone booth and, voilà, a new set of civilian clothes."

Romeo crossed one leg over the other, his foot resting on his knee. "Handy."

I leaned back in my chair and tented my fingers as I gave him the once-over. Young, wet behind the ears, cute in a puppy-dog kind of way, and, while I had changed my clothes, he looked as though he'd slept in his. "You look like you could use one of my phone booths. Have you even been to sleep?"

"Not yet."

Next to his night, my measly three hours of sleep looked positively self-indulgent. "So, what can I do for you?"

He uncrossed his legs and leaned forward. Earnest was the only way to describe him. "I came to apologize for Detective Richards. He was a bit abrasive last night."

"I thought this whole good cop/bad cop thing was supposed to be done as a tag team." I felt the edges of that bad mood start to wrap around me again.

He looked wounded. "Is it just me, or do you throw darts at everyone?"

"Everyone with a badge in his pocket."

"We're the good guys, remember?" He really was as young as he seemed.

"I keep trying to remember that," I explained. The kid was overdue for a dose of the real world. "But look at it from where I'm sitting. I found the helicopter. You can't seem to deliver the pilot. You take up not only my time, but other employees' time as well, not to mention the chilling effect your skulking around has on our guests. If you have some info, you won't share it with me."

The hangdog look on his face told me I was getting through.

"And, if—and that's a big if—you solve the case, I'll find out about it by reading the morning newspaper. So, tell me, why am I supposed to be happy to see you?"

Deflated, he sank back into the deep chair. "Well, when you put it that way..."

"I'll tell you what, Romeo. I like you. I really do. What do you say we work together to solve this thing? I think, between the two of us, we could do it."

He perked right up. "You think so?"

Like taking candy from a baby. "I know so."

At my beckoning, he leaned in closer.

"I've got something I need you to do," I told him.

~

THE CHAOS IN THE LOBBY HAD RATCHETED UP AT LEAST THREE notches by the time I had sent Romeo on his way, then hit the stairwell door and added my body to the teeming mass of humanity. I pushed my way through, then stepped back into an alcove near the front doors, flipped open my cell and hit the number two key.

Teddie answered on the first ring. "Yo."

"If you're not awake, you should be."

"Hello to you, Miss Sunshine. I'll have you know I'm up, dressed, and actually heading out the door to come find you. What's up?"

A scrum of intoxicated males invaded my alcove, laughing and high-fiving each other. They seemed unaware of my existence as I pressed back against the wall.

"I've got a mission for you," I shouted.

"A what? Speak up. You sound like you're in a riot. Where are you and what am I missing?"

I cupped my hand around my mouth and the phone, which was pressed tightly to my lips. "I'm in the lobby. If you get here quick, you'll be in time to greet the Hollywood crowd."

"They're worth the price of admission. I'll hurry."

"Great, but I want you to think about something, and it's a secret."

His voice took on a conspiratorial timbre. "What did you have in mind?"

~

AT THE STROKE OF THREE, A BUS PULLED UP OUT FRONT, WHIPPING the crowd to a fevered pitch. Caught in a rip current of humanity,

I elbowed and shoved, but couldn't make any headway from my alcove near the front door toward the bus.

"Here, let me." Paxton Dane appeared at my side. He grabbed my elbow and eased me forward. "This is one of my strengths, remember?"

He didn't say a word and magically the sea of people parted.

"Where'd you learn how to do that?"

"Chivalry school."

"So, chivalry isn't dead?"

"Not in Texas, and most certainly not in my mother's house." Dane stepped over the rope holding the crowd back and deposited me curbside at the unopened door of the bus.

"Your mother sounds like my kind of woman."

"She'd like you, too. You two are more alike than you could imagine."

I'm not sure if that was a good thing or not. I guess it depended on how Dane felt about his mother. And how I felt about Dane.

I had no time to dwell on it as the door of the bus opened.

A roar from the crowd greeted Subway Jones as he appeared on the top step.

Everything about Subway was average—well, not everything. Everything about his *appearance* was average. Average height, average weight, brown hair, brown eyes, pasty white skin that still bore the ravages of a serious teenage acne problem. Not yet forty, he had the beginnings of a slight paunch. Dressed in a loud Hawaiian shirt, khakis, and sandals, he looked like an insurance salesman from Duluth.

He did an exaggerated bump and grind, and I thought several of the girls at the front of the crowd were in danger of fainting.

"Who's that?" Dane shouted into my ear.

"Subway Jones."

The look on Dane's face was truly a Kodak moment.

I grabbed his shirt and pulled him down so I could shout into his ear. "Being a porn star is like being a writer—only one talent is needed, and nobody cares what you look like."

Dane's mouth, which had been hanging open, snapped shut, and he swallowed hard.

The boy was clearly in over his head.

Subway's eyes zeroed in on me, and I braced myself.

He launched himself down the steps. "Lucky!" He grabbed me and, to the roar of the crowd, planted a big kiss on my lips as he dipped me over his bended knee. After a few moments milking the crowd, he righted me. "How the hell are ya?"

"Never better."

He held me at arm's length. "Woman, you look fabulous."

"Liar." I motioned toward Dane, who was standing next to me like a dumbstruck child. "Subway, I'd like you to meet Paxton Dane, one of our new Security guys."

The men shook hands, but Subway barely gave Dane a glance before turning his attention back to me. Subway had little time for men taller and more handsome than himself, which meant he spent most of his time in the company of women. He hooked his arm through mine. "Where's Theodore?"

"He'll be here any minute." Security held back the crowd as we made our way to the lobby. I felt Dane right behind me. "He had a late night last night."

"Theodore?" Dane asked.

As if on cue, Teddie materialized in front of us.

"Hands off my woman!"

Subway dropped my arm and grabbed Teddie in a bear hug. "Theodore!"

Beside me, Dane leaned in, his mouth close to my ear. "How could you let that man kiss you?"

"Jealous?" His cologne was subtle, masculine, intoxicating. I tried holding my breath, but that was a short-term resistance method. I could do it only so long before fainting, so I quit.

"Now, that's a loaded question. Sorta damned if I do, damned if I don't kind of thing." He reddened and ground to a halt.

Amused, I crossed my arms and waited. I'd be damned if I was going to rescue him.

Dane took a deep breath. "It's just, well...you don't know where his lips have been."

"Oh, for heaven's sake!" I stopped for a moment. "If you think about it, Subway doesn't do anything without a camera rolling, so everybody knows exactly where his lips have been."

"That's precisely my point." Dane spread his arms wide, hitting a tall redhead smack in the boobs. He retracted his arm as if he'd been burned. "Sorry," he mumbled, his face flushed in embarrassment.

She gave him a withering stare, then moved on.

"If I'm to catch a dreaded disease, it'll have to be from someone else. Miranda would kill him if he put his lips anywhere she hadn't fully vetted. He's still walking and talking, so I feel pretty safe in assuming he's been a good boy."

"Who's Miranda?"

"Subway's wife."

"He has a *wife?*"

"Well, more like a keeper than a wife."

We both watched Subway as he wiggled and squirmed for the women, then pinched one little blonde on the ass. She giggled then lifted her shirt, showing off perfect, surgically mounted, EEE cantaloupes. The crowd roared its approval.

Dane shook his head. "If I pinched that girl on the ass, she'd break my nose."

"Nobody said life was fair. You're beautiful, he's...good —apparently."

Dane leaned down, looking me right in the eye, his voice low and seductive. "How do you know I'm not...good?"

Miranda Jones, who had appeared at my side, answered the question, rescuing me from my own stupidity. "Cowboy, in our business, good means you have a twelve-inch dick, can get it up on demand in front of a crowd, and keep it up until we've finished doing whatever we want with it."

Dane straightened as if he'd been touched with a cattle prod. "Well…" He swallowed hard, then clamped his mouth shut.

I didn't blame him. I wouldn't have known how to respond either.

Miranda continued. "You have no idea how long it took me to find him—Subway, I mean. I auditioned probably over a thousand guys." She put her hand on Dane's arm. I thought I saw him flinch. "Do you know how I met the little creep? In the produce aisle at the Piggly Wiggly! Can you believe it?"

Mute, we both shook our heads.

I could only imagine how an audition for a porn film would go. I had never found the courage to ask her, so I was left with my imaginings. The mental images were impossible to chase away. It was a good thing I'd already had lunch. One look at Dane's color-less face and I knew he was thinking the same thing.

We stood there for a moment, then I snapped out of it. "Miranda." I gave her a hug. "So good to see you. You two really know how to liven things up."

"Honey, that's our job." I'd known Miranda since grade school, and she constantly surprised me with her many incarnations. Today, she was the personification of the predatory female. Tall, buff and well-lipoed, she sported jet black hair as straight and as coarse as a horse's tail, and piercing gray eyes. She changed her hair color and her eye color as often as film stars changed spouses. Miranda had told me that contact lenses allowed her to fully coordinate. I was in awe. Each morning, I found it next to impossible to find a dress and a pair of shoes that matched.

Sporting a shiny black cat suit that adhered to her every curve, long hot pink nails, black stilettos, and makeup that looked like it had been applied by one of Cleopatra's handmaidens, Miranda liked to think of herself as a Hollywood creation. In my mind,

Burbank creation was more like it, but we all have our private little fantasies. She had been an adult star herself, until she realized the money was in producing the films, not performing in them.

While Subway did it for the fun, Miranda did it for the money.

She still had a grip on Dane's arm. "Honey, who is this beefcake?" She pinched his biceps and narrowed her eyes, as if sizing up a stud horse at auction.

Dane looked like he'd been stung by a scorpion. I half thought about leaving him to be feasted on, but then relented—good security guards are so hard to find.

"Down, girl. I can assure you The Big Boss would take a dim view of one of our Security hunks moonlighting as one of your screwing machines."

"Pity." She gave him a little slap on the ass as she looked him up and down. "You let me know if you ever want to change careers, cowboy." Miranda let go of Dane's arm.

Once released, Dane bolted toward the casino. He didn't even say good-bye.

We watched him go. "Miranda, you have got to stop terrorizing the help."

She looked at me, her eyes wide with innocence, then she burst out laughing.

"And you can drop the Vampira act now," I added. "Nobody's looking at you. Subway's got them all mesmerized."

"I know, but it's so much fun." She twirled in front of me. "What do you think of the outfit? Is it too much?"

"All you're missing are the whips and chains."

She giggled then hooked her arm through mine. "I know. Subway loves it. At home, I put this on and—"

I held up my hand. "Whoa. Stop. Too much information, dear. And I shock easily."

"You always were the Goody Two-shoes."

"And look how far it's gotten me."

"Yes, but you look a bit ragged around the edges." This time my friend looked me right in the eye, her smile fading a bit. "Not getting any, are you?"

I gave her a dirty look.

"What?" she asked, trying to look innocent, which was about as impossible as Angelina Jolie trying to look virginal. "I know, none of my business. But, are you having *any* fun?"

"Life's just shits and giggles."

"Bullshit," Teddie announced, as he appeared at my elbow and threw his arm around my shoulder. "Miranda, you talk to our girl here; she's losing her smile."

Miranda nodded, her forehead scrunched in concentration. "I can see that."

I shrugged out from under Teddie's arm. "Enough out of you two. I've got a casino full of people to keep happy, a weasel to locate, and two large parties to coordinate. The Big Boss is riding my ass. And the police are snooping around, spooking the guests."

"Well, look who's gone and gotten all grown-up," Miranda huffed, as she grabbed Teddie's hand. "Come with me, Peter Pan. Leave old Wendy here to wallow in her worries. I happen to know where the bar is, and I'm in desperate need of some liquid fortification. We'll put it on Wendy's tab." She pulled him with her as she disappeared into the crowd. Neither one of them looked back.

Great, I'd just been told off by a woman who screwed for a living and a guy who looked better in my clothes than I did. I thought I'd hit rock bottom when my Nextel vibrated to life.

"Lucky?" Miss Patterson's voice sounded a bit strained.

"Right here. Whatcha got?"

"Remember Mr. Ballantine?"

"Ballantine?" I thought for a second, then the light dawned. "The cockroach man?"

"Yes."

"Don't tell me he's back."

"He's back all right." She paused. "And this time he has a snake."

CHAPTER SEVEN

I FOUND Dane licking his wounds in the casino. He didn't look happy.

"You know anything about snakes?" I asked. "You mean other than what I just learned from your friend, Miranda, back there?" He hooked a thumb over his shoulder. "Are you sure she doesn't crawl on her belly and live under a rock?"

"Well, I don't know about living under a rock, but one time she decided to live in a mud hut on the beach next to the Santa Monica pier. Something about showing the world the plight of some obscure tribe of cannibals in the Amazon."

"She would like cannibals. I bet she's still chewing on the hunk she took out of my ass." Dane threw a quick look over his shoulder toward the lobby. "I hope she chokes on it."

"You're a big boy. I'm sure you'll find a way to get even." And I wanted ringside seats. I grabbed his hand and tugged him with me as I headed for the elevators. "Right now, we have a more pressing problem. What do you know about real, slither-through-the-grass snakes?"

We skidded to a stop in front of the elevators. I punched the up button. Reluctantly, I let go of Dane's hand.

"What kind of snake?"

"How the heck should I know?" The elevator hadn't come, so I punched the button again, then again and again.

"Punching the button a zillion times won't make it come faster," he said.

"Maybe not, but it makes me feel better. I'd take the stairs, but we're going all the way to the top." I turned and looked at him. "You haven't answered my question. What do you know about snakes? I can do rodents, but I'm not well versed in reptiles."

"We had an annual rattlesnake roundup back in my hometown. I participated a couple of times until a buddy of mine got bit and damned near lost a leg. Does that help?"

"It's better than nothing." The elevator door finally opened, and I dodged the people trying to get off as I pulled Dane inside. I inserted my card in the slot and punched the button for the penthouse floor.

"So, where's the snake?" Dane asked, after the doors had closed and we'd started skyward.

"In Mr. Ballantine's suite."

"Ballantine? You sound like you know this guy."

"Oh, yeah." I crossed my arms and leaned against the side of the elevator. Just thinking about Mr. Ballantine set my blood to boil. "Our first meeting concerned cockroaches. Now it's a snake. He's moving up the food chain."

Dane chuckled. "You gotta tell me about the cockroach."

"Cockroaches, plural. Hundreds of them."

"I think I'm going to like this story."

"Are you familiar with the hotel rating system?" At Dane's affirmative nod, I continued. "Like all top hotels, the Babylon jealously guards its rating. We opened at the top of the heap, and we intend to stay there." The elevator slowed its ascent, then dinged its arrival at the fifty-second floor. "Some of our guests try to blackmail us by doing things that might threaten the rating."

"Blackmail? How?"

We stepped out of the elevator and turned right, heading for the King David suite. "They stage some unpleasantness, then threaten to report it to the rating services unless we pay for their room and whatever."

"Hence the cockroaches."

"Five-star hotels are not infested with bugs."

"But they could be," Dane said. "How did you know it wasn't legit?"

"The bugs were technically water bugs, indigenous to the coastal states. They couldn't survive in the desert. They were brought in and planted in that room. I could have wrung Mr. Ballantine's neck, but I stifled myself. This time, he may not be so lucky."

"So we're on our way to a potential homicide?"

"Don't encourage me," I said, as we rounded the last corner. "He's one of the few people I'd like to meet on the edge of a cliff with no witnesses."

"Remind me not to get on your bad side."

Three big, tough-looking Security guys were standing outside Mr. Ballantine's suite, peering in through the doorway when Dane and I arrived.

"It's got Denny," one of them said when he caught sight of us.

Dane and I pushed past the guards. What we saw stopped us in our tracks.

"Holy shit," Dane mumbled.

In the middle of a beautiful, hand-knotted, silk Persian carpet writhed one of our Security guards, presumably Denny.

Wrapped around his middle was the largest snake I had ever seen.

The thing looked to be every inch of twenty feet, although it was hard to tell. It had already circled Denny's waist twice and was going for a third coil.

"Get this thing off of me!" Denny grunted. "I can't breathe!" He looked a little blue.

I grabbed the nearest guard and pointed to his gun. "Give me that thing."

Wordlessly, he handed it over.

"Dane, grab the snake's head and hold it still," I ordered, as I chambered a round and made sure the safety was on. "Everybody back."

Dane dropped to one knee and grabbed the reptile's head. Muscles bulging, he wrestled with the thing as it writhed. Twice, he lost his footing. "Damn. This thing even has teeth."

I tucked the gun in my belt, shouldered in next to Dane, and grabbed the snake with both hands. Finally, the two of us managed to pull the writhing body away from Denny just enough. Dane put his knee on the snake, holding its head to the floor. "Hurry," he growled through gritted teeth.

I let go and grabbed the gun. Thumbing off the safety, I pressed the barrel to the snake's head. I shut my eyes and pulled the trigger.

The recoil knocked me on my ass.

For a moment, time stood still.

I was still deaf from the report when I opened my eyes. Breathing heavily, Dane knelt on hands and knees, his head hanging between his arms. Denny pushed weakly at the now inert body of the snake.

I crawled over to him, grabbed the slippery beast, and tried to move it. Dead weight, the thing weighed a ton. "Help me here," I said to Dane.

It took us a couple of minutes to unwrap Denny.

"You okay?" I asked him as he took deep, measured lungfuls of air.

He nodded.

Dane stood, then grabbed my hand and pulled me to my feet.

We escorted Denny to the gaggle of Security guards who still filled the doorway. One took Denny's arm.

My Nextel vibrated at my hip. I grabbed it. "What?"

"I got reports of gunfire on one of the upper floors in the north wing." Jerry stated rather matter-of-factly, as if gunfire erupted in the hotel every day. "You know anything about it?"

"Yeah, it was me."

"You?"

"Yeah, me. I pulled the trigger."

"Cool. Who'd you shoot?"

I turned and surveyed the room through slitty eyes. "Nobody." Ballantine lurked in the far corner behind a chair that looked like King David's throne. The minute I saw him, my blood boiled over, my temper erupted, and I could almost feel his spindly little neck in my hands. "Yet."

I dropped my Nextel in my pocket as I stormed toward Ballantine.

The creep shrunk behind the chair.

I was a few feet from him when Dane grabbed my arm, pulling me to a halt. "Whoa there," he whispered in my ear. "He's not worth it."

Ballantine peeked around the edge of the chair.

I felt like making a lunge for him, but common sense slapped a lid on my temper. I straightened, threw my shoulders back, and slowly smoothed my dress. I took a deep breath, then blew several strands of hair out of my eyes. I stepped away from Dane.

He let me go, but stayed close. I guess he was worried my temper might erupt again. He needn't have worried. Past getting mad, I was well on my way to getting even.

Ballantine shrank back.

I crooked a finger at him. "Come here, little man." I waited until, visibly shaking, he stood in front of me, staring at his toes. "What kind of snake was that?

"Anaconda."

"Where on earth did you get it?"

"From a guy I know here in Vegas."

"How'd you get it into the hotel?"

"In a trunk. It took three bellmen to get it on the cart." A tinge of pride crept into his voice.

For a moment, I saw red again. Dane must've sensed it. He grabbed my arm, but I shook him off.

I leaned down and put my mouth next to Ballantine's ear. He flinched, but stood his ground. "Listen to me and listen good. Pack your things. Stop at the front desk and pay your bill, which will be large, as it will include damages for this attempted extortion." I lowered my voice. "Then get the hell out of my hotel. If you darken my doorway again, or if I get even a hint that you have said anything unsavory about this hotel or any of its employees, I will hunt you down myself. And when I'm through with you, I will personally deliver your sorry carcass to the police."

Ballantine visibly paled.

"I don't think you'd like being a boy toy for some lifer in the state pen." I turned on my heel, shouldered past Dane, then retrieved the gun from the floor where I had left it.

At the doorway, I slapped the gun in the chest of its owner. "Why do you carry this thing if you're afraid to use it?"

The guard grabbed the gun with both his hands and stared at me as if I had two heads.

"Men," I muttered, as I stalked off down the hall.

～

MY PHONE RANG AS THE ELEVATOR DOORS OPENED, AND I STEPPED into the lobby. I glanced at the caller's number. I flipped the phone open, pressed it to one ear and stuck a finger in the other. "Mother, aren't you in Carson City? I'm really busy."

"Too busy for your mother?" Her tone was colder than ice.

I took the finger out of my ear. That single phrase told me there wasn't going to be much about this phone call I wanted to hear. "Mother, contrary to what you may think, the earth does not stop rotating when you call. This is a bad time." Why I let her punch my buttons, I don't know.

"Sweetheart, with that attitude, you're going to grow old by yourself."

"That's not looking like a bad option right now."

"If you run off that nice Mr. Dane..." Clearly, the concepts of bad timing and an unreceptive audience were lost on my mother.

"Mother, if you called to talk about my love life, this is not a good time."

"What love life?"

I sighed and counted to ten. As I counted, I watched the people milling around the lobby. Did any of them have a mother like Mona? If they did, maybe we could form a support group. The first session could deal with stifling thoughts of matricide. "Mother, is this really why you called me?"

"Of course not."

I waited, but she said nothing. She was waiting for an apology, and the only way to get her off the phone without hanging up on her was to give her one. I guess I had been a bit harsh. "Sorry, Mother. What can I do for you?"

"I only have your best interests at heart."

"I know."

"Why do we take our frustrations out on each other?"

An interesting observation from my mother.

"Because it's safe."

"That must be it." Mother paused for a minute. I could almost hear her thinking. "Lucky, sweetheart, the reason I called is to tell you that the man Lyda Sue met at my place is no worry of yours. He had nothing to do with her falling out of the helicopter."

"Well, that's a relief." Sarcasm crept into my voice, but I didn't care. "How do you know?"

"I just know."

"I'm sure that will be compelling testimony in a court of law, Mother." I knew what was coming next. I could read my mother like my dog-eared copy of *Atlas Shrugged.* "You're not going to tell me who she met, are you?"

"Honey, it's not important. He's not involved."

"You're withholding evidence."

"You're not the police, and, if it's any consolation, I wouldn't tell them either."

"Mother, you can be mean and really, really irritating, but you've never been stupid."

"I knew you wouldn't like it, but you'll have to trust me on this one, dear."

"So, why did you call if you weren't going to tell me anyway?"

"I want you to be careful, that's all."

"That's not all, Mother; we both know it."

Sorry I'd apologized to her and more than a little pissed, I snapped my phone shut. I'm supposed to trust her? What about her trusting me? And she was willing to stonewall the police for this mysterious guy. Why? Who could she care about that much?

In a blinding flash of unusual introspection, I realized one very sad and unsettling thing—while I could read my mother like a book, I didn't really know her at all.

My Nextel vibrated. "What?" I practically shouted into the device.

"I heard you shot somebody." Miss Patterson had the annoying habit of making an announcement sound like a question.

"*Something*, not *somebody*, although the day is still young."

"Before you pull the trigger, think of me. I'm just getting you trained. It would be such a pain to break in a new head of customer relations." I heard the smile in her voice.

"I'll keep that in mind. I'm in the lobby ready to greet the Trendmakers."

"Got it. I didn't have anything else beyond wondering whether I needed to find you a good defense lawyer."

"An oxymoron, if not an impossibility," I said as I shut the phone, proud of myself for resisting the temptation to toss the thing into the trash and bolt out the front door screaming. Instead, I rehooked the device at my waist, arranged my features in what I hoped was a pleasant expression, and girded myself for my next task.

Truth be told, the Trendmakers made me nervous.

I watched them as they arrived to check in at the special desk set up for them in the far corner of the lobby. Short ones, fat ones, tall ones, skinny ones, the Trendmakers came in all shapes and sizes. It was like watching middle-class America trooping to Home Depot for a gallon of paint. But they weren't coming to Home Depot. And they weren't coming for paint.

They were in Vegas for a weekend of casual sex with one another's spouses.

And they didn't care if the whole world knew. Well, some of them didn't care.

As I watched them, I wondered who was sizing up whom, and for what. Who had already slept with whom? Were they back for more of the same, or did they want fresh meat this time around? Images chased through my mind. How could they stand there talking to each other as if they were bridge players attending their annual convention?

A few moments of that line of thinking was all I could stand. I needed a drink. After greeting the Trendmakers, I was heading to Delilah's for some personal time with a bottle of Wild Turkey.

I plastered on a smile and started toward the registration table. A tap on my shoulder stopped me.

"Ms. O'Toole?"

I recognized the voice that came from behind me. I turned. "Jeep. How are you?"

The Most Reverend Peterson J. Peabody loomed in front of me blocking the light, but his smile shed a light of its own. "Fine, doing much better, thank you. I'd like you to meet the missus." He pulled forward a small lady with a cropped hairdo and big eyes. Her smile was almost as wide as her husband's. Thankfully for the

Mrs. Most Reverend, that was the only thing about her as wide as her husband.

"Nice to meet you," I said.

She grabbed my hand in both of hers and looked at me with those big eyes. "Thank you so much for taking such good care of my husband last night."

Last night? Had it really only been last night? I felt like I'd aged ten years since then. "That's what we're here for." My voice sounded stiff, even to me. As I stood there, my hand held tightly in hers, I couldn't help wondering whose husband she had picked to start her weekend with. Did she like them older, or younger? Fat or buff? One at a time, or two?

I really needed to get a grip.

"Would you care to join us tonight?" Mrs. Peabody asked. "A group of us are going to Carne for drinks and dinner."

I extracted my hand. "Thank you, you're most kind, but I'm afraid I can't get away." I made a sweeping motion with my arm. "As you can see, things are a bit crazy here today."

"I can see that." Her smile lit her eyes. "But, if you change your mind, we'd love to have you."

I shivered. Coming from her, that innocent phrase took on a whole new meaning.

～

FORTY-FIVE MINUTES OF MEETING AND GREETING THE SWINGERS, directing them to the corner of the bar where libations would be served, and I was more than ready to drown myself in that bottle of Wild Turkey. I sidled onto the last remaining stool at Delilah's.

"The usual, Ms. O'Toole?"

I looked into the smiling eyes of Sean Finnegan, one of our head bartenders. "Make it a double, and if you put more than one very small cube of ice in there, I'll come across this bar and strangle you myself."

"Good day, huh?" Sean and I went way back. He liked to tell people, women in particular, that he was Black Irish. I guess they found that sexy or something; I don't know. What I did know was Sean's name wasn't Finnegan, it was Pollack, and he was from New Jersey, not the Emerald Isle.

We all had our little secrets.

"Terrific," I growled. For some reason, I had a burr under my saddle, and I couldn't figure out exactly why.

Cupping my hands around the double old-fashioned glass Sean set in front of me, I swirled the amber liquid and the one lonely ice cube around in the glass. Normally, I could blow through a day like today and not be fazed, but for some reason I felt out of kilter, not myself. Surrounded by people, I felt strangely alone, disconnected.

"I've heard of people trying to divine the future from the leaves at the bottom of a tea cup," Teddie said as he appeared out of nowhere. "But never from a glass—a very large glass, I might add, of Wild Turkey."

He sounded way too chipper for me to deal with right now. "Go away."

He leaned in and shouted down the bar. "Hey, would you guys mind moving down so I can sit next to my lady here?"

I felt all eyes turn my way. Terrific. Now I was the center of attention—just what I wanted.

After much grumbling and scrambling about, everyone moved down one seat, leaving an empty stool to my left. Teddie straddled it.

I felt the reassuring warmth of his shoulder next to mine. Grudgingly, I had to admit, cheery mood and all, it felt good to be with Teddie. It always did. Especially, like today, when he was just Ted and not wearing a dress and my high heels. "I think I'm supposed to be mad at you."

"Moi?" He feigned innocence. "What did I do?"

I tried not to smile at his big blue eyes and exaggerated expression. When he was just Ted Kowalski, he was damned attractive. He still wore his torn Harvard sweatshirt and a pair of faded jeans that were just tight enough to spark interest, but still leave a lot to the imagination. A hint of Old Spice aftershave wafted around him. I liked that—so old school.

"Nothing, really." His crack about losing my smile had stung. As they say, the truth hurts.

"I have your best interest at heart." So he knew. He draped his arm around my shoulders and pulled me a bit closer.

"You're the second person who told me that today," I said, enjoying the feel of his arm holding me.

"Who was the first?"

"Mother. Right after she stuck a knife in my back."

"Your mother is a piece of work."

"That's putting it mildly." I pushed the drink away. I didn't want it anymore. "But you know the weirdest thing?" I leaned against Teddie. Solid, and male, he felt safe—and not a bit like Cher. "She's my mother and I don't even know her, not really. You know what I mean?"

"People build walls. Vegas can do that to you."

I thought about that for a moment. "Do I do that?"

He took a deep breath, then let it out slowly. "Honey, you learned at the foot of the master. Mona is the most isolating person I know."

"But I have a ton of friends."

"You have a few friends and you keep us all at a safe distance."

"That sounds so sad." I didn't want to be the gal Teddie described. "I must not be a very good friend, then."

"Well it wouldn't hurt if you took a couple of rows of bricks out of that wall."

"I have no idea how. You help me, okay?"

"Your wish is my command."

We both said nothing, letting the noise of the bar close in around us. Tired of resisting, I let my head rest on his shoulder. I didn't want to think about building walls, tearing them down, keeping people out, or letting them in, but those thoughts buzzed around the edge of my consciousness.

"So how many years do you have to go without sex before they declare you a virgin again?" I mused aloud.

"What?" Teddie dropped his arm and leaned away to get a better look at me.

I darn near fell off my stool.

"Well." I pushed myself back upright and refused to look him in the eye. "I read somewhere that if a person hadn't had sex in ten years, then that person could be declared some sort of a *de facto* virgin again."

He looked at me aghast. "Why would anyone want that?" He made becoming a virgin again sound as appealing as contracting the Ebola virus.

"I'm serious. I was just wondering about the ten-year thing." I thought back to the last time I'd had sex. I wasn't close to the ten-year mark. Well, not perilously close anyway. I'd worked hard enough to lose my virginity the first time; I didn't think I needed to push through that barrier again.

Teddie said nothing for a moment, and thankfully he didn't laugh—or ask me how long it had been. Finally, he took my hand in his and looked me in the eye. "If you want to have sex, all you have to do is ask."

I snatched my hand away. "Why is casual sex a guy's answer to every problem?"

He reared back. With one hand he tapped himself on the chest. "Me? Men? You brought it up!"

"So to speak."

We stared at each other. Then we both burst out laughing. Tears rolled down our faces, and we both were gasping for air before we could stop. In between fits of laughter, Teddie took a big slurp from my abandoned drink. I thought for a second, then did the same.

We both sat there trying to breathe and fighting the giggles that threatened to erupt again. Finally, I could take a deep breath and trust myself not to dissolve into hysterics.

Teddie had quieted beside me when he turned on his stool so he was facing me. He pulled my knees around so we were staggered knee-to-knee, face-to-face.

I started to say something, but the look on his face stopped me. The laughter had disappeared, replaced by something else.

Holding my hands in one of his, he reached up with the other, running his fingers over my cheek. Slowly, he traced my jaw. I gasped as he brushed his thumb lightly over my lips.

Then he kissed me.

His lips felt soft, yet insistent, exciting. A long forgotten feeling stirred inside me. I wanted to resist, then I didn't want to. Thoughts and emotions tumbled.

I kissed him back.

The world disappeared.

He pulled back. His lips next to my ear, he whispered, "Lucky, my love. I'll make love to you anytime you want, and I can assure you, it will not be casual."

With that, he backed off his stool and strolled away.

Trying to catch my breath, I watched him go. I sat perfectly still as my heart pounded.

What had gotten into him? And me? I felt a grin tickle my lips. Typical guy. Where finesse was needed, brute force was applied. Why dismantle a wall brick by brick when you can run a bulldozer right through it?

Then, my smile faded as reality reared its ugly head. I liked my life just the way it was. I liked my friendship with Teddie, our ease around each other. Sex just complicated things. I didn't want complicated. Especially not with Teddie.

Teddie dodged a group of women, who all turned and looked at him, their admiration evident, their lust poorly concealed. He seemed oblivious as he walked down the steps, out of the bar, and shouldered right past Paxton Dane.

Dane didn't watch Teddie as he left. Instead, he stared right at me.

Terrific. I whirled around to face the bar.

Dane parked himself on the empty stool recently vacated by Teddie. "Wasn't that that Theodore guy we saw earlier? You told Mr. Jones that Theodore had had a late night, then he showed up. Right?"

"Yup." I refused to look at Dane. This day had morphed from just plain weird to totally out of control. My hand shook as I brushed my hair out of my eyes.

"How'd you know he had a late night?"

"He was coming in as I was leaving this morning."

"You live together?"

"Yeah." I gave Dane the wickedest smile I could muster. "Same building."

He seemed to accept that. "Bartender, give me a Bud Light." Dane rooted around in his pocket.

I put my hand on his arm, stopping him. "Sean, put the beer on my tab."

"You got it." Sean grabbed a bottle out of the cooler, twisted off the cap, then slid the bottle down the bar where it stopped, still upright, in front of Dane. Amazed, I wondered how much practice that skill had taken.

Dane grabbed the bottle, tipped it in my direction. "Thanks." He took a long pull. "You're having quite a day, Ms. O'Toole. You blow the head off a snake, making fools out of all the men in the room, by the way. Then you make out with your boyfriend in the bar. Then, when he leaves, you buy another guy a drink. Impressive."

"He's just a friend."

"You treat your friends well. Where can I sign up?"

"It's a select list—handpicked. Very difficult to earn your way on."

"I like a challenge."

I gave him what I hoped was a dirty look as I pushed myself to my feet. "None of this is any of your business. And I don't like being thought of as a game you're going to play."

"I'm very good at games." Leaving the bottle on the bar, he rose. He stood close to me, too close. I started to take a step back, but he grabbed my arm, holding me tight against him. "Want to play?"

"Does that line really work for you?" I raised my eyes to meet his. "What is up with all you men today? Is it a full moon? Did you overdose on testosterone? What?" I slapped his hand away. "I've been assaulted enough today."

He stepped back as if stung. "Excuse me."

"Damned straight. And a simple 'I'm sorry' will do."

"I'm sorry." He looked chagrined and half mad, a weird combination. "I really am. I don't know what got into me. Seeing you with that guy…" He looked as confused as I felt.

"Dane, go home. Your shift is over. It's been a long…weird… day. Get some sleep. God knows there won't be much time for rest later in the week."

Absentmindedly, he nodded. "Yeah, you're right. See you tomorrow. You'll be here?"

"I'll be here."

If I didn't shoot myself first.

CHAPTER EIGHT

$\mathcal{M}$ ISS PATTERSON still manned her desk when I pushed through my office door and sagged into a chair across from her. She looked at me over the top of her cheaters, which perched precariously on the end of her nose.

Today, her readers were white with black zebra stripes. Or was it black with white stripes? Who knew? Regardless, they matched her outfit, which also sported large patches of black-and-white zebra motif. Fairly daring for Miss Patterson.

"Well, you certainly cut a wide swath today," she announced, after I had settled myself.

I leaned my head back against the wall and closed my eyes. Kicking off my shoes, I stretched my legs out in front of me. Teddie's kiss had sent an electric shock down the length of my body, and every nerve still vibrated. Bits and pieces of the day raced through my head—Mother, Lyda Sue, Subway Jones, snakes, and swingers. Dane. Teddie. All of that on three hours sleep. "You know those days where everything seems to be telling you to go home, get in bed, pull the covers over your head, and wait until tomorrow?"

When Miss Patterson didn't respond, I lifted my head and

looked at her. She just sat there looking at me with a bemused expression.

"Today is one of those days." I leaned back again and shut my eyes.

"There's a rumor going around that some of the employees are starting a collection. They want to get the snake stuffed and give it to you."

"Like my golden cockroach trophy?"

"Mmm."

"A stuffed snake in my office wouldn't do much for my relationship with the PETA folks."

"What relationship?" she scoffed. "They threatened to shoot you on sight after the little incident with that actor and the farm animals, remember?"

Only too well. A practical joke gone very bad; it had made the front page of the morning paper. The actor had come out smelling like a rose, albeit with a kinky bit added to his reputation. As the representative for the hotel, I had been the scapegoat. I smiled at my own pun. "Thank you for reminding me."

"There's also another rumor going around."

"I'm not going to like this, am I?"

"Probably not. Were you and Theodore playing tonsil hockey in Delilah's Bar?"

I took a deep breath and let it out slowly. "If I stay here and keep my eyes closed, none of this will be real, will it? And you won't have used the term 'tonsil hockey'."

"I'm quoting the rumor mill," she huffed. "You want to talk about it?"

I sat up and forced myself to look at her. Actually, not wanting to meet her eyes, I focused on a spot on the wall behind her and just to the right of her head, but I didn't think she could tell. "No."

"If he's not in love with you already, he's well on his way."

I grabbed a paperweight off the corner of the desk and read

the inscription—her ten-year service award. I tossed it from hand to hand.

I forced myself to meet her eyes. "I said no."

"When you're ready."

Which would be never, but I chose not to tell her that. I pushed myself to my feet and replaced her paperweight carefully on the corner of the desk, arranging it just as it had been. "No use trying to do damage control on the kiss in the bar. I bet somebody has already pulled that from the security tapes, copied it, and has it running on the closed circuit. But, please get your hands on the snake and see that it is incinerated. Without a dead body, that story should blow over soon."

"I doubt it. It's the stuff legends are made of."

I went looking for my purse and found it where it should have been—in the bottom of the closet. I extracted the videotape and waved it at Miss Patterson as I headed for the door. "I'll be in Security if you need me."

∼

SECURITY WAS QUIET. NOT YET DINNERTIME, THE COCKTAIL HOUR had just begun. After stepping through the door and closing it silently behind me, I paused for a moment to let my eyes adjust to the dim interior. Security reminded me of the radar control room at McCarran. Rows and rows of monitors encompassed the far wall from desk height to the ceiling. This bank of monitors took feeds from all of the Security cameras throughout the hotel. Seated in front of the monitors, security personnel constantly scanned as the pictures flashed, held for a few seconds, then another picture took its place.

A separate bank of monitors on the adjacent wall took feeds from the casino. Here, the scrutiny was more intense, as specially trained personnel watched the games in progress, looking for cheaters. Some of these folks had even been in the business of cheating the casinos themselves—until they had been caught. We hired them for their special insight, but not until they had worked their way through the justice system.

All of the video fed into large recording machines in the back room.

That's where I found Jerry, alone, leaning back in his chair, his feet on the console of a big computer. Black as night, his head shaved and waxed until it shone, he wore a dark suit fitted to his wiry frame, dark gray shirt, silver tie, and Italian loafers. The gold Rolex on his left wrist was a new addition. Jerry puffed on a fake cigarette and eyed me through bloodshot eyes.

"Still trying to quit, I see," I said.

He pulled the cigarette out of his mouth, looked at it, then flipped it in disgust toward the trash can in the corner. He missed. "I don't have any choice now. They've made all the nonpublic portions of the hotel smoke-free. When they finally vote to make the whole damned thing a no-smoking zone, we're going to lose so many guests this place will be a mausoleum."

"I'll try to resist pointing out the irony in that statement." I waggled the tape at him. "Here's the video. Let's see what you can do."

"If The Big Boss finds out about this, he's going to fit us both with cement boots and toss us into Lake Mead. He's been calling down here all day looking for this thing. I hope you know what you're doing."

"I haven't a clue, but I'll take the heat if it goes south. What did you tell him?"

"I gave him the runaround, but I don't think we have much more time. He smells a rat." Jerry reached in his pocket and pulled out a packet of cigarettes. "And, if there's any heat, we'll both take it."

"He's not the only one who smells a rat." I watched Jerry pull a fake cigarette out of the packet. "Those things work?"

"I feel less homicidal when I use them."

"I'll take that as a 'yes'." I handed him the tape. "Let's get a look at this thing."

He kicked his feet off the console, took the tape, then turned and inserted it in the machine. As he worked, he asked, "Did you discover anything from those tapes you asked for?"

"Which ones?"

"The ones I sent down with Dane this morning."

"He didn't have any tapes. He told me they'd been lost."

Jerry and I looked at each other. I could tell he was thinking what I was thinking—The Big Boss was right—something about Dane stunk.

There wasn't anything we could do about Dane or the missing tapes right now, so we concentrated on the task at hand. A few seconds passed, then the screen came to life. We fast-forwarded through videos of an Asian family standing in front of various points of interest in Vegas.

"This is it," I said, as the camera panned the crowd in front of the Treasure Island, the pirate show ships in the background. "Slow it down." I grabbed a chair, pushed it in next to Jerry, and sat. Elbows on the console, nose inches from the screen, I watched as he advanced the tape frame by frame.

The pirate show progressed in all of its glory of lights, smoke, and noise. Scantily clad women brandishing swords leaped from the yardarms. A few women swung on ropes over the crowd. The helicopter came into view at the top of the picture. I pointed to it. "Can you zoom in on that?"

Jerry used the mouse to draw a square around the helicopter, then he worked through a couple of drop-down menus. When he finished, a slightly blurry image replaced the one we had been looking at.

I could make out the helicopter easily, and two people in the front seats. "Can you get the folks in the front seats to come in any clearer?"

"I'll try, although we're pushing the envelope. Thankfully, the guy taking the video was a techie." He worked through some more menus.

"How so?" I squinted, trying to make out the features of the two occupants as Jerry brought the image into increasingly sharper focus.

"He was using the latest in high-def. That camera alone must've set him back a couple a grand." He worked for a minute more. "I think I got it. Recognize anybody?"

"Willie, just as we suspected. And I'd bet my grandmother that's Felicia Reilly sitting next to him, even though she's changed her hair color and style." I squinted again, taking in every pixel.

"You don't have a grandmother."

"Details." My eyes never wavered from the picture in front of me. "What's that?"

"What?"

"See the white blur right behind Willie? It looks like something's in the backseat."

"Probably Lyda Sue."

"Maybe. But she fell out the door behind Felicia. Why would she be sitting behind Willie right before she fell? Doesn't make sense."

Transfixed by the image on the screen, I watched as Jerry worked. It was like watching a photograph develop. First there was nothing, then a blurry image of pixels, then...

"Holy shit." My stomach clenched. Cold dread rushed through every vein, freezing thought and emotion.

The Big Boss.

The man who had been my rock stared back at me, clear as day.

From the back seat of the helicopter.

Where he had been sitting next to Lyda Sue.

Seconds before she plunged to her death.

"Fuck," Jerry finally said. "We're so screwed."

I took a deep breath. *Think, Lucky, think.* Slowly, the shock wore off, and my brain, what was left of it, came back on line. "We're not screwed—we've been here too long. We're like family." I pointed at the images of Willie and Felicia. "They, on the other hand, are totally fucked."

Jerry nodded and I could see in his eyes we were on the same page.

I'd better find those two idiots before The Big Boss finds them first.

~

AS THE ELEVATOR ASCENDED FROM THE BASEMENT TOWARD THE BIG Boss's apartment, I felt like an astronaut being lifted up to the space shuttle, preparing to be blasted into oblivion. I tapped the tape against my thigh. Despite the cool air, beads of sweat popped, then trickled down between my breasts.

The Big Boss was expecting me.

I hoped he didn't have a gun.

Finally, the elevator slowed, then stopped. The doors opened and disgorged me into the middle of The Big Boss's apartment. This was the second unpleasant visit I'd had here in as many days.

"Where've you been?" His words measured, he sounded angry, which I expected. But he also sounded under control. I'm not sure that was a good thing.

"It's been a busy day."

I approached, stopping in front of him. For once, I was thankful for my height and heels. Being bigger made me feel stronger. Probably an illusion, but it was all I had, and I clung to it like the ledge of a ten-story building. "Here's your tape." I extended the package to him.

Instead of taking it, he cocked his head toward the bar. I put the video down where he'd indicated, then busied myself making two drinks. We both were going to need them.

"No copies?"

"Not that I'm aware of, and I looked under every bush I could think of. But the tape was out of our hands for a long time, so there's no guarantee."

"I'm counting on you, Lucky." His hard edge softened a bit.

I turned and handed him his drink. Taking a sip of mine, I eyed him over the top of my glass. Yeah, I'd been right before—he was nervous—as well he should be. "I'm good, Boss, but I'm not Superman."

The ice in his drink tinkled against the glass, betraying his shaking hand. "I heard you went to see your mother today."

"Yeah. Dane went with me." Funny, I didn't remember Miss Patterson telling me The Big Boss had called.

"How was she?"

"As good as she ever is."

That got a weak smile out of him, but his eyes remained hard.

I refused to let him redirect this conversation. "You going to tell me what happened?"

His eyes swiveled to mine, then skittered away. He turned and walked over to the wall of glass overlooking the Strip. Standing there, his back to me, he seemed to shrink inside himself.

"You looked at the tape." It wasn't a question.

"You knew I would." I walked over and stood beside him. The incredible view always took my breath away. Tonight was no exception.

He raised the drink to his lips and took a long pull. "Probably." He took another pull on the drink. This seemed to steady him.

Throwing back his shoulders, he raised his head, then turned and looked at me out of the corner of his eye. I saw a bit of the old fight there. "You really are going to be the death of me yet."

"Better you than me." This time I got a chuckle.

"Self-preservation, a critical Vegas skill. I taught you well."

I grabbed his arm, hard. "Don't do anything stupid. Those two idiots aren't worth it."

"I've ridded myself of lesser evils."

The cold edge to that statement sent chills down my spine. "Boss, this isn't Bugsy and the boys."

"No. Bugsy would never have had to bother with little shysters. He would have them taken care of and poof, no more pests."

Now, there's a new market for the Terminix folks. "It's not so easy anymore."

He shook his head. "Nothing ever is. I've heard from them, you know."

I turned to stare at him. "When?"

"Late last night. After you left."

"What's their game?" As if I didn't know.

"Blackmail."

"There's a lot of that going around."

"What?"

I motioned to the couch. "Let's sit. I've got a story to tell you."

So we sat there, shoulder to shoulder, surrounded by the best things life had to offer, looking out at a world of light and fun and promise, while I told The Big Boss about Willie the Weasel, Felicia Reilly, and the Most Reverend Peterson J. Peabody.

The Big Boss sat stock-still, his eyes narrowing to slits as he listened to my tale. "How is that related to me?" he asked when I had finished.

"I don't really know, but perhaps Reverend Peabody was a test run, so to speak. Then the opportunity to reel in a big fish presented itself."

"That would be me."

"Can you think of a bigger fish? But, I just can't shake the feeling there's something I'm missing here."

"How do you mean?"

"Willie the Weasel's a sneaky little creep, with about as much backbone as an earthworm. Blackmail fits, but I can't see him picking you as a viable target. Just the thought of you scared the pee out of him."

"What are you saying?"

"There must be somebody else."

"The woman?"

"Possibly." I stared out the window at the lights of the Strip. They shouted fun and excitement—until you scratched the surface and exposed the dark underbelly of the city. "You're not going to the police with this, are you?"

He shook his head. "I take care of my own problems."

Testosterone, the antidote to good sense. "If I'm going to help, I need to know everything. You need to come clean. What the hell happened?"

"Lyda Sue was a good kid. I was just trying to help her." He rose, pointed at my glass. At the shake of my head, he moved to the bar to replenish his drink. "She had a shot at a legitimate job."

"Doing what?"

"Management at one of the big hotels. Strictly entry level, but a foot in the door. Sorta like where you started."

"The big hotels aren't too big on hiring ex-hookers."

"Like I said, I was helping her."

He didn't have to spell it out. Helping her meant a new background, something respectable. The Big Boss held a lot of markers. I guess he'd called in a few. "How'd you meet Lyda Sue?"

"Through a friend."

"Anybody who could have a connection here?"

"No, they were from out of town."

"Think hard here, Boss. Do you think Lyda Sue was part of the blackmail?"

"Why would she do that? She had life by the tail."

"Maybe she was being blackmailed herself?"

The Big Boss's face darkened, his voice had a dangerous edge. "I thought of that."

"Secrets to hide, perfect bait for a couple of two-bit black-mailers."

Anger flared in his eyes. "All she did was invite me on a heli-copter ride."

"I'll bet she didn't know she was inviting you to her murder."
Now for the hard question. "So, how the hell did she go out that
door?"

The Big Boss ran a shaking hand over his eyes. "I don't know.
She'd moved over next to me. That other woman wanted to take
our picture. Then the helicopter rocked—violently and...she was
gone."

Poor Lyda Sue. She'd gotten herself in the middle of something
big—and she'd landed in the pirate's lagoon for her trouble.

"A bullet to the head would be too good for those two," The
Big Boss announced.

I had to agree with him—a bullet to the head would be good,
but only after prolonged torture.

"Boss, let me find them. The police will take it from there.
Promise me you won't do anything stupid."

He looked me right in the eye. "I promise," he said. We both
knew he was lying through his teeth.

～

STEPPING INTO THE ELEVATOR, I FLIPPED OPEN MY PHONE AND
called the office. After the fifth ring, I was about to hang up when
Miss Patterson answered. She sounded out of breath.

"The Beautiful Jeremy Whitlock doesn't happen to be there,
does he?"

"If he was, I wouldn't have picked up."

"Glad to see you're prioritizing." I rotated my head around. My
neck muscles were so tight I felt two inches shorter. "Could you
call him for me, please? I need to talk to him ASAP."

"My pleasure."

"Thanks. Then go home. I've got a few people to track down,
then I'm headed there myself."

"I was on my way, halfway down the hall, when I heard the
phone ringing."

"Good. Get some sleep."

"You, too."

Not likely.

~

JEREMY'S CALL CAUGHT ME STRIDING THROUGH THE LOBBY. "THANKS for getting back to me so fast." I dodged through the crowd toward the casino. I pressed the palm of my free hand over my other ear to block out the noise. I decided sticking my finger in my ear probably looked pretty silly. "Do you have anything yet?"

"Pushy broad, aren't you? It's been like, what, five hours?"

"Pushy and demanding." I stepped around an older man and woman who had stopped to gawk at the blown-glass ceiling. "Seriously, all joking aside, the ante has been upped. Can you put a couple of guys on this? I really need to find Willie and his sidekick —now."

"Haven't had any hits on those two, but I did get one on the other guy."

"Dane?"

"Yeah. He showed up at the Athena."

"The Athena? Interesting. What'd he do there?"

"I caught him coming in the front door. He went right to the elevators. Haven't found him on any of the floors yet. I'm going through the feeds now."

"Keep me posted. And put as many guys as you've got on this."

"Right-o."

~

THE CROWD IN THE CASINO WAS STARTING TO BUILD, BUT THE energy level still resembled that of a languid summer afternoon as it slipped toward dusk. The calm before the storm. The Beach Boys played through the speakers; the lights had yet to be dimmed for the evening. A couple of tables were full, but the play seemed apathetic. The cocktail waitresses looked bored— and cold. I knew how they felt. The casino was so cold they could hang meat in there. The crowds would warm it later, but for now it was almost uncomfortable—especially without much clothing.

I rubbed my bare arms as I wandered through the rows of slot machines, looking for Mr. Pascarelli. It was early yet, but I searched on the off chance he might be there. No luck.

Stymied, I put my hands on my hips and wondered what to do next. I couldn't think of a thing other than go look for those two idiots, Willie and Felicia, myself, which would be a waste of time. I'm sure the police had checked all the normal places, and I didn't know either Willie or his friend well enough to know what abnormal places they frequented. Although, with the little I did know about Willie, I'm sure there were many.

With Mr. Pascarelli nowhere to be found, I didn't know what to do. Go home or eat? My motto had always been "When in doubt, eat," so I decided to follow my gut.

Every hotel on the Strip has a buffet, some better than others. Ours was amazing. Located at the back of the building on the ground floor, looking out over our award-winning golf course, the buffet was a veritable feast fit for a king. Foods from every corner of the globe, desserts to die for, open twenty-four hours a day—my idea of heaven.

My plate laden with more food than I had any intention of eating, I scanned the room looking for a table. Mrs. Paisley and her friends filled a four-top in the middle of the room. They waved. Hands full, I nodded back. A table for two near the window called my name. Casinos being what they are, glimpses of the outside world are few and far between. When the opportunity presented itself, I was unable to resist.

I was sitting there, fork poised, trying to decide what to attack first when a voice interrupted. "May I join you?"

I looked up into the twinkling eyes of Mr. Pascarelli. Somehow, God had taken me off his shit list. "I would be honored."

"A beautiful lady such as yourself shouldn't be eating alone," the old smoothie said as he set his plate of spaghetti on the table.

"Don't be fooled by my mild-mannered exterior. I've been told I can be quite difficult."

"I like my women difficult. Challenges keep life interesting. If I were a few years younger, I'd give you a run for your money."

I smiled because I had no idea how to respond. "I've been looking for you." Talk about redirecting the conversation. I rooted around in my pocket for the photos. Then I moved the salt and pepper shakers, the Cholula sauce, the soy sauce, and a tub of green gunk I couldn't identify, clearing a space in the center of the table. I smoothed out the pictures. "Could you look at these? Tell me if you recognize anybody."

He took a bite of spaghetti, then moved his plate to the side, concentrating on the pictures.

He was so cute with his brow furrowed in concentration. Nice guys like him shouldn't be alone.

"I've seen all of these folks around. This guy..." He pointed at Willie. "He's the helicopter pilot, right?"

Not taking his finger from the photo, he looked up.

I nodded.

"I've seen him talking to this gal," he said, tapping Felicia's photo. "I think they got a thing going. But this other guy—I've seen him talking to her, too."

"Really?" Dane sure seemed to get around. "Did you see them together more than once?"

"Sure. And last time, their conversation looked heated."

"Heated, mad? Or heated, like...attraction?"

"He was mad. Real mad."

I gathered the pictures and stuffed them in my pocket. Leaning back in my chair, I surveyed Mr. Pascarelli. "Interesting."

He pulled his plate back in front of him and dove again into his pile of spaghetti, which was enough to feed a family of four. Something was wrong with the universe when skinny people could eat their weight in serious carbs and not gain an ounce. "Are you investigating Lyda Sue's murder?" he asked through a mouthful, his eyes twinkling. "Need some help?"

"Don't get any ideas." I grabbed a rib and dove in. "I'm leaving the investigating to the police. I was just curious, that's all."

"You know what they say about curiosity."

"They say a lot of things, none of them good."

I parked my brain in neutral as we both set to work in earnest. I was segueing from the ribs to the California rolls when I caught sight of Mrs. Paisley and her friends rising to leave. "Excuse me just a second. I've got somebody you should meet."

I stood and waved like a maniac until I caught Mrs. Paisley's eye, and motioned her over.

With the manners of a previous generation, Mr. Pascarelli rose to greet the ladies as they surrounded the table.

"Mr. Pascarelli, may I present Velma Paisley? You both share a love of playing the slots."

"Really?" Mrs. Paisley said, as she shook Mr. Pascarelli's hand. "Call me Velma."

"Velma, I'm Hank." Mr. Pascarelli looked shy. "Would you like to join us?"

I gathered up my plate. "Ladies, he's all yours. I'm calling it a day."

The five of them made quite a crowd around the small table. As I walked away, they fell into easy conversation. Mr. Pascarelli looked like the proverbial cat with the canary.

All's well that ends well, I guess. What was it with me and proverbs today?

Totally beat, and nothing pressing, I decided to check out early. I scrolled down the list of numbers on my Nextel, highlighted Jerry's, and pushed-to-talk. "Jer."

"Yo."

"I had three hours of sleep last night. I'm going home. Can you hold down the fort until the shift change?"

"Sure."

"I'll have my phone."

"And I know the drill. Call you only if there's a national emergency."

"You got it. And thanks. I owe you."

~

IN DESPERATE NEED OF CLEAN, FRESH AIR TO CLEAR MY THOUGHTS, I opted to walk home. Backlit by the setting sun, the Spring Mountains stood in stark relief. The air, still laden with the heat of the day, settled around me with a welcomed warmth. One lone bird circled in the darkening sky above. It looked like a vulture.

I needed rest. I needed to turn off my brain, take a good soaking bath, and crawl into bed—for the next week. However, rest would be impossible with Teddie waiting—and I'm sure he would be waiting. With the day still pinging around in my head, turning off my brain was probably not going to happen. And my next week had been bought and paid for by the Babylon. That left a bath.

The short walk home seemed shorter than normal tonight.

Forrest waved as I trudged through the foyer, but he didn't stop me with his usual small talk. I guess I looked as bad as I felt.

Silence greeted me as I stepped from the elevator. Newton wasn't cursing at me. There were no sounds from the kitchen. After hanging my purse on the peg by the door, I went in search of life.

Teddie was nowhere to be found. But he had been there. Newton's cage sported its cover, and I found a note on the kitchen counter. It read, "Take a bath. I'm upstairs, come on up if you feel like it. Washed the bird's mouth out with soap. He's sulking."

Even when he wasn't there, he could put a smile on my face.

Oh, what a problem I had! The mere memory of Teddie's kiss was enough to set my nerves afire again.

I wandered into the bathroom, dropping clothes as I went. Turning the tap to the "scald" setting, I watched as the tub began to fill. Maybe I was making this out to be a bigger problem than it really was. I mean, what's a little sex among friends?

Testing the water with a big toe, I yelped and leapt back. Okay, "scald" was a bit aggressive. I added cold water. I thought about adding bubbles, but tonight didn't feel like a bubble bath kind of night.

When the temperature was just right, I slid into the water until only my head remained above the surface. I sighed. The water felt delicious. I punched the button and jets of water and air massaged my body. The strain of the day started to let go. God, this was better than sex—at least better than the sex I remembered.

Who was I kidding? Sex among friends was a recipe for the double whammy—ruined friendships and bad sex.

I had no idea what to do. I parked my brain—thankfully it remained parked.

Something would come to me. It usually did.

⌁

THE BATH HAD BEEN HEAVEN, AND NOW I WAS FACING MY OWN IDEA of hell.

The elevator doors opened, and I stepped in for the short ride up one floor.

Would he be mad? Hurt? Would we have bad sex? Then everything would be different between us.

I didn't want different; I wanted the same.

But how could it be the same after that kiss? That kiss changed everything.

The elevator doors opened and I was assaulted with the smell of fresh-baked oatmeal raisin cookies.

"Mom's been here. She made a tin for you, too." Teddie stood in the middle of his kitchen holding a tin with a Christmas motif. It was open and I could see little spikes of wax paper sticking out.

"Are those what I think they are? The ones with the coconut?"

He nodded, stuffing his mouth full of cookie. Enticing me with the open tin of cookies, Teddie walked backward toward the couch. I followed him like a hound dog following the scent of a rabbit. We both plopped on the couch, the cookies between us.

I grabbed one. "Oh, God, they're still warm." I inhaled the first cookie and went for a second. "What's with the Christmas motif?"

"You know Mom—every day is Christmas."

Sorta like her son.

Teddie cleared his throat. "Listen, about today—"

He stopped at my raised hand.

I turned toward him. In my sweats and ripped T-shirt, with my hair piled on top of my head, I'm sure I wasn't exactly the stuff male fantasies are made of, but I needed to have my say. "Today was a weird day." His face fell, but I wasn't finished. "Your kiss— our kiss—was the highlight." Whoa, did I just say that?

"For you, too?"

"It was good, really good. It's just that we went from A to Z all in one fell swoop."

"Actually, we probably went from D to S, but I get your drift. How about we do one letter at a time and see where it gets us?"

I moved the tin of cookies to the floor, sidled in next to him, and put my head on his shoulder. "One letter at a time, I can handle that."

CHAPTER NINE

I AWOKE slowly, savoring the feel of Teddie's body wrapped in mine. One hand on his chest, a leg casually thrown across his, my body stretched the length of him. He felt warm, and hard in all the right places.

"Good morning," Teddie said, his voice tender and low. I smiled and opened my eyes. We'd fallen asleep on the couch. This wasn't the first time, yet somehow this time seemed different. I wasn't sure I was comfortable with different. "How'd you know I was awake?"

"Your breathing changed."

I left my head on his shoulder. I didn't want to move, not ever. He reached over and brushed a strand of hair out of my eyes, then he kissed my forehead.

So this is what D looked like—fully clothed on the couch, a peck on the forehead. I could handle that, but part of me liked his kiss yesterday better. However, I'd asked for one letter at a time; I guess that's what I was going to get. *Be careful what you wish for,* sprung to mind.

One of these days I should listen to all these proverbs I'd been spouting. Sorta like rumors, proverbs had a grain of truth in there somewhere. Wasn't there one about friends and lovers? As I recall, it ended badly.

"Hungry?"

"Stupid question." I groaned and tentatively stretched my legs. The one on the bottom was asleep. "What time is it?"

"Rise-and-shine time." Teddie sounded way too chipper, as if he'd been awake quite a while.

"We need to set some ground rules," I mumbled. "If we are going to sleep together, my first rule is 'no perkiness.' At least not until I'm fully caffeinated."

He gave me a lopsided grin. "*Are* we going to sleep together?"

I pushed myself up, catching myself before I slid off the couch to the floor. My hand met warm skin where his sweatshirt gapped away from his chest, sending a jolt through me. First my hormones were all out of whack, now my nerves were jangling. If I kept going down this path, pretty soon I'd be totally nonfunctional. "Technically, that's what we just did—sleep together."

"Technically, you're right. I was asking euphemistically."

"Oh, those big Ivy League words. I think, *euphemistically speaking*, that would come way down the alphabet."

"Drat." This time he pulled me to him and kissed me on the mouth. "Are there any more rules I should know about?"

His kiss lit every nerve that wasn't already on fire. In very real danger of giving in, shucking my clothes and getting on with it, I needed to put some distance between us. Both hands on his chest, one foot on the floor, I pushed myself upright. "More rules? Not that spring immediately to mind, but I'm in virgin territory here, so some will probably come to me."

"Virgin territory?"

"Do you have any coffee in this place?" I turned and padded toward the kitchen. "Bad choice of words—I may have slept with guys, but I don't wake up with them."

Teddie followed me to the kitchen where he pulled a canister of my favorite coffee from the cupboard. "Too bad. The waking up part can be one of the best parts."

He whistled while he filled the coffeepot and punched the button.

I watched him go through the preparations for breakfast, just as I had watched him do a hundred times before, albeit not after having spent the night on his couch. Several times a week I'd come up or he'd come down. We'd fix something and talk, share the news. I didn't want to lose that. It was the only good thing I had.

"Teddie, I'm not sure I can do this." I grabbed one of the empty mugs he had set on the counter and pretended to be fascinated with it.

"Can't do what? Have coffee?"

"You know what I mean." I sat across from him watching him make me eggs and bacon, just as I had yesterday. That breakfast seemed eons ago. "This could really screw up a great friendship. I need you."

Teddie leaned across the counter, took the empty coffee mug from my grasp, then held both of my hands in his. "I need you, too. But I don't want to be just your friend. Let go, Lucky. Give up control. Let me in. I won't disappoint you."

"Can't we stay the same as we've always been?"

"No."

"Why?"

"Because I don't do platonic—at least not with you. And not forever. It's not enough for me. And it's not enough for you either —you just don't know it yet." He let go of my hands and poured us both some coffee. He took a sip and eyed me over the top of his mug. "You don't know what you want. You spend your days fixing everybody else's lives, while ignoring your own."

"I don't *have* a life."

"My point exactly. If you don't pay attention, by the time you figure out what you want, you'll be too old to get it."

"Geez, haven't you heard of the soft sell?"

He gave me an exasperated look. "I've been soft-selling this for months now. Hasn't worked so far." He walked around the counter until he stood close to me—too close.

I could swear the man was surrounded by an energy field. A field that, once he got close enough, set my every nerve afire.

He touched my cheek. For a moment our eyes locked and held.

"Look, I may not be the guy, I know that," he said, as he brushed a hair from my eyes. "Just give me a chance. You can't keep locking people out, Lucky. It's not good for the soul."

I thought about what Teddie said through breakfast, my shower, getting dressed, and racing to work. In fact, that was practically all I could think about, until Miss Patterson walked through the office door.

"Mr. Fujikara is in the city jail. He wants you to bail him out."

Impeccable timing. She caught me mid-slurp on my fifth cup of java. I managed to spill only a little bit. "What?"

She handed me a tissue, then stood there looking all composed and efficient. The opposite of how I felt. What was it with me lately? My self-control had apparently gone on vacation—along with my self-respect.

I dabbed at the wet spot on my slacks. Thankfully, I had picked my dark blue Dana Buchman's and a matching silk top today.

"Nice earrings, necklace and belt, by the way. You actually match," said Miss Patterson.

"I accessorize and everybody notices. A sad commentary." Actually, Teddie had accessorized me, but Miss Patterson didn't need to know about that. "Tell me about Mr. Fujikara. Why's he at the jail and not the detention center?"

"They picked him up driving erratically way out on Charleston. Booked him on a DUI. His blood alcohol level was twice the legal limit."

"He wasn't in one of our Ferraris again, was he?"

Miss Patterson looked at her notes. "No. He'd rented an H2

from one of those fancy rental-car places. The car is okay. It's in the impound lot."

"Better call one of our lawyers. Get him down there to take care of the paperwork." I stopped dabbing at the spilled coffee. I was making it worse, leaving little bits of white tissue on my dark pants.

"Do lawyers make the world better or worse?" Miss Patterson asked. "I've never been able to figure that out."

"They're like mosquitos—no matter how many you swat, you're never going to rid the world of the bloodsuckers—so why worry about it?" I leaned back in my chair and took a good look at Miss Patterson. Yes, a makeover would do wonders. Not to mention what it would do for me. I'd been avoiding mirrors for a long time now. "The lawyer can go get Mr. Fujikara. Were you able to get us in to be beautified?"

"First, Mr. Fujikara wants you—only you."

"Terrific."

"He called the hotel about an hour ago. Security couldn't reach you on your cell; they found me. I found you."

"I couldn't find that damned phone this morning." I lifted a few papers on my desk looking for it. "I don't know where it is."

"Teddie has it."

"Oh."

"I called it looking for you. He answered. Said you must've left it there when you left this morning."

"Oh."

"He'll bring it by later." She looked at me with a deadpan expression. "I want you to notice that I am not asking for details. And, as to your second question, Linda can fit us both in today at noon."

"Good." She may not have asked for details, but she wanted them—would telling her be better than leaving everything to her imagination? I opted for the latter—probably a mistake. "May I borrow your car? This situation calls for low-profile, and my car is at home."

"I would hardly call your car low-profile."

A late 1970s vintage Porsche isn't even close to flashy by Vegas standards, but I wasn't going to argue.

I followed Miss Patterson into the outer office and waited while she found her keys. She flipped them to me. "Take care of my baby."

"Will do."

Miss Patterson's "baby" was a light blue Prius. I knew where to find it without asking—she always parked in my designated spot in the garage.

~

DETECTIVE ROMEO WAS WAITING FOR ME WHEN I ARRIVED AT THE city jail. He wore the same crinkled suit and weary expression. "Miss Patterson called and said you were on your way."

I fell in step beside him. "Have you had any sleep yet?"

"A little." He gave me a tired smile as he flashed his badge at the security checkpoint. The guards didn't even look up as they waved us through. "They brought your guy in just after midnight on a DUI. He was babbling about some woman trying to get money out of him. I tried to talk to him, but he was pretty wasted. Thought I'd let him sleep it off and talk to him this morning."

"Does he want a lawyer?" I tried to ignore the fact that, as we walked, various barred doors opened, then slammed shut behind us after we stepped through.

"He was in no shape last night to assess his situation. Your name was the only one he could tell us." Romeo stopped in front of a door marked "Interrogation Room 1." He opened the door and waved me inside. "They're going to bring him in here."

"I hope you guys are processing him for release." I stepped into the small room and felt like I'd walked onto a set right out of *CSI*.

Empty except for a grungy metal table and four chairs, the room was gray and lifeless. It reeked of disillusionment and despair. A shiver chased down my spine.

"Of course." Romeo pulled out a chair for me. "I thought we could talk here. By then they ought to have his paperwork done."

I sat and crossed my arms, trying to forget that I was in a small room, behind several sets of bars. I felt as if I should check my purse for a "get out of jail free" card, but they'd taken my bag from me at the front desk.

Romeo didn't sit. Instead, he leaned against the wall in the far corner—which wasn't far. "You seem antsy."

Like warning lights flashing a message of trouble ahead, the red lights on the video cameras in the corners blinked. "I'm not a big fan of jails." I stood and started pacing. Five steps by five steps didn't ease much tension. "I don't know what game you're playing here, Romeo, or why you're taping this, but you'd better do this by the book."

We stared at each other for a moment.

"Don't mess with me." I tried to sound threatening, but it's sorta hard to do when the person you're threatening holds all the cards.

The door squeaked open, interrupting the tension. A guard held Mr. Fujikara by the arm.

Wrinkled and mussed, he looked tired and more than a little scared. "Ms. O'Toole! Thank heavens!" Breaking free from the guard, he rushed to me and gave me a hug.

I detected faint odors of vomit and urine. A night in the Vegas drunk tank was probably quite an experience. "Are you okay?"

He nodded.

I pulled away from him. "Let's get you out of here."

"I need to take his statement now that he's sober." Romeo pushed himself away from the wall.

We each took a seat at the table.

I leveled my gaze at Romeo. "By the book."

Romeo nodded, read Mr. Fujikara his rights, then asked if he wanted a lawyer.

Mr. Fujikara shook his head. "I really don't have anything to say. My head is killing me. Somebody must've slipped something in my drink last night. I don't remember anything really—only bits and pieces."

Romeo's face fell. "You can't tell us anything?"

"Nothing more than you already know. I ate dinner at Carne by myself. My friends wanted to gamble, so they stayed at the hotel. A girl approached me in the bar at Carne. I invited her to share a drink with me. That is the last thing I remember."

"Had you ever seen this girl before?"

"No."

"Would you recognize her again?"

"I doubt it."

Romeo reached in his pocket and extracted a card. Extending it to Mr. Fujikara he said, "Here's my card. Call me if you think of anything else."

～

AN HOUR LATER, I FINALLY HAD MR. FUJIKARA AND HIS POSSESSIONS occupying the passenger seat of Miss Patterson's green-mobile. "Okay, give it up. What really happened?"

He opened his mouth to speak, then clamped it shut. His eyes widened as his gaze fixated on something over my shoulder.

I whirled around at the tap on my window.

Romeo motioned for me to lower the glass. "Sorry about the show inside. I had to take his statement so the higher-ups will think I am actually doing my job."

"I know how the game is played."

"Better than me, I should think." He grinned, then he handed me several folded sheets of paper. "Here's what you asked for. Remember, we're playing on the same team. The police stuff is there along with some personal info I got off the Internet." With that, he was gone.

I stuffed the papers in my purse and turned my attention back to Mr. Fujikara. "Your turn. And make it good."

"What?"

"You and me, we've been playing games for some time now, and I'm not as stupid as I look. That little charade back there may have fooled the young detective, but you can't fool me."

I watched him war with himself.

Finally, he gave in. "You're one tough broad." The guy had clearly been watching too many Bogart movies.

"You have no idea."

He settled in and fastened his seat belt as I piloted the car out of the lot.

He took a deep breath, then let it out slowly. "It's very simple really. As I told the detective, I ate dinner at Carne."

"But not by yourself."

"No." He fiddled with the handle of my purse, which rested between us. "I will tell you something, but if you repeat it, I will deny it. My wife, well…she would be disappointed."

"Understood."

"When I come here, I like to find some female company. I didn't want to hire a comfort girl—too risky, in many ways." He stared out the side window as he talked.

Comfort girl? Leave it to the Japanese to make a whore sound like Florence Nightingale. "So, what did you do?"

"One evening I was eating in the bar at Carne with a young lady from the hotel. A couple approached us and asked if we were swingers. I had no idea what they meant, but the young lady I was with did, and she told them we were."

"I have a feeling I know what young woman you are talking about. If I'm right, she's no lady." While stopped at the next red light, I pulled the copy of the employee photo of Felicia Reilly from my purse and handed it to Mr. Fujikara.

He took the photo, but didn't meet my eyes. "That's her! How'd you know?"

"She's been cutting a swath through the hotel." The light turned green, and I accelerated away from the intersection.

"I guess that should make me feel better, but I still feel very foolish." He hung his head.

"Why don't you tell me the rest of it?"

"The couple invited us to a party at a private estate somewhere south of town. I thought I'd died and gone to Nirvana—willing women, as many as I wanted, with their husbands' complicity. I didn't see any downside. I was wrong."

"Your young lady hit you up for money, didn't she?"

"At first, I thought she only wanted money for going to the party with me. You see, a single man cannot get in. I had to bring a woman with me."

"But then she wanted more?"

"She threatened to tell not only my wife, but my business associates as well if I didn't pay her." He turned to look at me. This time his eyes held mine. "That would ruin me."

Why did the people with the most to lose, play the riskiest games? "What did you do?"

"I bought a little time."

"What happened last night?"

"I was supposed to meet her in the bar at Carne. While I waited, I saw her—she didn't see me. She was having a heated conversation with a large man."

"A large man? Like my height and four hundred pounds, give or take, balding?"

"Yes."

The Most Reverend most likely. He and his wife had said they were going to Carne for dinner. "What then?"

"She spotted me and came over to the table. She didn't stay long. She was angry, and she looked scared. She said she needed the money right now. Something about leaving town."

"Did you give it to her?" I eased the car up the ramp into the cool darkness of the parking garage.

"Not all of it." He returned to looking out the side window.

"How much?"

"A grand. She took it, even though she wanted more. I have a feeling that's not the last of her, is it?"

"It will be if I get my hands on her." My grip tightened on the steering wheel. I wanted to get hold of those two so bad I could almost taste it. "And the DUI? Did she put something in your drink or did you do it to yourself?"

"I don't know. I usually can handle my liquor pretty well. Of course, I was upset, I didn't eat very much and probably drank more than normal."

Mr. Fujikara may have had one heck of a night, but little did he know, he had made my day.

I knew where to start looking for the Weasel. When Carne opened at five, I would be there.

Mr. Fujikara and I parted at the elevators. He went to his room after assuring me he would contact my office and make arrangements to meet with a lawyer.

The Beautiful Jeremy Whitlock caught me heading toward the casino. "Hey, I've been trying to get ahold of you. Some guy keeps answering your cell." He fell into step beside me.

"Yeah, I hired a guy to take my calls. I was getting tired of the ringing, pushing the buttons, the missed calls, the messages, all of it." Next time I saw Teddie I was going to shoot him.

"Sure. New boyfriend?"

"Old friend, but we're not going there." I stopped at the entrance to the casino. A few stragglers occupied stools in front of the occasional slot machine. For the most part, the tables were abandoned. However, a heated game of poker was still underway with Subway Jones in the thick of it.

"I'm an ace investigator. You can't keep secrets from me."

I narrowed my eyes at him. "Apparently, you have a strong death wish."

"Thought that would get a rise out of you."

"You were right." Jeremy looked impeccable in his creased slacks and tailored button-down. Each hair was in place and I couldn't see even a hint of five o'clock shadow. I knew the guy had been up most of the night. Subconsciously, I measured myself against his perfection and came up woefully short. I found that irritating. "You said you were looking for me?"

"Yeah. You know your guy we talked about last night? He never reappeared on any of the floors. I checked every one."

That could mean only one thing. "He went all the way to the top, then."

"Right. The elevator stops at Mr. Irv Gittings' office suite. He owns the Athena."

"I *know* who owns the Athena—I've only been in this business half a lifetime." Why can't a man resist telling me stuff I already know, as if my IQ drops a hundred points when I'm in his presence? "Why would Dane go see him?"

"Sorry, I didn't mean to insult you. I'm so used to talking to the blondes around here—most of whom are bimbos and flakes—the Vegas cliché."

"You're digging yourself a hole here." I glared at him.

"And after seeing the look on your face, I'm considering jumping in it." He shot me that dimpled grin. "Charming smart women—one of my many talents."

My bad mood began to melt as I started to get all gooey inside. One grin and I was a mess. I really needed to stifle myself. Why is it when your mind opens the door to sex that's all you can think about? Nothing like being betrayed by your own body part— several of them actually "You haven't answered my question."

"I don't know why your boy would go visit the competition, but I intend to find out. Could you get a copy of the background check you guys run on all new hires?"

"I've got something even better." I rooted in my bag for the papers Romeo had given me. "Security keeps all the checks, for obvious reasons. Since Dane works in Security, I didn't want to go that route. So, I asked another source to run one for me. He gave it to me this morning." I waved the papers at Jeremy, then smoothed them out on the nearest empty craps table. We hunched over them.

Jeremy whistled low when he realized what he was looking at. "Where did you get a copy of a police report and background check on Paxton Dane?"

"I have low friends in high places."

"Impressive."

Romeo had been thorough. I read through it twice. One glaring fact leapt out: Dane didn't have a kid sister. So, why did he tell Mother and me he did? What game was he playing? And, whose side was he on?

A half hour later I was still wandering aimlessly through the casino, lost in thought. Jeremy had scurried off to visit Miss Patterson before heading home for some sleep, leaving me to worry by myself. All I had were bits and pieces of the puzzle, but so far, none of them fit together. Lyda Sue was dead, The Big Boss was in trouble, Willie the Weasel and his female buddy were blackmailing half the guests at the Babylon, the new Security guy —with access to everything—was lying to everybody, Security tapes were disappearing, my best friend wanted to be my lover, and I couldn't get my libido under control.

Somehow, life had gotten away from me.

"You know, if you keep scowling like that, you'll get those little lines between your eyes. Then you'll look like you're a hundred." Subway Jones, sporting a day's worth of stubble and still dressed in his Hawaiian shirt, khakis, and sandals from yesterday, stepped in front of me.

"Now there's a happy thought." Teddie said I'd *be* too old to get what I wanted. Subway told me I'd *look* too old. I sensed a theme.

He hooked his arm through mine and steered me toward the lobby. "You look way too serious. Let's go watch Miranda's interview with CNBC."

"CNBC? The stock market channel?"

"She's a media mogul. Didn't you know? An American success story." Subway gave me a sly chuckle. "I don't know what those stock nerds are thinking—Miranda eats little boys like that for breakfast." At my startled look, he continued, "Not literally, of course."

With Miranda, one never knew.

We had given the media several conference rooms on the mezzanine for their base of operations. CNBC had set up shop in the Golden Fleece room, which somehow seemed appropriate.

Miranda preened at all the attention. She had traded her black Lycra number from yesterday for a blue pinstripe suit. Trying to look professional, I guess. Of course, her five-inch-long skirt and the sheer camisole with no bra kept respectability at bay. I sympathized with the guy who was following her around, trying to figure out where to attach her mike.

She caught sight of us and rushed over, trailed by the guy with the mike, a girl with a makeup kit, and another girl I thought might be the producer. They all came to a stop in front of us.

"Lucky, you came to watch my interview. How wonderful of you, darling!" I didn't know who she was channeling, but she sounded like Greta Garbo. Miranda was clearly going to make the most of her latest fifteen minutes of fame.

"Wouldn't miss it," I said.

"You are such a dear. Stuffy, but a real dear." With that, she caught sight of her interviewer and glided off in his direction, still trailed by her minions.

The two of them, Miranda and the interviewer—shark and bait—settled into chairs opposite each other. The mike guy waved the little device over her chest, clearly at a loss. Miranda grabbed the thing from him with a frown and attached it to her left boob, then lifted her face for a dusting by the makeup artist.

The temperature in the small space rose rapidly, fueled by the bright lights and the sheer number of people crammed in there. Subway and I pressed up against the back wall by the door, taking it all in.

Subway watched his wife, his eyes alight. "This is going to be good," he whispered.

"I don't know," I said. "Miranda tends to suck the witty right out of the repartee."

Subway laughed. "Yes, but the girl does know a sound bite."

The interview started with a seemingly innocuous question: "So Miranda, how did you get into the adult movie business?"

Miranda leaned into her young questioner, the full force of her cleavage displayed for the camera. She placed a hand on his knee and purred, "Well, I really, really love to screw."

Every man in the room was instantly struck dumb.

Every man except Subway, who whispered in my ear, "Sound bite number one."

∼

THE INTERVIEW WENT DOWNHILL FROM THERE. ACTUALLY, I THINK CNBC got what they wanted—I just wasn't sure they could show the whole thing on national TV.

Miss Patterson met me as I headed across the lobby. She looked flustered. "You really do need to get your phone back. I had to ask Security to find you." She pushed a strand of hair out of her face as she skidded to a stop in front of me.

"Where's the fire?"

She arched her eyebrows at me. "The Big Boss called. He was upset that he couldn't reach you on your phone."

I cringed, hoping Teddie hadn't answered that call.

"The Big Boss doesn't understand why Teddie is fielding all of your calls."

"That makes two of us. What did The Big Boss want?"

"He wants, and I quote, 'Lucky's ass in the bar in five minutes.' That was ten minutes ago."

My eyes got all slitty. I don't handle high-handed very well, and I most certainly don't like being summoned like a disobedient dog. "I assume he was talking about Delilah's? We only have five bars in this hotel."

My voice must've betrayed my anger, since Miss Patterson took a step back. Clutching her notepad to her chest like a shield, she nodded, then retreated with valor.

≈

THE BIG BOSS HUDDLED IN THE FAR CORNER OF DELILAH'S NURSING a Diet Coke. His mouth set in a grim line, he motioned for me to take the seat opposite him. I was ready for a fight, but this didn't seem like the time or the place, or even the correct opponent, so I did as he asked.

Dispensing with the pleasantries, The Big Boss started in. "A little while ago I got an interesting call from Irv Gittings. He was practically gloating."

"He has a copy of the tape, doesn't he?" The pieces were starting to fit together, but I asked just to make sure.

The Big Boss looked surprised. "How'd you know?"

I shrugged. "I didn't. It fits, though. What did Mr. Gittings say?"

The Big Boss picked up the Diet Coke can and poured the last bit into his glass. Then he put the can on its side and absentmindedly twirled it around. "He's been trying to get my hotels away from me for a number of years."

"I had no idea."

"I'm the last of a dying breed. A holdout against consolidated corporate ownership."

"You do have the prime location on the Strip."

He nodded and shrugged. "Now they have the leverage to drive me out."

I reached over and grabbed the can—the spinning was driving me nuts. "Give me two days."

"What are you going to accomplish in two days? My guys can't even find a scent of a trail left by William and his friend."

I pointed my finger at him. "I knew you were lying when you told me you wouldn't do anything stupid. And, Boss, it would be real stupid to get rid of Willie and Felicia—they're your only witnesses."

"I just want them roughed up a little."

"I want them roughed up more than a little, but only after we get what we want out of them, okay?"

"You know where they are?" For the first time since I'd sat down, he looked hopeful.

"I got a pretty good idea where Willie is. I'll know more this afternoon."

"You'll tell me when you find out?"

I snorted. "Not on a bet."

I rose to leave, but was stopped short when The Big Boss announced, "By the way, you asked if anyone else was there when I got into the helicopter with Lyda Sue."

I turned to look at him. "Yeah?"

"Somebody else was there—I'd half forgotten. He did the walkaround with Willie, then helped us get into the helicopter, positioning us for the whole weight-and-balance thing."

One more piece fell into place.

"Paxton Dane," I said.

The look on his face told me I was right.

CHAPTER TEN

$\mathcal{D}$ANE HAD a knack for turning up in all the wrong places.

And doing all the wrong things.

I ticked off his sins as I made my way back to the office. Let's see, he lied to me—twice. First about the videotapes. Second about the kid sister. He was seen having an angry exchange with Felicia Reilly—prime suspect number two. He'd loaded everyone into the helicopter on that fateful night. Then, he'd been caught going to see Irv Gittings at the Athena—who was locked in a duel to the death with The Big Boss.

No doubt about it, Dane had added his name to the suspect list and was working hard to hit numero uno on my shit list.

I should've known he'd turn out to be a bum—or worse. Could I pick them or what? Of course I hadn't actually picked Dane, but I had felt an attraction to him. Truth be told, I'd been feeling an attraction to almost any male who could walk and talk without drooling on himself. I realized I was in trouble when the gardener, who was married with eight kids and knew four words of English —one of them being "fuck" (which he used with relish)—started looking hot to me. Obviously, the holes in my sieve of discernment had gotten quite large. Perhaps the lack of meaningful sex had something to do with it.

So, the bum meter was malfunctioning a bit. I felt adrift.

But I didn't need to be a genius to figure out Dane was trouble.

"Lucky! There you are. I've been looking for you." Dane!

A shiver of fear shot through me. Like I said, he had a knack for turning up in all the wrong places. "You found me."

He wore a tired look, a green polo shirt that accentuated the color of his eyes, creased jeans, and a pair of broken-in cowboy boots made out of some exotic skin. They looked expensive. He stopped in front of me. "Do you know some guy keeps answering your phone? What's up with that?"

"Of course I know, and nothing is up with that." He looked sexy as hell. I tried my old trick of repeating *All men are pigs* over and over. This time it worked. I stepped around him and kept marching across the lobby toward the elevators.

He kept pace with me. "Why are you in such an all-fired hurry?" He grabbed my arm, spinning me around and holding me in place. "I need to talk to you."

Facing him, I yanked my arm out of his grasp. I took a deep breath and tried to arrange my features in a benign expression. Showing him my anger wouldn't help me see through his little charade. "Sorry, my day took off out of the gate at a full gallop. What can I do for you?"

"Have dinner with me."

"What?" I don't know what I was expecting, but that wasn't it.

"As I recall, I owe you a dinner. How about tonight? I can get us a table for two at Tigris."

I could only stare at him. Dinner with a traitor—I'd probably get the firing squad at dawn. But maybe I could get some answers from him without giving away what I already knew—as The Big Boss always said, hold your cards tight. And if it didn't work out, at least I'd have a great meal. "Today is Tuesday, right?"

"All day."

"How about tomorrow?" Tuesdays are movie night with Teddie.

"That'll work. I'll pick you up around seven. You have to tell me where you live."

"I'll meet you at Tigris." No way was he coming to my apartment. What would Teddie say? Was I hiding from him now, too?

God, life had gotten so complicated.

~

THE BEAUTIFUL JEREMY WHITLOCK AGAIN OCCUPIED THE CORNER of Miss Patterson's desk when I burst through the door. This time, however, he didn't move.

"Jeremy, if you're not careful we're going to stencil your name right where you sit, permanently reserving that spot for you."

He showed me those damned dimples. "I'd like that."

Miss Patterson looked thrilled as well.

"I don't mean to be a spoilsport, but take pity on me—this office grinds to a halt when you're here."

"Understood. Just a few minutes more, okay?"

I nodded. "Besides, Miss Patterson and I have an important appointment very shortly."

They both nodded at me like guilty schoolchildren.

I stifled a smile and shook my head. Kids.

"The Most Reverend is waiting for you in your office," Miss Patterson said, as I dropped my purse in the closet.

"Got it."

Jeep stood at the window, his back to me, his bulk blocking the light. "Reverend Peabody."

He turned at the sound of my voice. "Ms. O'Toole, call me Jeep, please."

I took a seat behind my desk. "Sorry. Hard habit to break. And it's Lucky."

"What's lucky?" he asked, his face clouded in confusion.

"Me."

"You're lucky?"

"My name."

"Oh." He nodded. "Somebody had a sense of humor."

The Most Reverend had gone Vegas. Today, he sported flip-flops, Bermuda shorts, a muscle shirt, and Maui Jim's. While I believe in "live and let live," seeing Jeep in a muscle shirt gave me an insight into the thinking behind a proposed Vegas city ordinance against men going without shirts.

Jeep remained standing, his elephantine legs spread, his hands clasped behind his back, his eyes hidden behind the dark glasses. "I saw the blackmailer last night."

I raised my finger. "Wait a minute." I stepped out of the office and retrieved Ms. Reilly's picture from my purse. I extended it to Jeep. "Is that her?"

He nodded.

"Felicia Reilly."

"That's her name?"

"If that's her, it is. Was she at Carne?" I knew the answer already, but would he tell me the truth? There seemed to be a serious epidemic of lying going around.

"Yeah." He flushed, and I didn't think it was from embarrassment. "She wanted her money."

"Did you give it to her?"

"No. I put her off. She was furious. But she's a greedy little cuss." A smile lifted the corners of his mouth. "She's going to meet me at a party we're having this Thursday night."

"Really?"

He nodded and took off his dark glasses. His eyes twinkled in anticipation. "We're going to get that conniving little bitch, aren't we?"

I raised my eyebrows, then nodded. "Just tell me where." He

wrote the address down for me. I recognized it—a toffee-nose address for sure—in the Estates...at Spanish Trail. Another piece of the puzzle dropped into place.

I escorted Jeep out. After the door closed behind him, I rubbed my hands in glee and danced a little jig. In a little more than forty-eight hours, I'd have Felicia Reilly, boiled, diced and ready to serve. If my luck held, and if my hunch was right, I'd have my hands around Willie's neck sooner than that. Both Miss Patterson and Jeremy looked at me like I'd lost a nut. I didn't feel the need to explain.

"Jeremy, you got anything for me?"

"No, not yet."

"Okay. You about ready?" I asked Miss Patterson.

She looked at me, her forehead wrinkled with concern. "Almost. Give me three minutes."

"You got it," I said, as I dashed into my office. "I need to make a phone call." I shut the door behind me.

Parking one cheek on the corner of my desk, I picked up the phone, dialed nine for an outside line, then I thought for a moment. *Damn.* I depressed the button on the intercom. "Miss Patterson?"

"He's just leaving."

"Fine. Do you know my cell number? I never call myself." Why I feel the need to explain my own stupidities, I don't know.

"Of course."

I waited...but giggling was all I heard. "Why don't you tell me, then we'll both know?" What is it about infatuation that turns a normally competent woman into a giggling school girl? I'd rather be caught dead.

Okay, even I don't believe me sometimes.

"Oh, sorry." She rattled off the numbers.

"Thanks." I dialed my cell.

As I figured he would, Teddie answered on the first ring. "Hey, good-lookin'."

"Hey, yourself. Where are you? And why do you keep answering my phone?"

"I'm three minutes from Samson's. And if I didn't answer, how would you have found me?"

Samson's was The Big Boss's attempt at humor. He thought it funny to name the hair salon after a guy with long hair. "If you weren't fielding every call to my cell, I would have called *your* cell."

"I'm not answering *mine*, only yours," Teddie answered, as if any of this made sense. "Are you ladies on your way?"

"We will be shortly. Is everything set up?"

"Most of it. I'll put the finishing touches on our plan while you do the hair thing." Excitement infused Teddie's voice. "This is going to be fun."

"And the other thing? Have you had time to work on that yet?"

"I've made some calls, but no one's gotten back to me yet."

"How can they when you're not answering your phone?"

He laughed. "You have me there."

"I don't know what I'd do without you," I said it and meant it. That was precisely my hang-up. One rather huge pothole in the rocky road to love.

"I'm working very hard at making myself indispensable."

"Are you going to give me back my phone?"

"I'd pay you good money to take it off my hands," Teddie said. "It rings incessantly—I have reams of messages for you. How do you handle it?"

"I have the patience of Job."

He laughed as if I were joking. "See you in a minute." Then he rang off.

Despite my best mental efforts to override it, my heart picked up its pace at the prospect.

~

SAMSON'S OCCUPIED A ZIGGURAT AT THE END OF THE BAZAAR. IT boasted a stair-stepped stone exterior with various trailing plants cascading from each step, most of them in riotous bloom. The ziggurat looked like it had been disassembled in some remote jungle, then reassembled for our pleasure in Vegas. Which was, funny enough, the truth. The Big Boss had found it in ruins in some obscure South American country. Money changed hands, an international incident had been doused—most likely with a great deal more money—and, voilà, one genuine ziggurat on the Las Vegas Strip.

Cascading waterfalls framed the fourteen-foot-tall, rustic wooden doors, which were decorated with huge brass rings for door pulls and a bar that could be lowered to secure the doors against invading hordes—which was superfluous, since Samson's never closed and was rarely invaded. The doors stood open, inviting me into the front lobby, where gorgeous young women waited to satisfy my every beauty need.

I felt the frisson of excitement before I registered a presence at my elbow. I didn't even have to look to know who it was—Teddie. My body clearly wasn't listening to my brain where he was concerned. "Hey."

"How'd you know it was me?" He circled my waist with one arm and pulled me to him. Teddie had traded his sweatshirt for a fitted, collarless cotton shirt. He still wore those damned blue jeans that made it almost impossible to resist running my hands over his ass or sticking them in his back pockets, which, while a bit more subtle, was almost as good. Apparently, I had blown right by pathetic and was now completely hopeless—a new low.

"You told me you'd meet us here," I said, trying to sound nonchalant.

"Right."

With both of my hands on his chest, I pushed him away. "Would you behave? We've given the grapevine enough to talk about for a while."

"They all talk about you anyway," said Miss Patterson, who stood off to the side waiting patiently with a grin on her face.

"*You're* no help. I'll remember that comment when it's time for your next raise."

She didn't seem fazed. I was losing my touch.

I shot her a look as I straightened my shirt and brushed a hand down my slacks, hoping against hope that straightening the outer would straighten the inner. It didn't work.

A young woman wearing a very short, off-the-shoulder toga cinched at the waist with a golden rope greeted us. "Ms. O'Toole, Linda is ready for you both now."

Long blonde hair, perky breasts, dimple-free thighs, an unlined face, she looked about sixteen and made me feel old and ugly. While nobody short of a skilled surgeon could do anything about the old part, I was counting on Linda to solve the ugly part. I nodded to Miss Patterson. "You go first, but a word to the wise about Linda. She can be a bit abrupt—rude even—so don't let her scare you."

Blinking, her eyes wide with fear, she said, "I could use some moral support here."

"You go on. I'll be right there."

For once, Miss Patterson did as I asked without a sardonic comment. I watched as she disappeared around another waterfall into the salon where Linda waited to work her magic. I turned to Teddie. "What's the plan?"

"Linda said she needed about two hours—she said you didn't have the patience for more than that."

I shrugged. Beauty wasn't really my thing.

"Meet me at the Palace at two. They're closing the store for us."

"You know Miss Patterson's size and everything?"

Teddie stepped in close to me, and leaned in, his mouth close to my ear. He didn't touch me, but it seemed as if I could feel every inch of his body with mine. "Lucky, my love, I'm an expert in two things. One of them is women's clothing." His seductive tone left no doubt as to what he considered his other area of expertise.

My body tingled all over. Teddie seemed determined to work us through the alphabet—and to make sure I was a wreck by the time we got to Z. His plan was working.

He had almost made it out the door when my brain returned to minimal functioning. "My phone?"

He waved it at me. "I'll keep it. You relax. Don't worry, if the building burns down or the SWAT team bursts through the front doors, I know where to find you." Then he disappeared into the crowd.

A young Samson look-alike appeared at my elbow. Samson's was famous for its army of namesake look-alikes. I could hear The Big Boss's voice in my head: "A beauty salon is a place for ladies, so let's give the ladies what they want." Apparently, women wanted an army of young, buff males to do their bidding. I had no argument with that.

Tall and sculpted, this young Samson sported a mini toga that looked as if it was designed to cover the essentials and nothing more. A brass ring circled one bicep. Gladiator sandals graced his feet, the straps winding around his calves. He had long dark hair and an otherwise completely hairless body. At least as far as I could tell—and that was pretty far, given his lack of clothing. I wanted to ask him if he'd been lasered or waxed, but thought better of it.

"Miss, would you like a mimosa?"

I looked at his tray laden with tall fluted glasses. I thought about Teddie. "One? Hell no, I'll take two."

~

I'D POLISHED OFF THE FIRST AND WAS HALF DONE WITH THE SECOND when I found Miss Patterson already seated in Linda's chair. Tapping her stilettoed foot, Linda, a trim, natural blonde with sharp features arranged in an ever-present frown, stood behind Miss Patterson surveying her in the mirror. Occasionally, she would pick up a lock of Miss Patterson's mop of frizzy, mousy brown hair suffused with streaks of gray and shake her head, tut-tutting.

I continued sipping my mimosa. Hands clutching the arms of the chair in a white-knuckled grip, Miss Patterson looked paralyzed with fear. Both of us were smart enough to know one didn't disturb the master while she was thinking, so we remained mute.

Finally, Linda stepped back and clapped her hands, shattering the subdued quiet.

I darn near dropped my glass. Miss Patterson looked ready to bolt.

A bevy of assistants materialized at Linda's summons. She gave them hurried, unintelligible instructions. They disappeared as fast as they had come.

"I know what you need," Linda announced. "You will like it."

Before Miss Patterson found her voice, a Samson appeared at her elbow and led her away. She threw a questioning look over her shoulder. I gave her a reassuring nod. The poor woman looked like a wide-eyed tourist seeing Vegas for the first time—awestruck and overwhelmed, but excited.

"Now you," Linda announced. "Take a seat."

I gulped the last of the mimosa, depositing the empty glass on the tray of a passing Samson, and did as I was told. Linda didn't scare me—much.

"You're a mess," Linda declared, as she surveyed my hair.

"That's why I'm here. Make me feel good about myself."

She nodded and tapped that stilettoed foot.

How could she stand in those things all day? Ten minutes in them and I'd offer up every secret I knew. Now there's a market as yet unexplored by Jimmy Choo—torture and interrogation. I waited while Linda thought.

"God, I live for challenges like this," she announced after a minute or two of careful observation. "Do you have any particular desires as to what I do with...*this?*" She motioned to my hair and looked as if she'd taken a bite of something awful.

"Whatever you want." I said it calmly, my resolve fortified by multiple ounces of champagne diluted only slightly with orange juice. I needed a new look to match the new me I hoped to be.

My pronouncement clearly startled the hair-meister. Her eyes grew just a smidgen wider. One corner of her mouth lifted briefly —or maybe I imagined that part. "Really?"

I nodded and snagged another mimosa from a passing Samson. "No weird colors or asymmetrical cuts—other than that, consider me your blank canvas."

The next hour and forty-five minutes passed in a flurry of activity—washing, dying, cutting, styling—even a stop at the makeup artist while my color set. The only time I almost lost my nerve was when Linda brought out the scissors. I shut my eyes while she worked her magic. She took my hint and turned me away from the mirror.

Sometimes Linda chatted while she worked, sometimes not. Today was one of her chatty days.

"How's your life going?" she asked as she took a big snip. "You have a different glow about you."

"Same ol', same ol'." A big lock of newly dark hair fell into my lap.

"I'm not sure I believe that, but I'll let you off the hook." She took another snip. Another lock of hair fell in my lap.

"I am going to have some hair left, right?"

"A strand or two. So, anything new about Lyda Sue?"

"You knew her, too?" That girl really got around.

"Not well. I used to run into her at Carne."

"Really?" I tried to keep my voice in a conversational tone. "What was she doing there?"

"What almost everyone does there—trying to find another couple interested in switching."

"Really?" I squeaked. So much for the conversational tone.

Linda didn't seem to notice. "The bar at Carne is the place local swingers look for action. I only saw her there a couple of times, both of them within the last two weeks or so. She was always with a tall, dark and handsome type who had the whole aw-shucks cowboy thing going."

I grabbed my bag and pulled out Dane's picture. "This the guy?"

She tapped it with her comb. "Yeah. Real smooth, that one."

"Did they ever find any action?"

"Didn't notice." Linda went back to her snipping.

"Did they want to switch with you and your husband?"

"Us?" Linda laughed. "Hell, Joe would kill me if I even thought about doin' it with another guy. And he knows I'd Bobbitize him if he ever put his weenie where it shouldn't be. The bar is our local watering hole."

I squeezed my eyes shut, but all I could see was Linda with a huge knife chasing poor Joe. Then a picture of Dane and Lyda Sue together. For Dane's sake, when I had dinner with him, I hoped the knives were kept out of my reach.

"Almost done," Linda announced.

Every now and then I caught a glimpse of Miss Patterson in passing. Each time she was clutching a mimosa in one hand and a Samson in the other.

Finally, it was time for the unveiling. I sat in Linda's chair, my eyes closed. I felt her turn me, so when I opened my eyes, I'd be looking at myself in the mirror. I could hear Miss Patterson in the chair next to me. I assumed she also had her eyes closed and was facing the mirror.

"Voila!" Linda announced.

I opened my eyes. For a moment I couldn't say anything. I didn't recognize the woman staring back at me. The rat's nest of over-processed blonde hair had been replaced by a cloud of soft, shiny, medium-brown curls with golden highlights. A few tendrils drifted across my forehead, drawing attention to my eyes. I'd forgotten they were such a deep blue. The understated makeup accentuated my cheekbones. Where had they been hiding? While not stunning, I was actually...pretty.

Who knew?

"Wow." Words longer than three letters had momentarily abandoned me.

Linda smiled. She was standing between Miss Patterson's chair and mine. With a satisfied nod, she crossed her arms and stepped aside.

Miss Patterson was radiant. Gone were the gray and the granny curls. She now sported a sleek, blonde style that took a decade off her appearance and made her eyes look as big as salad plates. She reached up and touched her face, a smile tickling her lips. Her eyes glistened.

She looked at me, but she didn't have to say anything—I knew exactly how she felt. "Linda," I said. "I know you charge a king's ransom, but you are worth every penny."

She nodded, acknowledging the compliment. "I just let out the real you. You've been fighting with yourself for years, Lucky." So how come everyone knew that but me?

~

PUTTING MY CLOTHES BACK ON FELT LIKE DONNING SOMEBODY else's old coat. I kept looking at myself in the mirror as I dressed. Everything about me was different—the old didn't quite fit anymore.

Although she didn't say so, I could tell Miss Patterson felt the same way. When she emerged from the changing room, she looked like a teenager dressed in her mother's clothes.

After I paid, and added generous tips for everyone, I grabbed her elbow and steered her out into the Bazaar. Instead of turning toward the hotel, we took a right, heading deeper into retail-land.

"Where are we going?" she asked.

"The makeover isn't yet complete." We stopped in front of the Palace. A large closed sign hung in the door. I knocked.

Miss Patterson hung back. "I can't afford this place."

"No worries. We're getting the Ted Kowalski discount. He's one of their most important customers."

She looked doubtful, but after a saleswoman opened the door, she stepped inside with me.

Designed to provide each customer with the royal treatment, the Palace was every inch a retail oasis. From the deep couches scattered liberally around the cozy space, to the small cafe in the corner, to the ever-present sales staff that bordered on obsequious, the Palace provided a customer-centric shopping experience. None of the store's inventory was on display. Instead, the customers—or as the staff referred to them, the clients—took a seat on one of the lovely sofas. The staff then brought out various, carefully selected items, one at a time.

I sank into the nearest couch, pulling Miss Patterson down with me. This wasn't exactly my normal shopping experience either. Sitting there was like waiting for a show to begin. I half expected the lights to dim and the music to start.

Instead, Teddie appeared, dressed in a rather risqué gown. Iridescent, beaded and practically see-through, it was reminiscent of the stuff Bob Mackie used to design for Cher in her heyday. He started to pirouette, then stopped in his tracks. He walked over to me and extended his hand, a smile splitting his face. His eyes locked on mine like a tractor beam.

Nervous as to what he thought of my new look, but powerless to resist, I let him pull me up. He turned me around in front of him. When I again faced him, he stepped in close, and very tenderly kissed me.

I'd never been kissed by a man in a dress before. I think I liked it. I'm not sure what that meant.

"You look fabulous," he whispered. He led me to a mirror.

"Look at the you you've kept hidden behind that wall of feigned indifference. You blow me away."

Blow him away? For sure I liked that.

I lost myself in our reflection—me in my pants, Teddie in his dress, and for some odd reason, nothing about us struck me as unusual.

Miss Patterson cleared her throat. "You guys are attracting some attention."

She was indeed correct. A small crowd, their noses pressed to the glass, lined the storefront. Teddie stepped toward them and turned slowly for their perusal. His performance elicited cheers and an occasional wolf whistle.

The show was on.

As he strode by me on his way to the changing room, he winked and asked, "How do you like my dress? Think it'll look good in the show?"

I pointed to his chest. "You don't have the right equipment to really take advantage of the design."

He looked down, then grinned. "I left my boobs at the theatre."

"At least you know where yours are," I said, as I surveyed my own inadequate cleavage.

He laughed, then ducked around the corner. "I'll be right back. Just let me change."

The minute he left, the parade began—dresses, pants, and silky tops—all in a riot of color. Tentative at first, then warming to the fun, Miss Patterson pointed to the ones she liked, and waved her hand dismissively at those she didn't. She even wrinkled her nose at a particularly offensive pantsuit.

Arms crossed and a serious expression on his face, Teddie watched as he leaned against the wall. All the original selections had been his. He had a wonderful eye.

Finally, Miss Patterson had narrowed her items down to about twenty. After she made her selections, Teddie grabbed her hand, pulling her with him around the curtain to the dressing rooms.

I took full advantage of the intermission. Up to this point, lunch had consisted of champagne and orange juice—not exactly the meal of champions. I wandered over to the cafe tucked discretely in the corner of the shop behind a counter sporting a few barstools in front, and snagged a sandwich and two Diet Cokes. I returned quickly, settling back in my place on the sofa and promptly inhaled half the sandwich. The other half was for Miss Patterson.

Teddie appeared from behind the curtain and, like Ed McMahon introducing Johnny Carson, mimicked a drumroll, gestured toward the curtain and said, "Heeeere's Miss Patterson."

The salesgirls, the crowd, Teddie, me, we all waited. But nobody appeared.

Teddie disappeared around the curtain, then reappeared with a very reluctant and blushing Miss Patterson in tow. He released her hand and stepped back.

For a moment there was silence, then all of us erupted in loud cheering—even the crowd outside.

Miss Patterson was a vision in a silky peach shirt and loosely fitted white slacks. She had a beautiful figure, curvy in all the right places. Why in the world had she hidden it under those old sacks? Why indeed? Only those not guilty of the same sin could question and criticize, so I kept my mouth shut, but added a few wolf whistles of my own to her applause.

Miss Patterson couldn't keep the grin off her face as she modeled all the outfits she had chosen. At the end of the show, we decided there were five absolute must-haves—two shirt-and-pant ensembles and one very flirty little black dress.

She didn't need much time to find shoes to match.

We congregated at the cash register, and Miss Patterson swallowed hard as the salesgirl presented her with the bill—seven hundred dollars. Her eyebrows shot upward. "That's all?" she asked. She looked first at me, then at Teddie.

We both shrugged and kept our expressions bland.

"Wow. That's one heck of discount you get, Mr. Kowalski," she said, as she proffered her credit card.

I noticed a sign on the counter that read, "Return policy: All items may be returned for full refund within ten days EXCEPT for any lingerie that has touched your choochilala."

"Is 'choochilala' a word?" I asked.

The salesgirl shook her head. "I made it up, but everybody knows what it means."

I couldn't argue with that.

Miss Patterson walked with the saleslady to the front door. Teddie and I followed, his arm hooked through mine. Just before the doors opened and the hordes descended, he whispered in my ear. "You're pretty sneaky. I don't get that big of a discount."

I just smiled and extracted my arm from his as the crowd surrounded him, all asking for his autograph.

I had made it out into the mall when Dane appeared at my elbow. God, he was worse than a bad penny.

"Do you know what time it is? Are you actually going to work today?" he asked.

I glanced at my watch. Four o'clock! Shoot! I needed to get a move on.

"Like the hair, by the way," he added.

That was a long way from "You look fabulous" and "You blow me away," but he got points for noticing—even though he played for the opposition. "Why are you always where I am? Is there something you need?"

"I work here. And, no, not really." He nodded toward Teddie. "You're an interesting lady, Ms. O'Toole. First you let a porn star kiss you and then a gay guy who wears women's clothes for a living. When are you going to let a real man in on the action?"

I put my hands on my hips and looked at him. "That is the sleaziest line I've heard since I talked to you yesterday. Did you take a course in creepiness?"

That wiped the grin off his face.

"Do you ever get anywhere with a line like that?"

He shook his head. "No."

I nodded toward Teddie. "And what makes you think he's gay?"

CHAPTER ELEVEN

ILLIE WAS close—I could feel it.

I needed one more piece of information, then I'd be sure.

I screeched to a stop in front of the valet stand at Carne, jumped out of the car, and tossed the keys to a startled kid in black pants and a vest. I assumed he was there to look after the cars—I didn't stop to find out. The Ferrari had covered the distance in record time, but I was still late.

Detective Romeo stood by the front door, looking studiedly patient. I'd called him as I'd left—I was back in possession of my phone, which Teddie had given to Miss Patterson and she had given to me. And I had just started to like being unavailable. "Wow, you look...different," Romeo said, as I joined him by the entrance.

"High praise, indeed." I smiled at him. "We're going to have to work on your delivery—smooth up those rough edges—if you want to make any time with the ladies in Vegas."

"Is that another service you provide?" His face colored a little.

"For a small fee, you can get Lucky O'Toole's *Lessons in Love*."

"Was that a bestseller?"

"Very small print run—not worth the cover price." I opened the mirrored glass door and motioned him inside. "What I know about love, you could put in your eye and not impair your vision."

He looked like he didn't believe me.

I nodded. "Sad, but true."

Carne was your typical high-end restaurant, specializing in a myriad of animal parts cooked to your liking. With dark paneled walls, high, overstuffed leather booths, brass accents and subdued lighting, it was both a place to be seen and a place to hide, depending on your mood.

No one manned the hostess station, so I stepped inside the main dining room. Waiters, clad in black with long white aprons, carefully wiped down stemware and flatware, then meticulously arranged each piece in its place on a white-clothed table.

Along the right-hand wall and extending the full length of the restaurant was an open kitchen with a huge charcoal grill. The chefs were busy chopping and arranging, preparing for the dinner rush.

I caught the eye of one of the waiters. "Where's the bar?"

"Right through there." He pointed to an opening along the wall to my left, which divided the building into the main room—the restaurant—and a side portion, obviously the bar. "We don't open until five."

I ignored him and headed for the bar.

Romeo dogged my heels. "What are we looking for?"

"A connection."

In contrast to the restaurant, the bar was an open and inviting space populated by a dozen high-topped tables, each with three chairs—which I thought odd; I couldn't imagine a scenario where three chairs would be appropriate, but apparently, there were a lot of things I couldn't imagine. A row of stools lined the bar, completing the seating opportunities. Lotsa room to mix and mingle—and trade spouses. A shiver of revulsion darted through me.

The place was as empty as a graveyard after dark.

I leaned across the bar and shouted, "Hey! Anybody back there?"

A tall blonde woman appeared around the corner, drying her hands with a bar towel. "We don't open until five."

The clock above her head read five minutes until five.

If I owned this place…I took a deep breath and smiled. "I know. And I can see you're busy, sorry. Would you mind answering a question or two? It won't take a minute."

The woman adopted a wary attitude. "What kind of question?"

I pulled the pictures of Felicia, Willie, and Dane out of my bag and spread them on the counter. "Do you remember seeing any of these people in here before?"

The bartender glanced at the photos, then back at me. "I might."

I knew what she wanted—good thing I had taken time to hit the ATM on my way out of the hotel. I reached for my wallet, but Romeo's hand on my arm stopped me.

He extracted his badge from his coat pocket and flashed it at the woman. "Does this help you remember?"

She shrugged. "No offense. Just working all the angles." She bent over the photos.

"Playing it straight usually gets you further," I said, unable to keep my mouth shut.

She gave me the once-over, then returned to the photos.

Romeo shot me a warning look.

I know. I know. Don't piss them off until *after* they give you what you want. I never was very good at playing games.

I shifted from foot to foot while blondie took her time with the photos.

Finally, she looked up. "I don't know about handsome there and the woman. I may have seen them in here. But this guy—" She tapped Willie's photo. "He's a regular."

My luck was holding! "Does he usually come in alone or with

anybody else?" I tried to adopt an attitude of casual indifference—whatever that was.

"I saw him a lot with this greasy guy with a wandering hand. Always touching what he shouldn't, like I'm some kinda chattel, you know?"

I nodded, wondering, among other things, where she came across that word. "You wouldn't happen to know his name?"

"Phil something." A smile tickled her lips. "Give me a minute. I'll get it for you. The dick was in here last Friday—alone."

"You remember back to last Friday?" I wasn't sure if she was stringing us along or not. "I'd think all the nights would run together."

"Oh, I remember, all right. I don't normally work on Fridays, but my rent was due, and I was a little short. I was lookin' good until your jerk left me a five-dollar tip on a two-hundred-dollar tab."

I shrugged in understanding. Vegas had more than its share of pretenders.

"Hold on a sec." She disappeared into the back.

Money and revenge—universal motivators.

She reappeared with a sheet of paper in her hand. "I was right. Phil Stewart—that's your guy."

I slapped my hands on the counter. "Great! Thanks." I turned to go, then stopped. I pulled five twenties out of my wallet and gave them to her.

"Whoa. Thanks." She seemed genuinely surprised. "I don't know what he's done, but get that creep, okay?"

"My pleasure."

∾

"Nice wheels," Romeo said, as he slipped into the Ferrari's passenger seat.

"Thanks." The kid was more comfortable complimenting cars than women. Typical.

"Clearly, I picked the wrong profession." Romeo traced the stitching in the leather seats. "Of course, nobody goes into police work looking to get rich."

"Some do," I countered, as I fired the engine and steered the car out on Charleston. "Vegas has a history of cops on the take. It can be quite lucrative, so I'm told."

"I wouldn't know," Romeo said, unable to take his eyes off the car.

"You stay on the force long enough, you'll learn." I gunned the engine and the car leapt forward—nothing like almost five hundred horses under the hood. If I didn't know half the cops in this town, I would've lost my license years ago.

Romeo wasn't paying attention. He had a stupid grin on his face as he watched me work through the gears with the paddle shifters. Put a guy in a fast car and his IQ plummets.

"That's cool. No clutch, huh?"

"Romeo, we can discuss the merits of clutchless manual transmissions some other time. Pay attention—we have work to do."

"Right." He pushed himself up in the seat. "Okay." He looked at me, his brow furrowed, as though he was trying to force brain cells back online. "Did that bartender give you the connection you were looking for?"

"Partly—but not completely." I let the speed bleed off as I approached the intersection of Charleston and Durango. The light was green. I threw the car to the right and accelerated through the turn—just like they'd taught me to do at the Richard Petty Driving Experience.

Romeo braced himself, but the smile never left his face. "You know, I'm completely at sea here. I don't know what we're looking for or what connections we're trying to make."

"Do one thing for me, then I'll connect all the dots."

"What's that?"

"I want you to call whoever it is at Metro that can put a name and an address together. I want to know if Phil Stewart lives in Spanish Trail and, if so, if this is his house number."

I gave him the piece of paper on which Jeep had written the location for the upcoming Trendmakers' party.

Romeo pulled out his phone and went to work, while I enjoyed the ride, the beautiful day, and the fact that soon I would have my hands around Willie the Weasel's neck—I was sure of it.

This time I made a more sedate left turn onto Tropicana— Romeo was still on the phone—I passed the first entrance, then turned into the second—the east entrance—of Spanish Trail.

Willie was there. I could feel it.

I whistled a jaunty tune as I motored past the elaborate entrance fountain and came to a halt next to the guard shack at the east gate.

I cast a beatific smile on Romeo when he announced, "You were right!"

I had known it all along—not actually, mind you, but...well, I just knew. Maybe my bum meter now had a GPS finder feature, or something. God, that would be interesting—not only would I attract the bums, but I could track them down as well! If the customer relations business ever went bad, I had another line of work to pursue—bum vigilante. Of course, there were probably a few legal hurdles to get over.

A heavyset woman in a Spanish Trail security uniform, gun holstered at her hip, sauntered over to the car, clipboard in hand. "Who are you?"

"Lucky O'Toole. This is Detective Romeo. We're here on police business."

"Uh-huh." The guard bent down and looked at us both, then scanned her clipboard. "You're not on the list."

"I know we're not on the list. We—"

"I can't let nobody in who's not on the list."

I motioned to Romeo to do his magic. Again, he flashed his

badge. This time, the woman took it and disappeared inside the guard's station. I saw her watching us warily as she talked on the phone.

She reappeared a few minutes later. "I thought you were lyin'," she said, as she handed the badge back to Romeo. She stepped back and pressed a button to open the gate. "You police sure have nice rides these days. Next time you guys want money from the voters, you can count me out."

Romeo shot me a smile as I accelerated away. "Hanging out with you could give the police a bad name."

∿

SPANISH TRAIL OCCUPIED THE TOP OF THE LIST OF VEGAS' MOST wonderful residential oases. Stucco and tile homes surrounded a twenty-seven-hole golf course with double-wide fairways and numerous signature water features. Grass and water—the symbols of wealth in the desert—and Spanish Trail had them in spades. Rumor had it that the temperature actually fell ten degrees once inside the gates, as if even the weather gods bowed to the show of money and power.

The first gated community in Vegas—most of the original power brokers had lived here at one time or another. To establish the appropriate hierarchy, the architects designed a series of gated communities within the gated community. The more money you had, the greater the number of gates protecting you from the riffraff.

Phil Stewart apparently had money.

We'd made it through the first obstacle and now found ourselves facing the second. This was like some kind of quest or something, where only the clever would pass—which, apparently, did not include me at the moment. Out of patience and out of ideas, I drummed my fingers on the steering wheel while I scrutinized the keypad, then glared at the closed gate blocking our entrance.

"Try five seven four two," Romeo said.

"What?"

"Five seven four two. It's written right here." He pointed to the piece of paper I had given him.

"Jeez." I poked at the numbers. "Nuance apparently flies right by me."

The gate moaned, then began its slow journey.

A Mediterranean-style McMansion, Phil Stewart's abode covered two lots at the end of a cul-de-sac. From glimpses through the shrubbery, I surmised it backed up to the golf course and had a wonderful view all the way to Mount Charleston to the north and the Spring Mountains to the west—a very pricey backdrop.

Romeo and I decided to attack on foot. I parked the car two houses down.

"We don't have a search warrant," Romeo announced, as he tried to keep up. He had to take two steps for my one.

"Amazingly enough, I did manage to capture *that* nuance." So, he had a habit of stating the obvious—I could identify.

"I have the tape recorder you told me to bring." He pulled it out of his pocket and showed it to me. It was identical to the one I brought. "I don't know how I'm going to take his statement and all that—if he's even here." Romeo shot me a look.

"Oh, he's here. Trust me."

"What do you think I'm doing?" Romeo clicked the button on the tape recorder to on, pressed the record button, made sure the tape was turning and the red light was on, then deposited the thing in his shirt pocket and pulled his jacket over to cover it.

I did the same, but put my recorder in my pants pocket. "Here's how we're going to play it. I'll take the lead—"

"I figured that much out already," Romeo groused.

"You're not going to take his statement," I continued. "In fact, you will not ask him anything."

"I won't?"

"Think, Romeo. I'll do the talking. I'll ask the questions and get the confession out of him. I'm not the police—I'm a private citizen. There are no rules on me questioning him and..." I held up my finger for emphasis. "And this is the most important part—I tape my own conversation with him and the tape can be used against him in a court of law."

"Right. I knew that." He cast me a sheepish grin. "I've never done this before, you know."

"You're doing fine. Keep your badge in your pocket, follow my lead, and we'll be cool."

We hiked up the curved driveway to the front of the house. We stopped before the huge copper door, which was decorated with etchings of naked women frolicking about. Just the kind of place where Willie the Weasel would hole up. I could picture him by the pool, a cool beverage in one hand, bikini-clad women slathering his body in oil. Oh, yeah, he'd burrow in here like a tick on a dog.

My eyes got all slitty.

"I've seen that look before." Romeo took a step back.

I smiled a tight smile. "Let me handle this. I haven't met a man yet who wouldn't at least open the door to a woman in a Ferrari."

"The car's down the street."

"Right." I shrugged. "I can talk my way in. Just watch." I pressed the bell. It played some tune—something about "let's get it on"—as it echoed inside Phil Stewart's party palace.

"Showtime," I whispered to Romeo, as somebody threw back the bolt.

The door opened.

Willie!

I could tell he didn't recognize me right off—one unexpected benefit of that makeover.

"Hello, Weasel," I said.

The light dawned in his eyes. "Oh, God, it's the Babylon's Amazon!"

I threw an elbow, hitting him smack in the nose. "That is for Lyda Sue."

Willie staggered back—his hands clutching his nose.

I followed him inside. I put my hands on his shoulders and brought my knee up as hard as I could into the soft flesh of his crotch. "And that's for me."

Willie crumpled to the floor—his mouth formed a circle, but no sound came out. On his back, one hand on his nose, the other holding his privates, he writhed in pain. Blood splattered the beautiful white, Italian marble floor, forming an interesting Rorschach pattern.

I put a foot in the middle of his chest. "Don't move." Adrenaline and the sweet thrill of revenge coursed through my veins. Exacting revenge was even better than I had imagined, a high no drug could match.

Blood oozed between the Weasel's fingers. "I think you broke my nose."

His words came out nasally sounding and high-pitched, tinged with pain. I liked that.

"No doubt." I put pressure on his chest to get his attention. "And that's not the only part of you I'll break if you mess with me. Now, be still." I motioned to Romeo. "Find a towel or something, would you? And take a quick look around. See if anybody else is here. Be careful."

He disappeared into the house.

"Who's the boyfriend?" Willie asked, as he motioned after Romeo.

"Just a trainee along for the ride."

"I didn't have anything to do with the whore who fell out of the helicopter." He actually sounded sincere. Lying was one of Willie's best things.

"We'll get to that. Where's your friend, Phil?"

"Out of town," Willie said, then spat some blood.

I was actually enjoying this—tiptoeing along the line between saint and sinner. I wondered what that said about my character—or lack thereof. "How long has he been gone?"

"A couple of weeks. Nobody with any money spends the summers in Vegas." Willie tried to wipe the blood away, but it was gushing too fast. "I look after the place while he's gone."

Willie was lying. The bartender had put Phil Stewart in town last Friday. "And the party on Thursday?"

Willie's eyes widened with pain or surprise, I wasn't sure which. "He'll be back for that."

"You know when?"

"Whenever he wants. He has his own jet."

I increased the pressure on Willie's chest.

"Ow. Okay, okay. Sometime tomorrow. He's coming from Jackson Hole."

Romeo reappeared with what looked to be a guest towel. He looked sheepish. I grabbed the towel and looked at it, then snorted. Several naked men, penises erect, comprised the beautifully embroidered border. Guess he'd gotten it from the girls' bathroom. I tossed it to Willie.

Willie caught it in one hand and pressed it to his nose. His eyes never left me. I saw hate in them—and fear.

"How'd you learn to do that?" Romeo asked, his voice tinged with awe as he nodded at Willie.

"I grew up in a whorehouse. A girl learns how to protect herself pretty quick. First time I broke a guy's nose, I also broke my hand. Used my elbow ever since."

"Wow."

Romeo and I each grabbed an arm and pulled Willie out to the patio. He was making way too much of a mess in the house. We tossed him onto a plastic chaise by the pool.

I took a good hard look at Willie the Weasel. Everything about him was bland, from his lifeless brown hair, to his small, close-set eyes, to his thick lips that matched his thick waist—and thick head. He'd been a wart on my ass for years—a tough-guy wannabe with rich friends who had powerful lawyers.

A guppy trying to swim with the big fish.

Why The Big Boss kept him around, I never could understand. You didn't have to be a rocket scientist to fly a helicopter. I almost had him once—but slick lawyers got him off—I still don't know how. The Big Boss had almost fired him then, but for some reason, he didn't pull the trigger. What had he said? It was better to keep your enemies close, that way you knew what they were up to.

And Willie was the kind to get even—with me. He'd almost pulled it off, too. I'd sworn I'd kill him the next time I saw him—an idle threat since he wasn't worth jail time. But breaking his nose? I clearly wasn't above that. And busting his balls? Not above that either. Add the prospect of a murder indictment on top, well—that was a rich dessert after an exquisite dinner—a triumvirate of decadent pleasure.

"You know you can't just barge in here and assault an honest citizen." Willie had propped himself up on one elbow, the hand towel still pressed to his nose. "I'll sue you again."

"Brave words from an idiot," I said. "First, we didn't barge in—you opened the door. Second, you aren't even close to being an honest citizen—you're wanted for murder. Remember?"

Willie, acting bored, flopped back on his chaise. "Oh that. I didn't do it."

"You were flying, pilot-in-command and all of that. If it wasn't your fault, whose was it?" I could feel the slight vibration of the tape recorder in my pocket.

Romeo stood to the side, making himself small, but he was close enough for his recorder to catch Willie's every word as well.

"Look, all I did was agree to take the three of them for a ride. Lyda Sue knew Felicia and knew that we'd been dating—me and

Felicia." Willie pulled the hand towel away from his nose. The blood started to flow again.

"Keep the pressure on it." I mashed the hand towel back on his nose.

"Ow." He glared at me. He looked even stupider than usual with the embroidered little men, their penises erect, dancing around his nose.

"Go on."

"Anyway, Lyda Sue thought it would be fun to go for a ride over the Strip after dark. So, I agreed to take them."

"And The Big Boss? How'd he end up in the helicopter?"

"Like I said, it was Felicia's idea. She knew he and Lyda Sue were chummy—if you get my drift?"

I resisted the urge to break more of his body parts. "I get your drift."

"Felicia thought it would be fun to have the great man himself along, so she suggested it to Lyda Sue. The rest is history."

"So, The Big Boss was just along for the ride?"

"Yeah, the dickhead was clueless."

Brave man, Willie—calling The Big Boss names when he wasn't around. "So, exactly how did Lyda Sue end up in the pirates' lagoon? Wasn't she belted in?"

"When we were over the pirate show, Felicia pulled out a camera. She said she'd take their picture if Lyda Sue would move over right next to The Big Boss." Willie swallowed hard, his mask of bravado slipping. "I guess she undid her seat belt and did as Felicia asked, or started to anyway. Right about that time, Felicia reached over, grabbed the cyclic and banked the helicopter hard to the side. We all lost our balance. Lyda Sue was thrown against the door. I guess the latch popped."

Right. "And?"

"I turned around and she was gone."

"What then?"

"The Big Boss freaked out—started screaming at us. I was

numb. And you know the weirdest thing?" Willie looked at me, his eyes wide.

"I can't imagine."

"Felicia just laughed."

"Tell me the rest."

"I took The Big Boss to Northtown. Then Felicia came with me to Spanish Trail—where you found the helicopter. I was watching you, you know."

No wonder I'd been so creeped out that night.

"All the way here, Felicia kept talking about how we had The Big Boss and how that was going to be worth big money."

"Was she going to shake down The Big Boss?"

Willie shook his head. "Maybe, I'm not real sure. I got the idea there was somebody else, but she never said who."

"Did she hole up here with you?"

"No, she split. She had a car stashed outside the Hacienda gate. Said she'd be back."

"And you believed her? You really are a putz, Willie."

Anger flared in his eyes.

"She set you up." I stopped. "No, she didn't set you up—she served you up on a platter."

"Nobody sets me up."

"Yeah? You've just given me this song and dance about being led around by some harebrained female. You're a candidate for that stupid criminal show. And what an idiotic idea in the first place—the whole thing was captured on film."

"You mean we'll be famous—like Bonnie and Clyde?"

I could see Willie's pea brain working—in the crowd he hung with, murder was the ultimate status symbol.

"Not you—Felicia. You didn't know anything about it. You were just the dupe along for the ride."

"What if I wasn't?" he said slowly, after eyeing me for a moment.

"Are you telling me you're smarter than you look? That the

plan was your idea, too?" Assigning any smarts to Willie was an insult to all the smart people of the world, but it was all I had, so I went with it.

He thought for a moment, which was a real stretch for Willie the Weasel. "Yeah, that's exactly what I'm telling you. It was part my idea."

I heard Romeo gasp behind me. I flopped down in the chair across from Willie's.

I never expected the Perry Mason thing to work. Not in a million years. That stuff only happened on television and in Agatha Christie novels.

I'd already gotten what I came for—The Big Boss was off the hook.

But I'd reeled in Willie as well.

All in all, this was a most satisfying day.

Apparently, Willie saw the look of satisfaction on my face. "You turn me in, I'll deny everything I said. I just wanted you to know the truth."

"You mean about what a tough guy you are?"

"Yeah." If someone could have a swagger in his voice, Willie had it.

"You'll deny it all?"

Willie tried to snort, then winced. "Whaddya think, I'm stupid or something?"

I reached in my pocket and slowly extracted the tape recorder. I saw reality dawn in Willie the Weasel's tiny little eyes as his predicament registered in his tiny little brain.

"Yeah, stupid or something, for sure," I said with a very satis-fied grin. "You are *so* up shit creek." I stood and bent over him. For a moment, we were eye to eye.

Then I hit him again with an elbow to his nose.

He screamed in pain as his body instinctively curled into the fetal position.

"And don't you ever, ever fuck with me or my friends again."

~

ROMEO CALLED FOR BACKUP.

I called the office. "Anybody looking for me?" I asked Miss Patterson when she answered.

"Funny you should ask. Irv Gittings himself called looking for you. He wants you to call him back. He'll be at the office until late."

Interesting. I had one of the three stooges, I had a line on the second, and now I get a call from the third. At least I had a hunch he was the third—everything pointed to him. So far today, I was batting a thousand on my hunches. It was time to test my average and see if it held up.

"Anybody else?"

"Teddie wanted me to remind you it's movie night, but that's it. Where are you anyway?"

"Oh, just taking a little personal time. I'll be back in about an hour and a half, maybe two. Can you hold down the fort until then?"

"Of course, but I'll have to leave soon after that. Jeremy's picking me up at nine-thirty."

"I see." I didn't try to keep the grin out of my voice.

"I was hoping you could get back in time to help me freshen my makeup."

"Need a little moral support?"

"Sorta."

"When do you want me back?"

"Could you be back by nine?"

That gave me two and half hours. "Count on it." I reclipped my Nextel at my hip.

~

SIREN BLARING, THE SQUAD CAR SQUEALED TO A STOP OUT FRONT, followed in loose formation by two Spanish Trail security vehicles. The uniforms now stepped in and cuffed Willie, leading him out of the house. They even put their hand on his head, pushing him down and into the back seat of the waiting squad car, just like on television.

Willie glared at me through the car's window.

I waggled my fingers at him. "Have a nice life."

Romeo appeared at my shoulder. "You look like the cat who ate the canary."

"I just got to live every woman's dream."

"Women have dreams like that?"

"I don't know a woman who doesn't fantasize about breaking some asshole's nose and busting him in the balls. Legal ramifications aside, it's okay for men to settle their issues with a shot to the nose, but women are supposed to be ladies—society's way of making us powerless." I shrugged. "I never really bought into that."

"I can see that." Romeo pursed his lips in thought. "I'll get credit for a big bust, thanks to you."

"You held up your end."

"Hangin' with you sure is educational."

"Kid, if I couldn't handle the weasels of the world, they would've run me out of town on a rail years ago." I put my arm around his shoulder and adopted a collegial attitude. "Louie, this is the start of a beautiful friendship."

"*Casablanca*, right?"

"Romeo, you got real potential."

"I'm beginning to understand why you're the go-to guy at the Babylon." Romeo grinned as he pointed to the uniforms in their squad car. "I'm going to ride with them. I'm not letting the Weasel out of my sight."

"I don't blame you." I wasn't sure I wanted to let the asshole out of my sight either.

"One question, though."

"Fire away."

"How'd you know your boss was in the helicopter as well?"

Yep, the kid had real potential.

"Hang around me long enough, I'll show you some of my tricks. You think you can keep a lid on the Weasel's arrest while I try to get a line on Felicia Reilly?"

Romeo nodded slowly as he eyed me. "I'll do my best, but if the reporters get wind of this, damage control is up to you."

"Damage control—that's my thing. Detective Richards is going to chew you up and spit you out for not bringing him in the loop."

"Not when I walk through the door with Willie the Weasel." Romeo grinned.

"That does add a couple of aces to your hand, doesn't it?" The kid even had a backbone. Not a bad friend to have in the police department.

Yes, this had been a most satisfying day.

"So, where are you going next?" Romeo asked. "You look like you have something up your sleeve."

"Oh, I got another hunch."

"You *need* some help?"

"No, this one I have to do on my own."

"You be careful."

"I can take care of myself," I said with a grin.

"No shit," the kid said, not even trying to hide the awe in his voice.

Romeo and I stood there a moment, shoulder to shoulder, each savoring the moment as we surveyed the neighborhood. The squad car, along with the Spanish Trail security trucks, hadn't attracted any attention at all. Not one neighbor had even bothered to saunter by to ask what was going on.

"Where is everybody?" asked Romeo.

"Like Willie said, nobody with somewhere else to go stays here in the summer. But those who can't escape to cooler climes all hide inside—I've seen it before. These places aren't like real neighborhoods; they're like a movie set, each house carefully constructed to reflect its owner's wealth. Neighbors separated by their own sense of self-importance."

"Weird."

"Welcome to Vegas, baby."

I watched the squad car, trailed by the security vehicles, as it left the neighborhood; then I locked the front door behind me and walked to the Ferrari.

Irv Gittings said he'd be in his office.

CHAPTER TWELVE

ONE OF the few remaining grand dames of the Vegas Strip, the Athena was an aging star—a throwback to the fifties.

The growth of the megaresorts had taken off at the other end of the Strip. Stranded at the wrong end of the action, the Athena was an island surrounded by a sea of lesser properties gone to seed. Ripe for a cash infusion—or demolition—the Athena was sinking.

I had a hunch Irv Gittings was a desperate man, and desperate men do desperate things.

Braking the Ferrari to a stop at the front entrance, I threw open the door, leapt out, and tossed the keys to the female valet. "Don't move it. Don't touch it. I'll be back shortly."

"You got it, Ms. O'Toole." A young woman with long, dark hair and a runner's physique caught the keys in one hand as I dashed by her and through the front doors. I thought I recognized her from a class I had taught at UNLV in the hotel and restaurant management program.

Dark and stale, the lobby was almost empty, even during this, the busiest week of the year. Off to the right, the casino was eerily quiet. I'm sure the rooms were booked, the whole town was bursting at the seams, but obviously nobody wanted to stay and play here, which was the kiss of death to a casino. Vegas rule number one—you can't make any money if you can't keep it in the house.

In need of freshening up, I decided to hit the ladies' lounge near the main bank of elevators. To be honest, my resolve needed a little fortifying as well.

I was about to come face-to-face with one of my biggest mistakes.

Back when I was young and stupid and still believed in fairy tales, I'd had an affair with the dashing Mr. Gittings. A whole year of sleeping with him, dining with him, appearing on his arm at fabulous parties attended by a whole parade of celebrities, our pictures in the society pages—I still don't know how I could've been so naive. Gullible, and inexperienced, I had been blinded by his star power, flattered by his attention, and seduced by his stories of us being the power couple of Vegas.

The sex hadn't been bad either.

I clamped my mind shut to those memories—they could get me in trouble, especially in light of my current libido problem.

Twenty years older than me, Irv was every inch the successful Vegas casino owner. Tall, trim, perpetually tanned, he was the center of female attention wherever he went. A touch of gray in his hair, chiseled features and eyes that danced with delight every time he saw me, I was a goner the first time I met him. It had taken me a whole year to get the stars out of my eyes and to see through his well-oiled veneer.

But, whether he knew it or not, Irv Gittings had taught me a few hard lessons.

Irv liked his women pretty, young and stupid. Once, I had fit that bill. Not anymore.

I pondered the made-over me who stared back at me from the mirror. I squinted my eyes. In a dim light, I could still pass for pretty, but I needed a touch-up. The cosmetics I had purchased at Samson's as part of the whole makeover thing were in a small pouch at the bottom of my Birkin. Now, if I just remembered how to use them.

Finished, I surveyed the result. Sultry eyes, lips painted in come-on red, I poofed my hair and pulled a few strands down so they covered my eyes.

Not bad.

I threw back my shoulders. *You can do this, O'Toole.*

Even I didn't believe it.

I wet a towel and dabbed at the blood on my elbow—Willie's blood. I couldn't do anything about the red splotches staining the white leather of my shoes—no matter how hard I scrubbed, they didn't budge. This had certainly been a day of men from the past.

After popping Willie's tape out of the recorder, I secured it in a zippered pocket in my bag. I shoved a new tape in the device, checked the battery level, then turned the thing on and put it in my pocket.

Showtime.

～

IRV'S OFFICE OCCUPIED THE BEST CORNER, WITH THE BEST VIEW ON the best floor—the top one. "Nothing but the best for Ol' Irv," he used to say, his arm wrapped around my shoulders as we stood before the wall of glass in his office—Vegas at our feet. As smooth as he was, Irv had the irritating habit of referring to himself in the third person. Back then, he'd included me on his list of "bests for Ol' Irv."

The elevator deposited me on my requested floor. The doors closed, leaving me stranded and, apparently, alone. As I moved down the corridor toward Irv's office, I felt like a condemned woman making her last walk.

The outer office was empty. Irv's assistant had apparently gone home for the night. No witnesses. Luck still perched on my shoulder.

"Anybody here?" Light came from Irv's office, so I headed that way.

Irv stepped through the door.

Damn, still gorgeous. A little worn around edges, but handsome as ever.

"Lucky?"

"My assistant gave me your message. I thought I'd stop by instead of calling."

"Sure." If he was surprised, he hid it well. Stepping aside, he motioned me through the doorway. "Have you been getting my e-mails?"

"Yes." I walked through the outer office and into his inner sanctum.

Large, even by Vegas standards, Irv's office had changed little over the years. The same monstrous antique desk occupied its place in the corner. According to Ol' Irv, some important document in American history had been signed on that desk. I didn't believe that, but I could name at least five women who had been screwed on the thing. Irv probably still etched his conquests' names in the wood on the inside. Thankfully, mine wasn't one of them—I drew the line at doing it on desks.

Photos of Irv with every celebrity imaginable from the last two decades competed for wall space with clever forgeries of a few lesser works by the great Masters and a few strategically placed mirrors. That was Irv Gittings—all show and no substance.

I took a chair in front of the desk.

"So, if you got Ol' Irv's e-mails, why haven't you answered?" He parked his butt on the corner of his desk. Fingers interlocking, he held one knee with his hands as he surveyed me with those inscrutable gray eyes.

"I don't discuss future employment opportunities on my

current employer's time. And I certainly don't negotiate by e-mail." I crossed my legs and leaned back.

"Negotiate?" His gaze wandered to my legs, then back. "So you're open to discussions?"

"Why else would I be here?" I leaned forward. "Look, Irv, let's get this out of the way. You and I were over a long time ago." He had tossed me aside for twin blonde gymnasts who could apparently do amazing things with their tongues.

He shifted uneasily.

"No hard feelings," I added, even though he'd thrown me out for the trash. "I assume you aren't offering me money to be your girlfriend. If this is business, I'm always open to bettering my financial position."

"So, you wouldn't be Ol' Irv's squeeze again?"

"I'm about ten years too old for you." *And much too smart.*

"So true," the asshole said, but not to me. He was looking at his own reflection in the mirror on the wall behind me when he said it.

What had Mother used to say? A man in love with himself could never love anybody else? Of course, I hadn't paid attention to her, so that had been the first of Ol' Irv's hard lessons.

"I've got to get back to work, so if you have a proposal, I'm all ears." I leaned back again, this time crossing my arms in front of my chest. "But I warn you, it's going to take an obscene amount of money to lure me from the Babylon. Frankly, the Athena would be a step down for me—a big step down."

One dart straight to the ego.

Irv's cheeks flushed.

Bulls-eye.

He jumped off the corner of the desk. "Wild Turkey, neat. Right?"

"Right."

Hidden behind a secret panel in the corner of his office, the bar boasted a variety of top-shelf liquor. Only the best for Ol' Irv,

I thought, as I watched him busy himself with bottles, glasses, and ice.

"Do you remember how we used to talk about being the Vegas power couple?"

I nodded. Like an old dog howling at the moon, he was going to make me sit through the same old song.

"We could still do that." Worse than a self-conscious teenager, he glanced at himself in the mirrored glass behind the bar as he finished our drinks.

I raised an eyebrow as he handed me my whiskey.

"Not as a couple, but as business partners," he continued, his eyes on my face. He took a sip of the clear liquid in his glass.

He drank very expensive tequila, if I remembered correctly. "At the Athena?"

"Oh, hell, not in this dump. Our talents would be wasted here."

I didn't want to point out the obvious—Irv's talent had run the Athena into the ground. Of course, it was probably somebody else's fault. With Irv, it always was.

He set his drink down, then grabbed the arms of my chair and turned me so I was facing slightly away from the desk. Like a lawyer delivering his summation, he paced back and forth in front of me. "Ol' Irv has bigger plans."

"Really?"

Second dart straight to the ego.

"Yeah, really." His tone turned defensive.

So far, I was batting a thousand. I waited, my heart in my mouth. Come on, Irv!

"You don't think Ol' Irv can pull it off, do you?" He stopped in front of me, a hint of bruised ego in his eyes.

I calmly took a sip of my drink, then lowered the glass and looked into it as I slowly swirled the bourbon around. His face had turned a deeper shade of pink when I again looked at him.

"You're blowing smoke, as usual," I said, trying to look mildly disinterested.

Third dart to the ego.

Irv's face flushed crimson.

Home run.

"I'm going to make a tender offer for the Babylon," he announced, pride oozing from every pore.

"What?" I felt the glass slipping through my fingers. I caught it just in time.

"That got you, didn't it?" A self-satisfied smirk split his face as he pulled a chair close to mine and took a seat on the edge. He leaned into me and said softly, "I've got the money all lined up. And..." He took my free hand in his. "I want you to run the place after I take over."

"You want me to run the Babylon...for you?" I looked at my hand in his. His flesh on mine.

And I felt...nothing.

Could Irv the Creep have been the cure for my libido problem?

I slowly extracted my hand from his grip. I'm not sure he even noticed.

"You're the key," he said. I know how important you are over there. Everybody likes you—the employees, the guests, the entertainers—you charm them all." He jumped to his feet and started pacing again. "You make the Babylon work. You know how to run a casino. If you stay after Ol' Irv becomes the boss, everyone else will stay."

"I'm flattered."

"I'll make it worth your while."

"How worth my while?"

"I'll double your salary and give you a bonus of one percent of the pretax profit."

I looked him straight in the eye. "A tender offer for the Babylon will require a serious chunk of change."

"As I said, the money is there. Some foreign money, some venture capital, and I've been setting some aside from the operations here."

I took another sip of my drink as I looked him over. Impeccably turned out, every *i* dotted, every *t* crossed, he still gave off a hint of quiet desperation. Hang around Vegas long enough and you develop a nose for it. "The Big Boss will never sell."

"The board of directors will force him to," Irv announced, a look of triumph on his face. "You see, Lucky my dear, Ol' Irv has your Big Boss by the balls."

"You?" I asked, putting some skepticism in my voice. "Have The Big Boss by the balls?"

"I'm going to bury him."

"How?"

"He's mixed up in something really bad. So bad, he'll go to jail. And you know how the Gaming Commission frowns on felons running casinos. They'll jerk his license for sure."

"It'll take more than your word to bring down The Big Boss."

"I have it all on tape. Your boss is a goner." Leaning back in his chair, he crossed his arms, a look of immense satisfaction on his face. "Yeah, Ol' Irv is going to be running the show."

I paused for a moment, as if in careful deliberation. "Okay, I'll play. Assuming what you told me is true, let's talk money. The older I get, the more I like it. Now, tell me about this one percent."

～

TWENTY MINUTES LATER, I FOUND THE FERRARI WHERE I'D LEFT IT, the nervous valet at its side. I exchanged a twenty for the keys and folded myself into the car.

"Thanks, Ms. O'Toole!"

"You bet. You're Brandy, aren't you? From my class at UNLV last fall?"

"Yes." A shy grin tugged at the corners of her mouth. "I'm surprised you remember."

"Hard not to. You were one of the brightest in the class." I pulled a card out of my wallet and handed it to her. "If you ever consider changing jobs, come see me."

"For sure!" Her grin grew wider. "Thanks!"

At the turn of the key, the engine growled to life. Like a big cat, the car waited, coiled to spring into action. Unfortunately, the drive up Las Vegas Boulevard to the Babylon would be slow and short, but it would give me time to think.

The lights of the Strip competed with the fading sunlight, beating it into submission as day marched relentlessly toward night. As I eased the car into traffic, a few clusters of people wandered the streets, drinks in hand. The night was young and laden with the expectations of untold delights—food, fun, entertainment—maybe some luck at the tables or with the opposite sex —or the same, depending on your preference. I drove with the window down, drinking in the dry, fresh desert air, trying to wash away the sour taste left by Irv Gittings.

While it would make interesting listening, the tape I'd made of our conversation didn't provide direct proof that Ol' Irv had added murder to his resume. And I wasn't sure that it mattered. Whether Irv instigated the murder or merely took advantage of the opportunity when Felicia appeared with the tape, the Babylon's board of directors would take a dim view of his shenanigans.

Something else he'd said niggled at me. Some of his tender-offer funds were monies he'd set aside from the operations of the Athena. How does one set aside money when the hotel operates in the red? Either I knew nothing about operating a casino, or Irv Gittings had been skimming from the house, which was a definite no-no with the Gaming Control Board, not to mention the IRS.

The light at Flamingo turned red, so I eased the Ferrari to a stop. Whistling their appreciation for the car, a group of young men passed in front of me. I smiled back at them. They raised their beers in a salute before they disappeared around the corner.

The light turned green. I kept the car at a slow crawl. The huge, illuminated signs lining the Strip flashed their come-ons. Magic shows, a popular singer at Caesar's, various Cirque du Soleil extravaganzas, an impersonator at the Venetian, Teddie at the Babylon, each sign painted the car with multicolored lights as I passed.

I didn't believe for a minute that those two petty blackmailers, Felicia and Willie, could dream up, much less pull off, a plot against The Big Boss. No, it had Ol' Irv's stink all over it. But that wasn't my problem—the police could sort it out.

Irv would have been a fool to actually pay Felicia Reilly for the tape. Giving money to a murderer would be a quick pass to the slammer. Irv was slimy, but he wasn't completely stupid. No doubt he had promised money, then stiffed her.

That meant Felicia was on her own, with only the grand from Mr. Fujikara—these days even if you travel light, a grand won't take you far.

I smiled as I tapped my hand to the beat of the song playing on the radio. Since she had no money, Felicia Reilly would probably go back to doing what she did best, blackmail. The Trendmakers party on Thursday night would be irresistible—she'd already told Jeep she'd be there to get her dough. Oh, yeah, she'd show all right. And we'd be waiting.

~

THE BIG BOSS WAS WAITING FOR ME WHEN THE ELEVATOR deposited me in his apartment.

"Have I got a story for you," I announced, as I brushed past him and headed straight for the bar.

"I'm out of Wild Turkey," The Big Boss said, as he punched the hold button for the elevator then followed me. "You drank the last of it last time you were here. I forgot to call down for more. Want me to do it now?"

"I don't need a drink, just a bottle of water." I grabbed one from the fridge and drained the whole thing in two long sessions before coming up for air. The empty bottle sailed into the trash can, dead center. "Two points."

The Big Boss eyed me warily. "You're in a fine humor this evening."

I plopped on his couch facing the window and the lights of Vegas and patted the place beside me. "Sit. You're going to like this story."

He did as I asked.

"Here." I took his hand and spread it open, palm up, putting the two tapes and the recorder into it. "I think you'll find these... most enlightening."

He started to close his hand.

"Wait." I grabbed the tapes and pried off the little tabs on the back of them. Now they couldn't be recorded over. Notoriously technophobic and inept when it came to small electronic devices, The Big Boss couldn't be trusted.

"Listen to those when you have a chance," I said, "but I'll give you the CliffsNotes version now, if you want."

"What is that on your shoes?" The Big Boss deposited the tapes and recorder in his pocket.

"Blood." Perfectly good Chanel flats ruined. A small price to pay for the opportunity to break Willie's nose.

"Not yours?" The Big Boss looked genuinely alarmed.

I shook my head. "Willie's."

"You found Willie?" The Big Boss's head swiveled to me.

"Yep." I leaned my head back and let the feeling of immense satisfaction wash over me.

"How'd you get his blood on you?"

"I broke his nose."

"That's my girl," The Big Boss said with a chuckle. "Where is he now?"

"The police have him, but they're keeping a lid on that fact for a couple of days." I crossed my hands behind my head. "One of those tapes I gave you is Willie's confession. He said you knew nothing about the murder of Lyda Sue."

The Big Boss grew very still beside me. He didn't answer right away. When he did, his words were soft and full of emotion. "I owe you."

"Seems to me you've had my back several times through the years." I reached down and squeezed his knee.

"The police are keeping the lid on Willie's arrest as a favor to me." I sat up and looked at the lights of the Strip. The sun had almost disappeared behind the mountains, shooting the sky full of oranges and pinks. I had no more than thirty minutes before I'd promised Miss Patterson I'd be back. "I need some time to find Felicia Reilly."

"You know where she is?"

"No." My elbows resting on my knees, I cupped my chin in my hands. "But I have a good hunch where she's going to be."

"You're going to tell me?"

"Not on a bet. You'll send your goons after her."

"No, I won't."

I gave The Big Boss a disbelieving look. "Let me handle this."

He eyed me for a moment. "I owe you that much. Besides, you're doing fine on your own."

We both stared out the window for a minute, the reality of the day washing over us.

The Big Boss reached in his pocket and pulled out his wallet, extracted a hundred-dollar bill, then returned the wallet to his pocket. As I'd watched him do a thousand times, he began creasing and folding.

"You gave me two tapes. What's on the other one?" he asked, his eyes never leaving the small shape taking form in his hands.

"A very enlightening conversation I had with Irv Gittings."

"Gittings?" The Big Boss kept his voice flat, which I figured cost him dearly. When I'd taken up with the competition years ago, The Big Boss had been practically apoplectic. "Where'd you see that ass?"

"In his office. I went to see him." I watched as The Big Boss focused on his creation. "He'd been sending me a bunch of e-mails. He offered me an obscene amount of money to come work for him."

"Damn," The Big Boss muttered as he dropped the small shape. He bent over and snatched it from the floor.

"He wants me to run the Babylon for him."

The Big Boss's eyes locked onto mine, the small figure in his hand forgotten.

"He's going to make a tender offer for the Babylon. He says he has the money lined up and you over a barrel."

"That son of a bitch!" The Big Boss's voice had murder in it. Jamming the folded bill into his pocket, he leapt to his feet. He stood very still in front of the window, hands clasped behind his back.

I thought he was being fairly charitable in his assessment of Irv Gittings' character. Maybe he was protecting my delicate sensibilities.

"Who do you know on the Gaming Control Board?"

"Bentley Beckwith is the head of the thing now. We go way back. Why?" The Big Boss swiveled his head around to look at me.

"Some of the funds for the tender offer came from money Irv said he had been setting aside from operations."

"The Athena has been running underwater for the last two years."

"My point exactly."

"You think he's been skimming?" The Big Boss turned to face me. The fire of the setting sun behind him outlined him in shadow, hiding his features.

I didn't need to see his face to know what was lurking there. "Wouldn't put it past him."

"The Control Board won't like that."

"I thought so, too. Wouldn't hurt to mention the possibility to Beckwith."

"Nothing like a woman scorned, eh?"

I deserved that. The Big Boss had taken my sleeping with Ol' Irv as a personal affront. Actually, I didn't give a damn what happened to Irv Gittings—he'd get what was coming to him eventually.

"I'll make the call," The Big Boss said. "Bentley will be all ears." He paused, then said with the old fire in his voice, "There's a board of directors meeting on Friday. It's time we went on the offensive, don't you think?"

"Offensive is my middle name." I smiled at the double meaning —both sometimes appropriate—and rose to go. Miss Patterson would be on pins and needles. "Listen to the tapes, then we'll strategize."

"That sounds like a plan. How about breakfast? Say, nine thirty at Nebuchadnezzar's?" The Big Boss took my elbow as he walked me to the elevator.

"I'll meet you there." My hand on the button, I paused. "Do me a favor, will you?"

"Anything."

"Don't call the police asking about Willie. Don't send a lawyer down there or take a hit out on him. Don't take any calls from the media, and, whatever you do, don't tell Dane about those tapes. You and I are the only ones around here who know of their existence. Let's keep it that way."

"That's four favors, actually," The Big Boss said with a smile.

I gave him a withering look.

He put up his hands. "You have my word."

~

BEFORE I COULD PUT THE DAY OFFICIALLY TO BED, I HAD ONE MORE call to make.

Fredericka "Flash" Gordon was the *Las Vegas Review-Journal's* top investigative journalist and my ace in the hole. We'd met at UNLV where Flash was known as Freddie. The moniker "Flash" had been hung on her after an incident with a bus full of professional basketball players—but I'd been sworn to secrecy.

I grabbed my Nextel and dialed a number I knew by heart.

"Hey, girl," she said. "What's up? You going to tell me about the new man in your life?"

"Which one?" I asked.

"You lying or bragging?"

"You're the ace reporter—you find out." I shifted the phone to my other ear as I stepped into the elevator and pressed the button for the mezzanine. My watch read ten till nine. "I need a favor."

"Does this have anything to do with the swan dive out of the helicopter?" All business, Flash's voice had lost its playful tone.

"It has everything to do with that." The elevator stopped at the fifth floor and two couples got on. "Hang on a minute, will you?"

"Sure."

I waited until I stepped out into the empty mezzanine before continuing. "Listen, I can't give you any details right now, but this story is going to be huge when it breaks."

"I'm all ears."

I could picture Flash grabbing her ever-present notebook and pen, yanking off the cap of the pen with her teeth, then scribbling notes in her own shorthand that nobody else could read.

"If you get wind of anything that has to do with this case—and I mean anything—I need you to sit on it." I strode down the hall toward my office.

"How long?"

"Forty-eight hours. Then I'll give you the whole story, start to finish."

"I'll have the exclusive?"

"Of course. That goes without saying." I could almost hear the wheels turning.

She whistled low. "Man, this story is threatening to pop, you know? It's big. I don't run this newspaper—I can't promise anything. And if the television heads break it, we have to go with whatever we can find."

"I'm just asking you to give it your best shot."

"I'll do what I can."

"You won't regret it."

"Lucky, I never have."

CHAPTER THIRTEEN

"*I* CAN'T believe it!" Miss Patterson announced, as I walked through the door. "You're three minutes early."

"Alert the media," I said, racing through her office to mine. "Give me a minute, will you?"

"You've got three, why not use them all?"

"I promise, I'll be right there. Okay?" I deposited my bag on the couch, then kicked off my shoes, flipping open my phone as I did so.

I flopped into a chair, my legs splayed in front of me as I dialed.

Teddie answered on the first ring. "I'm thinking a good, rousing musical," he said without preliminaries, "where pretty people sing and dance, fall in love, and live happily ever after—all to a score written by Rodgers and Hammerstein. What do you think?"

Instantly, everything I was going to say flew out of my head.

Just the sound of his voice knocked me off balance and sent an arrow of delight arcing through me. "Which one? I can think of a lot of musicals that fit that bill."

"Here's one possibility." In a rousing tenor, Teddie sang, *"Ok...lahoma..."*

Enjoying the entertainment, I let him work through a couple of stanzas, before I stopped him. "You sound just like Gordon MacRae. But I'm not in the mood for *Oklahoma!* It's too cornpone."

"Cornpone?" Teddie laughed—he had such a great laugh. "That's a first. Okay, how about this one?" He cleared his throat, then sang in his famous falsetto, *"There were bells, on the hill, but I never heard them ringing."*

This time I cut him off with a snort. "No. *The Music Man* isn't right either. Too depressing."

"The guy gets the girl—what's depressing about that?"

"He's a con man. He doesn't deserve her."

"Boy, you're picky."

"Not picky, shallow. Pretty people, singing and dancing, happily ever after—I am *so* there. Robert Preston is a hunk, though. You're getting closer."

"Robert Preston? So you're the older man type. Here's one you'll like." Doing a perfect Rossano Brazzi impersonation, he sang, *"Some enchanted evening..."*

"*South Pacific.* Perfect! You've got the men down, but your Shirley Jones needs work."

"I know. Her soprano is a bit too...soprano. I have to reach for it."

"I don't really think that's a bad thing." The only males who could sing a good soprano were either not my type or they were under the age of twelve—which weren't my type either.

"You have a point. There are aspects to being a heterosexual male I particularly enjoy. If not being able to do a good Shirley Jones impersonation is the price I have to pay, so be it."

"That's what I love about you—you're so well-adjusted."

"I'll have you know, you are the only person besides my mother who uses the term 'well-adjusted' when describing a man who makes his living dressed in ball gowns impersonating females."

"Okay, if well-adjusted is too big a stretch, let's just say you're comfortable in your own skin."

"I think I like well-adjusted better."

'They both fit. You're an entertainer."

"Precisely!"

"All that being said, I still have a problem with the fact that you look better in my clothes than I do."

He paused, then said, his voice low and warm, "Not from where I'm sitting."

I could almost feel the caress in his words. I closed my eyes and remembered the feel of him next to me, his lips on mine. "Teddie, you make me feel…good. Nervous, but good."

"*Now* we're getting somewhere. Are you coming home?"

My hand shook as I pushed the hair out of my face. All of a sudden I was tired, so tired. And all I wanted was to be home, safe in Teddie's arms. "I'll be there in an hour. Will that be too late?"

"You're the one who has to work tomorrow. I'm off this week. Remember? They've put some raunchy sex show in my theatre for the ElectroniCon crowd. I don't even want to think about it."

"Then don't. And say, would you mind ordering some food? I'm famished." That half a sandwich I ate while Miss Patterson tried on clothes was too little, too long ago.

"Sure. What ethnicity?"

"Surprise me."

"So, we're at S already?" Teddie asked. "S is for surprise."

"To be honest, I don't know where we are." I glanced through the open doorway. Miss Patterson paced nervously back and forth. "I'll see you in an hour."

"I'll be ready."

"If R is for ready, then you're going backward," I said as I disconnected.

Teddie would be ready for what? I thought, as I shut my phone and tossed it into my bag.

What was it about Teddie that made me feel centered and yet off balance at the same time? And what was it about him that made me *like* feeling that way?

~

"Okay!" I CLAPPED MY HANDS, THEN RUBBED THEM TOGETHER, startling Miss Patterson as I walked back into her office. "Lucky O'Toole, magic makeover touch-up artist at your service." I bowed low. "Your wish is my command."

She managed a tight smile.

"I can see we're in need of a little loosening up. I have just the thing," I motioned for her to stay where she was. "Stay there, I'll be right back."

I ducked behind the partition, opened the fridge, and grabbed the bottle of bubbly I had been saving. The cork popped with a loud boom and flew across the office. Champagne erupted out of the bottle, leaving a trail, as I grabbed two glasses and returned to a startled Miss Patterson.

"You've been saving that."

"Yes." I set the glasses down on her desk—they were old jelly jars with scenes from *The Flintstones* on them. "For a day worth celebrating."

She watched as I filled them.

"These are the best I could do," I said. "It doesn't matter—even from a jelly jar, Dom Perignon is the nectar of the gods." I raised mine in a toast. "To good friends, good luck, a life filled with joy, a future filled with promise, and some really great sex thrown in for good measure."

We clinked glasses and went to work on the champagne. Miss Patterson drained her glass, held it out for a refill, then dove into the second glassful.

"Easy. Those bubbles have a bite."

She nodded, then set her glass down on her desk and plopped back in her chair. "I'm a wreck."

"We can fix that. Bring your glass and all the stuff we got at Samson's and follow me." The blind leading the blind, we paraded into my office, me in the lead, Miss Patterson trailing. I placed a chair in front of the mirror, leaving room for me to work. "Sit."

I knelt in front of her and opened her bag of goodies.

"I've wanted to go out with Jeremy for so long," she confessed. "And, now that it's here, I'm beside myself."

I arranged all of the cosmetics on the floor at her feet, then, sitting back on my heels I gave her the once-over.

"That's the thing about dreams," I said, taking a deep breath, "they're safe until they come true." I ought to know. I was taking the short course in that theory myself.

I brushed her hair into place, then squirted a dab of goo into my palm and rubbed my hands together. Running my hands lightly over her hair, I added a bit of shine to her already perfect 'do.

Very carefully, I added some thickness to her lashes. I sat on my heels, surveying my handiwork. Yes, she was coming together nicely, but the eyes needed more pop.

"Jeremy's one lucky guy—you're pretty damned terrific." I handed her a tissue. "Let's get a little of that shine off your face, touch up your powder and blush, then we'll go to work on your clothes."

"Okay, I'm not too hard on the eyes—which is a new experience— thanks to you. Every time I walk by a mirror, I wonder who that is looking back at me."

"I know the feeling."

"But none of that changes the fact I'm a good bit older than Jeremy."

"It's very trendy being a cougar."

"I never thought of myself as a feline before. An old shoe, yes, but a predatory cat? No."

"A whole new you."

"The outside may have changed, but inside I'm still the same old me."

"The one Jeremy was attracted to in the first place. Now, come with me. We need to choose what you'll wear into battle."

Like brightly colored rugs at a bazaar, each of her purchases hung side by side across one wall of my office—a couture rainbow of subtle color and elegance.

"Where is he taking you?"

"To Picasso's at the Bellagio."

I whistled low. "A classy place, for a classy lady. How do you feel about the little black dress and my 'knock me down and fuck me' Jimmy Choos?"

"You'd lend me your Jimmy Choos?"

"Of course. We're the same size, right?"

"Close enough. I can tighten the straps a bit."

I grabbed the shoes from the closet and the black dress and handed them both to her. "I hope you're better at walking in those shoes than I am."

Miss Patterson stepped into her office and ducked around the partition to change. When she reappeared, I was momentarily speechless.

The Beautiful Jeremy Whitlock didn't stand a chance.

The simple black dress hugged Miss Patterson's curves in all the right places, stopping just short of her knees. The silver Jimmy Choos sparkled on her feet accentuating her dainty ankles. Her new blonde hairdo shone like a sleek cap of gold, highlighting those big blue eyes and rosy cheeks. Painted a lush shade of pink, her lips looked full and inviting.

Something was missing, though—something subtle.

I unscrewed the square-cut diamond earrings I wore every

day. "Here, wear these. They are the piece de resistance—the cherry on top, so to speak."

Miss Patterson hesitated. "Weren't those a gift from your mother?"

I nodded. "And now the gift of their use from me to a good friend. They'll bring you luck, not that you'll need any."

Clearly unused to the large stones and their screw backs, she fumbled with them.

"Here, let me." When I finished, I stepped back.

She twirled in front of me. And she didn't even bobble on those heels. Amazing.

"So, tell me about Theodore." She stood in front of me, hands on hips, her smile lighting her eyes.

"Not much to tell." Busying myself gathering her other outfits hanging on the wall, I avoided eye contact.

"Liar."

"I really don't know what to say." I hung each of the outfits carefully in the closet, then stepped around my desk and sagged into my chair. Today had been a day of highs and lows—a real roller coaster ride. And right now, I found myself suffering from a severe shortage of adrenaline.

"I've been wondering one thing," Miss Patterson mused aloud. "How'd a good-looking guy like Teddie end up doing female impersonations?"

"The Hasty Pudding Show at Harvard. It's all in drag. A star was born." I motioned to the chair across from me. "You can sit, you know. That dress is gabardine, it won't wrinkle."

Carefully, she perched on the edge of the chair. "Teddie went to Harvard?"

"Grad school. He got his MBA there, after he studied at Juilliard. His father had his heart set on his son taking his rightful place in the family investment banking firm on Wall Street."

"I guess Theodore had other plans" Miss Patterson smiled. "The guy's got gumption. Hard not to like that."

211

"Apparently, his father didn't take the news very well. I don't guess an investment type from New York would know how to handle a son who channels Cher five nights a week to a sold-out house. His father's a bit of an empty suit—I have a feeling he can be a real ass when he wants to. His mother's a peach, though—Harvard MBA, runs her family's business."

I steepled my fingers, put them to my lips, and looked at Miss Patterson. "When Teddie bought the penthouse at the Presidio, he talked me into buying the apartment below his. He said it was a really great investment. The rest is history."

"Sounds like an interesting family. Any siblings?"

I shook my head. "What if we're not any good together? No way could I have sex with him then go back to being buddies. So, where would that leave me? No boyfriend, and, worse—no best friend."

"Well, all I know is relationships take courage." Miss Patterson announced bravely. The irony of that remark was apparently lost on her. I stifled a smile.

"My courage seems to be in short supply," I responded truthfully. I played with one of the paperweights on my desk. A cockroach encased in Lucite containing flecks of gold—my golden cockroach trophy—a gift from the employees after Mr. Ballantine's first extortion attempt. Creepy, but I liked it. "You make all this sound like some high-stakes poker game."

"Not a perfect analogy, but it'll do," said my expert in love. "Both require calculated gambles."

"I suck at poker." Not to mention love. I put the cockroach trophy back on my desk where it secured a pile of papers, from what I don't know.

"You are one of the best poker players I've ever seen." She smoothed her dress nervously. "I know you can handle a relationship with Theodore—you just have to want to. Lucky, he's the kind of guy gals like me dream about."

Me, too, but I wasn't going to tell her that.

"To quote a wise and wonderful friend of mine, 'That's the thing about dreams—they're scary when they come true.'"

"You're paraphrasing."

"And you're avoiding yourself," Miss Patterson announced. How come she knew me so well?

"One of my better skills."

Miss Patterson shot out of the chair at the sound of the outer office door opening.

"Anybody here?"

Why did such a simple question sound so intoxicating in an Australian accent?

"Back here," I said, then whispered to Miss Patterson, "Your knight is here, and I hope he didn't bring his white horse or that dress won't work at all."

She giggled, all traces of her nervousness gone.

We both turned as the Beautiful Jeremy Whitlock walked in.

"Your timing is impeccable," I said, glad for the interruption. Too much introspection on an empty stomach.

When he caught sight of his date, he stopped dead in his tracks. I recognized the expression on his face—I'd seen it before. This afternoon. On Teddie's face. When he looked at me.

Jeremy reached for her hands and tenderly held them in his

Suddenly shy, Miss Patterson looked down.

"You look fabulous!" Jeremy didn't even try to hide his delight.

Miss Patterson raised her eyes to his and flashed a megawatt smile. "Thank you. So do you."

Good girl. "Mr. Whitlock, treat her well, and I expect you to have her home at a reasonable hour."

They both grinned like high school kids on their way to the prom.

"Yes, Mother," they said in unison, then laughed.

They turned to go, Jeremy keeping hold of one of Miss Patterson's hands.

"Have fun, kids. Be good. And, if you can't be good, be careful."

The door smothered their giggling as it shut behind them.

~

FRESHENING MY OWN MAKEUP HAD TAKEN A BIT LONGER THAN I realized—all this girly-girl stuff sure took time, and Teddie was waiting. I hurried as I tossed my cosmetics in my bag, flipped off the lights, and closed and locked the door behind me.

I took the stairs.

As I hit the lobby, my heart was thudding faster than a quick trip down the stairs would warrant. No matter how much I wished to deny it, Teddie had quite an effect even when he wasn't there. The memory of his touch alone sent a river of warmth washing through me.

Damn.

I burst through the front doors and came face-to-face with Teddie coming the other way.

My heart tripped even faster at the sight of him. Any more of this and the sucker would probably leap right out of my chest.

"Whoa, there." He grabbed my arm. "Where's the fire?"

"Wasn't I supposed to meet you at home?"

He hooked his arm through mine, holding me tight against his side, as we turned to walk out the front drive. "Yes, but I didn't want you to walk by yourself, so I started out to meet you."

"I'm glad you did."

"The truth of it is, my actions weren't completely altruistic—I had an ulterior motive."

"Really?"

"I couldn't wait any longer to see you."

~

WARM AND SENSUOUS, THE NIGHT ENVELOPED US AS WE STROLLED the length of the long curved drive. Magically, a few brave stars pierced the dome of light above Las Vegas. I'd never noticed them before.

A sleek, black limo waited at the end of the drive.

"Your chariot awaits." Teddie opened the back door with a flourish.

"We only have a few blocks. The walk will do us good."

"We're not going home."

"What happened to movie night?" I slipped inside the cavernous darkness of the big car.

"Change of plans." Teddie settled in next to me, his shoulder warm against mine. Holding my hand in his, a self-satisfied grin splitting his face, he announced, "We're going on a real date—our first."

A date? A bolt of excitement shot through me. "Where are we going?"

A finger to his lips, Teddie made a shushing sound. "Relax. I've taken care of everything."

I rested my head on his shoulder, closed my eyes, and let go.

~

LIKE A BUTTERFLY IN A COCOON, SAFE AND QUIET, I LOST ALL SENSE of time and place, aware only of Teddie next to me, the warmth of his hand in mine, the rhythmic rise and fall of his chest.

A soft kiss to my forehead, then Teddie whispered, "We're here."

"I don't want to move."

"I'm sure Andre would serve us out here, but it's not quite the ambiance I was hoping for."

My head still on his shoulder, eyes closed to the world, savoring the moment, I sighed, "Andre's."

A throwback to another time, Andre's had been the place to go when Las Vegas served up glamour rather than glitz. Squirreled away on a nondescript street in a seedy section of downtown, the restaurant still reeked of movie stars, clandestine affairs, and well-dressed ladies and gents who thought a proper dinner wasn't complete without a touch of beluga and a fine Bordeaux.

Bejeweled with twinkling white lights, trees stood like soldiers on guard beside the entrance. Through a small courtyard and a weathered wooden door, Andre's exuded the warmth of a good friend's home.

A small man with discretion etched in every feature, the maître d' greeted us warmly. We followed him through several small rooms filled with the hush of diners enjoying an exquisite meal, to a cozy, private space in the back.

One table robed in white and decorated with silver and crystal occupied the small room lit only by candlelight. Subtle, sexy music wafted from unseen speakers. A waiter, gloved hands and a white cloth over one arm, pulled out a chair with an expectant look in my direction.

Once Teddie and I had taken our places, the waiter disappeared, leaving us alone.

"You don't mind skipping popcorn and *South Pacific*, do you?" Teddie still held my hand, and he squeezed it.

"This is our own enchanted evening."

Everything about Andre's was perfect, from the upholstered walls, to the plants tastefully arranged to provide privacy without being claustrophobic, to the personal attention and the five-star food.

All of the momentous occasions in my life had been celebrated within the confines of these small rooms—my high school and college graduations with my mother, my various promotions with The Big Boss.

And now, my first date with Teddie.

"How did you choose Andre's?"

"You mentioned once it was your favorite place."

"Don't they close shortly?"

"Not tonight."

A waiter appeared, holding a bottle of wine as if he bore gold to the king.

Teddie and the waiter went through the wine dance—sniffing corks, testing the bouquet. Teddie caught my eye and winked as he listened to the litany of attributes particular to his chosen vintage.

Tonight, his eyes seemed bluer than I remembered as they danced with delight, his smile brighter, his lips—that kiss had changed everything.

I no longer had a libido problem—I had a Teddie problem.

Raising his glass, Teddie said, "To beginnings."

THE NEXT TWO HOURS PASSED IN A FLURRY OF ACTIVITY AS WAITERS filed in with wonderful dishes, each one an exquisite work of art. Teddie had ordered everything in advance, relegating me to pampered delight.

We ate. We laughed. We talked. We got to know each other in a subtly different way.

The restaurant was quiet and our appetites sated, when the waiters cleared the table and disappeared.

Music played softly in the background.

"Dance with me?" Teddie rose and extended his hand.

I let him pull me to my feet. "Don't the waiters want to go home?"

"Lucky, let it go."

As the first strains of "Till I Loved You" wafted around us, he pulled me close.

Like two pieces of the same puzzle, we fit together—my curves filling his hollows.

Cheek to cheek, heart to heart, we swayed to the music, as Barbra Streisand sang a song of friendship growing into love.

~

OUR FOOTSTEPS ECHOED IN THE EMPTY LOBBY OF THE PRESIDIO AS Teddie and I strolled through, hand in hand. Even Forrest had abandoned his post. I had no idea what time it was, and I didn't care.

"What a perfect evening." I leaned into Teddie as we settled into the elevator and he pressed the button for my floor. "Thank you."

"My pleasure."

Teddie shifted my hand to his other one, then circled my shoulders, pulling me tight to him.

"I've never been treated like that before," I said from somewhere near his shoulder.

The doors opened to my living room. For once, the bird didn't shout an obscene greeting.

"Want to come in?"

Teddie shook his head as he turned me to face him. "You've had a long day, and have another one facing you tomorrow."

Both hands framing my face, he kissed me.

I stepped into him and lost myself as he deepened his kiss.

After lingering, he finally stepped away.

"Sweet dreams, Lucky, my love."

CHAPTER FOURTEEN

*T*HE SOFT light of early morning slipped into my bedroom, seeping around the shades, bathing everything in the golden promise of a new day, and gently rousing me from a fabulous dream.

Teddie. Andre's. The night came flooding back to me in waves of joy.

The dream wasn't a dream at all. I smiled at the memory.

Stretching, I luxuriated in the soft caress of fine linen sheets and the downy comfort of my feather mattress, then I sat up and swiveled my feet over the edge.

My room looked the same—gleaming hardwood floors, whitewashed walls graced by a few brightly colored pastels of desert scenes. The thick rug felt the same under my toes—I wiggled them, enjoying the feel.

Everything was the same—yet different.

Like a soaking rain in the forest, the hint of love brought a sparkle to the day. The colors were brighter. The air shimmered with the sun's energy, as if the world—no longer muted by the mundane—held untold promise.

While the world sparkled at this ungodly hour of the morning, I did not. I needed caffeine.

Reality washed over me as I padded to the kitchen.

Teddie really was serious. He didn't want to be just my friend anymore—he wanted more, much more, and sooner rather than later. Even though he had been restrained last night, his full-court press belied the lip service he'd been giving to the whole one-letter-at-a-time thing. He was leaping letters on his way to Z.

I punched the button on the coffee machine and the grinder whirred as its blades bit into thin air. Damn, I'd forgotten to fill the thing last night. I busied myself with serious coffee preparation.

Warm cup cradled in my hands, I stared out at my city as the sunlight pushed the darkness of night over the mountains.

I loved Vegas—the city of dreams.

People came here to escape a life defined by all their previous choices—a brief respite from the burden of reality. For a scant moment in time, they were no longer a used car salesman from Dallas, a plumber from Chicago, or a factory worker from Detroit. They could be anything they wanted to be in the fantasy world of Vegas—handsome, virile, beautiful, rich...in love.

Like boulders pushed ahead of a flood my thoughts came tumbling back. I was powerless to stop them. For me, Vegas wasn't a fantasy world—it was my reality—a carefully constructed box with me on the inside and everybody else on the outside.

Teddie was banging on the door—a door hanging on one hinge.

Did I have the courage to let him in? Could I keep him out?

I took a sip of the warm brew and felt the caffeine jump start.

Who was I kidding? Like fine sand, the illusion of control slipped through my fingers, and triggered a distant memory—my mother, the specter of pain behind her eyes, announcing in a tired, resigned voice, "We can't pick who we fall in love with, little one. Love picks us." I didn't remember the conversation or what had triggered it. Too young to understand my mother's pain, the memory haunted me for years.

Would love pick me?

Would it bring the pain it had brought to my mother?

Was that really what I was afraid of?

The shriek of my alarm startled me as it echoed through the apartment. I'd forgotten to turn the thing off. Spilling coffee as I went, I trotted to the bedroom and silenced the offending device with one slap.

Enough thinking.

Time to face the day.

～

As TWIN JETS OF WARM WATER PUMMELED MY BODY, KNEADING THE tension from my neck and shoulders, I swiveled my head from side to side—no pain—a minor miracle. Turning the temperature to cold, I forced myself to stand there. The jolt added to the coffee jump start.

Adrenaline and caffeine—my drugs of choice.

After scouring myself dry, I wrapped myself in a thick, Turkish terry-cloth towel. Unfortunately, through the years, I had developed an appreciation for the finer things in life. Some time ago, a boyfriend had announced that I was officially "high-maintenance."

I took that as a compliment.

I set to work doing battle with myself. The makeup I could handle, but the hair eluded me. The front part was easy, but without three hands, the back was impossible. That was the problem with styled hair—Linda's creation was fabulous, but I could never duplicate it. All that money to end up feeling somehow inadequate and slightly disappointed.

Still, it was a vast improvement over my former shoddy self.

My dressing room beckoned—all five hundred square feet of

it. Larger than my first apartment, it was lined with closet doors on two walls. Another wall held a full-length mirror, angled so I could see my rear view—on the off chance I could stomach it. Shelves of shoes rounded out the fourth wall.

An unrepentant clotheshorse, I'd been collecting designer clothes a piece at a time, as money allowed, for practically forever. Today, I was in the mood for something flirty and fun, and maybe a little bit naughty.

Escada. And I knew just the piece.

I twirled in front of the mirror. A pretty beige suit, with a delicate fitted jacket and a swing skirt with a sheer bright orange cami underneath. Bronze Dolce & Gabbana peep-toes, a cascade of David Yurman silver and gold, and I was set.

I fed the bird, my thoughtfulness rewarded with a "Get lost, bitch," grabbed my Birkin, and, surrounded by a balloon of happy memories—all thanks to the kind Mr. Kowalski—floated out the door to meet the day.

～

THE SHARP POINT OF REALITY PUNCTURED MY BALLOON THE MINUTE I walked through the front door of the Babylon.

"Ms. O'Toole! Could I have your assistance, please?" The hint of panic in Sergio's voice matched the look on his face. With frantic waving, he beckoned me to the front desk.

"How can I help?"

He gestured to a woman standing in front of him. "This is Ms. Hetherington. She is staying with us—"

"This man won't help me," the woman interrupted. "I have a problem and I need it fixed. Now!"

The woman, dressed in black from head to toe, smacked her gum as she talked. She didn't smile. I wasn't sure she could. A study in too much plastic surgery, her face was pulled as tight as a canvas on a frame. The heavily applied makeup didn't help.

She motioned to a Louis Vuitton trunk open at her feet. "Honestly, I can't see *why* this is so hard!" Hand on hip, she looked from me to Sergio and back again, then pointed to the contents of the trunk. "Smell that."

Bending low, I was assaulted by the unmistakable stench of cat urine.

"Whoa!" The ammonia made my eyes water. "How did that happen?"

"The cats, of course." She rolled her eyes, apparently put out at having to deal with me and my double-digit IQ.

"Whose cats?" My voice took on a flat tone. She didn't notice.

"Mine, of course. Two Bengals and a long-haired Siamese." She blew a bubble with the gum, then smacked it loudly. "I thought they'd be fine, but I guess they got nervous or something."

"You packed your cats?"

"Well, yeah," she said, sounding like a teenager in desperate need of a parent to draw some boundaries. "What else was I to do? The airlines wouldn't let me carry on more than one—even in first class."

"Where are the cats now?"

She waved her hand, indicating the lobby. "Somewhere out there. I don't know. They ran when I opened the trunk."

"Sergio, get ahold of Jerry. Tell him to find those cats. They're probably hungry, and if they get into the baby ducks swimming in the Euphrates—" I stopped. I could visualize the carnage—feathers flying, blood in the river, children screaming—traumatized for life. "Just tell him it's really important."

Sergio disappeared into the back.

"Now," Ms. Hetherington said, as she picked up an article of clothing from the trunk. Holding it between two fingers, arm extended, she wrinkled her nose in disgust. "I need all of this cleaned, immediately. I'm standing in the only outfit I have that's wearable, and it's totally unacceptable for the party tonight."

"Fine." I forced a smile. "We'll be glad to take care of it. You should have your clothes in a couple of hours. The trunk may take a bit longer."

"What about the cats?"

"This hotel has a policy against animals in the rooms. We will see the cats are taken care of during your stay—when we find them."

"What do you mean I can't have my cats? Do you know who my husband is?"

"A very lucky man, I am sure. But, still, no pets." She dismissed me with a sneer, and turned to Sergio, who had reappeared. "I want to speak to your supervisor—now!"

Sergio gave me a glance, then said, "I'm the front desk manager."

"Surely you answer to somebody?" Ms. Hetherington huffed. I half expected her to stamp her foot.

"In matters like this, I would go to the head of customer relations."

"And that would be me," I interjected. "Have you checked in?" She waggled her key in front of my face. "Helloooo..." I motioned one of the bellmen over. "This gentleman will escort you to your room. I can assure you, your cats will be well tended. We'll deliver your clothes when they are ready.

"I should think so," she huffed. "Really, that's the least you could do."

~

THE OFFICE DOOR WAS LOCKED WHEN I GOT THERE.

That was odd—Miss Patterson usually beat me.

I checked my watch—9:15.

Miraculously, I found my keys lurking on the bottom of my bag. Turning on the lights as I went, I walked through to my office and shrugged off my purse as I deposited myself on the couch.

Scrolling through the list of contacts in my Nextel, I high-lighted Miss Patterson's cell number and pushed send.

The Beautiful Jeremy Whitlock answered on the fifth ring. "Hello?"

"Hey, Jeremy." I struggled to keep the smile out of my voice. I didn't even try to keep it off my face. "You wouldn't happen to know where my fearless assistant is, would you?"

"Oh, hey! She just left. She was running late—I guess she forgot her phone."

"Apparently."

"I'm totally glad I cracked into her. I thought she'd fob me off, for sure."

"Is that a good thing or a bad thing?" I asked hesitantly. To me, his statement sounded as if it bordered on too much information.

"Bugger. I forget sometimes you people don't talk right over here. I'm glad I asked her out. I thought she wouldn't give me a chance."

"You had a good time, then?"

"The best. Tell her I'll lob in after a bit with her phone."

"Sure," I said, not completely sure what it was I was supposed to tell her.

Jeremy had just rung off, when I heard the outer door open.

Miss Patterson appeared in my doorway. Her face red, her hair a bit mussed, she patted down her dress—the same little black number from yesterday. My Jimmy Choos sparkled on her feet. "I'm sorry I'm late."

"A bit overdressed for work, wouldn't you say?" I bit back a smile.

Her brows crinkled as she looked down at the dress and the shoes. "Well, I..."

I held up my hand. "It's okay. I just wish you'd called. I was worried."

"I tried. I'm sorry. I can't seem to find my phone."

"Jeremy has it."

"Oh."

"I called. He said you'd just left."

"Oh."

"I would ask you whether you had a good time, but I'm pretty sure I know the answer already."

Gathering her dignity, Miss Patterson looked me in the eye. "Honey, I'm older than you. My time is running short." With that, she retreated.

I followed her into the outer office. Boy, get a makeover, release the cougar within.

"I hoped you and Jeremy would make some hay, but I never thought you'd roll around in it—not on the first date."

"You'd do well to follow my lead." She sat at her desk, unscrewed my earrings, and then handed them to me. "You know what they say about women over thirty—they have a better chance of being hit by lightning than getting married."

I reinstalled my earrings. "It's women over thirty-*five*, thank you very much. I still have plenty of time."

"Fine. But you and Teddie—"

I waggled my finger at her, cutting her off. "Oh no. This isn't about me. Besides, I'm already late for breakfast with The Big Boss."

"Chicken."

Her words followed me out the door. I didn't have an answer. How do you argue with the truth?

⁓

"YOU'RE LATE," THE BIG BOSS ANNOUNCED. A PLATE OF FOOD already in front of him, he occupied a two-top against the window, in a closed section of Nebuchadnezzar's.

"Two minutes." I flopped into the chair across from him. "Someone had to take care of a lady with some cats. Miss Patterson was late—"

"It's not important." The Big Boss forked in a bite of scrambled eggs and green chili. "You want some food?"

"No, thanks. I had a late dinner."

He looked at me for a second, but didn't ask the question I saw in his eyes. Thank God for small favors. I had too many questions and too few answers as it was.

"Your tapes were interesting listening," he said through another mouthful of egg. "Irv Gittings—I look forward to dealing with him in front of the board tomorrow."

That was probably the only thing keeping Ol' Irv from an appointment with his maker. I doubted if he knew how lucky he was.

"Did you have a chance to call your friend on the Gaming Control Board?" I asked.

"Yeah. He said they were on top of the discrepancies at the Athena, but he couldn't give me the details. Just confirming Gittings' problems was more than he should have revealed, but he owed me."

"Ol' Irv's got more problems than a mongrel has fleas."

"Well put." The Big Boss grinned, then pushed his plate away. He flipped his glasses down from their perch on top of his head, then grabbed some papers from his briefcase by his feet, and began to spread them on the table.

"Before we start in on our presentation to the board, I need to ask you a favor," I said.

"Fire away."

"I need to hire another assistant. I'm spending twenty hours here most days—Miss Patterson almost as many. I'm exhausted." I blew at some hair tickling my eyes. "And I need a life."

The Big Boss looked at me over his cheaters, which rested on the end of his nose. "Does this have anything to do with your late dinner last night?"

Did anything get by The Big Boss?

"Yes. No." I sighed. "I don't know. That's my problem. I'm too tired to think straight."

"I see." A smile tugged at the corner of his mouth. "You don't have to ask me for permission to hire an assistant. If you need one, hire one."

The Big Boss rooted through his stack of papers, extracted a page, and pushed it across the table to me. "Now, about tomorrow, we need to get our story straight on Willie and Lyda Sue. Irv's requested to address the board, so we'd better be able to counter his every move..."

～

THE COOKS WERE CLEARING THE BREAKFAST ITEMS FROM THE STEAM tables, replacing them with lunch when The Big Boss and I finally finished our meeting.

Miss Patterson caught me on my Nextel as I was climbing the wide staircase to the lobby "Lucky?"

"Whatcha got?"

"Miranda Jones wants to meet with you—something about going over the guest list for her table at the awards banquet."

"Right. Do you have the final workup from catering?"

Miss Patterson gave me the rundown.

"So, nothing new?"

"No. Miranda said she'd be at the pool, and you'd know where to find her."

～

THE HANGING GARDENS OF BABYLON WERE ONE OF THE SEVEN wonders of the ancient world. The Big Boss had spared no expense in re-creating them as our pool area. Vines and trailing flowering plants hung from every possible nook, cranny, crevice and ledge, creating a veritable cascade of greenery and blooms. A permanent staff of horticulturists tended to baskets and pots of riotous blooming plants.

You could cut the humidity with a knife.

Leave it to The Big Boss to create the only tropical climate zone in the desert.

Water cascaded from ledges and rocks, burbled up through rock features then rushed into the three pools, all connected by a lazy river dotted with caves. Each pool was a distinct area, with its own rules. One pool for families, one for adults only, and one for VIP adults, where tops were optional.

Even in my state of diminished IQ, I knew exactly where Miranda would hold court.

Protected from prying eyes by the tall palms surrounding the VIP section, Miranda had arranged herself in all her glory on a chaise in the sun. Her body slick with oil, she wore only a tiny black thong and a look of disdain.

I dragged a chair into a spot of shade near her. "You wanted to see me."

She put a hand to her eyes and squinted against the sun. "Yes, I need to go over the table for the awards ceremony."

No, "Thank you." No, "Good to see you." No, "Sorry for summoning you like staff." And she knew how much I hated discussing business with near naked people.

Her subtle put-down was a carefully designed maneuver in a game we'd been playing for as long as I could remember. Clawing and scratching, we both had fought like hell to escape the lives we were born to.

We both had mothers who whored. After a long battle with life-altering substances, Miranda's mom succumbed to her demons when Miranda was sixteen. In a way, I'd been lucky— Mona was a scrapper. If I'd learned anything from her it was how to fight—and how to fight dirty when necessary.

Miranda had made her escape from Vegas—and I hadn't, or so she thought. The ironic thing was, although Miranda lived in L.A.

she hadn't really escaped at all—the porn business was just a slightly different take on the prostitution trade. But that was a nuance apparently lost on her. Or maybe not—and that's what this was all about.

I shrugged out of my jacket then hung it over the arm of my chair. Settling back, my smile fixed, I began to rattle off the arrangements for her table. As I did so, I noticed a small mechanical device motoring our way.

Small as a mouse, it crept along on a base of tiny rubber wheels. A glass eye continually scanned, rotating from side to side. When it turned in Miranda's direction, all movement stopped.

Oblivious, Miranda stretched like a cat after a long nap.

As I finished my spiel, I looked around. Somebody had to be controlling the thing. On my second pass, I caught movement behind a palm tree to my right.

Paxton Dane. He had a little box in his hand with a joystick jutting from the top and a shit-eating grin on his face. Payback time. I knew somehow he'd get even with Miranda for taking a bite out of his ass.

Leaning back, I crossed my arms, kept my expression neutral, and watched as the show began.

Miranda sat up. Facing me, she held a breast in each hand and proffered them for my inspection. "So, what do you think? I just got them redone. I think they look really nice."

Nice for prized watermelons at the state fair. "Lovely." I kept my expression bland.

"And the wax jobs they're doing these days! They make it possible to wear a thong like this and not be tacky."

Clearly we had a different definition of tacky.

She spread her legs and eyed the tiny triangle of cloth. "I have to have it done every three weeks."

"Sounds painful."

"Tell me about it." Miranda rolled over, exposing both her

cheeks. "And try keeping an aging ass dimple-free. They have this new machine. It sucks really hard on your skin. It's supposed to give it tone while eliminating the toxins trapped in the fat."

While bringing one to rears.

She wiggled her dimple-free booty around. "It works. You ought to try it."

"I have a low threshold for pain." And at least a shred of dignity left. I couldn't imagine lying there while some technician sucked on my butt.

"Too bad." On her stomach, propped up on her elbows, Miranda eyed me over her sunglasses. "Pain is a part of life."

I couldn't tell whether she meant to be profound, or she had missed her own point. "When I get desperate, I'll let you know."

She pushed her glasses back into place and hopped over on her back, her plastic boobs pointing toward the sky.

"Are we done?" I asked.

"Oh, yeah." She waved dismissively. "The arrangements sound fine."

I knew they would be. "Oh, Miranda? You've just given those guys a great show—for free."

"What?" She sprang to a sitting position, one leg on either side of the chaise—her crotch pointed directly at the little peeping Tom device. "What guys? And I never give a show for free."

I pointed to the little mouse. "There's always a first time."

The little device turned and sped away, but it wasn't nearly fast enough. I grabbed my jacket, and bolted after the thing. Two strides and I held it.

I waved the device at her. "Two can play your game, sweetheart."

She glared at me for a moment, then burst out laughing. "Okay, you win this round. Did you set the whole thing up?"

"Of course not. We don't do that to our guests here—I merely took advantage of the opportunity."

"Brilliant." She reached for the device. "Let me see that. Maybe we could use this in our next production—sort of a peeping Tom perspective. Wouldn't that be a turn-on?"

"You're the expert," I told her.

"You're coming to the opening gala tonight?" she asked.

I'd forgotten. Even when the cat-pee lady mentioned a party, it hadn't rung a bell. The trade show opened tonight to those in the business. "I'll be late. I have dinner plans."

"Come when you can."

I left her talking into the little eye.

My phone rang as I pushed through the heavy doors to the lobby. I smiled at the number. "Hey."

"Where are you?" Teddie asked. "It's lunchtime. Are you hungry?"

Butterflies took flight at the sound of his voice. "Getting there."

"They let me into my theatre. Me and the boys are working through a new number. We ordered pizza. Want some?"

"I've got to check on some cats, then I'm on my way."

"Cats?"

"Don't ask."

"Busy morning, then?"

"Uh-huh. Finished off by a very informal meeting with Miranda at the VIP pool."

"I can only imagine. Who won that round?" Teddie laughed that wonderful, warm laugh that sent shivers of delight down my spine.

"Miranda awarded the victory to me, but I think it was a draw."

"You two have the most interesting friendship."

"We have history, but I'm not sure it's a friendship."

I heard someone in the background call to him.

"I gotta go," Teddie said. "We just ordered the pizza. It'll be thirty minutes at least before it gets here."

"I'll be there."

"If you hurry, you can catch the run-through of our new number."

∽

As I strode through the lobby, I caught sight of a couple of Security guys crawling through the shrubbery. A few more patrolled the banks of the Euphrates.

I stopped by the river and pushed-to-talk. "Security. What's the status on the cats?"

"We have two. Still looking for the third." The low-timbred voice of Paxton Dane.

As I started to answer, a little girl walked by me holding a small cat, its fur bearing distinct leopard spots. "Dane, which cats do you have?"

"One with weird spots and another with long hair and blue eyes."

"I think I have a line on the third. I'll get back to you." I followed the little girl and stopped her before she reached the front desk. "Honey?" I squatted down so we were eye to eye. "That's a really pretty cat."

"It was over by the ducks. I wanted to take it home, but my mom said it probably belongs to somebody." She stroked the cat as she looked at me. "Do you think I can keep it?"

I had half a mind to let her have it—the animal would be much better off with the little girl than with the horror who had packed it in a trunk. "We'll see."

I knew better than to promise something I wasn't sure I should deliver, but I'm a sucker for happy endings. "Where's your mom?"

"Right over there." The girl nodded in the direction of a woman standing off to the side, watching us intently.

233

"You wait here while I talk to your mom, okay?"

"Sure."

The girl's mother smiled as I approached. "I try to let her handle people when I can—she's never out of my sight. I don't want her to be shy."

"I don't think you have to worry about that. Do you all live here?"

"Yes, in Green Valley," she said, her eyes on her daughter.

"When it gets too hot outside, I bring her here to see the ducks. We had a treat today with all the babies. And then she found the cat."

"How do you feel about taking a cat home with you?"

Her eyes darted to me, then swiveled back to her daughter. "I'd love it, but are you sure it doesn't belong to somebody?"

I cast a discrete glance around the lobby—no cat-pee lady. "Cats wander in here from time to time. We take them to the shelter—we have no other choice."

"Then we'll take that one with us." She shook her head with a smile. "I don't know whether I could get it away from my daughter anyway. You've made her day."

"You both have done wonders for mine."

The mother approached her daughter and bent down to whisper in her ear. The grin on the kid's face put a smile on my heart. I watched as the two of them disappeared out the front door, the sunlight swallowing them.

I turned and ran right into the hard and altogether wonderfully masculine chest of Paxton Dane. I seemed to have a habit of doing that. "Oh, sorry."

"My pleasure," he said, a hint of invitation in his voice.

Too bad he was playing for the opposition. Needing distance, I stepped away.

"Was that our third cat?" Dane nodded after the woman and her daughter.

Feeling a bit sheepish at being caught, I nodded. "You can call off the search."

"I thought the cats belonged to one of our guests?"

"The woman packed the three of them in a trunk for the flight here."

Dane's face clouded—his eyes got squinty.

I knew that look.

Then he gave me a lopsided grin—it was a good grin, for a bad guy. "Too bad we couldn't find that third cat. I guess it ran out the front doors or something."

"Yeah, too bad." Hoping I wasn't too late for the run-through, I turned toward Teddie's theatre.

Dane fell in step beside me. "We're still on for dinner?"

"I'll meet you at Tigris, but could we make it at six thirty instead of seven?"

"I'm okay with that. If I can't change the reservation, I'll call you."

"You did get the guys who designed that little spy-mobile thing, didn't you? We can't have those things running around the hotel capturing our guests at indelicate moments."

"Sure. I took the thing from them, but promised them leniency in exchange for its use." His glee was impossible to hide. "Pretty good, don't you think?"

"It was perfect, actually." Stepping around the No Admittance sign, I grabbed one of the handles of the theatre doors and threw my weight against it.

"You can't go in there," he said. "It says 'Private, rehearsal in session.'"

I gave Dane a look and stepped inside the darkened theatre. Starting down the steps toward the stage, I felt Dane's presence behind me, hanging back in the shadows.

CHAPTER FIFTEEN

*I*N A pair of pink stilettos, jeans, a ripped T-shirt, and with a pink boa around his neck, Teddie commanded the top tier of a mountain of stairs in the center of the stage. A series of staircases cascaded from Teddie's high point, each level populated by several of Teddie's boys—his ensemble of the most beautiful young men I've ever seen—each handpicked and a potential star in his own right.

But it was Teddie the spotlight loved.

Christo, Teddie's understudy, stood next to him. Tall, and lean, his blond hair long and wavy, Christo wore loose dance pants cinched at the waist, a body-hugging muscle shirt, his own pair of stilettos, and a boa—his was blue.

"Okay, everybody!" Teddie clapped his hands for attention. "Are you ready? This one's Christo's."

The boys snapped to attention.

Teddie gave the sign to key the music. As the first strains of Abba's "Dancing Queen" played, he shouted, "Lights!" Then he ducked out of the spotlight, leaving Christo in its beam.

The lights pulsed to the beating rhythm of the song. The boys danced, their gestures grand and campy. Christo sang as he descended the stairs. While it was a nice number—just the choice of song itself made me smile—the whole thing lacked the usual sparkle.

Teddie let them go for about thirty seconds before he shouted, "Stop! Everybody back to their places." He stepped in behind Christo on the top tier. "Remember, this is the huge ending production number. You're the star—you're the dancing queen. You gotta sell it. Make 'em believe!" Teddie threw the boa around his neck. "Here, I'll show you."

As Christo stepped out of the way, a transformation came over Teddie. His body loosened, relaxing into a female languidness. One hand on his hip, knees together, a come-hither look on his face, when the music started, Teddie sang as he descended the stairs. His gestures grand and sexy, he sparkled—his energy infusing the whole theatre.

Even as a woman, Teddie was sexy as hell. I must be losing it.

Toward the end of the number, in a salute to *Mamma Mia!* the boys invited the crowd to dance.

Being a large part of a very small crowd, I did as they said. Twirling down the aisle, arms overhead swaying to the music, I joined in the singing: *"You are the dancing queen."*

Up the stairs, I arrived at Teddie's side just as the final, frenzied notes played. His eyes alight, he twirled me around, then dipped me over one knee as the music faded.

The theatre fell silent as he pulled me out of the dip, holding my body against his. Then he kissed me.

Catcalls and wolf whistles erupted from the chorus.

Still holding my body tight to his, Teddie gave me a huge grin. "Hello."

"Are you going to add that to the show?"

"That's only for you," he whispered.

The few nerve endings that weren't already afire glowed hot.

"Show's not over. The boys deserve a bow," Teddie announced.

Hand in hand, we both turned and bowed for the chorus, who erupted in loud cheers and shouted, "Encore!"

We complied. This kiss left me breathless.

Finally, when I had somewhat regained my composure, I asked Teddie, "What does it mean that a kiss from a guy in stilettos and pink leather boa makes my toes curl?"

"You're very comfortable with your sexual orientation?"

"No, I think it means I'm very comfortable with *your* orientation."

Teddie threw back his head and laughed, his arm still around my waist.

I could feel the heat of him.

Christo pushed through the throng. "I see what you mean. That was brilliant!" He turned to me. "Teddie's the man!"

"I'm counting on it," I deadpanned.

That elicited another round of wolf whistles.

"Enough!" Teddie said, laughing. "Lunch break. Pizza's in the back. You have an hour."

He grabbed my hand. "Are you hungry, or can you wait a bit?"

"I'm good. Let the boys have their go."

We sat on the edge of the stage, the bright lights impossible to see beyond. The outer door opened, a square of light piercing the darkness, as someone stepped out of the theatre.

Dane. I'd forgotten about him.

"What'd you think of the number?" Teddie asked.

"With you, it was terrific. But, seriously, 'Dancing Queen'?"

"If you can laugh at yourself, the whole world can laugh with you." Teddie kicked his bare feet—he had ditched the stilettos and boa. "That's what this is all about—fun. I can sing ballads, imitate a good many of the famous singers of the last half century, dance, tell jokes, play seven instruments well, many more not so well— but all that is so normal it's almost banal."

"Maybe for you."

"This is where you're going to tell me I'm wasting my talent pretending to be women in a cheap show in Vegas, right?"

"Why would I say something like that? You're really good at it, and you seem to be having fun. Besides, we pay you a boatload. So, where's the problem?"

"You really are something special." Absentmindedly, Teddie picked up my hand and began tracing my fingers with his, sending shivers through me.

If he only knew the effect he had, he'd be dragging me off to a room—guess it was a good thing we worked in a hotel. Or maybe that was a bad thing.

"A straight guy channeling Cher and Bette Midler?" he said. "And surrounded by a bevy of the most beautiful men you've ever seen? Now that's a trip. Besides, swine that I am, I can't resist the huge sums of money you guys throw at me."

"Can't resist the siren call of success?"

"I'm easily bought, but don't let it get around. It's a novelty act —won't last forever. But for now, it pays the bills." Teddie looked around the darkened theatre, then checked over his shoulder.

"Who're you looking for?"

"Just wanted to make sure we're alone. I've got something I want you to hear."

He jumped to his feet and pulled me up and over to the bench at the white grand piano in the corner of the stage. "Sit." He patted the spot next to him. He cracked his knuckles, then he began to play and to sing in that wonderfully rich tenor of his.

I didn't recognize the song—a beautiful melody about love and yearning. Surely some pop star had ridden that tune to the top of the charts—and I was a sucker for songs of love. Very catchy yet touching, I wondered how I had missed it. Clearly, I had been working too much.

The final chords still lingered in the air when Teddie asked, "Any good?"

"Good? It's great! Who recorded it?"

"Nobody—yet." He stared out at the darkened theatre. "I wrote it for you."

My heart skipped a beat. "What?"

He shrugged, but still refused to meet my eyes. "I've been playing around with songs for years. I was okay at it, but the music didn't have any heart until I met you." Finally, he looked at me with a quizzical expression. "You really think it's good?"

"It takes my breath away."

~

TEDDIE'S SONG CHASED THROUGH MY HEAD AS I MADE MY WAY BACK to the office. Music—the language of love. I'd never thought of it as a weapon before, but it was—one that Teddie wielded with amazing accuracy. I'd spent an entire lifetime very carefully erecting a wall around my heart, and Teddie had opened the door with a kiss, then had proceeded to demolish a good chunk of the wall in the course of forty-eight hours. I felt exposed, vulnerable —yet safe, and somehow invigorated.

In short, I was a total mess.

I ran a shaky hand through my hair. How the hell was I going to make it through the rest of today?

Operating at slightly above barely functional, I took a deep breath and forced myself to focus—with marginal success. Dinner with Dane would require I be at the top of my game if I was going to worm his story out of him. Wandering around like a lovesick schoolgirl was so not me—at least not the me I used to know.

I so needed to get over myself.

Grabbing my Nextel, I dialed the office. "What do I have on my schedule this afternoon?" I asked Miss Patterson when she answered.

"Not much. A Miss Brandy Wine called. She said you had given her your card and told her to make an appointment. I penciled her in for four, but I can reschedule, if you wish."

"How would you feel about hiring an assistant?"

"Grateful beyond all measure."

"That bad, huh?"

"If you and I keep up this pace much longer, we'll be certifiable."

"I passed certifiable a long time ago and am well on my way to blithering idiot." I pushed through the office door, snapped the phone shut and continued the conversation with Miss Patterson in person. "Brandy aced my class at UNLV. She's young and inexperienced, but has good instincts. We'll have to train her, so it will mean more work to begin with—mainly for you."

"That's fine, as long as I can see the light at the end of the tunnel."

"Good. I'll need you to sit in on the meeting at four then. We both will have to agree or she doesn't get hired." I paced in front of her desk. "See if you can get ahold of the Most Reverend Peabody. I need a moment of his time when it's convenient—preferably sooner rather than later."

"And if he asks what this is about?"

"He shouldn't, but if he does, tell him it's about catching a rat."

One glance into my office made me cringe—papers were propagating at an alarming rate. I should tackle them, but nervous energy coursed through me. Thinking while sitting was out of the question. I needed to walk.

"I'll be in the lobby or the casino." I waved my phone at her as I reached for the door. "You know how to find me."

~

LIKE A FINELY TUNED ENGINE, A HIGH-END HOTEL HAS A SOUND ALL its own when its running well—each piston firing, the timing perfect, the gears meshing seamlessly. I paused at the railing of the mezzanine overlooking the lobby and the teeming mass of humanity. The bellmen with their carts rushed to greet guests and handle their luggage. The front desk—a smiling staff-person at each post—processed guests quickly. Cocktail waitresses trolled the crowd providing grease to any sticky cogs.

Closing my eyes, I listened. Under the ever-present music, the pulse of excitement throbbed in the voices below. No strident misfires. No angry backfires. Just the smooth sound of customers getting what they thought they'd paid for.

"You look like you're meditating. Very strange place to do that," said the Beautiful Jeremy Whitlock from behind me.

Keeping my eyes closed, not moving, I answered him. "Listen. What do you hear?"

I felt his presence next to me.

He was quiet for a moment. "Besides Sinatra?"

"Filter the music out."

"Voices, all mixed together—excitement."

"Precisely." I opened my eyes and looked at him. "That means my people are doing their jobs, which means my life is easier."

"Which means I could take your assistant for a gelato?"

"Okay with me."

"You know, she's bloody fantastic," he said in answer to my silent question.

"She has to be back for a meeting at four."

"Got it."

"I don't guess you and your gizmo have had any more sightings?"

"Just your cowboy bloke. He's been a real regular in Mr. Gittings' office. The other two are laying low."

"That's what I figured. But it does surprise me that a guy like Dane would hitch his team to Irv Gittings' wagon."

Jeremy snorted. "Man, when you've seen the stuff I see, nothing surprises you anymore."

"Really?" I watched the people below, and I wondered what had they come to Vegas looking for. And what were they willing to risk to get it. "People surprise the hell out of me all the time."

Jeremy turned to go.

"Have her back by four!" I said to his retreating back.

He disappeared into my office. Miss Patterson's excited greeting filtered down the hall before the door closed.

Looking for problems to solve, I spent the next hour wandering through all of the public areas on the main level of the hotel. Despite the huge crowds, the hotel ran with a precision that would make a Formula One team proud. At 3:25, having not uncovered even one minor misstep, I commandeered a corner table at Delilah's and watched the stairs for the arrival of the Most Reverend—Miss Patterson had said he would meet me here.

Jeep was as good as his word. On the stroke of the half hour, he lumbered up the steps. I waved him over.

He wedged himself into the chair across from me, mopping his brow with a handkerchief. "The Good Book says I'm probably going to hell for what I'm doing here, but at least I'll be prepared for the temperatures."

"There's always a price for pleasure."

"I'm just hoping eternal damnation isn't one of them," he huffed, as he waved to get a waitress's attention, then, once he had it, he mimicked a drinking motion with his hand and mouthed the word *beer*. He pointed at me and I shook my head. He gave me a grin. He didn't look too worried about riding the slippery slope to hell.

"Well, if you want to do a little penance for your sins, I have an idea."

"Really? What?"

"As you know, a certain young lady we both would like to get our hands on will most likely be at your party tomorrow night. I'd like to catch her and turn her over to the authorities, but I need your help."

His eyes locked on mine. "What can I do?"

$\sim$

Miss Patterson and Brandy were seated in front of my desk when I burst through the door at five minutes after four. "So, you two have gotten a chance to get to know each other a little bit? Good."

Both sets of eyes followed me as I took a seat behind my desk.

Miss Patterson's gaze held amusement. I was glad to see that my assistant had traded her little black dress and my Jimmy Choos for that pair of loose white slacks and peach shirt we had picked out yesterday. She looked cool and calm—the afterglow of a night of great sex with a handsome Australian. Mental pictures threatened to develop—my own private naughty movie featuring my friends. Terrific!

Focusing on Brandy, I closed my mind to the pictures. Brandy's dark hair was neatly tied back, her makeup flattering but subtle, accentuating her blue eyes and wide mouth. I remembered the flash of a megawatt grin that rivaled Julia Roberts's. Her dark suit was prim, but not too. Diamonds sparkled at her ears, and her shoes looked like this season's Christian Louboutins. She certainly knew how to dress the part.

And she was young—younger than I remembered. A pox on her.

"I didn't expect you to call so soon." Not exactly a stellar opening to the interview, but it was the best I could do.

"If this isn't a good time—" Brandy's eyes held concern.

"It's perfect. In fact, your timing couldn't be better." Miss Patterson handed me a piece of paper—Brandy's application. "Miss Patterson and I are about out of gas. We need some help."

The two across from me were quiet as I scanned the application. I see here you finished your hotel and restaurant degree last spring." I gave a low whistle. "Pretty gaudy grade point."

Brandy smiled. "I'm a hard worker."

"I remember that about you." I remembered other things about Brandy as well. On her own, with no real marketable assets other than her Marilyn Monroe figure, she'd worked her way through college.

Study by day, strip by night.

Technically, she had danced in a cage after hours in one of the local watering holes. She'd come to class with black eyes and assorted bruises from time to time after turning down demands for extracurricular activities. I'd offered help, but she'd refused— said she could handle them. I remember one guy she'd put in the hospital. "Wine isn't your real last name, is it?"

"No, it's Alexander."

Not much better, but at least Brandy Alexander sounded more like a real name rather than a stage name. "Well, Miss Alexander, with your degree and grades, how come I found you parking cars at the Athena?"

She straightened at my question, looked me unwaveringly in the eye, and said, "Most of the hotels don't want former strippers in their management."

"Ah, yes, the new saintly image of Sin City." All done to appease the delicate sensibilities of the corporate types at the home office in New York—as if covering the grime in a new coat of whitewash made the grime disappear. "I can assure you, you'll find none of that hypocrisy in this office. I carry the taint myself —my mother runs a whorehouse in Pahrump."

"Cool." The girl looked at Miss Patterson questioningly.

"I'm from Iowa," Miss Patterson said. "My mother milks cows and drives a tractor. Sorry."

"Here's the deal," I explained. "We're looking for an assistant for Miss Patterson—strictly customer relations. With your background, I would think you would be more inclined toward operations."

"Do you have any idea how many kids in the program would kill to work for you?"

I was taken aback. "Really? Whatever for?"

"You rock."

"I'll take that as a good thing." Today really was the weirdest day.

"We'll work you like a galley slave, and—" I nodded at her shoes. "The salary won't buy many pairs of Christian Louboutins."

"That's okay. I'll be learning from the best in the business."

I leveled my gaze at her, trying to muster a serious expression. "You can't put any of our guests in the hospital."

Miss Patterson's eyebrows shot up.

"You remember that." Brandy looked stricken.

"Her hands are registered lethal weapons," I explained to Miss Patterson.

Brandy waved her unassuming appendages. "Black belt, karate, and aikido."

I nodded to Miss Patterson. "Do you have any questions for Miss Alexander?"

She smiled and shook her head.

"Fine. Brandy, would you mind stepping outside? I need to confer with my assistant—this is a small office, we watch each other's backs here, so we need to feel comfortable with each other."

The girl closed the door behind her, but I could still see her through the glass side panels as she stood looking out at the teeming lobby below.

"She'd work for food." Miss Patterson and her bullshit meter.

"Yeah."

God, just looking at her transported me back. I was fifteen, fear tempering my brashness to a steel-like hardness. I'd had to convince The Big Boss that not only was I really eighteen, but I could do a good job with no training other than growing up in a whorehouse. He'd known I was lying, but he'd taken a flier on me. That foot in the door had made all the difference.

"So, what do you think?" I asked.

"How can we not hire her? I couldn't live with myself and you couldn't either."

"She worked her ass off and got doors slammed in her face for it," I said, shaking my head. "Vegas, the town that eats its young. She's your assistant if you can get her to accept your offer."

"And what is my offer?" Miss Patterson looked at me, her pencil poised above a notepad.

"Fifty grand to start, a review and possible raise after six months, the normal benefits. All in exchange for her soul and every second of her free time."

"Great." Miss Patterson rose to go. "But I think I'll leave out that last part. She can discover that on her own."

~

ONE ADVANTAGE, PROBABLY THE ONLY ADVANTAGE, OF PAPERWORK IS it demands my total attention. No thinking about Teddie...or Dane and his lies. No worrying whether Willie the Weasel, Ol' Irv, and Felicia Reilly would get what they deserved. And my mother? What was up with that last phone call? Did she really think she could put me off the scent? I'm a better hound dog than that—if anybody knows that it would be Mother.

Okay, clearly I had lost my powers of concentration. The pile of papers still commanded every square inch of surface area on my desk—I hadn't made much of a dent, and I'd been at it for over an hour.

Miss Patterson wasn't back from taking Brandy to Human Resources.

Leaning back in my chair, I put my feet on my desk and closed my eyes. Dog tired, I never realized how much energy emotion took.

The outer door opened and closed. Unable to muster even a scintilla of curiosity, I stayed where I was. If it was trouble, it would find me. Trouble knew where I lived.

"Hey." Not trouble—Teddie, to the extent those two were mutually exclusive.

"Practice over?" I asked, but didn't move.

"The sex show folks needed to get in. You wouldn't believe what they're doing."

I held up my hand. "I'm very visual."

He laughed. "That could be ugly. What do you say I buy you a drink, then maybe some dinner?"

"A drink would be good." I opened one eye and looked at the clock. Five forty-five. "But I'm meeting someone at Tigris for dinner in forty-five minutes."

"Really?" Teddie asked as he pulled me to my feet.

"Yeah, I'm having dinner with the Dark Side."

~

ONCE AGAIN SEATED SIDE BY SIDE AT THE BAR IN DELILAH'S, TEDDIE asked the question I was hoping he wouldn't. "Who is the Dark Side?"

"Paxton Dane."

"Oh."

The look on his face made me feel queasy, like I'd kicked a dog or something. "It's business."

"Interesting place for business."

"I won a bet."

"Really?"

"I can't explain. Not until I have a few more answers—" His hand on my arm stopped me.

"You don't have to explain." He smiled, but hurt still clouded his eyes. "Are you coming to the party later?"

"I'll try."

"Good." He pushed backward off the stool. "Maybe I'll see you there."

I watched him walk away.

I guess he'd forgotten about buying me that drink.

❧

RELATIONSHIPS—SO DAMNED DIFFICULT. I COULD HANDLE MY JOB with ease and confidence. My life was a whole other matter.

The Babylon had a sister hotel in Macau—taking any job there was looking really good right now. With time to kill, I wandered toward my office. Miss Patterson should go home, and I needed to think about what corner of the office would become Brandy's domain.

My two assistants were way ahead of me. They had already moved furniture, pushing Miss Patterson's desk closer to the front door, and clearing a corner near the entrance to my office.

"We ordered a desk, a chair, and some supplies," Miss Patterson announced as I walked in. "The desk can go here." She stood with her back to the wall, her arms extended. "I think it all fits without blocking any of us. What do you think?"

"That's fine." I waved at them as I disappeared into my office. "Whatever makes you guys happy is fine with me."

Unable to sit, I stared glumly out the window at all the happy people below. And this day had started so well...

Miss Patterson stuck her head through the door. "You okay?"

Before I could answer, the outer door burst open. Teddie rushed in, almost knocking Miss Patterson down in the process.

"Sorry." He gently scooted Miss Patterson out of the doorway and pulled the office door shut. Walking over to me, he took my hands in his. "I really mishandled that whole thing in the bar."

I pulled my hands away—I couldn't say what I had to say with my skin on his. "*That* was exactly what I was afraid of. You're my best friend and now you have all these other expectations of me. What if I can't live up to them? Then you won't be my friend anymore?"

Reaching for me, he closed the distance between us.

I crossed my arms and stepped back. "Don't. I can't think straight when you're touching me."

Dropping his arms to his side, he stopped. He didn't have to say anything—I could see it in his eyes.

"I can't think straight when you look at me like that either."

"Don't try so hard, and don't worry so much. You're over-thinking this whole thing."

"Me? Overthink? That's a first." I managed a smile.

"Just relax. Let go."

"That's what men say just before they start working a hand up under my skirt."

"Clearly, you've been hanging out with the wrong men."

Despite my protests, he hugged me tight.

No longer willing to resist, I let him hold me, my head on his shoulder, my arms around his waist.

He felt solid and safe, calming yet exciting, the same yet so very different. How could one kiss have changed so much?

CHAPTER SIXTEEN

*D*ANE WAITED for me just outside the double bronze doors of Tigris.

I watched him from across the casino as he scanned the crowd, then checked his watch. Already purposely ten minutes late, I decided another few minutes of forcing Dane to cool his heels might get him hot under the collar—a distraction I could use.

Paxton Dane was a veritable living, breathing, reminder of the old adage: If something is too good to be true, it usually is. Tonight, he sported a pair of fitted, creased jeans, a plaid button-down under a camel blazer, a flash of gold on the wrist, and those expensive-looking kickers.

Wavy brown hair begged fingers to run through it. Emerald eyes softened the sharp planes of his face. Full lips, normally curved in wry amusement, now were pulled tight by anger. He wore a look of self-awareness—he was a hunk and he knew it.

I bet Dane hadn't been turned down by a female since grade school.

Good thing I no longer had that libido problem.

Anger flashed in Dane's eyes as I walked up, then he hid it

behind a forced smile. "There you are. You know, they'll only hold our reservation for fifteen minutes."

"I'm really sorry. This job of mine!" I shook my head as I hooked my arm through his.

If he could pretend to be a good guy, I could pretend to be happy to see him.

He visibly relaxed as he escorted me through the bronze doors into another world. The ceilings low, the lighting subtle, Tigris commanded the top of a very short list of exquisite five-star restaurants in Vegas.

Silk carpets in bright colors hung in loops from the ceiling, tightly woven straw mats covered mahogany floors, burnished to a dark shine, palm trees grew from patches of sandy soil—a Vegas interpretation of a sultan's luxurious tent. Torches, real flame under glass, lit the path through the tables. Sumerian treasures adorned the walls. Somewhere, there was a very early Greek reproduction of the Code of Hammurabi, but I didn't see it as we followed a young woman to our table next to the window.

In contrast to the slick elegance of most top restaurants, the tables in Tigris were made of intricate inlaid mosaic. The glassware was sturdy and blue. Omer, the culinary genius in charge of Tigris, was an unknown, self-taught, Turkish chef when The Big Boss had found him slaving away at a very nice restaurant in Oman.

Now the toast of Vegas, Omer was no longer little known.

Roham, our waiter tonight, waited at my chair with a big grin. "Miss O'Toole, so good to see you!"

I let him seat me. "I see they haven't sent you back to Iran."

"Not yet," he said. His smile lit his dark eyes. "You want Wild Turkey, neat." A statement, not a question. He nodded at Dane. "May I offer you a beverage?"

"Bring me a Bud in a cold glass."

"Ah, Budweiser—full-bodied, with a delicate bouquet and light finish. We recommend that in a pairing with the sea bass tonight —most excellent."

A smile tugging at one side of his mouth, Dane watched Roham retreat. "Friend of yours?"

"Acquaintance. Why?"

"Same sense of humor." Dane shook out his napkin and placed it in his lap. "Is he really from Iran? Aren't we at war with them or something?"

"Not yet. And he's an American citizen, born in Phoenix to Iranian parents. Roham enjoys pretending he's the real deal—the girls find it 'exotic and dangerous'—his words, not mine."

"You seem to know a lot about him."

"You'd be amazed at what I know."

If Dane had a guilty conscience, that didn't prick it. He was either very good, or totally amoral. Neither of those gave me warm fuzzies.

Fishing for a foothold, I said, "Thanks for backing me up on the cat this morning."

"Our secret." He opened his menu, then looked at me over the top of it. "Do you know what you want already?"

"No." Nervous, I played with my forks. "I usually let Roham order for me."

"Really?" Dane scanned down the menu. "I don't even know what some of this stuff is. He could bring you eye of newt and hair of frog and you'd never know."

"Not if he knows what's good for him." I forced myself to quit playing with the flatware. Instead, I folded my hands in my lap. "You, on the other hand, have already offended his sensibilities with your Bud, so I'd be careful."

He returned to scanning his menu for a moment, then snapped it shut. "There's only one thing to do."

"And that is?"

"Throw myself on your mercy and hope that Roham will treat me kindly," he stated, still avoiding my eyes.

"Coward."

Dane grinned. "Could you just make sure that, whatever he brings me, I can identify it?"

I assumed he could identify sheep's eyes and the pigs' penises (apparently both delicacies), but I didn't think that was what he had in mind.

Roham returned with our drinks—mine he set before me with a flourish, Dane's he held between two fingers, a look of disgust on his face.

"Would you quit?" I laughed. "It's not like he's the first Texan you've served."

"Texas! The Lone Star State?" A smile split Roham's face. His black eyes danced with merriment. "I knew a girl from Texas once. She...how do you say it?" He thought for a moment, then announced, "I know! She filled my hands!"

Dane stared at him blankly.

I burst out laughing—that visual thing again. "I think you mean she was a handful."

"Yes! That's it!" His grin disappeared as his brows crinkled. "That's not what I said?" The kid had the whole Iranian, English-is-my-second-language charade down pat. I wondered if he'd ever thought of doing stand-up.

"Almost, but not quite."

Roham gestured toward Dane and spoke as if he couldn't hear. "Who is this man, this Texan, to you?"

"This is Mr. Dane. He works in Security."

"So sorry, I thought maybe this dinner wasn't business." Roham's face fell as he bowed his head slightly toward Dane. "My pleasure. I am Roham."

"The pleasure is all mine," Dane said, with a trace of a smile.

My thoughts whirled as I struggled against falling into an easy camaraderie with him. Something about the whole bum thing didn't feel right. Maybe my libido was leading me astray again, but smart men like Dane were usually as adept as women with a few bums under their belts at sniffing out creeps like Irv Gittings.

"Roham, why don't you bring me the sea bass and Mr. Dane a steak? Salads to start?"

"You are not trusting Roham tonight?" He sounded offended.

"I'm not feeling very adventurous. No offense."

Roham gave me the eye, then turned to Dane and asked, "Mr. Texas, how would you like your steak prepared?"

"Rare."

"Very good."

"And your sea bass?" he asked me.

"Not rare."

Grumbling, but apparently satisfied, he left us.

Outside the window, the hanging gardens and their many waterfalls beckoned—a lush oasis in the desert. Like wild animals clustered around a single pool of freshwater, our guests jostled and jousted for a prime position, angling their chairs so the last ray of sunlight landed on their already bronzed skin. Servers darted between guests, their trays laden with frozen tropical drinks (minus the little umbrellas—The Big Boss hated those things), plates of mouthwatering fruit and bowls of sorbets and ice creams—all designed to sooth and refresh.

Still hours away, nightfall would change the whole feel of the gardens. As the sun disappeared over the horizon, pulling its trailing rays after it, peace would descend on the gardens. Birds would coo in the treetops as they prepared to rest for the night. Under the soft light, lovers would stroll hand in hand along the pathways under the lush vegetation, seeking the darkened corners or private pools.

"You didn't answer his question."

"What question?" I asked, still imagining lovers strolling through the gardens, safe from view, hidden by a cloak of darkness. So real was my imagining, I almost had to blink my eyes

255

against the brightness of the day as I fought to bring Dane into focus.

"What I am to you." Dane took a swig of his beer straight from the bottle. Roham had neglected to bring a glass.

"Now, that's a good question, isn't it?"

The rapt attention of an incredibly good-looking man, and I didn't feel a thing. For once, my body had not only received my brain memo about Dane, it actually listened. I leaned over the table. "Look around you. Do you see this place, these people?"

"Sure." A quizzical expression replaced his smile. "And your point is?"

"This is my home. These people are all my family—The Big Boss especially. He took me in and gave me a chance when no one else would."

"You still haven't made your point."

"I'll see you in hell before I let you or anybody jeopardize them."

"Why would you think I would do that?" He leaned over, putting a hand on top of mine, his eyes like green lasers locked onto mine. "Aren't you forgetting I work here, too?"

His hand on mine, and still I felt nothing. "You may work here, but you spend a fair amount of time with the competition."

"The competition?" His voice mocked me.

"Irv Gittings."

As if singed by a name, he jerked his hand away. "Why the hell would you think that?" His anger didn't completely hide his surprise.

"Because you visit him on a regular basis."

"How do you know that?"

"This is Vegas—you can find out anything if you know who to ask." I watched him working hard to control his temper. "What I can't figure out is, are you a good witch or a bad witch?"

"Look, I didn't want to lie to you, but I wasn't sure who I could trust."

"You said that before—after your first lie, right before your second." I placed my napkin on the table and stood to leave. "All I want to know is whose side are you on? Apparently, you aren't going to tell me. If that's the case, this dinner is over."

"Want to fill me in on those e-mails Irv's been sending to you? Those were pretty remarkable e-mails, by the way." Dane looked up at me, accusation in his eyes. "If you tell me what you two are planning, perhaps I can get the district attorney to go easy on you."

"What?" I said, my voice raised in indignation, the white-hot heat of fury barely contained. I felt rather than saw heads turn in our direction. "How dare you! Did you see any replies?"

"Only one." He glanced nervously around. "Would you sit down? Everyone is staring."

"And what was my reply?" My voice was low, cold. My eyes all slitty. The son of a bitch.

"I'm paraphrasing here, but pretty much you told him to go to hell—in a nice way, of course." He tossed the line off as if he didn't put any credence in my response.

"Of course, always the lady, just like my mother taught me to be," I sneered. "So, let me get this straight. You accuse me of the most vile form of betrayal imaginable based solely on several e-mails from Irv, which you took at face value. Yet, you declined to give the same consideration to my response, because it refuted what you wanted to believe—that I was a traitor to those I hold dear?"

Dane eyed me calmly, his arms crossed over his chest.

For once, I was glad the steak knife was out of my reach.

"Irv's e-mails implied you two were negotiating—he kept upping the ante. For all I know, you could have been meeting him somewhere."

I was standing there, my face flushed, my breathing rapid, weighing the punishment for homicide against the benefits, when Cindy, the head cocktail waitress, tapped me on the shoulder.

"Ms. O'Toole, if you're looking for the ladies room, head toward the bar and hang a left. It's down the hall on your right."

"Thanks, but I'm not looking for the bathroom," I said. "I'm debating whether to throw my drink on my dinner partner or just leave with my dignity intact. The latter would be classier, but the first option would be so much more satisfying. What do you think? The drink in his face or the high road?"

A smile tugged at the corner of the girl's mouth as she put a hand on her hip and gave Dane the once-over. "Good-lookin' guys are the worst, but no reason to sacrifice your dignity, you know."

"So, the high road?"

"Yeah, don't give him the satisfaction." With that, she stuck her nose in the air, whirled on her heels, and retreated to the bar.

"I'm beginning to understand the term 'rapier wit,'" Dane said with a grimace.

"Anger sharpens it to a fine point," I snarled.

"Would you sit down? People are watching," Dane asked again.

"You said that before." I looked around the room. Nobody would meet my eye. "Do you think I give a rat's ass?"

"You are the most difficult woman." Dane took a deep breath then let it out. "Look, I've missed a lot in this investigation—there's a bunch about Vegas I don't understand. And, I've gotten a girl killed. So please, sit, listen to me." He tugged my hand. "I was wrong about you in the beginning. Tonight, I wanted to punch your buttons, see how you reacted. Look at it from my position—"

"Everyone's guilty until proven innocent?" Tired of being the center of attention and secretly afraid someone would call Security—which would be rather interesting, but not exactly what I wanted to deal with right now, I sat back down and refolded my napkin in my lap.

"I walked in here cold—I didn't know who I could trust, so I trusted no one." Dane sighed and ran his fingers through his wavy hair. Under the facade he presented, he looked worn out, ragged around the edges. "I would like the chance to tell you the truth—I hope you believe me."

"I'll listen, but if I get even a whiff of bullshit, I'm outta here."

"I understand your feelings—" Dane started.

"Patronizing a woman hovering on the brink of homicide is not wise."

He took a deep breath and glanced around at the people near us. "I'm one of the good guys."

His timing impeccable, Roham interrupted with our salads, which he placed before us with a flourish. "Would you like fresh ground pepper?"

We both shook our heads. Neither one of us picked up a fork as we watched him walk away. And then, as if all the lights of understanding lit in my head at once, all the pieces of the puzzle came together, and I saw it whole for the first time.

"You work undercover for the Gaming Control Board," I said when we were again alone.

Dane looked at me for a moment. Was he weighing whether to tell me the truth, or inventing another lie? "How'd you know?"

"I didn't, and I still don't know it for sure—if you think I'm going to take your word for it, then I got a bridge in Brooklyn to sell you. But it fits." I picked up my fork and attacked my salad. "I'll check out your story tomorrow."

"Check away." Dane crinkled his brow. "Fits with what?"

"The Control Board knew about the irregularities at the Athena—"

"How did you—?" Dane interrupted.

"This is Vegas..."

"You can find out anything if you know who to ask," he finished my sentence.

"Anyway," I continued. "If they knew about the fancy book-keeping and no arrests had been made, then it figures they have an investigator in place."

I forked in another bite of salad. I never knew goat cheese, pine nuts, pears and avocado, all on a bed of tender baby spinach and dripped in balsamic vinaigrette worked so well together. "Lyda Sue tipped you guys off, then she became your insider."

"Did she tell you that?"

I shook my head. "She didn't have to. She was in line for a management job at a hotel on the Strip. I'm guessing it was the Athena. But she had a problem—a less than stellar background. The Big Boss was helping her fix that."

"Fix it?" Dane cocked one eyebrow at me.

"Erase it, change it. Why should Lyda Sue be punished for a bad choice circumstances forced on her when she was a kid?"

"I'll overlook the obvious illegality of tampering with state records."

"Sometimes—"

"You need to do the wrong thing for the right reasons?" Again, Dane completed my sentence. I wasn't sure I liked it.

"Lyda Sue met you out at Mona's place, didn't she?"

He nodded.

"So, how come you were surprised she was a former hooker?" I asked. "One would suspect that anyone who had intimate knowledge of a whorehouse used to work there."

"She told me the madam was the mother of a friend of hers. I had no reason not to believe her—and it wasn't important enough to check out anyway," Dane said, as he concentrated on pushing the spinach leaves around his plate.

After polishing off the last bite of my salad, I shoved my plate to the side. *Some friend I turned out to be.* "Irv got wise to The Big Boss and Lyda Sue—Willie probably told Felicia, who took it to Irv."

"How would Willie know?" Dane was clearly interested in the story now.

"He sat in Security every time he waited to fly."

Dane nodded as the light dawned. "If you have access to Security, you have access to the world. You see a lot of stuff."

"Felicia has worked here a long time—long enough to know Lyda Sue's former profession. Irv used it to blackmail Lyda Sue into getting The Big Boss on that helicopter." I smiled and shook my head. "I'd even be willing to bet she told The Big Boss the whole scheme as she knew it, and he agreed to play along, hoping to turn the tables on Ol' Irv."

"So, did Irv plot the murder or was it Felicia Reilly?" Dane asked.

"That we don't know—not without Miss Reilly."

"She's long gone," Dane said, then waited while Roham delivered fresh drinks and whisked away the empties. "She didn't strike me as stupid—she's smart enough to know she's up shit creek without a paddle."

"Maybe so, but it's hard to go far without any cash."

"How do you know she's short on cash?"

"Let's just say I've made an educated guess."

Dane took a sip of beer, his eyes never leaving mine. "You know where she is?"

"I'm working on that."

"You're not going to tell me?"

I held his gaze. "No."

Roham interrupted the tension with our dinner. We both sat in silence as he placed our plates in front of us, then removed the covers with a flourish. My mouth watered at the aroma rising from the sea bass. One bite and I knew the master himself had assisted in the preparation.

When we were alone again, I asked Dane, "Did The Big Boss know you were playing both sides?"

"No, but to his credit, he didn't trust me. He made you my keeper. I'll have to remember to thank him for that." Dane forked in a bite of the bloodiest piece of steak I'd ever seen, a look of gustatory delight on his face.

"Does cannibalism run in your family?"

"No? We're Methodists," he said. "Why?"

I motioned to the steak.

"Oh, it's a Texas thing."

As I settled into my meal, I said, "Why don't you tell me about Texas?"

~

WE LINGERED OVER THE EXQUISITE FOOD. OMER WOULD HAVE HAD my head if I'd rushed, so it was a good thing Dane was a fairly adept conversationalist—for a Texan. And he could spin the tale tall about three boys growing up in west Texas.

Dane polished off dessert and two cups of fully leaded coffee, both of which would have kept me awake into next week. I watched in awe.

Finally, when the plates were cleared, I rose to go and said, "Come with me. I need to make a quick trip through the kitchen."

Dane followed as I burst through the kitchen doors. "Omer! What a feast! You outdid yourself once again."

The rotund chef bristled with pride. He bowed his head, acknowledging my praise.

"And Roham—a delight as always." I turned and applauded the entire staff in the kitchen. "Bravo to all and many thanks."

Dane again trailed in my wake as I made my way through the bar, calling each of the wait staff and bartenders by name. I paused at the hostess stand to add a tip to the bill and sign it.

"Do you know everybody in this hotel?" Dane whispered.

"Almost. These folks are my family"

"Hey, the dinner was supposed to be on me," Dane said, when he realized what I was doing.

"Tonight it's on The Big Boss. I figure he owes us."

"How so? He's still in up to his eyeballs." Dane reached for my hand.

I shook my head and put my hands in my pockets as we

pushed out the doors and into the barely controlled chaos of another night just getting underway in the casino.

"He's in the clear—at least that's what Willie told the police."

Dane stopped midstride, then he shook his head and chuckled. "You really play your cards close to the vest, don't you?"

I didn't feel the need to answer. The question was probably rhetorical anyway.

"So, what about Felicia Reilly?" Dane put a hand on my elbow, steering me through the crowd. "What do we do about her?"

"I have a plan, but I need to work on it a bit before I tell you."

"Still don't trust me?"

"Would you trust you if you were me?"

"Somewhere in that fractured syntax lurks a good question." Dane's lips curled into a smile, this time one that actually reached his eyes. "And my answer would be no; I wouldn't trust me if I were you."

At least he'd dropped the lying thing.

"So, you left Pahrump when you were fifteen?" Dane maneuvered me around the blackjack tables toward the rear doors.

"If you really must know?"

"I must."

"I'll give you the short history of Lucky O'Toole, then I want to talk about something else. I moved here when I was fifteen and started working for The Big Boss as a cabana girl. Worked my way up from there. Got a college degree. Kept moving up the food chain."

"And your mother?"

"She waved good-bye as I left."

"I see."

He didn't see at all, but I didn't want to discuss it. What kind of mother would let her fifteen-year-old daughter move to Vegas, lie about her age, and go to work every day in a bikini?

"Any other family?"

"You got the short history. Now, pick another topic."

"Okay." Dane stood and extended his hand. "Let's walk."

Again, I ignored his proffered hand. "A walk would be good, then I need to hit the trade show opening."

"Trade show?"

"In conjunction with the adult movie awards. Sex-a-Rama. You might want to come; I understand Miranda's doing a pole dance."

He shot me a pained look. "I think I've reached my humiliation quota for the week."

~

WE DECIDED ON A STROLL THROUGH THE HANGING GARDENS. DUSK diffused the sunlight into gossamer shimmers that filtered through the leaves of the trees high above. A few straggling sun worshipers, either desperate to catch the waning sunlight or comatose after an afternoon of margaritas, lay prostrate on the lounge chairs in the few remaining pockets of sunlight. Soon, the shadows would chase them inside.

The deck hands and cabana girls busied themselves with cleanup. One cocktail waitress wandered through the dwindling crowd.

"Can I ask you a personal question?" Dane said.

"Another one?" I bent down to retrieve a plastic cup from under one of the chairs. "One was your quota."

"What's up with you and Theodore?"

I searched for a trash can and disposed of the cup.

"Avoiding the question?" he asked when I returned.

"No, formulating an answer."

We sat on boulders next to one of the waterfalls. The sound of cascading water had a primal effect on me—I could sit for hours listening to the gurgles and crashes as if the water could wash my soul clean. Trailing my fingers through the cool water, I smiled at its sensuous feel as it tripped past.

"I really don't know what's up with Teddie and me."

"That's not an answer, that's evasion."

"No, it's honesty," I replied. "Teddie is my best friend, but he wants to be more. I don't know if I can handle that."

"So, you're still fair game?"

CHAPTER SEVENTEEN

*T*HIS YEAR, the organizers of Sex-a-Rama had titled the show, "The State Fair." Being fairly provincial, I couldn't imagine a state fair focused on fornication, but one thing was certain—if they had any farm animals in there, I was leaving.

A man in a leather G-string, boots and mask, with a whip tied at his waist, greeted Dane and me at the door. "Your names?"

I tried to remain focused on the S&M guy's eyes, but I was having my troubles. All rippling muscle—buff, polished and denuded—his body begged to be stared at—and touched. I resisted that part. "O'Toole and guest."

This was a private party, so the guest list would be relatively short—hundreds rather than thousands—I took solace in that. My name associated with this bang fest probably put me on some FBI list of perverts. At the very least, I was sure my presence earned me a black mark on my soul.

The sadist or masochist—I never could keep the two of those straight—checked his clipboard, and motioned us inside.

We pushed through the slit in the curtains covering the doorway—no peeping Toms allowed at this peep show. A stage on risers commanded the center of the room. Half of a Ferris wheel, complete with hanging chairs, arced over it, attached by a single pole rising out of the center of the stage. A wall of speakers, pumping out a pulsating rhythm, formed the backdrop.

Drinks in hand, people wandered the hall in various stages of undress. The ones angling to catch the eyes of a movie producer were the easiest to spot—siliconed, sculpted, and swathed in spandex and Lycra and fake tans. Knots of people gathered around celebrities, most of whom were there to pitch products or their latest celluloid adventure.

"What's through there?" asked Dane, nodding toward an arched doorway to the right of the stage. Above it a large banner announced The Midway.

"All manner of toys and games, I would suspect." I extended my arm in that direction. "Shall we?"

We ducked under the arch and joined the flow of people wandering from booth to booth.

"I think we're overdressed," Dane said, as his head swiveled to catch the rear view of a young woman, her breasts like ripe fruit under her wet T-shirt, as she passed. "That woman's shirt is completely see-through."

"The invitation did say 'clothing optional.'"

Danes head swiveled back to me, his eyes huge. "Really?"

I nodded as I tried not to look at him, focusing instead on the products displayed in the first booth. Big mistake.

As I surveyed the devices on the table, a lady who could've been the pre-makeover Miss Patterson's sister picked one up and said, "Honey, this little lovely will rock your world."

"You think?" About ten inches long with a fork at the end, the thing looked more like something a shaman would use to divine the location of water than a pleasure device. The forks, one longer and thicker than the other and strategically curved, ended in bristled rubber nubs.

"Watch," the lady said as she flipped a switch. "This will hit all of your pleasure points. You can do yourself."

"Where's the fun in that?" I groused, as I grudgingly watched. The rubber nubs twirled and the whole thing vibrated. All it lacked was a pulsing red light and a siren.

Dane appeared at my elbow. "Did you know there's a whole army of women wandering around who make that T-shirt girl seem dressed for the prom? This place is amazing." He glanced down at the table. "What're you doing?"

"Here." The lady thrust the device at Dane. "It's great for foreplay."

"What am I supposed to do to it?" Dane asked, a twinkle in his eye.

I laughed and pushed him on down the aisle. One booth halfway down on the other side caught my attention. "Oh, I like this one," I said as I got a good look. "It's just like the water guns at the fair when I was a kid."

Only the guns were shaped like erect penises, the testicles forming the grip. When you squeezed hard, water shot out of the end, inflating the balloon end of the condom attached over the penis-gun. The harder you squeezed, the larger the volume of water squirting and inflating the condom—the person holding the first one to break won.

"New game's starting," announced the hawker—a woman who looked to be barely legal—clad only in a thong.

"Want to play?" I asked Dane, as I grabbed one of the two open guns.

"I can't," he said, as he shook his head. "There's something about squeezing that thing's balls…"

"Yeah, it's fun." I grinned, then turned to focus on the battle.

A bell rang, and we were off. Two guys on the end were ahead early, their condoms expanding at an alarming rate. The blonde to my right and the redhead to my left and I grinned at each other and squeezed as hard as we could. We caught the guys and left them in the dust.

I braced myself for the inevitable explosion, but it didn't come

—the balloon on the end of my gun growing to the size of a basketball. Who knew a condom could stretch that far?

And who would need it to?

When I thought it wasn't possible for the thin rubber to expand further, mine burst—seconds ahead of the redhead's. Everyone put down their guns and congratulated me. Ever gracious in victory, I raised my arms and did a Rocky-esque dance.

The young lady, wearing little more than a big smile, awarded me my prize—a box of thirty-six Always Ready glow-in-the-dark condoms, size large—for the "big guy."

I clutched them to my chest and turned to Dane. "I won!"

"So I see." He grinned at me.

"I have no idea what I'm going to do with these." I looked at the picture on the cover of the box. "Seriously, glow in the dark?" I fought back the image of a dark room, a glowing, disembodied penis...

Dane laughed and started to say something, but I cut him off.

"Not a word out of you." I looked around. "Have you seen a bar? I could use a drink."

We found the bar along the back wall, bracketed by huge, free-standing edifices erected by the film companies, complete with giant screens showing trailers for upcoming releases. Young, buxom women and well-muscled men, all of them shirtless, signed autographs for their adoring fans.

Dane dove into the crowd at the bar and reappeared with two glasses of wine, one of which he handed to me. "This looks interesting," he said, as he motioned to one of the overhead screens. "God, there isn't enough pubic hair there to cover a mouse."

"Miranda told me wax jobs like that are all the rage." I watched the pile of writhing flesh. Four bodies, and I counted two penises, two choochilalas, and three sets of boobs. "Aw, same old stuff—I've seen it all before," I said, as I took a sip of my wine. "Come on, we haven't tried the Emporium."

"What do you think we'll find in here?" Dane asked as we ducked inside.

"Lotions and potions."

A mirror image of the Midway, the Emporium also consisted of rows of booths. However, unlike the sex-toy folks, who let their devices sell themselves, the lotion and potion purveyors usually hired stars to hawk their products. Needless to say, the crowd had packed in pretty tight.

The largest gathering arced around a booth hawking "Wonder Woodie Crème." Pushing through the throng, we found Subway Jones holding court.

Brandishing a small tub of crème, he addressed the throng. "Men, do you want to be ready in a hurry?" Subway put his hand to his ear. "I can't hear you! Want to be ready in a hurry?"

A chorus of male voices shouted, "Yes!"

"Ladies, does your man have the stamina you crave?" Again he put his hand to his ear and waited.

The ladies shouted, "No!"

"I guarantee you both can have what you want!" He thrust the tub of goo in the air. "Wonder Woodie Crème is the answer! Male enhancement in three seconds, guaranteed! This stuff works! I should know." He winked and rocked his hips suggestively. "Buy three for the price of two and get a photograph of good old me and Wonder Woodie Crème in action. I'll personalize it for you."

The crowd went wild and almost all of them bellied up to the table, money in hand. Subway stepped aside, letting them pass, then he moved our way.

"I thought they outlawed snake oil salesmen years ago," Dane whispered as Subway approached.

"Lucky!" Subway grabbed me, twirling me around. "How ya doin'? Don't you want an autograph?"

"Only if you sign my panties."

"You know I don't do underwear." Subway gave me a devilish grin.

"Bummer."

"Where's Theodore? I thought he'd be with you," Subway asked, as he gave Dane the once-over.

"He said he might see me here." I resisted the temptation to explain Dane's presence. "You haven't seen him?"

"I saw him earlier. He was looking for you."

Dane nodded to the product Subway still clutched. "Does that stuff really work?"

"Sex happens between the ears." Subway answered with a shrug. "If you think it works, then it usually does."

"What works?" Miranda asked as she materialized at Subway's shoulder. "Hi, handsome," she cooed to Dane.

He actually blushed. "I was asking your husband about his product."

Sidling up to Dane, she put her hand on his arm and leaned against him. "Did you know Wonder Woodie comes in flavors? I really like the passion fruit."

"Knock it off, Miranda," I said.

"Why?" She gave me a wicked grin. "Have you already laid claim to him?"

I narrowed my eyes at her—a feeble attempt at delay while I struggled to formulate a pithy reply.

Pointing to the box I held, she asked, "What's that?"

"I won a prize."

"How lucky."

"No, how Miranda? I thought of you when they gave it to me." I held it out to her. "My gift to you. It's not much—you'll probably go through the whole box in under an hour."

She looked at it then purred, "Honey, even I'm not *that* good."

"Strangely, I'm comforted by that." Hooking my arm through Dane's, I said to him, "Come on. Let's leave these two to their...business."

"You *are* going to stay for my dance?" Miranda asked, a subtle pleading in her voice.

"We'll be there." I pulled Dane into the crowd.

And came face to face with the cat-pee lady.

I managed a stiff smile. "Oh, Ms. Hetherington. Nice to see you."

She wore the same stretched expression, but the outfit looked different. The faint aroma of cat urine still clung to her—or maybe I imagined it.

"I know you." She gave me the eye. "You're the lady who wouldn't let me keep my cats."

"Guilty as charged." I motioned to Dane standing at my side. "This is Mr. Dane, one of our Security team. He helped search for your cats. Dane, this is Ms. Hetherington."

"Ma'am." Dane nodded, but didn't extend his hand.

"Are you enjoying the party?" I asked her. If she didn't know she now owned two cats instead of three, I sure wasn't going to break the news to her—at least not here and not now.

"My husband and I are working it." She grabbed Dane's hand. "*You,* come with me."

Dane threw a "rescue me" look my direction as he allowed himself to be dragged down the aisle.

He was a big boy—I had no doubt he could handle the Ms. Hetheringtons of the world by himself. The crowd had almost swallowed them when I reluctantly followed.

Shoulder to shoulder they stood in front of a booth, which, according to the banner above it, sold Klimaxx—a pleasure enhancer for both sexes.

Great, not only could I buy a gizmo to "do myself" as the lady had so delicately put it; if that didn't work, I could buy an orgasm in a bottle. I wondered what they'd come up with next—actually, after a moment's thought, I didn't think I really wanted to know.

Ms. Hetherington held tightly to Dane's arm as she addressed the man behind the counter. "Honey, this is Mr. Dane. He's interested in our product."

So the bigwig Ms. Hetherington had threatened me with

wasn't a bigwig at all—he was nothing more than a man who sold what looked like dried grass clippings to the sexually frustrated.

There was a god.

I shouldered in next to Dane.

"Here." Ms. Hetherington thrust two tubes of gel at me. "This is our other product—sexual lubricant, one for him, one for her."

I held one tube in one hand, one in the other. "You need two?"

She gave me a wink and a conspiratorial nudge with her elbow. "When these two gels mix, there's a chemical reaction—instant heat that really lights your fire."

"Like peeling jalapeños then touching your eyes?" I asked as I handed the tubes back to her.

Dane grabbed my elbow, dragging me away before she went for my throat.

"That stuff reminds me too much of epoxy," I said, as we wandered down the aisle, dodging nearly naked young women and men and those more fully clothed who followed them. "Don't you remember as a kid watching your parents mix that stuff—two tubes of goo that when mixed formed a glue so strong it could hold the space shuttle together?"

"Probably not the image they're looking for, but I know what you mean. My brother glued himself to Sally Wiler when they were both ten. She wasn't pleased."

"Really? I think I'd like your brother. Did young Sally ever forgive him?"

"She married him."

"A guy who likes you so much he glues himself to you *would* be hard to resist."

"I'll have to remember that," Dane said, as he took hold of my elbow, steering me through the crowd.

We wandered a while longer. The products were interesting, but the people were the real show. Around each corner, I looked for Teddie, but I never found him. Where could he be?

At the stroke of eleven, a voice over the loudspeakers encouraged us to assemble in front of the stage for Miranda's show. She didn't perform often—she no longer had to—so tonight was a special treat, eagerly anticipated by aficionados of this sort of thing.

I wasn't one of them.

However, I'd told Miranda I would be there, so Dane and I joined the throng as they chanted, "Miranda! Miranda!"

The lights went dark. The music started—the volume so loud, each note shot right through me, turning my innards to jelly. A single spotlight flashed on, its beam capturing Miranda dressed in the top part of a nurse's uniform. Trapped in the beam of light, Miranda wiggled and writhed—presenting various body parts for the crowd—which roared its approval. Periodically, she shed an article of clothing, whipping the throng to a fevered pitch.

She really did have something special.

Dane stared, transfixed by the show.

Me? I just wanted to go home. "I'll see you tomorrow. I'm going home," I shouted at him, my voice competing with the seductive beat.

His mouth half open, he glanced at me and nodded, then turned back to the show.

∼

WHERE WAS TEDDIE?

I ducked out through the curtains and past the leather-clad guy with the clipboard, then flipped open my cell and pushed number two on the speed dial. My call immediately rolled to Teddie's voice mail. Even his recorded voice made me go all melty inside.

I had it bad.

Slowly, I closed the phone without leaving a message.

He wasn't at the party. He wasn't answering his phone. I glanced at my watch—eleven thirty—early yet.

Maybe he'd left me a note at the office.

That idea propelled me through the casino—I barely registered the crowds at the tables, the quiet throngs in the poker room concentrating on the game as if it wasn't a game of chance, the bubbling of happy voices at the bar, the choking cigarette smoke.

I had almost made it to the other side when I heard my name shouted above the noise. Turning, I scanned the crowd.

Mr. Pascarelli emerged from a row of slot machines, a hand raised trying to flag me down. "Glad I caught you," he said as he arrived, huffing and puffing, by my side. "Velma has something she wants to tell you. Is this a good time? You looked like you were in a big hurry."

"Not at all."

"Good, Velma'll be right along. She was money ahead and had to cash out." A sparkle in his eye, a grin on his face, the man looked like he had a new lease on life.

"You haven't been asking me for a good luck hug recently," I teased. "Have you thrown me over for somebody else?"

His face turned bright pink.

"Good for you!" I said, as Mrs. Paisley appeared at his side.

"Lucky!" she cried as she grabbed my arm. "The best thing has happened!"

"You hit the mega-millions again?"

"Even better." Her eyes were bright with delight. "My grandson got a call today from the director of admissions at Harvard. It seems there had been a mix-up with his application records."

"Really?"

She nodded vigorously. "Not only was he admitted, they awarded him a partial scholarship as well! He's over the moon!"

"That's wonderful!"

She narrowed her eyes at me. "I give you his name and three days later he gets a call? Sure is a coincidence, don't you think?"

"Life's full of funny coincidences."

~

As I KNEW IT WOULD BE, MY OFFICE WAS DARK WHEN I ARRIVED, BUT Miss Patterson had left it unlocked. A good thing, since my keys were in my Birkin, which was in my office.

There was a note taped to the inner door. My heart skipped a beat as I opened it.

It wasn't from Teddie.

In what I assumed was Brandy's handwriting, the note consisted of a list of phone calls I had received, beginning with Detective Romeo and ending with Flash Gordon.

Teddie's name wasn't listed.

Since it was too late to start returning the calls, I opted to head home. Grabbing my phone, I highlighted Jerry's number and pushed-to-talk. "Jer?"

"Hey, Lucky. You heading home?"

"If everything's under control."

"So far." Jerry's voice sounded tired. "We've got a couple of rowdies in the holding cell, but that's about it."

"Night's still young. You know how to find me."

~

I TRIED TEDDIE'S NUMBER AGAIN AS I RODE DOWN IN THE ELEVATOR after locking up the office. Again, it rolled directly to voice mail.

Pocketing the damn phone, I pushed through the front doors into the eternal twilight created by the lights of the Strip. My head low as I hurried down the entranceway, I sought the anonymity of darkness.

Had it only been last night when Teddie met me coming the other direction? Hopeful, I glanced up—no Teddie.

I was alone.

Like the hug of a dear friend, I welcomed the embrace of darkness as the lights of the Strip faded behind me. If I wasn't careful, the comfort of darkness would be the only comfort I would have. Thinking back on my relationship with Teddie, I saw now he had been angling for more than a platonic friendship for some time. I hadn't seen it...no, that wasn't true—I *had* seen it. I hadn't acknowledged it—because I was afraid.

Pushing people away was a bad habit of mine.

Had I managed to push Teddie away as well? The thought of losing him hit me like a sucker punch to the stomach, making it hard to breathe. Lost in thought, I stopped. Somehow, thinking and walking at the same time seemed impossible.

Standing there, in the quiet solitude, fighting the growing ache inside me, I was hit by a blinding flash of truth—somewhere along the way, despite my best efforts not to, I had fallen in love with Ted Kowalski.

And that scared the hell out of me.

I didn't want to be in love—I wanted to be in control.

~

FAITHFUL FORREST MANNED HIS POST AS I STRODE THROUGH THE lobby toward the elevators. "Hey, Ms. Lucky. How was your day?"

How was my day? Good question. I paused to answer him. "Interesting. And yours?"

"Good. Me and my son took the boat out on Lake Mead. Did some skiing, drank some beer. We don't get to do that too often, just the two of us."

"He starts law school in the fall, doesn't he?"

"Yes, ma'am."

"You must be so proud." I made a mental note to ask the home-owners association if there was something we could do to help with the boy's tuition. "Is Teddie home?"

"No, ma'am. He went out some time ago and hasn't come back."

"I see." I pulled my key card out of a pocket in my purse. "Thanks."

The elevator ride seemed interminable—Teddie's absence left a black hole that had sucked all the joy and energy out of the day.

Apparently happy to see me, Newton ran through his whole repertoire of foul epithets as I deposited my purse on the couch and kicked off my shoes. Some of the words I'd never heard before—I could only imagine what they meant. I arrived in front of his cage as he wound down. Face to beak, we stared at each other.

"You'd better be careful. I hear fricassee of parrot is all the rage in the finer culinary establishments this year," I growled because I felt like growling at someone and Newton was the only one handy.

"Asshole."

I resisted the urge to wring his neck and baste his carcass over an open fire. Instead, I busied myself with his food and water. Feeling guilty for my murderous thoughts, I even changed the papers in the bottom of his cage. Somehow, I remembered to clean the coffeepot and fill it for the morning before I staggered off to bed.

As I slipped between the sheets, I thought how nice it would be to find Teddie waiting.

But he wasn't.

I'd never felt so alone.

CHAPTER EIGHTEEN

$\mathcal{A}$ FTER A miserable night's sleep, I rose with the sun. Six a.m. in the shower. Seven a.m. on the road, the Porsche happy to blow some carbon off the plugs. The little car hummed nicely as it settled in at eighty-five on the long, open stretch of highway between Vegas and Pahrump. Born in the same year, my car and I were equally high-maintenance—one of the traits I both admired and hated. Apparently today was one of the Porsche's better days even if it wasn't one of mine.

Although early, the heat of the day radiated from the blacktop. I flipped on the CD player and sang along in Spanish to Luis Miguel's ballads of love and loss, as the road flashed beneath the car.

I didn't want to think. I didn't want to feel. I just wanted to be. At this hour of the morning, Mona's looked abandoned, the parking lot empty, the shades drawn. However, I knew the proprietress would be awake—I'd never known Mother to need more than three or four hours of sleep a night. I parked the car, made sure I locked it, then bounded up the steps and through the unlocked door. Mother rarely slept, and Mona's never closed.

Following the lure of wonderful aromas, I found the kitchen staff busy with breakfast preparations.

Trudi, a whippet-thin lady who'd run the staff for years, noticed me first. "Miss Lucky! Your mother didn't tell us you were coming."

"She doesn't know." I snagged a piece of bacon from a big platter next to the stove. One bite and I groaned in delight. "Crispy! Just the way I like it." I held the remaining piece of bacon aloft. "This is why I could never be a vegetarian."

The staff rewarded me with a few grins.

"We're just finishing your mother's tray," Trudi said. "She was expecting it ten minutes ago, and you know how she is without her coffee."

"Let me take it. I don't mind wading into the line of fire." Grabbing the tray from the counter, I smiled at the white linen tea towel under china and crystal. "Guess we're still doing the Southern-belle thing."

Trudi answered with a tired smile. "Would you like a plate?"

"If it's not too much trouble." Holding the tray in both hands, I used my butt to push open the swinging door that separated the kitchen from the rest of the house. "Could I get extra bacon—perhaps as hazardous duty pay?"

"Sure. I'll bring it up in a minute."

Mother's suite occupied the attic of the old Victorian. After hiking the four flights of stairs, I paused to catch my breath, then used my foot to knock on the door.

"Come!" Even this early, my mother's voice had an edge to it.

"Don't shoot. I come bearing gifts." Balancing the tray on one knee, I freed one hand, turned the knob, and pushed open the door.

Mona sat cross-legged on the floor in the middle of the room, hundreds of old photographs scattered around her. Wearing short-shorts, a tank top, no bra, and no makeup, she looked so young…and sad. Focused on a picture in her hand, she didn't look up when I entered.

"Hey, Mother. Where would you like your tray?"

"Oh!" Her head turned away from me, she wiped at her eyes with the heel of one hand, then turned toward me, her face in the shadows. "Nobody told me you were coming, dear!"

"Good to see you, too, Mother." I proffered the tray. "Where do you want this?"

She pointed to a small round table with two chairs in front of one of the dormer windows.

"Don't be mad at your staff—they couldn't tell you what they didn't know." I poured a cup of coffee from the carafe. "Milk, no sugar, right?"

Mona nodded and stayed where she was on the floor. "Come, sit with me."

The room took me back—the four-poster bed covered with the same floral Laura Ashley print that also covered the walls—my mother's own secret garden. A memory of me as a little girl, lounging on Mother's bed—the two of us chatting like the best of friends—chased through my head. That had been so long ago.

"Be careful. It's hot." I handed the mug to Mother and sat, Indian style, on the floor next to her. I motioned to the old black-and-white photos. "What's all this?"

"I don't know." Mother surreptitiously swiped at her eyes again. "I guess I needed a trip down memory lane."

I finally got a closer look at my mother—her red eyes, dark circles framing them, her ratty ponytail. "Mother, what's wrong?"

"Remembering old times always makes me sad." She rooted through the pictures, selecting one and handing it to me. "You were about eight there—my little best friend. Life was so simple then."

The photo showed me—all long brown legs, pigtails and a big smile—sitting on a pony. "I remember that pony—blind in one eye and mean as hell. The bugger bit me on the ass—left a scar."

We both smiled at the memory.

"And then this one." She stared at the dog-eared photo in her hand as she took a tentative sip of her coffee.

I leaned over to get a look. "That's my favorite. I have it on my credenza." She handed me the one with Dean Martin, Sammy Davis Jr., Mom, and me.

"Your father took it. Those were happy days." She stared at the picture, transported back to another time.

"What?" I asked when I found my voice. "My father took it? You never told me."

Mother looked up, her eyes coming back into focus. "Oh!" She waved dismissively. "It's not important."

"Maybe not to you. You never told me you even knew who my father was."

"Honey, that's insulting." Mona had made it her life's work to dodge my questions—she'd become quite adept.

"But a hazard of your former profession."

Mona didn't say anything, as if she hadn't heard a word I'd said. Instead, she stared at the photo, lost in the past. Her face had a look I'd never seen before.

"You loved him, didn't you?"

She nodded and her eyes filled—not only with tears, but also with sadness—and pain. "Very much."

"So, what happened?"

"Life got in the way," she said with a sigh. "If I have one regret, and I don't have many—living in the past is useless—I regret letting him go—not fighting harder."

I didn't have to imagine how painful that had been—I saw it, etched in Mother's every feature. It wasn't hard to figure out what had happened. What family would want their son to bring home a young woman with nothing more than raw beauty and an irrepressible spirit, who lived on the streets and sold herself to survive? With no education and no family, she must've been the barest hint of the vibrant, adult personality she would become. The two of them hadn't had a chance.

Reaching out, I grabbed her hand and squeezed. "I'm so sorry."

"We were young. We thought we could change the world." She looked up at me, her eyes shone with intensity. A single tear streaked down each cheek. "If love finds you, hang on tight, child. Your father and I thought we'd get another chance. We were wrong."

I leaned back on my hands and looked at her. "That's what you've done all these years? You've waited?"

She shrugged and wiped at her eyes. "The memories with him were always better than reality with somebody else."

"Wow." Didn't Mother just tell me living in the past was useless? I thought about asking her who he was, this man who had stolen her heart, then abandoned the mother of his child, but she'd wallowed in grief long enough. She wouldn't tell me anyway. Despite all my questions through the years, she had steadfastly refused to answer.

When I was younger, I thought my father's identity would provide a critical key to my own. Now, I realized he didn't matter at all. As Mother said, living in the past is useless. Strangely though, I found comfort in the fact that I was born out of love and wasn't the product of poor protection.

I forced a smile. "So, what prompted this little blast from the past?"

Mona took a deep breath, composing herself. She sat up straight and surveyed the room. "I've been thinking about redecorating. Laura Ashley is so seventies, don't you think?"

I reached over to the nightstand, grabbed a tissue from the box, and handed it to her. "Awful lot of memories in this room," I said. "Maybe it's time you cleaned house—banished the ghosts, so to speak."

"That's what I was trying to do when I came across that damned box of old pictures." Mona wiped her eyes.

We both jumped at the soft knock on the door.

Trudi poked her head in. "I brought two plates—I figured you would start talking and forget about the food."

"You were right." I jumped to my feet and relieved her of the heavy tray. "Thanks."

"There's a fresh pot of coffee there, too." She picked up the old tray and disappeared out the door.

"Come on, Mother. A little food should put a smile on your face—it always does with me."

"You always were a big eater." Mona brought her now cold coffee, warmed it from the new carafe, and joined me.

Mother and daughter, we sat by the window at the little table with the Laura Ashley skirt and the matching upholstered chairs, as we had done so many times before. I remembered when my feet didn't even touch the floor. The same Tiffany lamp cast its feeble light, which was all but lost in the sunlight streaming through the window.

Nothing had changed, but everything was different.

Mother took a few halfhearted bites of egg, then abandoned her fork and settled back in her chair, her coffee mug cradled in both hands. "I like your hair. It becomes you."

High praise from Mona. "Thanks."

Mother eyed me over the lip of her mug. "So, to what do I owe the pleasure of this visit?"

"I wanted to ask you a question."

"Oh?" Mother said, as if she didn't know what was coming next.

"Who did you think came to visit Lyda Sue here in the Babylon's helicopter?"

"The minute I hung up the phone, I knew I'd made a mistake calling you. You never could do as you were told."

"Like mother, like daughter." I picked up another piece of bacon—my third—and started in on it. "You're avoiding my question, Mother."

"I was worried it was that nice Mr. Dane. He seemed smitten with you, and I didn't want you to screw it up." Mother gave me a bland look.

She was bullshitting me. I had known she would, so it came as no surprise. So, if I had known the odds were stacked against me getting the straight skinny from my mother, why did I come? What was I looking for? Even I wasn't sure of the answer.

"What makes you think I would screw up a relationship with Dane?"

"Honey, I've watched you for years. Just when it looks like a man is interested, you do something to push him away. I've never understood why." Mother took another sip of coffee.

"It's not like I've had a lot of people in my life who stuck with me, Mother. I learned early on I was the only one I could count on."

Hurt flashed in her eyes, then disappeared. Adopting a familiar air of feigned indifference, she said, "Perhaps you're right. But, as to Mr. Dane, I got the feeling he was a good guy. Poking your nose into his business was sure to irritate him."

"You've got to stop meddling, Mother." That was like telling a zebra to stop being black-and-white, but I had to say it anyway—just in case, one of these days, she'd surprise me.

"If I don't meddle, you'll end up by yourself, Lucky. No lover. No child. I wouldn't wish that on anyone."

"You're alone. You seem to be doing fine." Other than sagging under the weight of a torch she'd carried for far too long, for some empty suit who had abandoned her when she'd needed him most.

"I have you," Mona said, her voice a whisper. "That's the only thing that gets me from one day to the next."

"Oh," I said, fighting for the right words. The truth of it was, I had no idea whether Mother meant what she said or whether she was working another angle—which was more like her. This whole morning had been weird—I felt like I'd entered a parallel universe the minute I'd set foot into my mother's room.

If I was so important to her, then why did she let me go—so young, so inexperienced, with no one to guide me? That's a question I'd wanted answered for a long time, but I didn't ask. Not now, maybe not ever. There was no really good answer, so what was the point? Though, I'd be lying if I said it didn't hurt, even still.

"How's Theodore?" Jumping from one uncomfortable topic to another was Mother's best thing.

"He's good. Real good." Avoiding her eyes, I dove into my eggs.

"Have you figured out yet he's in love with you?"

That stopped me, my fork halfway to my mouth. Carefully, I set the utensil back down on my plate. "So, everybody could see it but me?"

"When you're in the eye of the tornado, the world looks blurry —especially when you're working hard to avoid clear vision." Mona eyed me for a moment. "What are you going to do about him?"

"I'd like to know that myself," I grumbled.

"You do know, at least ninety-five percent of the men who wear women's clothing have issues with their sexuality, don't you?"

Ah, Mona was back. I regained my footing. "Thank you, Mother. Might I ask where you got that little tidbit? *Prostitution Today? Cross-Dressers Weekly?*" I forked in that abandoned bite of egg. "I can assure you, Teddie has no issues in that regard—he's an actor playing a role."

"You don't need to get mad," Mother said with a grin.

"Besides, we can wear the same clothes, so with Teddie I not only get a lover, but I get a fabulous new wardrobe."

"Ah, sarcasm, your defense of last resort. Hit a nerve, did I?"

The woman would be the death of me—or I'd end up in prison after having strangled her in a fit of frustration.

I sighed and looked out the window. Heat shimmered from everything, diffusing the light. The trees, what few there were, bowed in supplication to the assault of the sun.

Kindred spirits, me and those trees. Like them, I was beaten down and tired. Tired of being angry. Tired of running. Tired of being alone.

"You hit a nerve." I shrugged as I looked at my mother. "The truth is, I have no idea what to do about Teddie."

"Honey," she said as she reached over, putting her hand on mine. "I think you do."

~

PARKING THE CAR WITH THE SUNLIGHT BEATING ON THE DRIVER'S side violated a cardinal rule of summer desert living. I knew it, and I'd done it anyway. The door handle was so hot I couldn't even touch it, much less hold on to it long enough to actually open the door. Shirttails came in handy in situations like this— luckily, mine just reached. Popping the handle, I opened the door, then walked around and opened the other door to let what tepid little breeze there was, blow through.

Stepping back into the shade while my car cooled, I opened my phone and hit the speed dial.

Teddie answered before I even heard it ring. "Where are you? I went down to your place—the bird had been fed, but no you. I tried your cell, you didn't answer, and there's nobody at your office yet."

Relief flooded through me—he wasn't mad—at least he didn't sound mad. "I got up early—didn't sleep well. I've been to see Mother and am just starting back."

"You didn't sleep well?"

"No." I listened to him breathing on the other end of the line while I debated what to say next. What the heck—now was as good a time as any to fall on my sword. "It didn't seem right to go to sleep without at least talking to you. Last night, I called, but I kept getting your voice mail. "

"My battery died—you know how I am about plugging the damned thing in. I didn't realize you had called until this morning. I'm sorry."

"I was worried."

"I was running errands and came in late. Forrest said you looked tired, so I didn't bother you," Teddie added. "I'm sorry I worried you. What exactly was it you were worried about?"

Worried you were with another woman. Worried you were mad at me. Worried I'd screwed everything up. Worried I'd lost you before I even knew what I had. All were true, but I couldn't find the courage to tell him. Instead, I said, "Are we okay?"

"Sure, what makes you ask that?" Teddie sounded guarded.

"I thought I'd see you at the trade show last night. Subway said you'd been there."

Silence stretched over the line. I could hear myself breathing. Time slowed to a crawl.

Finally, Teddie broke the silence. "I was there. I saw you with that Dane guy. You guys were laughing—it looked like you were having fun. He didn't look like the Dark Side."

"I was looking for you." My heart leapt into my throat. So this was it—Teddie and I were over before we really began?

"I know. Stupid of me, really, but it just hit me right between the eyes."

"What?" I could barely get the word out.

"The reality of your world. You see handsome men all day long —and are probably hit on more than I care to think about."

I took a few moments to formulate my reply. "My job puts me in that position, as does yours. No way around that." I squeezed the phone so hard I thought I would break it. "Teddie, you have to trust the one you hand your heart to."

"I know. And I'd trust you with my life and my heart—it wasn't that."

"What then?"

"It's a guy thing, all that primal chest-beating and ownership stuff."

My death grip on the phone loosened a bit. "So, we're still good?"

"Honey, we are perfect," Teddie said with a chuckle. "It was me who needed fixing."

"And are you fixed?"

This time Teddie laughed. "In a manner of speaking."

"Glad to hear it." His laugh melted my tension. "Listen, if you'll be around in about an hour, I need to bring the Porsche home, and in addition to having something to say to you, I have something to thank you for, and a favor to ask—actually two favors to ask."

"Sounds interesting. Do you want me to cook breakfast?"

"Only if you're hungry—I stuffed myself on Trudi's bacon."

"How was your mother, by the way?"

"Different."

"That goes without saying."

I laughed and didn't feel the need to explain. At some point, I'd get around to telling him about Mother and my father, but not now. "I'll see you in about an hour."

"I'll be waiting."

∽

THE DRIVE PASSED WITH ME TRYING NOT TO THINK ABOUT TEDDIE. Sounding like an in-control adult, and not an addlepated schoolgirl, took all of my energy as I made and fielded calls. Somehow, the workday had started without my presence.

My office was functioning. I held Flash off until tonight when, hopefully, I would have more of the story. A good friend of mine on the investigative staff of the Gaming Control Board was looking into Paxton Dane's story. Detective Romeo wanted to talk to me—we settled on a late lunch. Other than that, Miss Patterson and Brandy seemed to be keeping the lid on. They were doing so well, in fact, I was feeling a bit superfluous by the time I pulled into the garage at the Presidio and parked the Porsche in its normal spot.

My heart beat a rapid rhythm as I rode the elevator from the garage straight to the top. Almost losing my nerve, I stepped out into the vast cavern of Teddie's apartment.

He met me halfway across the large room. Unfortunately, his attire—shorts and nothing else—did little to help me keep my composure. One look at him, and my carefully planned speech went out the window. Instead, I closed the distance between us with a few measured strides.

He watched with a bemused expression as I took his coffee mug from his hand and placed it, very carefully, on the side table to the sofa.

My hands found his bare chest. I let them roam with a freedom I hadn't indulged in before.

"Lucky..."

My finger on his lips silenced him.

Stepping into him, my body pressed to his, I savored the feel of him. His skin smooth beneath my fingers—his body hard and hot. Teddie's arms circled my waist, crushing me to him.

I saw my future in his eyes as his mouth found mine.

He deepened his kiss and time stopped.

I have no idea how long we stood there like that, and I didn't care. The whole world could have imploded, and I wouldn't have missed a beat. My skin on his, his mouth on mine—that was enough—almost.

His voice was rough when he finally spoke. "We take this much further, I won't be able to stop."

"I don't want you to."

A ragged breath escaped him, as if he were fighting with

himself for control. "I want your passion, Lucky, but it's not enough. I want more—I want the whole fairy tale."

I stepped back—just a few inches, but it gave me a moment of clarity. "Tell me what you want."

Somehow, his hands found my skin under my shirt. His fingers traced my spine, making it almost impossible to think.

"I want to be your best friend and your lover," he began. "I want to make love to you so slowly that you beg for it. I want to watch Sunday night football with you—debating whether John and Al are truly the best who ever called a game. I want to ride through Tuscany on a motorbike, your arms around my waist, and your voice in my ear. I want to hold your hand and weep through wonderful love stories while we live our own for real. I want you to be the last one I talk to at night and the first one I see in the morning. And when our journey is done, when I travel from this world into the next, I want to be holding your hand. In short, I want it all."

Like the blow from a hammer, each word, laden with emotion, assaulted the wall around my heart. And when he was done, all that remained of that barrier was a pile of rubble.

"Sounds perfect."

"You sure?"

"I've never been surer of anything in my life." I meant every word.

With a big grin, he swooped down and picked me up, then started toward the bedroom.

"Put me down. You'll herniate yourself." Was that me giggling?

At that precise moment, my phone rang.

Teddie paused.

"Ignore it. I'm good, but the Babylon will not stop functioning without me."

After two rings, it stopped. "See?"

I waited, one heartbeat, two heartbeats, and then three. Just when I thought we'd made a clean getaway, Miss Patterson's voice came over the walkie-talkie. "Lucky, pick up. I know it's a bad time for an interruption, but it's important."

Teddie eased my feet to the floor, but he kept his arm around my waist, holding me to him. I closed my eyes and just for a brief flash of time, savored that moment—the one with Teddie next to me, neither of us having a care in the world. That moment just before I discovered the calamity so serious that Miss Patterson felt compelled to call—even when she knew where I was and probably what I was doing.

I unclipped the Nextel and pushed-to-talk. "How bad is it?"

"It's The Big Boss. They've airlifted him to UMC. He lost consciousness—Delores found him when she came to clean. His heartbeat is irregular—they don't know if he's had a heart attack or not."

The news knocked the breath from me. The Big Boss? Heart attack? That couldn't be right. The guy was a horse.

Just when I felt I'd lost my center, I felt Teddie's arm around my waist—strong and comforting.

"Lucky?" Miss Patterson's voice sounded as taut and as tight as the shortest string on a finely tuned piano.

For some odd reason, I found myself wondering what key that would be—it's funny what your mind turns to when overloaded. "I'm here. When did they take him?"

"Just now. He called from the helicopter, if you can believe that."

"I can believe it."

"He wants you there."

My brain cleared, life came back into focus—I always was a crisis performer. The Big Boss used to say that if he ever was in an airplane that had lost all its engines and was on fire, he would want me at the controls. The Big Boss...

Focus, O'Toole. "I'm on my way, but first get a pencil and paper and let me know when you're ready."

I heard her shuffling around, then her voice came back. This time more in control, calmer. "Ready."

"Call Detective Romeo. Tell him lunch is off, don't tell him why —we need to keep The Big Boss's situation under wraps. Got it?"

"Got it."

"Tell Romeo to meet me at that address in Spanish Trail—the one I gave you yesterday—at seven o'clock tonight. Tell him to bring wires for four and whatever the device is that will let me listen and talk to whoever is wired."

"Okay."

"Call the Most Reverend Peterson J. Peabody. Tell him my list of party attendees is final—he'll know what to do."

"Got it."

"Call Flash. Tell her to wait for my call tonight. Don't give her any more information than that. And call Dane, give him the Spanish Trail address. Tell him to meet me there at eight o'clock. No, make it seven thirty. When he bitches, tell him I said to just do it—I'll make it worth his while."

"I think I will enjoy that."

"Did The Big Boss say anything about the paperwork for the board of directors meeting tomorrow?"

"He has it with him."

I shook my head. "He would." Nothing was more important than his hotel. "Can you prepare a proxy for him to sign, allowing me to vote for him tomorrow?"

"Already done."

"Have Brandy bring it to UMC. Have her wait in the ladies' room on the fifth floor. Call me when she arrives—I'll meet her." I stopped for a moment. Had I thought of everything? Probably not, but it would have to do. "See if you can find Mr. Fujikara. Have him call me on my cell."

"Anything else?"

"Pray." I rang off.

Teddie turned me to face him, then kissed me gently. "It'll be okay," he murmured as he held me close.

"One way or the other." I let him hold me. "I'm not ready to lose him."

"We never are."

Allowing myself a moment of weakness, I gathered strength from Teddie as I rested my head on his shoulder. A moment was all I had. I pushed myself upright and stepped away. "I need to ask you a favor."

"Anything."

UMC, the University Medical Center, didn't look like much from the street. In fact, it looked like the last place a person with a serious medical condition would want to end up. Nothing could be further from the truth. State of the art and staffed with the best doctors money could buy, UMC took care of most of Vegas' old guard.

A nurse waited for me as I burst through the doors. "Ms. O'Toole?" she verified.

I nodded.

"This way." She whisked me through a labyrinth of hallways, keeping me out of sight—half the cub reporters in town hung out at UMC looking for a juicy tidbit when news was sparse. "We have Mr. Rothstein in a private suite. Everyone is under strict instructions to keep it quiet."

"Is he okay?" I asked, as we wound our way through the corridors.

"He has some fairly major heart problems, but he's stable. The doctors can give you more details."

The private suite wasn't much. Still industrial with its laminated floors and stark white walls, it was private and had a few touches of hominess—a sitting area, plants softening the corners, and something passing for art on the walls. But nobody had done anything about the smell. Reeking of ammonia, medicine, and sickness, the odor was alternately depressing and horrifying. I fought the urge to turn tail and run.

I hated hospitals. And I hated that The Big Boss was stuck in one.

Still wearing his business shirt, slacks, and a frown, he sat upright in a hospital bed parked against the far wall and angled so its occupant could get a glimpse out the window—if one felt inclined to look across and into another patient's room in the wing opposite. A pallor lurked under the angry flush on his face as he clutched his left arm. His shirt open, leads attached to his chest tethered him to a machine that beeped in time with his heartbeat.

Dr. Knapp, his personal physician, stood next to the bed and, with the patience earned through years of practice, he explained The Big Boss's situation to him. "Al, you've known for years your heart is enlarged—this day was coming. You've put the surgery off too long. The specialist is on his way from the Mayo Clinic. When he gets here in a few hours, we'll know for sure what we're dealing with."

"Bloody hell. I'm fine."

"Sure. That's why you're having trouble breathing, you're sweating even though it's cold in here, your left arm hurts like hell, and your cleaning lady found you out cold on the floor."

The Big Boss stopped clutching his arm, lowered his eyebrows, and glared at Dr. Knapp.

"The surgery is touchy, but it is a complete solution to your problem. You should have a full recovery. It needs to be taken care of, Al." Dr. Knapp put his hand on The Big Boss's shoulder. "For now, I'm in charge, and you're to do as I tell you. I don't want to lose you, my friend."

"Me either." I moved from the doorway where I had been eavesdropping, into the room to stand beside Dr. Knapp at The Big Boss's bedside. So, it wasn't that serious! An operation and he'd be fine. I felt the tension ease a bit, my shoulders dropped from somewhere around my ears to their normal position.

Dr. Knapp spoke first. "Lucky, thank God. I'm going to need your help corralling this bull."

"Looks like you're doing okay so far."

Emotions chased across The Big Boss's face—anger, pain, and finally fear. "'Bout time you showed up," he groused at me, as he slapped the frown back in place.

"You okay?" I asked.

"No, I'm not okay! What does it look like?"

Even I could recognize a rhetorical question when I heard one, so I said nothing and waited.

Finally, The Big Boss sighed. The fight left him, a look of determined resignation replacing his scowl. "Doc, can you leave us a minute?" Dr. Knapp started to say something, but The Big Boss held up his hand, stopping him. "Let me talk with Lucky, then you can have your way with me."

Mollified for the moment, the doctor left.

"Close the door, will you?" The Big Boss asked. "We've got some things to talk about. That board meeting tomorrow—you're going to have to handle it."

CHAPTER NINETEEN

ATERING TRUCKS ringed the cul-de-sac in front of Phil Stewart's house when I arrived. From the looks of it, the Trendmakers expected a large turnout. I angled the Ferrari, which I had once again borrowed, between a truck from a local Mexican food restaurant and an RV that served as the home to the Traveling Fellatio Sisters—apparently the entertainment for the partygoers—when they weren't creating their own. Oh goody.

Not many things in Vegas reached the status of over-the-top, but I had a feeling, if the Fellatio Sisters lived up to their name, they came perilously close. That was one of the problems with Sin City—once you stepped out on that slippery slope, it was all downhill—and nobody knew where to draw the line or when they'd crossed it.

However, the lack of a taste arbiter in Vegas was the least of my worries as I tossed the keys to the startled valet. "Put it out of sight in the garage or something? Okay?"

"You're early. The party doesn't start for another hour or so." The kid stared at the car, practically drooling with delight. "I'll have to move Mr. Stewart's cars around."

"Fine."

It was déjà vu all over again as I hiked up the drive, now lined with luminarias, and paused in front of the door with the lewd etchings on it. Mr. Stewart must've paid a ton of money to get that approved by the architectural committee. I added good taste —right after love—to my list of things that couldn't be bought.

Half bracing myself to see the Weasel's blood still on the white marble floor of the foyer, I turned the knob, eased the door open, and took a peek. I needn't have worried, the floor was spotless, and the house and grounds beyond had been transformed. Walking through the house toward the backyard—the main focus of tonight's festivities—I took in all of the changes. Somebody, or a whole army of somebodies, had been busy.

A Mexican village had replaced the former studied Southern California charm. Colorful serapes and sombreros hung from the banisters. Brightly colored lanterns dangled from wires draped across the wide expanse of the den and the yard beyond. They danced in the early evening breeze, throwing splashes of colored light. Frozen margarita machines churned in strategic locations. Donkeys and goats nibbled hay in pens in the grassy area between the main house and the cabana, and chickens pecked at corn strewn on the pool deck surrounding the hot tub—which had room for at least twenty.

Any party that combined swingers and farm animals had me worried. I tried not to think about the possibilities.

Under the overhang to the cabana, the Naked Mariachis— thankfully still clothed—set up their sound equipment and tested their mikes. I wondered if the Mariachis and the Fellatio Sisters came as a package—a sort of two-for-one deal—but some things are better left unknown. In fact, a good many things about tonight would probably be better left to the imagination. Although, with that whole visual thing I had going on, I'm not sure that would be any better for me.

Pausing at the edge of the patio, I tried to focus—a task that was easier said than done as I watched a man on a ladder stuffing a huge piñata—shaped like a large pair of breasts—with small, square cellophane packets, which I recognized from the box of them I had won last night. Another man was stuffing the same pink-jacketed condoms into another piñata, this one shaped like a large derriere. Briefly, I wondered what the partygoers would use to break open the papier-mâché body parts, then decided I was better off left in the dark.

A lot rode on these next few hours. If we snagged Felicia Reilly, maybe we would get Irv Gittings. Then The Big Boss would keep his hotel without a fight, and I would keep my job.

A man with hair so black it looked like a bad toupee (assuming there was any other kind), an artificially whitened smile, and skin tanned until it was the color of shoe leather waved at me from across the yard and shouted, "Ms. O'Toole?"

I waited until he arrived in front of me to respond. "Yes."

"I'm Phil. Welcome to my home." Placing his hand on my elbow, he steered me back inside. "Why don't I show you around, then you can tell me exactly what you need?"

My skin crawled at his touch. "The most important thing is a position on the second floor, overlooking the pool—preferably a room that can be locked, so we will be undisturbed and unnoticed."

"Let me give you the whole layout, then I'll show you a couple of places that should work."

Phil's house was huge, easily twelve thousand square feet with another five thousand in the cabana by the pool. The Mexican theme extended throughout. We strolled down corridors, past numerous bedrooms, all individually numbered and sporting wicker baskets filled with condoms and tidy wipes on the night-stands. Each bathroom, also numbered, stood at the ready with piles of brightly colored towels and washcloths.

"You know, I grew up in a whorehouse in Pahrump, so this feels like home," I casually remarked. I didn't know whether I was trying to get a rise out of him or whether I was just creeped out.

Making the casual sex thing consensual didn't make it any more palatable.

"So you sorta know how this evening will go, then." Phil seemed nonplussed by the comparison.

"People pay money to come to the party?"

"Uh-huh." He steered me back toward the foyer of the house.

At least, that's where I thought we were headed—I'd gotten a bit turned around.

"Only the men pay, and they must be accompanied by a woman. Single females get in free."

"I'm not sure I'd say it was free—"

"This is our gym where we will be holding games tonight," Phil Stewart announced, as he pulled me to a stop in front of a set of large metal doors.

"Games?" I asked, then instantly regretted it.

"Yes. The most popular one is Hands On."

"Hmm." I tried to act disinterested.

"It's really fun, you ought to try it. We put about ten or fifteen people in there, let them mingle for fifteen minutes, then kill the lights." Phil's enthusiasm was evident. "They have to identify each other in the dark, by touch alone. Most get—how should I put it—distracted—before then. The one who gets the most identities correct wins."

This time I was smart enough not to ask the obvious question.

"Room three should suit your purposes." Phil tapped on the door with a large 3 on it as we passed by. "Just flip the switch by the door, and a red light will show in the hall. Nobody will bother you if that light is lit."

"You know who we're looking for?"

"I've seen her a couple of times, but I can't guarantee I'd recognize her. A lot of folks show up at these parties."

"And we're not here, right? You haven't seen me and my friends."

"Got it."

I stopped him at the top of the stairs. "Don't screw this up, Stewart. You won't like what happens if you do."

Our eyes locked. I saw anger in his—and arrogance. He'd covered both well.

"The police have made that crystal clear," he said with a touch of bitterness.

Descending the stairs, I caught sight of Detective Romeo, a bag over his shoulder, standing on the edge of the patio, surveying the debauchery to come and getting twitchy. Excusing myself, I left the sleazy Mr. Stewart and retrieved Romeo before he started flashing his badge, which would panic the natives.

Grabbing his sleeve, I said, "You and I need to get out of sight before the guests start arriving." I pulled him with me into the house and started up the stairs.

"Do you know what they're doing down there?" He swept a hand toward the backyard as he reluctantly let me pull him along. "This guy, Stewart, is charging folks to attend a party where they can have as much sex as they can stand." Distracted, he tripped on one of the stairs, nearly pulling us both down, but that didn't slow down his mouth. "On top of that, the entertainment for the evening are two sisters, presumably paid, who are to give blow jobs to all comers!"

"I'm not sure that's the best choice of words," I said, as I grabbed his arm, pulling him up and into room number three—the one directly over the pool with the best view of the whole party. Once in the room, I turned him to face me. "Focus, Romeo! We have more at stake than arresting a few sex addicts."

His eyes big as dinner plates, he nodded. He looked about twelve years old. Had the police lowered the minimum age requirement for the academy and I missed it?

I shut the door behind us and flipped on the red light. "Do you have the wires?"

"Yeah." He shrugged off the bag, set it on the floor, then

kneeled as he rooted in it, pulling out boxes and wires. "I brought a couple of extras. You never know."

Romeo explained the whole setup to me as we laid everything out on the bed and set up the base station by the window so I could listen, talk, and watch at the same time.

"You keep tabs on Phil Stewart. I don't want him tipping off Felicia. And, Romeo..." I made sure he was looking me in the eyes. "Be cool, okay? You're going to see some amazing stuff down there." I didn't feel the need to tell him he would be useless wandering agog through the party—I think he got my drift, though.

"You got it. I'll stick to him like stink on—"

"Got it." I glanced out the window. The caterers and party decorators still bustled around the yard, but no sign of any guests. "I can't be seen wandering through the party—Felicia Reilly would recognize me and smell a rat—she knows I wouldn't be caught dead playing with this crowd."

My phone rang. Grabbing it, I glanced at the caller's number— Teddie. A shot of warmth chased through me.

"Hey." Thinking of Teddie had apparently reduced me to single syllables—this was not a good thing.

"You've been out of my sight too long. How's The Big Boss?"

"He needs surgery, but it's not serious—apparently he has an enlarged heart. They've been watching it for years."

"So, no need to worry right now?" I could hear the concern in Teddie's voice—I knew it wasn't only for The Big Boss.

"No. He's stable and in good hands. They'll operate tomorrow. If things change, they'll let me know immediately."

"Good. Where are you? I'm out front—does the theme on the front door carry through inside?"

"You have no idea. This place is a veritable booby trap for the sexually unwary. We're in room three, top of the stairs."

"Sounds fascinating. I'll be right there."

Secretly, I was glad for Romeo's presence—I didn't trust myself alone in a bedroom with Teddie right now. Especially not in this sex palace. A few minutes surrounded by the promise of wild, unbridled sex that oozed from every inch of this house would resurrect even a nun's dormant libido. In this house, with Teddie around, mine threatened to go thermonuclear.

Teddie burst through the door without knocking, a big smile on his face. He carried some clothes on hangers over one shoulder, and a bag on the other. Two strides and he stopped in front of me, grabbed me with one arm around the waist, and kissed me long and slow.

God, he was good at that.

Pulling back, he gave me a lopsided grin, but didn't let me go. "I've missed you."

"So I see." I felt the color rise in my cheeks as I unwrapped his arm from around my waist. With my free arm, I directed his attention to the other person in the room. "This is Detective Romeo."

Teddie extended his hand. "Romeo. I'm Ted. I belong to Ms. O'Toole."

"Sir," Romeo said, as he shook Teddie's hand and shot a glance my way.

"Ted is helping us tonight," I explained, using the words to fill the awkward spaces. Teddie belonged to me? The thought made my heart soar and my mind wander—as if this night didn't pose enough challenges already. "I see you've raided my closet, Mr. Kowalski."

"I had no idea what one wears to one of these functions, so I brought several options." Teddie held out the clothes he'd brought for my inspection, showing me each one in turn. "A sundress with a pashmina. Casual slacks and sweater set. Or..." He waggled his eyebrows at me. "And this is my favorite. A tennis outfit."

"Gee, I don't know. Which one do you feel prettiest in?" I couldn't keep the smile off my face.

Teddie stuck out his tongue at me.

Romeo stared at us as if we'd lost our minds.

"Surprise me," I said.

As Teddie disappeared into the bathroom, I turned to answer the questions I saw on Romeo's face. "Since single men can't get into the party, and since I can't be seen as a guest, Ted is going to be Mr. Dane's date tonight."

"Oh." Romeo's brows crinkled.

"He's also known as the Great Teddie Divine..." I offered as further explanation, hoping I didn't have to spell it out.

"Oh!" The light dawned in Romeo's eyes. "I thought that guy was gay."

"Not hardly."

The Nextel vibrated at my hip, and Dane's voice came over the walkie-talkie. "O'Toole, I'm in the foyer, but I don't see anyone waiting for me."

From the tone of his voice, I gathered he hadn't liked Miss Patterson summoning him at my behest with no explanation. "Room three. Top of the stairs."

In seconds, Dane burst through the door and caught sight of me. He pocketed his phone and kept talking. "Are you my date?"

"No. This is Detective Romeo." I raised my hand, shutting down Dane's question. "He's not your date either. While he fits you with a wire, I'll explain."

~

DANE HAD CALMED CONSIDERABLY WHEN I FINISHED MY explanation and we had fitted and tested his wire. "So, my date and I are going to wander, looking for Felicia?"

"Yup." I nodded.

"So, where is this date of mine?" Dane asked.

Somehow, I hadn't found the right words to tell him about Teddie.

At that moment, the bathroom door swung open. Teddie had

disappeared. In his place stood a stunning, statuesque woman, with long blonde hair, twinkling eyes, and a pouty pink mouth. He'd picked the orange sundress and soft peach pashmina to hide his shoulders. "That would be me, big guy." Teddie's soft, female tones were dulcet, intoxicating.

Dane's eyes widened, a satisfied smile tugging at the corners of his mouth. "O...kaaay," he said, drawing the word out as he nodded appreciatively.

Teddie gave me a wink, then said in his normal voice, "But don't get any ideas."

"Whoa!" Dane glanced between Teddie and me. "Theodore?"

"You can call me Ted."

"Damn, you look just like a dame!"

"I believe that's the point."

"Sorry, you surprised me." Training his emerald greens on me, Dane shook his head. "And so did you." His voice had lost that angry edge. "So, Ted's my keeper tonight?"

Stupid was apparently not one of Dane's character flaws.

Even though my source at the Control Board had confirmed Dane's position there, he'd proven himself about as trustworthy as a career politician running for reelection. He'd been tight with Irv Gittings, and anybody who had cast his lot with Ol' Irv crawled on his belly like a reptile. I should know.

"Let's get this party started," I said. "Romeo, fit Teddie with one of those things and we'll send the cute couple on their way."

Ten minutes later, all of us satisfied the equipment worked, Teddie turned to me. "How 'bout a kiss for the road?"

"My pleasure." I complied, then licked my lips. "Nice lip gloss. Is it strawberry?"

"You like it? It's new. I think it's called Strawberry Smack," Teddie said with a smile and the conspiratorial tones of a woman sharing her makeup secrets. "I read this book about how not to look older—the author said to wear light-colored lipstick. She also said side-swept bangs were a plus."

"Okay, now you're worrying me. Go play, but one word of advice—you might want to stay out of the gym." I pushed him toward the door where Dane waited. My voice turned serious. "Find Felicia Reilly."

"Will do. And no gym," Teddie said.

With a chivalrous bow, Dane motioned Teddie to precede him through the door, then said to me, "I still can't believe you turned me down for a guy who wears a dress."

Teddie's head snapped around. He didn't say anything—he didn't need to—I saw it all in his eyes.

After turning off all of the lights, Romeo and I took our position by the window. A few couples roamed the yard. Teddie and Dane joined them. I still couldn't get over how the Trendmakers looked like the folks you'd see coming out of church on Sunday. Old, young, tall, short, fat, thin—a perfect cross section of middle-class America.

"Did anything about that kiss creep you out, or was it just me?" Romeo asked, then colored when I looked at him. "Of course, it's none of my business really."

"Guess you're not one of your breed who find women-on-women action a turn-on?"

Romeo flushed crimson. "I—"

I held up my hand, stopping him. "Ignore me." I knew the kid needed baby steps, but I couldn't help myself. I mean, who wouldn't swing at a hanging curveball out over the plate like that? "Everyone else sees a beautiful woman when they look at Teddie because that's what he wants them to see," I explained. "I just see Teddie."

A knock at the door made us both jump. "Lucky?"

I recognized Jeep's voice. I opened the door and was glad to see him standing there with Mr. Fujikara—the last two actors in tonight's drama.

In the dwindling light leaking through the windows, Romeo fitted them with their mikes.

"If either of you see Felicia Reilly, I better be the first to hear about it," I informed them, then sent them on their way.

Let the party begin.

~

ALL TRACES OF LIGHT IN THE WEST HAD DISAPPEARED BY THE TIME the party gained momentum. Easily two hundred or more guests wandered the grounds—who knew there were that many willing to part with five hundred dollars for as much sex as they could handle with people they didn't know?

A full moon added to the light from the lanterns and luminarias, bathing even the shadows in a soft light that made the recognition of the players easy—my luck was holding. I caught snippets of conversation as Teddie, Dane, Jeep, and Mr. Fujikara worked the party. So far, Teddie had fended off three propositions. Dane had given his number to four women and promised to meet another in room five at midnight. Mr. Fujikara exchanged pleasantries with other partygoers—many of whom he appeared to know well.

Several couples were all over each other in the hot tub—I tried not to watch. Others clustered in knots around the yard.

Jeep and his wife were in deep conversation with another couple by the bar—I could hear snatches of it—something about joining with another couple they'd met last year. They weren't planning just drinks and dinner. I turned the volume down on his mike—way too much information.

The Naked Mariachis, sans clothing, their instruments strategically positioned, started into their second set. The Fellatio Sisters were laying low.

And, so far, Ms. Reilly was a no-show.

I was getting antsy when I caught sight of Teddie leaning on an elbow on the bar—he was alone. "Hey, Teddie, ladies don't lean on the bar like that."

He straightened as if he'd been poked in the ass with a sharp object. "Sorry, I don't normally play a lady, so this is new territory for me. Anything else ladies don't do?" He lifted a mug of frozen margarita to his lips.

"A number of things, but good thing for you..." I said, my voice low and suggestive, "...I'm no lady."

Making a gargled sound, he choked on his drink.

"I had no idea this could be so much fun," I remarked to Romeo, my hand covering my mike.

He gave me a pained expression.

"Oh, sorry!" Dane said to someone. Then to me: "Unless Miss Reilly is interested in a blow job, we don't need to keep an eye on the library."

"Got it." I stifled a grin. So that's where the Fellatio Sisters were holding court.

We both snapped to attention at Mr. Fujikara's hushed whisper. "She's here!"

Adrenaline shot through me. I raised the volume on Jeep's mike back to normal. "Okay, everybody, it's show time. Where is she?"

"The back bar—the one by the gym," Mr. Fujikara replied.

"Everybody act normal. Anybody near the gym?" I asked, fighting to keep my voice calm and my mind clear, as my heart raced.

"Damn," Dane said. "I'm in the gym—somebody just killed the lights."

Did the guy just not listen or did he intentionally ignore me? Talking to him was like doing business with appliance repairmen who, to a one, acted as if "competent female" was an oxymoron.

"Whoa! What're you doing?" Dane exclaimed, before I could give him a short and sweet ass chewing.

"Oh! You're that handsome cowboy dude. I knew you'd be hung like a horse," a woman purred. She must've been practically in Dane's lap for me to hear her that clearly.

"Dane, quit fooling around. Find the door—get after Felicia now!" I ordered.

"She's headed toward the den," Mr. Fujikara whispered. "I'm following her."

"Romeo, where's Phil Stewart?"

"Cabana."

"Keep him there." One less thing to worry about.

"Wilco." The kid was by-the-book. If he started spouting all those police codes, I was screwed.

"I got her. She's crossing through the den. Looks like she's headed outside toward the pool," Dane said, his voice hard and angry.

"Teddie?" I glanced out the window and could still see him waiting by the bar.

"I see her. Tell Dane to follow her, I'll try to close them off from the opposite direction."

"Dane—"

"Got it." So, he wasn't by-the-book—I liked "Wilco" better. At least then I knew what he was going to do.

A few seconds—which seemed like an eternity—passed. Then I caught sight of Felicia, dark hair flying, as she stalked around the pool, rigid with anger. She glanced over her shoulder once, but other than that, she didn't seem nervous or wary—just mad.

"I see her," Jeep answered in his soft, Midwestern tones. "Looks like she's heading my way."

"Act normal. Get her talking. The others need a minute or two to close in."

He didn't have time to answer as Felicia Reilly advanced on him.

"Teddie, work your way by the cabana," I directed. "Let me know when you have them in sight." I saw him move. "Dane, where are you?"

"Working my way around the other end of the pool, keeping

my distance from Ms. Reilly. I don't want to spook her before Ted's in place."

Jeep held off Felicia for the moment, but she was getting angry, their conversation heated.

"Fat man, I want my money—fifty grand. You said you'd have it tonight." Felicia's voice was shrill.

I couldn't tell whether she was just mad or starting to panic.

"I'm a man of God—a shepherd of the people. I don't have that kind of money. I'll need more time," Jeep pleaded.

"A man of God! That's rare!" Felicia scoffed. "You'll be without a flock soon unless you give me the money now!"

"Please, you must understand," Jeep implored, his arms spread wide. "You'll ruin me."

"I intend to, if you don't pay up. Now!" Felicia gestured wildly as she shifted from foot to foot in front of him.

Jeep shook his head. "I don't have the money. I can't get it until day after tomorrow."

Felicia glanced over Jeep's shoulder and she froze—she'd caught sight of Dane advancing on her.

A quick glance told me Teddie was in place, cutting off her escape route around the end of the pool opposite the one Dane rounded.

Effectively, the two men had Felicia trapped in a chute between the pool and the fence separating the property from the golf course.

Felicia glanced over her shoulder. She looked right past Teddie.

Jeep grabbed her. They struggled. Felicia wiggled free and gave Jeep a huge push. Arms whirling as he fought for balance, Jeep teetered on the edge of the pool.

Then he toppled over into the water.

All heads turned at the huge splash.

For a moment, no one did anything, then a "hooray" arose

from the crowd and guests began darting for the pool and cannon-balling in.

"Shit," Dane said, as he was caught in the lemming-like chain reaction. Fighting through the surge of people, he'd never reach Felicia in time.

"Teddie—"

"I got her."

Just as I thought she would get by him, he grabbed her arm, whirling her around.

He reared back, cocked his fist...

And hit her right in the face.

She staggered back, then dropped like a heart-shot deer.

Right into the Naked Mariachis.

Men and instruments went flying—ass over teakettle—in an abundance of exposed flesh.

Some women screamed. Some cheered.

"Interesting party, don't you think?" I said, as Romeo and I ripped off our headsets and ran.

❧

FELICIA REILLY STILL LAY ON THE GROUND, BUT WAS SHOWING SIGNS of life when Romeo and I pushed through the crowd. Teddie shook his hand, a grimace on his face.

"You're going to have to tell him about the elbow thing," Romeo said, as he dropped to his knee, rolled the good Miss Reilly over and clasped her hands in a pair of handcuffs.

The crowd gasped as Teddie removed his wig and grinned at me. Several folks applauded.

I looped my arms around his neck. "You did it!"

He laughed as, a hand under each of my arms, he lifted me up, then let my body slide slowly down his—firing every nerve.

"This is the first time I've been the heroine *and* gotten the girl," he said, just before his mouth closed over mine.

Dane fought through the crowd, arriving beside us and cutting short a rather delicious kiss. He stared down at the now trussed Ms. Reilly, then at Teddie, his admiration evident. "Ted, you are my kind of gal!"

I grabbed someone's mug of half-frozen libations and tossed the contents in Felicia Reilly's face. As she sputtered and spewed, I felt a small sense of satisfaction. Teddie was right—letting go felt good—although I don't think this was exactly what he had in mind.

Romeo jerked her to her feet and escorted her toward the house. Teddie, my hand in his, Dane, and I followed.

As we passed the hot tub, I noticed the occupants—still hard at it—hadn't even noticed the commotion. "Would we still be considered voyeurs even though they don't care if we watch?" I whispered to Teddie.

He shot me a grin. "You are the most amazing woman," he said, sending shivers down my spine. "Where do you come up with that stuff?"

"Sorta scary, huh?" I returned his grin. "Living with me is a cross I bear."

"Why don't you let me help you carry the load?" he whispered in my ear, breaking the tenuous thread of control I had over my imagination.

A few moments alone with my imaginative wanderings and I needed a cold shower—or a locked room.

Standing under the porte cochere, Teddie pressed behind me, his arms around my waist, and his chin on my shoulder. Dane standing to one side, we watched Romeo stuff Felicia Reilly into the back of an unmarked squad car. He said something to the uniformed cops, then strode back toward our little group.

"I don't care if you have to use the thumbscrews and the water board, I need to know her story by ten o'clock tomorrow morning," I said to Romeo when he was close enough. "I'm counting on you—everything hangs in the balance."

"I won't let you down." His intensity showed in his eyes, earnestness adding weight to his words.

The kid would do his best. I only hoped it would be enough.

~

LONG AFTER ROMEO HAD COLLECTED HIS EQUIPMENT FROM ROOM three and both he and the squad car had disappeared through the gate, the three of us stood there, lost in our own thoughts. Everything was out of my hands now. Either Felicia Reilly would give up Irv Gittings or she wouldn't. I prayed for the latter, but The Big Boss and I had prepared for either. There was nothing more I could do.

Leaning back into Teddie, I shut my eyes as he nuzzled my neck, sending delicious shivers through me. Almost gasping out loud, I smiled as a ball of warmth exploded inside me, invading every crevice. "Cut that out!"

Teddie ignored me.

I didn't pull away.

"You guys need to find a room," Dane groused, as he disappeared back inside the house, leaving us to ourselves.

"That's the best idea I've heard all day," Teddie whispered as he nibbled my ear.

"I already have a room," I whispered back. "But we need to get you out of that dress."

CHAPTER TWENTY

ONCE INSIDE room three—which, by the way, I now saw in a totally different light—Teddie dropped the pashmina in a chair, shucked the sundress over his head as well as his underpinnings, and dropped the whole mess on the floor en route to the bathroom. At the door, he turned, dressed only in his swing easies, and said, "Don't move! I'll be right back." Was he kidding?

Even I don't have that kind of superhuman control. I followed him.

His back to me, Teddie bent over the sink, washing the makeup off—an interesting pose, with myriad possibilities. Stepping in behind him, I pressed myself against him, running my hands along the muscles in his back.

"Jesus," Teddie swore under his breath as he glanced up at me and scrubbed faster.

"Don't hurry on my account," I said, as I slid my fingers under the elastic waistband, then slowly worked from back to front—teasing, tantalizing. "I'm having a great time."

Splashing his face quickly, he pulled me around in front of him. Face-to-face, I let my hands roam lower, as—one by one—he popped the buttons on my shirt. Wanting—needing—to feel his hands on me, I reached to help him.

He shook his head and knocked my hands away. "My turn to play," he murmured, as he found the last button, then pushed my open shirt back over my shoulders, pinning my arms. His mouth closed over mine as his hands found my skin, taking the breath from me.

Wallowing in the sensations of him, the feel of his hands on me, his mouth on mine, rational thought vanished like an early morning mist under the assault of the midday sun.

Complete surrender was imminent...

My Nextel rang, shattering the moment like a hammer on fine crystal.

"Damn," I cursed, as I wondered if the thing had a built-in blood pressure monitor.

Teddie sagged against me. "If I have to stop now, I'm going to explode."

"That's an old wives' tale."

Leaning back to get a good look at me, he arched one eyebrow and said, "I know I shouldn't ask." He paused while the phone rang a second time. "But *what* is an old wives' tale?"

"That men will explode if they don't have sex, thereby doing damage to vital organs."

The phone rang a third time as Teddie stared at me. He looked as if he couldn't decide whether to laugh or cry. "Maybe so, but I'm going to have the damnedest case of blue balls you ever saw."

Blue balls—that didn't sound good. I decided retreat was the better part of valor—especially since I was already in over my head.

"You're going to have to answer the thing. I can't seem to move my arms," I calmly explained. "It could be about The Big Boss. If it's not important, get rid of them...quickly."

He narrowed his eyes as he ripped the offending device from

its carrier at my hip. "Gladly." Flipping it open, he said, "Ms. O'Toole is taking some personal time and unless you've nicked a major artery or body parts are falling off, she'll have to talk to you later—much later."

Teddie listened for a moment and his grin vanished. "Oh, I see...Yes, Sir...Right away." Slowly, he closed the phone.

My heart stopped at the look on his face.

"That was Dr. Knapp. Apparently, The Big Boss had another incident during one of the tests. They had to use the paddles to bring him back." Hastily, Teddie helped me shrug into my shirt and started closing the buttons as he talked. "They have him prepped for surgery, but he refuses to go. He's insisting on talking to you first—face-to-face."

Finished with the buttons, I tucked in my shirttail and caught a quick glance in the mirror. Unfortunately, I looked like a woman suffering from *coitus interruptus*, but it would have to do. "For Chrissake, he's prepped for surgery? And he won't go until he talks to me? Face-to-face? Is he crazy?"

~

AT THE WHEEL OF THE FERRARI, TEDDIE SEEMED INTENT ON breaking multiple land-speed records as he turned north on Rainbow, a long stretch of straight road, and floored it. My fingers drummed on the armrest, my heart pounded. The night still held the warmth of the day, but my skin felt cold and clammy.

In full coping mode, I asked myself what the worst-case scenario would be. If I could handle that, then I could handle the problem.

Okay, worst case—The Big Boss didn't make it.

A few seconds of mulling that over and I realized I was up to my eyebrows in quicksand—I couldn't handle a world without The Big Boss. Totally impossible.

So he had to make it.

"Can't you go any faster?" I shouted above the whine of the engine, knowing Teddie was doing his best, but I had to do something.

Instead of answering, Teddie reached over and squeezed my hand.

I hated being out of control.

Control? Who was I kidding? I couldn't make The Big Boss healthy, I couldn't force Felicia Reilly to roll over on Irv Gittings...Hell, I couldn't even find time between phone calls to have some meaningful sex. My life was running me—a sad state of affairs, yet I didn't seem to be able to do anything about it.

Dodging traffic and running a couple of red lights, Teddie flew up Rainbow, screeched around the corner onto Charleston, then hammered the last couple of miles to the hospital. The car had barely come to a stop when we both jumped out.

"This way," I shouted, as I bolted through the front door. I turned and saw Teddie toss the keys to the valet, then run after me.

Ignoring the stares of the people in the hallways, we ran, shoulder to shoulder. The elevator would take too long, so we hit the stairs. Out of breath and truly terrified as to what I would find, I stopped in front of the closed door of The Big Boss's suite. Teddie beside me, I paused, summoning some semblance of composure. Taking several deep breaths, I settled my heart rate and cleared my mind.

One last breath and I pushed open the heavy door.

The Big Boss, his eyes closed, lay quiet and still in the dim room. The only sign of life was the machine beeping in time to his heart rate. He seemed to have shrunk inside of himself, as if his body, virtually devoid of its life force, had shriveled like a balloon after its air had escaped. His skin looked gray, almost translucent.

Lowering myself into the chair next to his bed, I put my hand on his arm and whispered, "Boss?"

Teddie perched on the arm of my chair, and we both watched as The Big Boss's eyes fluttered open then came into focus.

He turned his head, looked at me and smiled. "You came."

"As fast as I could."

His eyes wandered to Teddie. "Theodore."

"Sir."

The Big Boss licked his lips and looked around. "Would you mind pouring me a glass of water? I'd really like a stiff shot of single malt, but that seems to be off limits for me right now."

"I'm not sure you can have water. We should ask someone," I said.

Teddie jumped up. "I'll go find the nurse." He disappeared through the door.

"Help me sit up, will you?" The Big Boss directed the question to me.

I found the controls that lifted the head of his bed, then helped him scooch until he found a comfortable upright position.

"We got Felicia Reilly," I said when he had gotten settled. "I don't know yet if she'll give us what we want—the police are questioning her now."

"Another nail in a particular someone's coffin, I hope."

Teddie walked back in a small cup in his hand. "No can do on the water. Not before surgery. You can have a few ice chips though."

The Big Boss took the cup Teddie proffered, shaking a few chips into his mouth. He parked them in a cheek. "But, however it turns out, I know you can handle it. The Babylon is in good hands."

Teddie again sat on the armrest. I sought his hand and held on tight.

The Big Boss looked at our clasped hands and smiled. "I have a story to tell you, but I don't quite know where to start."

His tired eyes met mine, holding them.

"Remember when I was a kid and I'd screw up and my supervisor sent me to talk to you?" I said. "Remember what you always told me?"

"The beginning is always a good place to start." He smiled. "Those were great days…" He trailed off.

For an awkward moment, nobody said anything. "Look, why don't I leave you two alone for a bit?"

The Big Boss made a fluttering motion with his hand. "No, no. Sit." He grabbed my free hand and squeezed. Looking me in the eye, he said. "This is a personal story. If Lucky wants you here, then so do I."

I grabbed Teddie's hand, pulling him back down.

There I sat, between the two most important men in my life—one had shepherded me through the first half of my life, the other I wanted by my side through the second half.

For the first time, it dawned on me that my name was no longer some kind of cosmic joke—I truly was lucky.

"The beginning?" I encouraged The Big Boss. "And, please, work quickly to the punch line. You've got me so worried, I'm going to stroke out right here if you don't get on with it."

"No need to worry—it's all good. Theodore, my wallet is in the inside pocket of my jacket over there." He nodded toward the chair in the far corner of the room. "Would you be so kind as to get it for me?"

"You want to do hundred-dollar-bill origami now?" I couldn't contain myself. "You're driving me nuts—"

"Hush, child. You sound just like your mother. I never could get her to be quiet either."

"My mother?"

The Big Boss took the wallet from Teddie, opened it, and pulled out a small, tattered scrap of paper and extended it toward me. A tic worked in his jaw, his hand shook a little bit.

I took the paper from him.

"Recognize it?" The Big Boss asked, his voice a whisper.

I looked down.

It was a photograph, an old photograph—my favorite photograph.

My mother, Sammy Davis, Dean Martin, and me, reaching for the person behind the camera.

"Where did you get this?" For a moment, I stopped breathing, my chest tight.

"I took that picture. That was one of the best, and worst, days of my life."

I sat stock-still, unable to move.

The Big Boss's face was taut with fear, but I saw the love in his eyes—it had been there all along.

"It was me you were reaching for," he said with a self-conscious shrug.

My eyes welled with tears. I leaned against Teddie—he felt solid, strong.

His arm circled my shoulders, pulling me tight as he angled his head to look down at me. "I'm a bit behind the eight ball here," Teddie said. "Why are you crying? I don't like it when you cry."

I handed the photo to him. "That's me and my mother a long time ago."

"I've seen it before. Don't you have a copy in your office?"

I nodded. "My father took that picture."

"But I thought The Big Boss just said he..." Seconds ticked by. "You're Lucky's father?" he asked The Big Boss.

"Yes."

I gasped as the whole truth hit me. This was the man Mona had waited all these years for. He'd been so close, almost within reach, yet a whole world away. Had he known how much she loved him?

"My mother?" My voice sounded tight.

"She's the last person I talk to every night."

"Oh!" My heart broke for them. Tears chased down my cheeks.

Teddie held me tight as sobs racked my body. "Why are you telling her this now?" he demanded of The Big Boss.

"I died this afternoon. I could die again tonight." He choked, then cleared his throat. "I needed to explain."

I squeezed his hand, fighting to get myself under control. "No need to explain. Mother was fifteen—even back then it was a felony to have sex with a minor."

"I thought—" The Big Boss started, but I stopped him short. I wanted to swipe at my tears, but I couldn't let go of either hand I held—one gave me strength, one I hoped to give strength to.

"I know," I continued. "You thought she was twenty—that's what she told everyone. I remember her twenty-sixth birthday. She thought it great fun that she was really only twenty-one and officially legal. I had to swear on a Bible I would keep her secret. She was taking an awful risk—I wasn't yet six."

The Big Boss and I smiled at the memories—the ties that bind a family. Family! Wow!

"You were trustworthy even then," he said.

I shrugged. "Don't get me wrong, I had a great childhood, but when you have a child for a mother, you grow up fast."

The Big Boss gave me a guilty smile framed with sadness, but said nothing. What was there to say?

"Anyway," I said, continuing the explanation. "Not only was Mother underage, but you were climbing the food chain at the casinos. The Mob was very much in control and, as I recall, they would not have taken kindly to an ex-hooker becoming the wife of their golden boy. Then there was the sticky matter of a child out of wedlock—all those Catholics would have had a stroke. After the Mob, the corporate holier-than-thous took over—same problem. Do I have it right?"

"Your batting average is so high, you could be a leadoff hitter in the majors." He took a deep breath. "Are you mad at me?"

"Mad?" I shook my head. "Horribly sad for you and Mona, but mad? No." I moved to sit on the bed so I faced him. "Look at me. For my whole life, you have been there for me. You even came to my basketball games in high school."

His eyes widened. "How did you know? I always hid in the back."

"You are the head of the power elite—when you show up anywhere, it's like Moses parting the Red Sea. Anyway, my point is, you were better than any father could be. Whether I was aware of the biological connection is irrelevant—I always loved you like a daughter."

Leaning back, he sighed as a smile lifted the corners of his mouth. "I thought I'd lost you again."

"Again?"

"That day the picture was taken. I knew I wouldn't see you again for a long time—perhaps forever. I wouldn't hold your mother again." He squinted his eyes shut tight, but a single tear escaped and trickled down his cheek. "You both were so important…"

He angrily swiped at the tear. "I thought I'd been given a life sentence to a living hell, but, when you were fifteen, your mother called. She said you couldn't live with her anymore—it just wasn't right for a young lady to live around that sort of thing. On top of that, the inspector we'd bribed for years to overlook the fact a child lived in a whorehouse was retiring. Then, when you told her you wanted to move to Vegas, she took it as a sign she really had to do something. Fate forced her hand."

"Mother called you?"

"Yeah. It was her idea that you come work for me—that way I could watch over you, keep you safe, offer help when you needed it." He opened his eyes and looked at me. "She didn't abandon you, Lucky. She waited until the last possible minute to let you go— even then she cried for months. I know how mad you've been at her all these years, thinking she let you walk away—that she didn't care. Letting her take the fall for that is my biggest regret."

In one instant, it was all gone—all the anger, all the hurt. My heart was free.

"Call your mother. I want her holding my hand when I wake

up. I don't give a good goddamn if the sanctimonious asses on our board are offended by my choice."

"You make them tons of money," I scoffed. "With that crowd, morality is all well and good, as long as it doesn't negatively impact their bottom line."

That got a smile out of him. "Theodore, open the door. I'll bet there's a passel of white-coats out there waiting to cart me off." He raised a hand to my cheek. "You've exceeded every expectation I ever had by miles."

"You've done the same."

"Get that son of a bitch, if you can." Those were his last words to me as the orderlies filed in and wheeled him out the door.

The door swung shut behind them, and Teddie wrapped me in his arms.

"God, I've just found my father and I could lose him."

Teddie's voice came back strong and sure, "Lucky, you've had him all along."

~

AFTER THEY TOOK THE BIG BOSS TO SURGERY, TEDDIE AND I WENT in search of food—hopeless optimists that we were—thinking they actually had something resembling sustenance in a hospital. We'd settled for coffee and a day-old Danish in the cafeteria—a term only an administrator with a cockeyed sense of optimism would use to describe the drab, windowless room in the basement. Doctors and nurses, rumpled and wrinkled with deep fatigue etched in their faces, occupied several of the tables. Worried family members huddled in quiet clumps at others. We claimed a spot in the corner.

I picked at the roll as my thoughts wandered like wild horses in the desert, impossible to corral.

"If you don't mind me asking, what son of a bitch are you supposed to get?"

Teddie's question yanked me back to reality. "Sorry, I can't tell you. You'll have to read about it in the papers like everybody else."

"Right."

"It's important—the most important fight I've had, and I have no idea how it's going to turn out." I pushed myself to my feet. "But I do know I'd better quit mooning about. I've got a board of directors' meeting in a few hours. I need to call my mother—she is going to be positively apoplectic that she wasn't here when they took him to surgery. And my office—I'm totally out of that loop." I sighed as I thought of it all. "Then the media needs to be spun."

"I've never met anyone who has more of an existence and less of a life than you," Teddie said with a grin as he rose and took my hand. "What can I do to help?"

"Save me from myself."

~

USING THE BIG BOSS'S HOSPITAL SUITE AS A COMMAND CENTER, I went to work.

First, I'd tackle Mona. I grabbed the Nextel, scrolled through the numbers until I found the one I wanted, then pushed-to-talk. "Jerry?"

"Well, if it isn't our fearless problem-solver. I hadn't heard from you in so long I thought they'd canned your ass."

"Then who would you dump all your problems on?" I paced back and forth in the small room as I talked. "Listen, do you have an empty helicopter and an available pilot?"

"Let me check." The connection went dead for a moment, then he came back. "We got both."

"Good. You know my mother's place, right?"

"No way am I answering that question," he scoffed. "I'm a married man. I plead the fifth."

"Send the chopper out to pick up my mother and bring her to UMC. She'll be waiting."

"You okay?" Jerry's voice turned serious—UMC had that effect on people.

"I'm fine. It's under control." I pushed End, flipped open the phone, and again scrolled through the list. This time I punched Send.

Mona answered on the first ring. "Lucky, is everything okay?"

Her voice sounded strained. I wondered if she'd had her nightly call from The Big Boss. Since he'd died once today, I doubted it. "No, Mom. Things aren't okay."

Amazingly, Mona didn't interrupt me once as I told her about The Big Boss. And more amazing still, she didn't yell at me for not calling her sooner.

"I will be waiting, honey. And, thank you."

Flabbergasted, I slowly closed the phone. I'd never heard a thank-you from Mona in my life.

Okay, Mona under control. Who next? I dialed my office—even at one in the morning I bet they were still there.

Miss Patterson picked up immediately. "Lucky?"

"Thank you for staying so late. I've got some things I need you to do."

After I'd finished giving her the list, I set the phone on the windowsill and sagged down on the couch, my legs stuck out in front of me.

"Tired?" Teddie asked. He sat in a chair on the other side of the room, legs crossed, and head back.

"What a day," I sighed, as I burrowed into the welcoming embrace of the soft cushions. "I'm so tired I don't know whether I'm coming or going."

Teddie unfolded himself and walked over to me. "Lie down." I looked up at him—he looked absolutely delicious—but there was no way. "As interested as I am, I can't muster the energy. Besides, there's no lock on the door."

"On your stomach," he said with a grin. "I can't solve your problems, but I can give a pretty fair back rub."

A half an hour later, and just as I was starting to loosen up a bit as Teddie kneaded the knots in my neck, Mona blew through the door like a cyclone. Her hair pulled back, her makeup understated, dressed in creased blue jeans and a starched white shirt, she looked like a nice little housewife from the suburbs. If only wishing could make it so.

"Lucky! Where is he? Is he okay?"

"Mother. He's still in surgery. It'll be couple of hours yet." I couldn't move—I didn't want to. Teddie's back rubs were even better than advertised.

"A little lower there on the right," I directed him. He did as I asked. "Oh, yeah. Right there."

"Lucky!" For a moment, I thought Mona was going to stamp her foot.

"Mother, relax. We've all had a hell of a day. Getting all worked up isn't going to make anything better."

She seemed to sag under the truth. "It makes *me* feel better, though."

"I know what you mean." Like mother, like daughter—scary thought. "Mother, you remember Teddie?"

My mother found her manners. "Theodore, I'm sorry. How are you?"

"In love with your daughter, but otherwise pretty good."

"Glad to hear it," Mona said with a grin, then shook her head. "Poor, poor fellow."

"Help me up." I rolled over and Teddie pulled me, groaning, to my feet. I ran a hand through my hair, then brushed down my blouse and slacks. I bet I looked as bad as I felt. "Okay, let's all try to get a little rest. They'll find us when they have any news."

I helped Mother unfold the chair into a bed, while Teddie rounded up blankets and pillows. After she was settled, I tucked a blanket around her, then bent down and kissed her cheek. "Good night, Mom."

"I've always loved you," she murmured, her eyes heavy with the weight of a long day. "Maybe I wasn't a good mother sometimes, but I always tried to do what was best for you."

"I know. You did great." I stood and looked down at her. What a bad hand she'd been dealt, and yet she had triumphed in her own way. She raised a daughter. Kept the daughter away from the pitfalls she herself had fallen into. She helped other young women escape their own bad choices. And she'd loved a good man. All together a fairly successful life. I only hoped I did as well.

"Mom, I need to know one thing."

"Only one?" She gave me a tight, worried smile.

"At some point, The Big Boss could've picked us, but he didn't. He chose his hotels instead."

"About twenty years ago, he wanted to give it all up. Throw it all away. I wouldn't let him." Mother's eyes shone with her conviction, but she couldn't mask the pain.

"You wouldn't?" I could only imagine how much that cost her. "Why not?"

"Both your father and I came from dirt-poor families. We both knew what it was like to not know when we'd eat again, to not have heat in the dead of winter, to struggle into clothes several sizes too small so that we would at least have something to cover us." Her eyes glazed for a moment, clouded with memories, none of which seemed pleasant. "We both were the products of alcoholic parents who couldn't cope with life."

She patted the chair beside her. As I sat next to her, she took my hand, turned it over, and absentmindedly traced the lines of my palm. "But, a tough life made tough adults out of us. When you came along, both of us would have given our lives to make sure you didn't have to go through what we had as children."

"You gave up your chance for me?"

"You were the bridge—even though we weren't together, we were joined. It was enough—it had to be." She turned my hand over and pressed it to her cheek as she shut her eyes. "And don't ever think I was unhappy. Having you was the best thing that ever happened to me. I love you so much."

"I love you too, Mom," I whispered, as I brushed a stray hair from her forehead. "You rest now. I doubt any of us will sleep, but try to relax."

Teddie had kicked off his shoes and was sitting on the edge of the bed. "Come here." He pulled a blanket over us as we lay together, his arms around me, my head on his shoulder, one leg tucked between his. I couldn't get any closer without crawling inside him.

"I never got to thank you," I said.

"For what?"

"Your phone call. Harvard not only accepted Mrs. Paisley's grandson, they awarded him a partial scholarship as well."

"What good is all that money I give them every year if it doesn't buy me some stroke with the old alma mater?" Teddie's voice reverberated in his chest under my ear. "He was well qualified, so it didn't take much."

"Thank you just the same. Mrs. Paisley is a peach—one of the good people of the world."

"You would know." He kissed my forehead. "Can I ask you something?"

"Only if it can be answered in short sentences and small words. Mental acuity is failing by the second."

"You turned down Dane?"

"Just the thought of you turns a bad day into a brilliant one. When something wonderful happens, you're the first person I want to share it with. When something bad happens, you're the only one who can make me feel better. You laugh at my jokes, even when they aren't that funny. In return, you make me laugh even when I don't feel like laughing. You are thoughtful and kind and the world is a better place because you're in it. And, perhaps best of all, you love me in spite of myself."

I found an opening in his shirt and touched his skin. I heard his sharp intake of breath. "In addition, as sort of an added benefit, do you feel that?" I asked.

"Yeah."

"Even the sound of your voice does that to me." I unbuttoned one button and put my hand flat on his stomach, and felt his skin warm under my touch.

Dane hadn't stood a chance.

CHAPTER TWENTY-ONE

*T*HE FRONT door to my office opened, and a heartbeat later Miss Patterson appeared in my doorway. Today, she wore brown slacks and a dusty-blue silk shirt, sexy heels and a single diamond drop around her neck, which matched the ones in her ears. Her short blonde 'do looked hip and fun. Her eyes shone brightly—even after only a few hours of sleep. Every time I looked at her, it was a bit of a shock—I still wasn't used to the total transformation.

"Whoa! How long have you been here?" She glanced around, taking in my uncluttered desk—you could now see the top—a rich, finely grained black walnut.

I held up my finger for her to wait a moment as I scanned down the page in my hand, signed my name, then carefully placed the paper on the top of a stack that was now at least six inches high. "All of those are ready to go." I glanced at the clock on the wall. Nine-thirty. "I've been here three hours or so. It's amazing how much you can get done when the office is quiet."

"How's The Big Boss?"

"The doctor awakened me at four thirty, just after they'd finished. The surgery went well. According to him, The Big Boss will be better than new—eventually. His recuperation could take a bit. Knowing The Big Boss, he'll love that."

I didn't tell her I'd left Mona in recovery holding The Big Boss's hand and waiting for him to wake up. I'd had to threaten all kinds of legal action and bodily harm to convince the staff to allow Mona in there, but The Big Boss would get his wish.

I also didn't tell her I'd left Teddie sleeping—I hadn't had the heart to wake him when the doctor came to get me. Of course, Teddie might not thank me for leaving him there—in that bed by himself, he was in danger of having some nurse walk in and jab a thermometer into an orifice. His problem, not mine. Right now, I had enough of my own.

I levered myself out of the chair. My butt was numb—I hadn't sat that long in forever. Stepping around the desk, I checked my appearance in the mirror—it was amazing what a hot shower and a change of clothes could do. Dark Chanel suit, red silk camisole to match my red Stuart Weitzman heels, enough gold and diamonds to impress the money crowd, soft hair, very little makeup, and, for once, no dark circles. I was ready. "Time to do battle."

~

THE BOARDROOM OCCUPIED A PRIME CORNER ON THE TOP FLOOR, just down the hall from The Big Boss's suite. As I readied myself, I couldn't remember a time I had been there without The Big Boss. Even though I knew I wouldn't find him. I still looked for him among the thirteen suits—four of them women—seated at the big oval table when I pushed through the door, then closed it behind me. Among the faces that turned toward me, I found Irv Gittings and gave him a smile.

He winked at me.

"Ladies and gentlemen, Mr. Rothstein will not be here today. For those of you I haven't met before, I am Lucky O'Toole, an executive of this hotel, and I will be serving in his stead. In the packet of papers in front of each of you, you will find the proper documentation to allow me to do that." I took The Big Boss's seat at the head of the table. "Before we begin, are there any questions?"

No one said a word as I glanced from face to face—some were old, some young, some pretty, some bland. Five directors were from New York and represented our corporate minority share-holders. Seven directors were local and generally sided with The Big Boss, the Babylon's controlling shareholder. Two of those seven were technically my superiors at the Babylon—the director of operations and the treasurer—although in actuality, I reported directly to The Big Boss. I nodded to them. Not being a director, Irv sat to the side.

"Very well then, let's begin." I watched the faces watching me as we went through the whole *Robert's Rules of Order* thing, calling the meeting to order and reciting the list of attendees, making sure we had a quorum. That out of the way, I dove into the meat of the meeting. "As you may have noticed, we have a guest, Mr. Irv Gittings." I watched the faces, looking for signs of Irv's coconspir-ators. I didn't know if he had infiltrated our board or not, but I suspected he'd at least made forays in that direction. And The Big Boss always told me to know my enemies.

"Mr. Gittings has asked to address the board, so, before we get down to business, I suggest we listen to what he has to say." I motioned to Irv. "Mr. Gittings."

Heads swiveled as Irv rose and walked over to my side.

Dressed in an exquisitely tailored gunmetal-gray suit, with the tiniest silver pinstripe, gray tie and light lavender shirt, Irv was the personification of a wolf in sheep's clothing. He rested his hand on my shoulder as he turned to address the assemblage.

"Gentlemen, I'm sure you're wondering why Mr. Rothstein isn't here today. I'm wondering the same thing, but I think I have an explanation for you." He pulled a DVD out of his coat pocket and held it up for the room to see. "This is video footage of the young woman falling to her death last weekend from a helicopter owned by this hotel. I'm sure you are all aware of the incident." He paused, looking at each director in turn for signs of assent.

Getting them, he squeezed my shoulder, and continued. "You may not know that the police have evidence that strongly suggests the young woman was murdered."

A collective gasp rose from Irv's audience. I had to hand it to him—he had them right where he wanted them.

"And..." He waggled the DVD for attention. "This footage shows that Mr. Rothstein was in the helicopter." With each word, Irv's voice rose to a final crescendo. "In fact, he was in the back seat of the helicopter with the young woman when she fell."

The room erupted in a chatter of voices. Irv had a satisfied grin on his face as he looked down at me. I grinned back.

Irv raised his voice to be heard. "In fact, I bet the police are looking for Mr. Rothstein right now. Isn't that right, Ms. O'Toole?"

That quieted the group, as all heads swiveled in my direction.

"The police don't tell me what they're doing," I said, taking a bit of wind out of Irv's sails. My Nextel vibrated at my hip. I looked down and smiled to myself as I read the text message.

On a roll, Irv barreled ahead. "Since Mr. Rothstein is up to his ass in alligators, this hotel is without solid stewardship to navigate these turbulent economic times. Therefore, my investors and I plan to make a tender offer for a controlling interest. Together with Ms.—"

"Irv?" I interrupted.

Startled, he looked at me, his eyebrows snapping into a scowl.

I rose from my chair and sidled around him. "Before you continue..." I opened the door and looked into the smiling face of Detective Romeo, two uniforms flanking him. "I believe these gentlemen want a word with you."

I stepped aside, allowing Romeo and the two cops into the room. Flash Gordon and a photographer followed them.

When in front of Ol' Irv, Romeo began, "Mr. Gittings, I am arresting you for the murder of Lyda Sue Stalnaker. You have the right to remain silent..."

I stopped listening as Romeo ran through his Miranda spiel. Instead, drinking in the moment, I watched the expressions flash across Irv's face: disbelief, anger, rage, then—glancing my direction— pure, unadulterated hatred.

My heart soared like a hawk. I had lied about not caring what happened to Irv Gittings. Revenge, as addictive as crack cocaine.

One of the cops fastened Irv's arms behind his back with a pair of handcuffs.

And Flash and her photographer caught it all.

I gave Romeo a nod and a smile as he led Gittings away.

After all of the non-directors trooped out, I shut the door and I turned to face the board. "That was exciting, wasn't it?" I grinned, receiving mostly grins in return. Calm replaced the tension. "I apologize for the drama, but sometimes you have to set a trap to catch a rat. Mr. Gittings, the rat in this story, left a few rather pertinent details out of his story."

I again took my seat and leaned back, savoring my victory. "This morning, Detective Romeo of the Las Vegas Metropolitan Police Department recovered an audiotape from one of the co-conspirators in the plot to kill Miss Stalnaker and to frame Mr. Rothstein for her murder. Mr. Gittings' voice could be heard on the tape as he planned the crime."

"Then, where is Mr. Rothstein?" asked one of the New York directors.

"Unfortunately, he was admitted to the hospital yesterday with an irregular heartbeat." I held up my hand to silence the disquieted murmurings. "He's fine. He had a pacemaker installed last night. He should be back at the helm in no time." I left out the part about dying once and the part about the myectomy and the specialist flown in from the Mayo Clinic.

I leaned forward, my hands on the table in front of me. "Now, let's get down to business, shall we?"

~

FEET ON MY DESK, HANDS BEHIND HIS HEAD, LEANING BACK IN MY chair, Teddie was holding court in my office when I arrived. I was aware of a crowd in the room, listening in rapt attention as Teddie regaled them with details of the Trendmakers party—some I was unaware of—but all of them were funny. Probably a bit funnier in the retelling.

Nobody noticed me as I hid in the doorway, shielding myself behind the broad shoulders of the Beautiful Jeremy Whitlock—who, I noticed, had his arms around Miss Patterson's waist, pulling her back against him. The others in the room were hidden from view, but it didn't matter—my focus was on Teddie.

He was a natural-born entertainer, his expressive face and eyes danced with merriment, holding the interest of his small audience the way the weaving flute of a snake charmer captured the cobra.

He stopped midsentence when his eyes caught mine. Kicking his feet off the desk, he sprang from the chair. "Hey! How'd the meeting go? We've all been on pins and needles."

"I can tell." In two strides, I was in front of him. I grabbed his shirt in both hands and pulled. "I missed you," I said, just before my mouth covered his.

He kissed me back. Now my day was perfect.

I pushed him away, and he dramatically flopped back into my chair.

"Do you think you can miss me more often?" he said as he grabbed my hand and pulled until I was sitting in his lap.

"I'll think about it." Arms looped around his neck, I scanned the others in my office. Brandy and Dane sat in the two chairs across from the desk. Jerry leaned against the wall, a sardonic smile lifting one side of his mouth. Jeremy still held Miss Patterson, a very satisfied grin on her face—I didn't know whether the grin was for me or for her; I suspected both.

"Are you going to tell us about the meeting?" Jerry asked, clearly nonplussed by all the frivolity.

"Sure, but first—is anybody hungry? I'm famished."

"We've ordered pizzas. They should be here in a few minutes," Teddie said. "I ordered a veggie delight extra sauce for you."

"Just the way I like it." I squeezed his neck then proceeded to give them my abbreviated version of Irv Gittings' fall from grace.

"All I can say is, the minutes from that meeting are going to make interesting reading," Teddie announced when I'd finished, eliciting another laugh from the crowd.

As promised, the pizza delivery man arrived, laden with enough pies to feed our little crowd and half the tourists lurking in the lobby, and enough soda pop to fill at least one of the pools out back. Everybody helped themselves, and Teddie and I fell to the task of sating at least one of our appetites.

I was on my second piece when Romeo burst through the door, then stopped, an embarrassed look on his face as we all turned toward him.

"Want some pizza?" I asked him through a mouthful.

He grabbed a plate, heaped five slices on it, then parked his butt on the corner of my desk. "That was fun, wasn't it?"

"Kid, you about gave me a coronary. Your text message came at literally the very last minute. I was about to be thrown into bed with Irv Gittings."

"Can we use another analogy?" Teddie interjected, in a shameless attempt to get a smile out of me.

It worked.

"I'm sorry we were so late. The tape was in a safe-deposit box at the main branch of the Bank of America on Charleston," Romeo explained. "It practically took an act of Congress to get the branch manager out of bed and down there with a guy to drill out the lock."

"You did good."

His face flushed at the compliment. "I want to know one thing —how'd you know Felicia Reilly would have a tape like that?"

"She was a pretty smart little felon, but neither she nor Willie had the balls to take on The Big Boss—Irv Gittings had to be a part of it." I took a slurp of Diet Coke. "The crooks I've known have always tried to get the dirt on their co-conspirators as insurance against a double cross. It stood to reason Felicia the blackmailer would tape Ol' Irv."

Romeo's brows creased in thought. "If she had a trump card like that, why didn't she play it?"

"She would have, once she was out of his reach. Even though his star was fading, Irv Gittings was still one of the power brokers in this town. If you value your life, you'd better be well hidden when you mess with one of those guys."

"It still works like that here?"

"With the old guard? You bet your ass."

Thankfully, Romeo had no more questions. On his last piece of pizza, he got up and wandered toward Brandy.

"Is your leg numb?" I asked Teddie as I moved my butt slightly in a vain attempt to get some blood back into the one spot that had been in contact with the muscles in his thigh.

"I don't know, I can't feel it."

I started to jump up, but he pulled me back down.

"I'm kidding. You're not moving."

I saw Flash standing in the doorway and motioned her over.

I didn't need to glance down at the newspaper in her hand— the self-satisfied look on her face told me all I needed to know. "The last nail in Irv's coffin," I said, just because it felt good to say it out loud.

Teddie took the paper and huddled over it.

"They held the run for me. I told them it would be worth their while." Flash parked herself in the spot recently vacated by Romeo.

"Bet they're not sorry."

"My boss gave me a raise on the spot." Flash gave me a grin. "Of course, that's just the afternoon paper. I'm getting a one-inch headline and my own byline in the *Review-Journal* tomorrow morning."

"We'll probably be watching you on the evening news as well. You hit a home run."

"I owe you."

"I'd say we're even," I said. "Now, go help yourself to some pizza."

Flash jumped up and went in search of food.

Teddie whistled low in my ear. "My, you've been a busy girl, chasing all the bad guys."

"You're reading between the lines."

"You aren't mentioned by name, that's true. But this whole caper has your fingerprints all over it." Teddie leaned me back so he could look me in the eye. "You flushed Irv Gittings, didn't you? The paper says your young Galahad—"

"Romeo."

"Right, your young Romeo put the whole thing together, but he didn't, did he? You did, and you personally delivered the *coup de grace*. Am I right?"

"What can I say? I'm multitalented."

"Hmmm, I think I would like to explore that further," he whispered in my ear. "But, seriously, all foreplay aside, you've made a powerful enemy."

"Not the first time." I rose, effectively cutting off that line of conversation. "Now, I know someone who would really like to see that paper."

Worry clouded his eyes as I met his gaze and held it. He shrugged. I knew he was only shelving the topic until later, but I'd take the small victory.

"The Ferrari's out front." Teddie grabbed my hand and pulled me toward the door. "Are you done pursuing truth, justice, and the American way this afternoon, or do you have to come back to the office?"

"I've hung up my cape for the day."

"Good. Give me that damned phone." Teddie grabbed my Nextel and handed it to Miss Patterson as we stepped by her and Jeremy. "Your fearless leader is taking the rest of the afternoon off. Don't call her unless the fate of the free world hangs in the balance."

She shot me a knowing grin as she pocketed my phone. "Don't worry, we've got everything under control. And, yes," she said in anticipation of my next question. "I'll make sure the board members are well taken care of."

"Thanks!" I shouted over my shoulder as Teddie pulled me through the door.

❧

WE FOUND THE BIG BOSS IN CARDIAC INTENSIVE CARE, MONA AT his side—his hand still clutched firmly in hers, if she hadn't let go of it since four thirty this morning, gangrene was going to set in.

My father smiled weakly at us. His eyes, intense black points of life in his otherwise wan face, followed my every movement. I sat on the other side of his bed. His hands on my shoulders, Teddie stood behind me.

For once in her life, my mother said nothing.

I cocked my head toward The Big Boss, but directed the question to my mother. "You thought it was him visiting Lyda Sue at your place, didn't you?"

"I'd introduced them. He was helping her."

I nodded at her confirmation of the last piece to the puzzle, then I held up the paper for The Big Boss to scan.

When he'd finished, he looked up at me, relief washing over his face. "I told you the Babylon was in good hands."

"Flash Gordon's boss gave her a raise on the spot."

"That's right, hit me while I'm down." The Big Boss grinned—this time his smile had some pop to it.

"What is it you used to say? 'Get 'em on the ropes, then hit 'em again'?" I teased.

"Using my own words against me? You are a cruel, cruel child." He laid his head back on the pillow and closed his eyes.

I squeezed his hand. "We'll leave you to rest. Mom, take good care of him."

Mona nodded at me, her eyes filled with tears. "Lucky, I…"

"I know, Mom. Now, we can all get on with the lives we were meant to have."

I always wondered how racehorses felt after they'd been loaded in the starting gate, but before the bell had rung—ready to go, but unable to race.

Now I knew.

As Teddie and I rode the elevator to his place, I was careful to keep my distance. One touch from him and, like those racehorses at the bell, I'd leap out of the gate—there'd be no holding me back. The tapes from the security cameras in the elevator would be blackmail material—or else some enterprising soul would sell them on the Internet—either result would not be good. Teddie might get some mileage out of them, though—a few minutes with me, and no one would wonder about his sexual orientation anymore. Clearly, my mind was grasping at stray thoughts—anything to keep from focusing on the moments to come. I had a loose enough rein on my body as it was without carnal thoughts to spur it on.

"I've got some champagne chilling," Teddie said, as we stepped into his apartment. "Want a glass?"

"I don't want champagne."

He looked at me and, for a moment, I thought he was fighting back a smile. "No?"

I shook my head as I shrugged out of my jacket and let it fall where I stood. "No champagne."

His eyes grew warm as I skinned my camisole over my head.

I heard his sharp intake of breath as I stepped out of my skirt — my mother had been right about the whole wearing sexy underwear thing. To hell with diamonds—lace and garters and real silk stockings were a girl's best friend.

"What then?" he asked.

"Just you."

He grinned as he reached down and picked me up. This time I didn't argue. Once inside the bedroom, he kicked the door shut, then let me slide slowly down his body. He had a habit of doing that, and it was absolutely mind-blowing—every nerve ending in my body caught fire.

"Teddie, my love," I said, as I reached for the top button of his jeans, "You are about to get Lucky."

CHAPTER TWENTY-TWO

*L*IKE A bubble rising to the surface of a languid pool, I slowly emerged from a sound sleep. The sweet vibrations of the last few hours still echoed through my body, carried on a current of pleasure. On my side, Teddie curled around me, one hand cupping my breast, one leg thrown possessively over mine, his breath soft on the back of my neck; I never wanted to move. Of course, after the last few hours, I wasn't sure I was still capable of movement.

I'd never known sex could be so utterly draining, yet invigorating. So incredibly intimate. So...perfect.

Rolling ever so gently, I twisted and turned, careful not to disturb his embrace, until I faced Teddie.

He was already awake. His eyes, now the blue of the deepest ocean waters, captured mine, and he gave me a lazy, lopsided grin. "That was friggin' fantastic."

"Which time?" I asked, as I rested my head on his shoulder and nuzzled into the crook of his neck.

"All of them." He casually stroked my arm.

I submerged myself in the sensation of his nearness—the hot

spark of excitement along each inch of my body where it touched his.

"I have something for you," Teddie whispered after a few moments.

"You've just given me the most perfect afternoon in recorded history."

"That was a mutual gift—this one is just for you."

"Do I have to move?" I reluctantly pushed myself to my elbow.

"Eventually." Teddie reached up and pulled me into his kiss.

After a few minutes, it took everything I had to break the embrace. "It's getting late. I'm going to have to go."

"We'll go together—Miranda made a place for me at her table. I understand you were supposed to be Subway's date, but Miranda said he wouldn't mind."

"That's the second best thing that's happened to me today." I felt like crowing as I crawled over Teddie, then swung my feet to the floor.

Teddie was right behind me. Grabbing a robe from the back of a chair, he helped me into it. "Follow me."

Admiring his long, lean lines, I gladly did as I was told.

His apartment had a huge dressing room, as mine did, lined with mirrors. He grabbed a large, gold box from the top of his dresser and presented it to me. Gold boxes meant only one thing —the Palace.

"Open it."

He held the box as I lifted off the top. I gasped when I saw what was inside. I lifted the delicate fabric and held it up.

Intricately beaded in teals, blues and purples on two layers of chiffon, so thin that each single layer was translucent, but together they were provocatively modest, it was the most beautiful gown I had ever seen.

I looked at him quizzically. "When did you get this?"

"I bought it the day we were there with Miss Patterson, but it needed some alteration. I picked it up the other night when you tried to call me on my cell and couldn't get me—the night I was trying to stifle my inner caveman." He set the box aside. "Put it on."

I shrugged out of the robe and stepped into the cloud of material, then pulled it up and snaked my arm through, careful not to rip the delicate fabric. Teddie, standing between me and the mirror, zipped me up. He brushed my hair back from my face, gave me a wink, then moved aside.

A beautiful—even sexy—woman stared back at me. My eyes grew wide. Off one shoulder, cut down the back and slit up one side to the very limit of good taste, the dress fit like a second skin until it draped in soft folds just below my hips.

Teddie moved behind me, his chin on my bare shoulder, his arms around my waist. "This is the you I've seen every time I've looked at you since the day we met. Remember that day?"

I smiled as I leaned back into him. "Backstage after your show at the Flamingo."

"You walked up to me and introduced yourself. You told me you wanted me, then you got all flustered when you realized what you'd said."

"You knew I meant to say I wanted your show, but you left me dangling in the wind."

"I'm shallow; I take my kicks where I find them." He waggled his eyebrows at me over my shoulder.

"That sounds like something I'd say."

"Anyway, this is how I see you—sloe-eyed, your mouth a little puffy and bruised after an afternoon of unbridled sex—with me, of course. Your hair loose and sexy." He nibbled on my ear for a moment, sending shivers through me. "You blow me away. You always have."

GOING FROM MY AFTERNOON WITH TEDDIE TO WATCHING THE procession of adult film stars parade down the red carpet was truly ruining the sublime with the ridiculous. Teddie, resplendent in his perfectly fitted tux, held my hand as we stood off to the side and watched the show.

"Welcome to the land of the Stepford porn stars," I whispered in Teddie's ear, as starlet after cookie-cutter starlet, all bleached, waxed and suitably siliconed, sashayed down the gauntlet to the raucous approval of the crowd gathered six deep.

Young men in varying states of inebriation hung over the velvet ropes shouting their favorite star's name. Occasionally, one of the women would grant a request for a photograph or a kiss. One particularly brazen young thing almost started a riot when she raised her dress and gave the crowd a money shot.

"That one clearly doesn't understand that some things are best left to the imagination," Teddie remarked.

"Did you truly expect subtlety from this crowd?"

"Do you know who any of these women are?" Teddie asked, God bless him.

"I don't really focus on faces when I watch porn."

He shot me a startled look.

"What?" I kept my face a mask of innocence.

The roar of the crowd drowned out his reply.

Miranda, a young man on either arm, posed for photographs and adulation. Tonight, she wore a flowing robe reminiscent of those worn by royalty in an earlier era—except for the fact that Miranda's royal wardrobe was completely see-through—sort of a modern take on the emperor's new clothes. Every square inch of her body was displayed for all to appreciate.

"Miranda is certainly very comfortable with her body," Teddie whispered.

"Nobody should be that comfortable."

Behind Miranda, Subway marched by himself—a good sport letting his wife have her fun.

Catching sight of us, Subway ducked under the ropes and wormed his way through the crowd. He wrapped me in a bear hug, then planted one of his famous kisses on me. "Lucky! You look remarkable!"

"Who knew?"

"Theodore." Subway shook Teddie's hand. "You have the most stunning date of all. One, I understand, you pilfered from me."

Teddie beamed in my direction. His grin shot a jolt of warmth through me—I didn't need to be clairvoyant to know what he was thinking.

Miranda with her boy toys muscled in beside Subway. "Theodore, you look good enough to eat." She waggled her eyebrows suggestively and said, "If I only had the time."

"My loss, I'm sure," Teddie shot back.

"Lucky, these are my friends." She proffered the boys for my inspection. "You remember, the ones with the little camera by the pool?"

"Right."

"They're going to be technical advisors on our next film."

"You boys be careful," I said. "She eats young men like you for dinner."

One of the youngsters looked over-the-moon with anticipation. The other one looked at me as if he couldn't decide whether I was being literal or figurative. Keeping my expression bland, I didn't give him a hint. He'd jumped into the cage with the tiger; he was on his own.

"Nice dress," Miranda said, I assumed to me, since I was the only one in our little throng wearing one.

"It's a wee bit conservative for you, don't you think?" I asked. "Who are you dressed as tonight?"

"I'm the Whore of Babylon," she announced, as she adopted a regal position, putting her assets on display. "What do you think?"

"Appropriate," I said. Momentarily at a loss, it was all I could think of.

Teddie leaned down to Subway and said, "Is this where I tell you your wife has a nice ass and you hit me in the nose?"

Subway laughed and put a hand to his wife's back, urging her to move. "Come on, Miranda. You and Lucky have dueled enough for now. Besides, we're wanted inside."

The four of them disappeared into the ballroom, leaving Teddie and me alone as the crowd rapidly thinned.

"Do you think Miranda knows that the Whore of Babylon is an allegorical figure of supreme evil associated with the Antichrist?" Teddie asked.

"Probably not, but if you told her that prophesy spoke of a beast with seven heads and ten horns taking down the Whore of Babylon, she would think that had a lot of interesting possibilities."

"Where did you learn that?" he asked after he stopped laughing.

"Harvard isn't the only institution of higher learning."

"They're going to be sad to hear that." Teddie hooked his thumb toward the ballroom. "Do you really want to go to the banquet and awards thing?"

"You're not dying to know who wins the award for the best up-and-comer?"

He shot me a look. "They don't really have an award for that, do they?"

"Subway wins it every year."

"I want to be like him when I'm his age," Teddie said with an evil grin.

"You'll need to find a new lover."

Teddie shook his head. "Too high a price to pay. Seriously, though, do you have to go?" He didn't even try to hide the fact that he hoped the answer was no.

I shook my head. "I don't think we'll even be missed."

"Good." He grabbed my elbow and steered me back toward the casino. "We're young, alive, in love, and all dressed up with money in our pockets. Where would you like to go?"

I thought for a minute. "I know just the place."

~

RIDING THE ELEVATOR, I WAITED UNTIL THE LAST GUEST GOT OFF before I stuck the key into the panel, then removed the cover over the button that said Babel, and pressed it. Fifty-three stories up, Babel, our new rooftop lounge, was set to open next weekend.

The construction crew had left thousands of lights twinkling in the branches of the potted trees surrounding the swimming pool, and the roof retracted, so the stars added their own sparkle — perfect. Babel had been designed to attract the younger, hip crowd, but tonight, we had it all to ourselves.

Hand in hand we walked to the edge of the rooftop terrace. Teddie put his arm around me as we drank in the view. Vegas stretched to the horizon in every direction—the flashing multi-colored lights of the Strip; the white lights of the neighborhoods where people lived quiet lives, raising families; the moving red and white lights of cars coming and going, tracing the highways and streets in lines of light; the landing lights of the planes on approach to McCarran, hanging like a string of pearls in the velvety blackness of night sky.

My town.

Teddie hugged me tight, then lifted my chin and kissed me deeply, awakening every cell in my body.

My life.

My Nextel rang.

Teddie groaned, then laughed a resigned sort of laugh as he fished the thing out of his pocket. "Can't the others cover for you tonight?"

"They were here all last night and all day today. I gave them both the rest of the weekend off." I flipped open the phone, put it on the speaker, and said, "O'Toole."

"Oh, Ms. O'Toole!" Sergio's voice sounded strained as he talked rapid-fire. "We have this man, in room 12107. He is spitting mad and naked as a jaybird. Housekeeping found him. There is this trapeze, and this rope, and duct tape around his...well, you will have to see him yourself."

"On my way."

"Nice to know your life is getting back to normal." Teddie took my hand and led me to the elevators. "A naked man, duct tape around his member, a trapeze, rope; how'd you get so lucky?"

I threw my arms around his neck and just before my mouth closed over his, I murmured, "Lover, I was born lucky."

ONLY THE BEGINNING...

THE END

Thank you so much for going on a Lucky adventure with me. I
hope you enjoyed the ride.

As you may know, reviews are SUPER helpful. They not only help
potential readers make a choice, but they also help me win
coveted spots on various advertising platforms.

So, if you would please, do me the favor of leaving a review at the
outlet of your choice.

NEXT UP FOR LUCKY...

Read a short excerpt below

CHAPTER ONE

Millions of enraged honeybees had done the impossible: Single-handedly they had brought the Las Vegas Strip to a standstill.

Alerted by our limo driver, who was stuck somewhere in the mess, I bolted out the front door of the Babylon, down the drive, and screeched to a halt at the Strip. Momentarily speechless, I joined several hundred Vegas revelers gathered in clumps. Gawking, they encircled a large tractor-trailer. The cab lay on its side—I could see the driver still trapped inside, staring out at us.

Momentum had wrapped the trailer around the cab. The thin aluminum skin had given way, exposing smashed and broken hives. A trickle of golden goo, which I assumed was honey, oozed from the trailer's open wound.

Clouds of bees launched themselves through the jagged tear into the cool night air. They swarmed over and through the crowd like tiny avenging angels. The mass of hurtling bodies and flashing wings reflected the multicolored signs on the Strip in a free-form light show that put the Fremont Street Experience to shame.

Lifting half-full glasses in salute, the crowd *oooohed* and *ahhh-hhed* as if this was another Las Vegas extravaganza provided for their benefit. The party atmosphere lasted but a minute or two—right up until the bees got angry. Swatting and twitching, the revelers did the bee dance. Then, realizing the bees meant business and outnumbered them by a large margin, they tossed their glasses and bolted. I never knew drunk people could run that fast.

Like a herd of wild horses in a mad panic, they stampeded past me, making a beeline for the relative safety of the hotel.

I was congratulating myself on my mixed metaphor when one of the little swarmers decided my neck was the perfect place to bury its stinger.

"Damn!" I slapped at the tiny creature, then plucked its squashed body from my skin and tossed it away. For such a small thing, it sure packed a punch. The pain galvanized me to action. I ran upstream through the crowd, heading for the truck.

Geoffrey David-Williston was right where I knew he'd be—in the thick of the action. Of course, I didn't have to be Einstein to figure that out—Geoffrey was the head of the World Association of Entomologists and their chief bee guy.

For months we'd been negotiating and planning the entomologists' conference at the Babylon, which would start the day after tomorrow. He had promised me we could populate an exhibit with millions of honeybees without incident. Fool that I am, I believed him—then.

Now I wanted a piece of his ass!

Reaching out, I grabbed his shirtsleeve, pulling him around to face me just as another little bugger planted a stinger in my left calf. Geoffrey's shirt still clutched in my fist, I bent down and swatted the bee away as I started in.

"You assured me no one would ever know you'd carted

millions of bees through the streets of Las Vegas. Well, they damn well know now! In fact, you told me honeybees were docile and wouldn't harm anyone." I waved my free hand toward the bees. "They sure as hell don't look docile now, do they?" I ducked, hiding as much of myself as possible behind Geoffrey as the angry swarm buzzed past.

Several inches taller than my six feet, with hawkish features and deep-set eyes, Geoffrey was so thin he looked as if he hadn't seen a good meal in decades, making it hard for me to hide much of my bulk behind him. He didn't look at me. Instead he concentrated on the bees, his eyes following them as they raced through the night. When he spoke, I had to strain to hear. "Be calm. You're agitating the bees."

"Calm?" I brushed a little gold and black body from the sleeve of my sweater. "Agitating the ..." I paused, closed my eyes, counted to ten, then opened them again. Nope, still seeing red; so I repeated the whole counting thing. This time, when I opened my eyes, I was only seeing a slight shade of pink. Better. "Geoffrey ..." I started again, but he wasn't listening.

"Do you think you could get someone to turn off all these lights?" he said, as he watched the buzzing cloud whirling around. "The bees are disoriented. We're going to have a hard time getting them back into their hives."

"Turn off the lights? On the Strip? Sure, it'll only take me a minute." My voice was deadly. "Fortunately, I've been entrusted with the secret code to the switch that will kill the power to the beating heart of Las Vegas."

Geoffrey looked at me, a quizzical look on his face. "You can't turn them off?"

What was it about sarcasm that eluded brilliant minds? "Of *course*, I can't turn them off. You'll have to think of something else."

"Get me something to burn, then. Quickly." His eyes again followed the billowing mass of bees.

"A jackknifed tractor-trailer, a cloud of angry insects, a first-class traffic jam, and a panicked mob aren't enough for you? You need to start a fire?" My eyes were getting slitty—a bad sign.

"The bees are starting to sting. When they sting, they release an alarm pheromone that attracts other bees to help in the fight. Smoke can sometimes mask that pheromone." He turned and gave me the benefit of his full attention. "I think stopping the stinging first would be a good thing, don't you?"

I slapped at another bugger attacking my neck, then stomped my feet. Maybe I was imagining it, but I felt bugs crawling all over me. Real or imagined, the bugs propelled me to action. Geoffrey's plan being the only viable one at the moment, I grabbed my push-to-talk and barked orders to Security for barrels filled with something flammable.

"Once we get the smoke going, that should stop the bees from attacking. Then call the fire department," Geoffrey said when I was done, his words heavy with defeat. "The bees are simply too riled-up."

"And, pray tell, what will the fire department do?"

"They'll have to knock the flying bees down with foam." A baleful expression settled over Geoffrey's features. "That will kill them."

"Don't look so hang dog. You're not going to make me feel guilty about massacring millions of bees," I lied. "That solves the flying bee problem. What about the crawling ones?"

"I've called my team. They should be here any minute with the bee suits. We have to try to put the hives together, and then, hopefully, the bees will return to them."

My hand began to cramp, so I let go of Geoffrey's shirt and swatted at a few bees crawling on my skirt. Since I knew nothing about taming bees (which sounded as improbable as teaching fleas to dance), and Geoffrey's plan was the only one we had, I decided to go with it. "Okay. Work your magic. I'll call the fire department." He started to speak, but I held up a finger to silence him.

"And the police department needs to cordon off this area before these bees do a real number on someone."

"I'm sorry," Geoffrey whispered, his eyes again turned toward the sky.

"That's okay. I'm sure you didn't envision the truck dumping its load."

He turned and looked at me, his eyes struggling to focus. "I was apologizing to the bees, not to you."

"Of course you were." I felt the color rise in my cheeks as I wrestled for self-control. "Get these bees out of here and clean up this mess." I poked Geoffrey in the chest for emphasis. "But first, get the driver out of that truck before the bees eat him alive. Do it now!"

He gave me a look that told me, in no uncertain terms, I had exhausted my usefulness, then turned back to his charges. I paused to make sure he was moving toward the cab of the truck, before I turned to stalk off in a vain attempt to keep my dignity intact. I refused to slap at a bee that had punctured my elbow.

Stung, dismissed, and more than a little browned-off, I fought the urge to wring Geoffrey's scrawny neck, which was a bad idea anyway.

Then the bees would be *my* problem.

You see, problems are what I do. My name is Lucky O'Toole, and I am the Head of Customer Relations for the Babylon, the most over-the-top resort/casino on the Las Vegas Strip. And as such, the hotel's entertainers, employees, and guests—oh yes, the guests; the weird, the wacko, the drunk and disorderly, the slightly naughty and the truly wicked—are all my responsibility.

I started in the business when I was fifteen. In the intervening years, I'd dealt with cockroaches, snakes, cats (both man-eating and domesticated), dogs, various reptiles (poisonous, venomous, and vile) and rodents (four-legged and two-legged), but tonight was my first experience with bees. And, frankly, I was at a bit of a loss.

Tired of offering my exposed skin to irate insects, I'd decided total retreat was the better part of valor when my phone rang. I flipped it open. "O'Toole."

"OhmyGod, ohmyGod, ohmyGod—"

"Paolo, calm down. What's wrong?" Paolo drove our limo on the late-night shift.

"The bees! The bees! They are coming after me! How do they get into the car? OhmyGod! Mary, Mother of God, protect me." A staccato mix of English and Spanish, he fired the words at me. "Help me!"

"Where are you?"

"In the limo. Behind the fallen-over truck."

I squinted my eyes and stared beyond the light into the darkness. I caught the glimmer of silver and the reflection of light on black, like a black hole in the night. "I see you. I'll be right there."

I bolted toward the car, my arms crossed in front of my face, breathing through the loose weave of my sweater. I had no intention of discovering what it would be like to inhale an enraged bee.

Bees crawled all over the car. I could just make out the filmy aura of Paolo's face peering at me through the driver's window. He waved his arms frantically as if fighting off an invading horde. Using the sleeve of my sweater, I brushed the bees off the handle and wrenched the door open.

Paolo recoiled at the cloud of insects that swarmed through the opening. I reached in, grabbed his lapels, and lifted the small man clear of the car, setting him on his feet. We both ran like hell up the drive and through the front door, which we slammed behind us. Our backs pressed to the glass, we sagged against it, fighting for breath.

Color was returning to Paolo's face. Dotting his otherwise flawless Latin complexion, I noticed several red welts. I'm sure I sported a set of my own.

"I don't know about you, but I'm asking for hazardous duty

pay," I said, when air again filled my lungs and I was no longer teetering on the brink of homicide.

"Hazardous duty pay? What is this?"

"Ask your boss when you insist on a raise."

Paolo crinkled his brows. *"You* are my boss."

"Oh, right." I straightened and smoothed my skirt. "Then forget what I said."

His eyes twinkled. "Paolo never forgets."

I raised one eyebrow as I looked at him. "Then you won't forget our limo which you abandoned in the middle of the Strip?"

"You want me to go back out there?"

I bit back a smile at his stricken look. "When it's safe, get the car."

~

The dispatcher at the fire department didn't miss a beat when I explained the problem—she rallied the troops. Their sirens already sounded in the distance. My call to the Metropolitan Police Department didn't go quite as smoothly. In a snippy voice, the dispatcher assured me Metro had the incident "under control," which I thought highly unlikely. Metro had a disdain for directing traffic and regularly left motorists to their own devices when dealing with gridlock—an interesting approach in a state with a Concealed Carry law.

As a precaution, I keyed Security again and asked for reinforcements outside to help untangle the snarled traffic before somebody started shooting.

My footsteps echoed off the marble floor as I strode through the lobby. The revelers chased inside by the bees had filtered away, leaving the vast space virtually empty. I paused for a moment, drinking it all in. I rarely saw the place this quiet—two thirty in the morning wasn't my usual gig.

A work of art, the Babylon had been designed to incorporate

all of the ancient wonders of the original Babylon—with a Vegas twist, of course. Large and grand, the lobby resembled an ancient temple with polished marble floors and walls inlaid with intricate, iridescent mosaics. Chihuly blown-glass hummingbirds and butterflies of all shapes, sizes, and colors covered the ceiling. Long and low, the registration desk hid under the colorful tents of a bazaar that formed the pathway into the casino.

The Bazaar, a vast array of high-end shops, the entrance to which was on the far side of the lobby opposite the registration desk, beckoned weary revelers, and big winners. What the gambling gods gave at the tables, the retail gods could take away. We had all the best names—Chanel, Louis Vuitton, Tiffany, Cartier, Jimmy Choo, Dolce&Gabbana, Hermes, Escada, Ferrari— to name but a few.

An indoor ski slope, replete with manmade snow and moguls, lurked behind a wall of glass adjacent to Registration. Of course, I rather doubted the ancient Babylonians strapped on a pair of K-2s and threw themselves down a snow-covered run, but, after all, this *was* Vegas, and some latitude with reality was expected. At this time of night, all the skiers were doing the après ski thing; the mountain was closed.

Completing the picture, a winding waterway—the Euphrates —snaked through the public areas of the ground floor. Lined with flowering plants and spanned by numerous footbridges, the Euphrates was home to myriad fish and fowl.

Sitting on one footbridge, half-hidden from view, a man and a woman caught my eye. Anger infused their posture. Even with their backs to me, I could tell their conversation was not a pleasant one. At this time of the morning the combination of too much alcohol and too little sleep was often incendiary. As the problem solver on duty, it fell to me to put out the fires.

I edged closer for a better look. The guy's wavy brown hair looked familiar. So, too, the tailored tweed jacket. Damn! The Beautiful Jeremy Whitlock! What was he doing here? And what was he doing with that petite woman with long strawberry blond hair? Actually, as Las Vegas's ace private investigator, Jeremy was often nosing around, so seeing him wasn't that unusual. But seeing him with this woman certainly was, since Jeremy was involved in a hot-and-heavy with Miss Patterson, my senior assistant, who was neither petite nor a redhead.

The woman stood. Jeremy leapt up and grabbed her arm. When she turned to yank her arm from his grasp, I got a good look at her face. With a sinking heart, I realized that I also knew her. Numbers Neidermeyer, the scourge of every bookie in town. Our very own sportsbook manager swore the woman had no soul. I agreed with him—she'd sold it to the Devil a long time ago.

Numbers and I had history. When she was a blossoming odds maker and I was the Director of Operations for one of the Big Boss's lesser properties, she'd tried to put us over a barrel. I'd won that round, and, luckily, our paths hadn't crossed since. But, if the grapevine could be relied upon, she'd continued playing the same game, although with bigger stakes. To hear it told, she'd ruined several dozen careers not only in the gaming industry but in professional athletics as well. Because she was the best in the business—such was her reputation that one word from her would cause the big money to jump in before the casinos could change the odds, leaving the casinos with their pants down—she'd emerged from the various wreckages unscathed.

With a glance toward the front door, Numbers turned on her heels and headed in the opposite direction, leaving Jeremy alone. We both watched as she disappeared into the casino.

I wandered over to Jeremy's side. "Slumming tonight?"

He jumped at the sound of my voice then shook his head. "You have no idea." He ran a hand over his eyes. "That woman. She's a bloody cow."

"Can you speak American rather than Australian?" Actually, I'd sit and listen to the Beautiful Jeremy Whitlock speak Swahili if he wanted—those brown eyes flecked with gold, the wavy hair begging to be touched, the dimples, the perpetual tan, the great ass, the delicious accent ... . If he and I weren't both already spoken for, I could definitely embarrass myself in his presence.

His dimples flashed then disappeared.

"Rubbed you the wrong way, did she?" I asked. "She has a habit of doing that. For all the years I've known her, I've been convinced she sees no reflection when she looks in the mirror." I took a good look at Jeremy. He looked whipped and more than a little peeved. "Is she involved in one of your investigations?"

"Up to her pretty little neck. I just can't prove it ... yet. She's as cunning as a shithouse rat."

"My thoughts exactly." I glanced at my watch—almost three hours into the new day. "Is there anything I can do?"

"No, but thanks."

I didn't think he'd accept—client confidentiality and all of that —but he looked so miserable I had to offer. "You look beat. Are you going home?"

"No, I'm bunking with your right-hand man these days."

"I'm not sure I'd put it quite that way. Somebody might get the wrong impression."

Clearly too tired to smile, Jeremy gave me a peck on each cheek and an unenthusiastic little wave as he turned to go.

I watched him until he disappeared into the casino.

I spent the next hour wandering among the tables and slot machines as the gambling day wound down. A cloud of smoke hovered above the thinning crowd. Having abandoned the rows of empty slots, the cocktail waitresses lurked near the few tables still hosting some action. At the beginning of the evening, the waitresses wore broad smiles and little else. Now the smiles were nowhere to be found, and the women looked cold and miserable as they shifted from one foot to another. I marveled at their composure. A long night in the mandatory stilettos would have reduced me to tears.

A small crowd of Babylon employees clustered around a lone slot machine. Paxton Dane, a long, tall drink of Texas charm and the Gaming Control Board's expert on cheating—actually he was an expert on lying *and* cheating, but that's another story—was holding forth on all the latest ways to rig slot machines for a large payout. The required presentations to the staff were always held at four o'clock in the morning, when the fewest number of quarter-pushers were around. While the gambler might sleep, the hotel staff merely changed shifts. Which reminded me, my shift was almost over.

Just when I was actually beginning to believe I might escape on time, my push-to-talk called my name. I flipped it open, glanced at the number, then said, "Hey, Jer. Whatcha got?" Jerry was my counterpart in Security.

"What'd you do, draw the short straw or something? How come the boss is working the graveyard?"

"You know how I like to be in the thick of the action."

"Right," he snorted. "Your main squeeze working tonight?"

"Playing piano in Delilah's Bar."

"Thought as much. I got a call you need to take."

"Sure," I said, with a sinking heart. The possibility of some shut-eye before dawn was diminishing by the second.

"A guy in 12410 locked himself out of his room. The typical story—he was heading for the bathroom in the dark and went out the wrong door. Apparently he's buck naked and hiding in the laundry room."

"You checked his name against our registration records?" I asked, my brain switching to autopilot.

"Yeah, they jibe."

"How am I supposed to ask him for ID before I give him the key?" I really didn't want to go into a room alone with a naked guy who was most likely three sheets to the wind.

"His name is Lovato. I think you can put two and two together."

I whistled low. "Interesting. How'd he get hold of you?" "Employee intercom." "On my way."

~

After a stop at the front desk to get a new key programmed for room 12410, I headed for the elevators. Standing in front of the main elevator bank and its shiny brass doors, I took stock of my reflection. A recent makeover had converted me from bottle-blonde to my natural light brown. Although I liked the transformation, I still wasn't used to the new old me.

I even wore a bit of makeup to accentuate my blue eyes and those darn cheekbones that had to be coaxed out of hiding. Still tall, I'd lost a few pounds—one of the effects of falling in love—that was recent, too. My mother told me I lost the weight because now I had something else to do with my hands. My mother, Mona, ran a bordello in Pahrump. Subtlety and gentility were not two of her stronger suits.

Once an elevator arrived, the ride was brief. I found the laundry room halfway down the hall on the right. I paused in front of the door. Should I knock? Feeling magnanimous, I decided I should.

Two taps and a voice called out, "You better goddamn well have my key. I'm freezing my butt off in here."

I paused, savoring the moment. I didn't get this sort of opportunity very often and I wasn't above making the most of it. This made staying up way past my bedtime almost worth it. I opened the door and froze in mid-stride.

Scrunched into the far corner of the small closet, swathed in white, with a scowl on his face, sat Las Vegas's own district attorney, Daniel Lovato. Most people called him Lovie—a nickname he well deserved—but Lovie Lovato the Lothario was too alliterative for me, so I stuck with Daniel.

"Daniel! Isn't this interesting?" My shit-eating grin would have been impossible to hide, so I didn't even try.

"Oh, Jesus, O'Toole. What are you doing here?" Lovie gathered the folds of sheet around him. "Shut the damn door."

"Does Glinda know you're here?" I shut the door behind me, then leaned against it, arms crossed across my chest. Glinda, in a fit of bad judgment I still didn't understand, married Daniel years ago. The fact that she hadn't killed him by now was a true testament to her self-control.

"I'm here with the bi—my wife." Daniel lowered his gaze and glared at me from under his bushy black eyebrows, which matched his thick black hair. Handsome, yes, but charming? To my knowledge, no one had ever accused him of that. "I beat on the door, but I couldn't wake her up. Now give me the damn key."

He extended his arm imperiously. With a sheet draped across his lap and over one shoulder, he looked just like a Roman Emperor—except the throne from which Lovie ruled was a pile of dirty laundry. Where was my camera when I needed it? Even my push-to-talk didn't have a camera feature. I resolved to do something about that.

I handed him the key. "We've got to stop meeting like this. People will start to talk, and I don't want to get on Glinda's bad side." Glinda was a bodybuilder and she scared me.

Daniel grabbed the key. Wrapping the folds of sheet around him, he levered himself to his feet, then brushed past me through the door.

"You're welcome," I said as I watched him stalk down the hall.

Here with his wife? *And I'm Mother Theresa.* When our great district attorney was out of earshot, I keyed security.

Jerry answered immediately. "You okay? Any problems with the naked guy?"

"Everything's fine, but do me a favor. Keep the last twenty-four hours of video from the hallway in front of 12410." I paused as I watched the district attorney let himself into his room. "And

363

you'd better keep the next twenty-four hours as well. I don't know what games are going on up here, but I have a hunch we had better do some prophylactic CYA."

~

"My day is officially over," I announced to no one as I rode the elevator to the lobby. Teddie would still be in Delilah's Bar tinkling the ivories, so I headed in that direction. Time to round him up and hit the trail.

Two months ago Teddie became the new man in my life. Actually, that's not really true. Two months ago he became the new man in my bed (not that there was an old one). Prior to that we'd been platonic best friends. Then, out of the blue, Teddie got a wild hair and kissed me right in the middle of Delilah's Bar. That kiss had changed everything.

Delilah's Bar—an oasis in a vast forest of machines and table games designed to relieve gamblers of their money—sat under a colorful tent on a raised platform in the center of the casino. Flowering bougainvillea streamed from latticework suspended between columns. Water gurgled from fountains and trickled down the wall behind the long bar. Thankfully, the televisions had been turned off. One lone patron, a cigarette dangling from his lips, played video poker at the far end of the counter.

Our head bartender, Sean, wiped down a glass with a bar rag. He nodded and smiled as I climbed the steps. "Your man's a real hit."

I took a seat on a stool and turned my full attention to Teddie, who was seated at the baby grand.

As Teddie played, he studiously ignored his audience of one, a lady seated close to him who had kicked off one shoe and was running her bare foot up his leg. In this day and age of rampant plastic surgery, I couldn't hazard a guess as to how old she was, but she was clearly trolling—and she had taken a shine to my man.

She had good taste—he *was* beautiful. Spiked blond hair, chiseled features, sparkling blue eyes surrounded by lashes females would kill for, broad shoulders, small waist, perfect ass. When near him, I found it next to impossible to keep my hands to myself.

Teddie's real name is Ted Kowalski, but when I brought his show to the Babylon, he was known as the Great Teddie Divine, Las Vegas's foremost female impersonator. Everybody assumed he was gay, but they were wrong big time. He's not even bisexual, which makes it nice for me.

Now Teddie busies himself writing songs and hoping for a music career. Juilliard-trained with a Harvard MBA, I had no doubt he'd get it. But in the meantime, he wrote music when the spirit moved him and played the piano in Delilah's on the nights I worked the graveyard. In addition, he still had his hand in the female impersonating thing. He now produced the show and was the headliner's understudy in case of an emergency.

I'd never tell Teddie this, but secretly I was glad when he hung up his dress. Having a lover who looked better in my clothes than I did was more pressure than I thought it would be. In addition, now I was the beneficiary of all his hand-me-downs—another plus.

His baby-blues closed as he sang an old Frank Sinatra ballad, Teddie wore his ubiquitous blue jeans. Tight, but not too, they always got my attention. In place of his favorite Harvard sweatshirt, he wore an open-collared shirt, the top several buttons undone. I could see the hint of chest hair, which I sorta liked. For a long time he waxed on a regular basis—chest hair and his Oscar de la Renta gown with the plunging neckline would not have been pretty.

Mid-ballad, Teddie stopped. "Mrs. Hitzelberger—"

"Norma," said the lady with her foot wedged up the leg of his blue jeans.

"Mrs. Hitzelberger," Teddie countered, this time a bit more forcefully.

Before he could continue, I slid onto the piano bench next to him. "Hey, handsome." With one hand, I turned his face fully toward me and gave him the very best kiss I could muster at almost four a.m.

Mrs. Hitzelberger grabbed my arm and tried to pull me away. "Honey, I was here first. This one's mine."

Like a flea trying to move an elephant, she had zero chance of pulling me away from Teddie, especially since he was kissing me back.

"Theodore," Mrs. Hitzelberger said imperiously, "Would a thousand dollars buy a few hours alone with you in my room?"

Words prevailed where force had failed. Teddie and I broke the kiss and turned to look at her, unsure whether we'd heard what we thought we'd heard.

"What?" Teddie asked.

"A cool grand for a few hours with you."

"What makes you think he's for sale?" I asked when I finally found my voice.

"Honey, everything in this place is for sale." Mrs. Hitzelberger waved her hand dismissively. "The only thing left to determine is the price."

I wasn't going to argue—she was closer to the truth than I cared to think about. "If that's the case, this one ..." I shrugged toward Teddie, "... was bought and paid for long ago."

Mrs. Hitzelberger sized me up for a moment. Then she drained her drink and slid off her stool as she worked her foot back into its shoe. "Lucky you." She gave me a squeeze on the shoulder, then turned and headed for the bar.

"Truer words were never spoken," I said as I leaned into Teddie. "Play something for me."

He cocked his head at me. Then, a smile tugging at his mouth, he began to play. Frank Sinatra gave way to Bryan Adams.

I put my head on his shoulder as he sang a beautiful song about lovers who had started out as friends. Closing my eyes, I smiled. The guy had a song for every occasion.

~

After I'd turned over the reins of power to my youngest assistant, Brandy, home beckoned. With Teddie's song in my heart and his hand firmly in mine, I pushed through the front door of the hotel and out into the cool night air. A few bees still buzzed against the glass. Thankfully, they ignored us.

At the end of the drive, we stopped to survey the damage. In full turnout gear with hastily rigged veils attached to their helmets and all openings bound with tape, the firefighters still manned the open hoses, washing dead bee bodies into the gutters. A commercial tow truck had righted the cab of the tractor-trailer. Men in white suits and veils worked on the shattered hives. Despite the conspicuous absence of the Metro police, traffic again crept down the Strip.

"What happened here?" Teddie asked.

I gave him a brief summary as I pulled him away from the lights of the Strip and into the velvety cloak of the darkest time of night.

"I was wondering about those red welts on your neck. I knew I hadn't put them there, and you aren't the type to engage in extracurricular necking." Teddie wrapped his arm around me, pulling me close.

The guy knew me pretty well. "Bees are going to be the least of my worries this weekend."

"How can I help?" He gave me a quick kiss on the temple for no apparent reason.

I liked it. "Keep me relaxed."

"They say sex is one of the great stress relievers."

"I like the way you think, Mr. Kowalski." I looped an arm around his waist. With my free hand, I grabbed his hand dangling over my shoulder.

The heat of the summer finally had broken, leaving the air as smooth and refreshing as a fine wine. We strolled the few remaining blocks in silence, savoring the quiet and the dark. Most of the stars had faded in anticipation of dawn, but one or two still twinkled valiantly. Except for a few bats winging in the darkness, the world was still.

Conveniently, home for both Teddie and me was a tower of glass and steel, called the Presidio, located behind the Babylon.

"Your place or mine?" Teddie inquired as he held open the front door for me.

"I like sleeping at your place—waking up in a man's bedroom makes me feel naughty."

"Naughty is good." Teddie shot me a grin as we stepped in the elevator. He inserted his card, and pressed the PH button, then folded me into his arms. "As long as you restrict yourself to this man's bedroom."

"Shouldn't be a problem. One man at a time is all I can handle," I murmured as his mouth closed over mine, setting my every nerve afire. How he did that remained an intoxicating mystery, but as they say, better not to look a gift horse in the mouth.

The ride to the top floor passed without notice. At the ding of the bell announcing our arrival, we unclenched and staggered out of the elevator into the middle of Teddie's great room.

I leaned one hip against the sofa and grabbed Teddie's shoulder. "Stand there a minute, will you?" I bent over and shucked off a shoe, then shifted feet and shucked the other. "Better."

"Let me help you." With a glint in his eye, Teddie boosted me so I was sitting on the back of his sofa, feet not touching the floor. He stepped between my legs and I wrapped them around his waist. He eased off my sweater then went to work on the buttons of my blouse.

I watched as he deftly worked through the lot of them. While the future with Teddie still looked a bit murky, the present was shaping up nicely.

"Woman, you have the most incredible underwear." He hooked a finger under the strap of my black lace bra and worked it down my arm. His breath caught when the sheer fabric fell away.

"My mother always told me fast cars and short skirts got a guy's attention, but the lingerie sealed the deal." His skin on mine shot sparks of warmth to my very core.

"She knew what she was talking about." Teddie looked at me, his eyes the deepest shade of blue. He looped one arm around my waist.

"She should." Warming to the game, I snaked my arms around his neck. "But I don't want to think about my mother right now. I don't want to think about anything."

"Have it your way." My body anchored to his, his arm firmly around my waist, Teddie bent me back.

When his mouth found my exposed breast, rational thought evaporated.

End of Sample
To continue reading, be sure to pick up *Lucky Stiff* at your favorite retailer.

ALSO BY DEBORAH COONTS

The Lucky O'Toole Vegas Adventure Series

Wanna Get Lucky? (Book 1)

Lucky Stiff (Book 2)

So Damn Lucky (Book 3)

Lucky Bastard (Book 4)

Lucky Catch (Book 5)

Lucky Break (Book 6)

Lucky the Hard Way (Book 7)

Lucky Ride (Book 8)

Lucky Score (Book 9)

Lucky Ce Soir (Book 10)

Lucky Enough (Book 11)

Other Lucky O'Toole Books

The Housewife Assassin Gets Lucky

(Co written with Josie Brown, author of the Housewife Assassin series)

Lucky O'Toole Original Novellas

Lucky in Love (Novella 1)

Lucky Bang (Novella 2)

Lucky Now and Then (Novella 3)

Lucky Flash (Novella 4)

The Brinda Rose Humorous Mystery Series

90 Days to Score (Book 1)

The Kate Sawyer Medical Thriller Series

After Me (Book 1)

Deadfall (Book 2)

Other Novels

Deep Water (romantic suspense)

Crushed (women's fiction)

ABOUT THE AUTHOR

Deborah Coonts swears she was switched at birth. Coming from a family of homebodies, Deborah is the odd woman out, happiest with a passport, a high-limit credit card, her computer, and changing scenery outside her window. Goaded by an insatiable curiosity, she flies airplanes, rides motorcycles, travels the world, and pretends to be more of a badass than she probably is. Deborah is the author of the Lucky O'Toole Vegas Adventure series, a romantic mystery romp through Sin City. *Wanna Get Lucky?*, the first in the series, was a *New York Times* Notable Crime Novel and a double RITA™ Award Finalist. She has also penned the Kate Sawyer Medical Thriller series, the Brinda Rose Humorous Mystery series, as well as a couple of standalones. Although often on an adventure, you can always track her down at:

www.deborahcoonts.com
deborah@deborahcoonts.com

facebook.com/deborahcoonts
twitter.com/DeborahCoonts
instagram.com/deborahcoonts
pinterest.com/debcoonts
bookbub.com/authors/deborah-coonts
amazon.com/author/debcoonts
goodreads.com/DeborahCoonts

CPSIA information can be obtained
at www.ICGtesting.com
Printed in the USA
LVHW051042271120
672831LV00015B/655